BEHIND BARS

A few minutes later, she was vaguely aware of the sound of a key turning in the lock of her cell door. Mitch Hughes stepped inside, taking up most of the available space. Slowly she raised her eyes to meet his and waited to see what he wanted.

"Your friends thought you might like these." He thrust a lace-edged pillow and a quilt at her and she bit back the automatic urge to thank him. Although he'd been the one to send for Lucy and Melinda, she wasn't feeling particularly grateful right now. Frightened, alone, terrified maybe. Gratitude didn't enter into it.

"Is there anything else?"

"No."

"Fine." Mitch stalked out, slamming the door behind him.

Somehow that little fit of temper pleased her. If he wasn't all that happy about having a woman in one of his cells, how did he think she felt? A lot of folks in Lee's Mill had looked down their noses at her for her whole life. Things were likely to be a whole lot worse now.

Despite the warmth of the jail, she shivered uncontrollably. Before the tears burning in her eyes broke loose, she grabbed the pillow and laid it at the head of the small cot. Curling up on her side, facing the back wall, she pulled the quilt over her until it covered her head. One by one, the tears fell silently onto Melinda's beautiful embroidery.

Somehow, Josie didn't think she'd mind.

A LAWMAN
FOR
CHRISTMAS

Pat Pritchard

ZEBRA BOOKS
Kensington Publishing Corp.
http://www.kensingtonbooks.com

ZEBRA BOOKS are published by

Kensington Publishing Corp.
850 Third Avenue
New York, NY 10022

First Printing: October 2003
10 9 8 7 6 5 4 3 2 1

Printed in the United States of America

One

Two quick raps of the gavel brought the meeting to attention. There wasn't a woman in the room who didn't look forward to the day that it was her turn to be the one wielding the power the gavel represented. Just the sharp sound of wood striking wood had Josie sitting up straight, excited that the meeting of the Luminary Society was about to begin.

"Good evening, ladies. We have much to accomplish, so let's get started."

Melinda Hayes, the pastor's new bride, stood at the front of the room, smiling as she prepared to take roll. While she called out names, Josie wondered if she'd ever be as comfortable in front of a room full of people as Melinda seemed to be. For the moment, she was content just to be accepted as a member of the Society.

That in itself was far more than she'd ever dared to hope for in her life, because she'd grown up as the daughter of the town drunk and was married to another one. It had taken every ounce of courage she could muster to apply for membership in the Society when it was first formed. To give the women of Lee's Mill credit, not a single one had objected to her presence.

Melinda, Lucy Mulroney, and Cora Lawford had been the three to organize the Society to offer women a chance to educate themselves. For some, it was a chance to share their love of books. For others, such as Josie, the meetings offered an opportunity to learn to read and write. The world seemed a wondrous place now that words and letters were no longer a baffling mystery to her.

Melinda had finished calling out names and was ready to move on to the business at hand.

"We will begin our discussion tonight shortly, but Cora and her aunt Henrietta have asked for a few minutes of our time to ask for our help in preparing for the Christmas celebration. Please give them your full attention."

Melinda took her seat at the front table as Cora and her aunt made their way to the front of the room. Josie was surprised to see Henrietta Dawson, because the older woman was not a member of the Society. In fact, there had been times when she'd threatened to force her niece to resign her membership.

Cora, a frequent speaker at the meetings, spoke first. "I'd like to thank everyone for granting us a few minutes of your time. Normally, we wouldn't bring church circle matters to Society meetings, but my aunt would like to ask a favor from you." She stepped aside to allow her formidable aunt to take charge.

With a single glance, Henrietta Dawson silenced a pair of women who had dared to start whispering in the back row. When she was satisfied that every eye in the room was firmly on her, she gave a satisfied nod and began to speak. "As many of you are aware, the church circle is working to make this year's Christmas celebration the best ever. Although most of our plans are moving ahead smoothly, we are in dire need of help with some special projects."

She looked around the room, as if weighing each person's ability to come to her aid. Her eyes slid past Josie and then came back. If Josie wasn't mistaken, Henrietta seemed to nod before moving on to the next person.

Maybe she was imagining things. Although she had attended a few church services since the pastor had come, she'd never once been a part of the annual Christmas service.

But she'd wanted to be, every year of her life as far back as she could remember.

Henrietta was talking again. "This year it is our goal to make sure that every child finds a surprise under the tree at the church. To that end, we need those of you who are handy with a needle to help make small bags for candy. If we have time, we'd also like to sew some clothes and such for some of the needier families in our midst."

Once again she seemed to be looking in Josie's direction. "We will provide all the fabric and patterns. I would appreciate any time you can give to help us out. I'll be in the back of the room to take names when the meeting is over."

The rest of the meeting seemed to fly by. When the gavel brought the evening to an end, Josie headed for the door. She was handy enough with a needle but wasn't at all sure that Henrietta would welcome help from her. Rather than risk the embarrassment of being turned away, she would simply leave.

Just as she reached the door, Henrietta's voice rang out over the room, stopping Josie's escape. "Mrs. Turner, don't disappointment me. I was counting on your help."

Josie's heart seemed to stop as she slowly turned to face Cora and her aunt. Her friend gave her an encouraging smile while Henrietta's expression seemed to be daring her to falter. The crowd parted like hot butter as Josie made her way back to where Henrietta waited. The older woman thrust a sack in Josie's hands.

"There's a sample bag in there for you to use as a pattern. If you get those done, come get more from me." She actually smiled briefly. "Cora has shown me some of

your work. You have a fine hand with a needle and
thread, young lady. Our church circle meets on Tuesday
afternoons, if you're able to come help plan the rest of
the Christmas program."

Just as abruptly Henrietta turned her attention to the
next woman in line. Josie clutched the sack of material
as she walked away. Had she heard Henrietta correctly?
That she actually wanted Josie to be part of her group?
Perhaps Christmas really was the season of miracles.

Still filled with the wonder of it all, Josie started on the
long walk to her cabin in the woods.

Damn it, he knew better.

That didn't keep Mitch from watching the clock,
counting the minutes until Thomas Mercantile down
the street opened for business. He resisted the urge to
watch out the window, telling himself that as sheriff he
should keep an eye on things, but that didn't justify spy-
ing on anyone. He shook his head in disgust directed
right at himself. It used to be that he bought the few supplies he needed once a month, but lately he'd taken to
spreading his purchases out over several trips to the
store and cursing himself for a fool each step of the way.

The hands on the clock approached eight o'clock and
then crept on until they reached half past the hour.
Shuffling a pile of papers from one side of his desk to
the other, Mitch forced himself to concentrate on his
monthly reports. The office remained oppressively
quiet, the soft rustle of paper the only noise other than
the occasional snore emanating from the cell in back.

The current resident was one of their more frequent
customers. Hardly a week went by without Mitch or his
deputy having to haul Oliver Turner in for disturbing
the peace. Hell, more than once Mitch had been

tempted to arrest the man just for setting foot in a saloon to save everyone from having to deal with a belligerent drunk later on.

The thought made Mitch smile. He'd have to run that idea past Mayor Bradford. Cletus couldn't approve officially, of course, but he'd enjoy the joke. Maybe he'd even get Cade Mulroney to write an editorial on the subject.

The sound of footsteps on the wooden porch of the jailhouse caught Mitch's attention. He was on his feet and pouring a second cup of coffee before his deputy came through the door.

"Morning, Mitch." Jake hung his hat and coat on a peg on the wall and took Mitch's place behind the desk. He glanced at the neat pile of reports and let out a low whistle. "You must have had a quiet night to get all that done." He leaned back in the chair, balancing it on two legs. "Figured that was the case, because you didn't roust me out of a good night's sleep. For once," he added with one of his quick smiles.

"Quiet enough," Mitch said, handing the younger man the coffee he'd poured. Nodding in response to the snores coming from the back of the jail, he brought his deputy up to date. "Just the usual. Oliver Turner tried pushing around the crew off a riverboat. By all accounts, they weren't bothering anybody, just made the mistake of sitting at the table Oliver considers his."

He shot a dirty look toward the sleeping form in the cell. "Luckily for me, the deckhands were due back at the boat, so they didn't put up much of an argument when I told them they'd have to leave, too. But you know Oliver: once he gets riled, he won't stop. I had to knock him cold to calm him down." Mitch smiled briefly. "A couple of those deckhands were only too glad to help drag the idiot down here to his favorite cell for the night."

Jake grinned. "I'll bet. Think he'll remember where all the bruises came from when he wakes up?"

Mitch shrugged his indifference, feeling fed up with the whole mess. He was damn sick and tired of Oliver and his problems. "If the fool is up to eating when he wakes up, send to the hotel for a meal. Otherwise, he's free to go."

"Any fines?"

"Not this time. He didn't last long enough to do any damage." Besides, despite his father's wealth, Oliver rarely had more than two dimes to rub together. The man's wife saw little enough of his money without Mitch taking any more of it.

"I'm going to get some breakfast and maybe stop by to see Cade." He picked up his hat and slipped on his duster. "This afternoon I need to take supplies out to my place that Ben asked me to pick up for him, so send word there if anything comes up. Otherwise, I'll be back to relieve you in the morning."

"Sure thing, Sheriff." Jake dropped the chair back down and propped his feet up on the desk. The man was smart enough to take advantage of the quiet times. Sometimes they were all too rare.

Mitch stepped out into the sharp chill of an Ozark morning. Although not unpleasantly cold, the taste of winter hung in the air. Out of habit, he took a careful look from one end of the street to the other. Lee's Mill had settled down considerably over the past couple of years. Before that, between the Yankees and the bush-whackers, the entire area had been in a constant uproar, but not anymore. Mitch saw to it.

He stepped off the porch and crossed the street, heading for the hotel and a hot meal. Several people called out greetings as he passed by. He spoke to some and waved at others. His job kept him from having much time to socialize, but he made a point of being on good terms with most of the town.

The route he'd chosen took him past the new building that housed Thomas Mercantile. Lucy, the owner, was now married to Cade Mulroney, although she'd kept the store's old name. A few months before, a madman had burned the old store to the ground trying to destroy the Luminary Society, the women's group Lucy had helped found.

The whole town had pitched in to help Lucy rebuild, but no one had worked harder than Lucy's new husband. Between helping with the store and running the newspaper, Cade never had more than a minute or two to call his own. Mitch had rarely seen a man happier with his lot in life.

Speaking of the devil, Cade stepped out of the newspaper office, just ahead. Mitch hurried his steps to catch up with him.

"Morning, Cade."

"Are you looking for me or just passing by?"

"Both. Are you going to be around later? I was going to stop in to see you."

His friend fell into step beside him. "That would be fine if you don't mind me working while we talk. I still have an editorial to write as well as an article on the town council meeting."

"I don't want to interrupt anything. It can wait until tomorrow if that would work better for you."

Cade frowned. "Where you headed now?"

"The hotel, for breakfast."

"Why don't I come with you? I had a late night last night, and then Mary decided we all needed to be up at first light. A cup of Belle's coffee sounds good about now."

Mitch grinned. Cade's daughter was one of his favorite

people. "How is my best girl these days? Is she still happy about sharing you with Lucy?"

"You've got it all wrong." Cade looked genuinely puzzled. "The truth is, Mary hates having to share Lucy with me." When Mitch laughed, Cade reluctantly joined in. Then he turned serious. "My real worry is how she'll feel about sharing both of us with a baby brother or sister."

That brought Mitch up short. "Really! You and Lucy?"

Cade looked understandably proud. "Yes, although you're the first one I've told. We wanted to keep it secret until we knew for sure. Lucy plans to make the big announcement when the Luminary Society meets next week, but I figure it's safe to tell you early."

"Well, congratulations! I'd buy you something stronger than coffee to celebrate, but it's too early in the day." He slapped his friend on the back. "And about Mary—she'll make a great big sister. Kind of like having a real doll to play with."

"I hope so."

They reached the door of the hotel. With unspoken agreement, they changed subjects as soon as they were within hearing of other people. Mitch led the way into the dining room and their favorite table. Before Cade's marriage, the two men had often shared a meal at the one table that afforded both of them a view of the entire room with their backs to the wall. Old habits died hard.

Once they were seated and Belle had taken their orders, Mitch brought up the reason he'd wanted to speak to Cade alone.

"I got a telegram from a sheriff upstate, asking if we'd had any trouble with a gang that had been working his area. Seems that they'd hit a few stagecoaches and such before moving on. There's a reward being posted, but he was also warning us that they might be headed our way."

"Did he give you specific numbers or any descriptions?"

"No. He did promise to send out posters as soon as he could, but they haven't gotten here yet."

Cade murmured a few choice curses under his breath. "What do you want me to do? Not much use putting a warning in the paper if we don't know any more than that."

"You're right. Actually, I wanted to know if you still trade news with other papers in the state."

"Sure, that's how we get most of our stories. I either get the information by telegraph or I get copies of their papers when the stage comes in."

Cade let his words trail off when Belle arrived with his coffee and Mitch's breakfast. As soon as she was gone, he picked up where he had left off. "Some of the news is too out of date to be of much use, but I still like to see what's going on elsewhere."

"I figured as much," Mitch said between bites. "Keep me posted if you see anything that makes you think this gang is working anywhere near Lee's Mill. If it does look like we're in their path, I want enough lead time to send for help. Jake is good, but not as experienced as I'd like. I don't want to have to face down a bunch like that by myself."

Cade's shoulders straightened, and his hand slipped down to the gun he always wore. "You know you only have to ask."

Mitch shook his head. "Thanks, but no thanks. Lucy would have my hide. Besides, with one child and another on the way, you've got no business riding in a posse."

Cade glared across the table at him. "It's because I do have a wife and family that I will be right there beside you."

Mitch knew there was no use in arguing with Cade, especially when trouble had yet to come their way. He turned his attention to finishing off the last of his bacon and eggs. Belle stopped by one more time with the coffeepot.

"Eggs all right, Sheriff?"

"Just like I like them. Thanks."

"More coffee, Mr. Mulroney?"

"No thanks, Belle. I've got to be going. If I don't keep an eye on Will, he'll be over at The River Lady before we put the paper to bed."

Although Will was a first-rate typesetter, his work suffered once he got more than two beers inside him. Cade often complained about the amount of effort it took to keep the man away from the saloon long enough to get the *Clarion* printed and delivered. Mitch found it entertaining to watch the two men work together.

Mitch tossed enough money down on the table to cover the bill before following Cade back outside. "Next time we're at The River Lady, I'll buy you a real drink."

"I'll let you." Cade looked down the street. "Damn it, there he goes." He hurried off down the sidewalk to catch up with his employee.

"Let me know if you hear anything!" Mitch called after him.

Cade raised his hand to acknowledge that he'd heard him. Mitch watched his friend hustle down the street to haul Will back to work. He noticed Cade was limping a bit, a sure sign he wasn't up to his best. The newspaperman had never talked much about his injury, other than that it happened during the war. Both men had fought on the same losing side, but neither of them dwelled on it much. Mitch figured their common experience was one reason they got along so well.

Now that he was alone again, Mitch had a decision to make. He did need to go out to the small farm he'd bought the previous year. The only question was whether he really needed to stop in the store beforehand. Ben, the old farmhand whom Mitch had inherited along with the property, had asked Mitch to pick up a few things, but there wasn't any rush.

Before he was aware that he'd even made a decision, Mitch turned back from the direction of the stable where he kept his horse and marched directly toward Thomas Mercantile. He carefully schooled his expression even as his gut twisted in anticipation. Drawing a deep breath, he turned the doorknob and stepped through the door.

A small bell chimed directly over his head. It was one of the few things that Mitch had been able to salvage for Lucy from the ashes of the fire. He'd spent several hours restoring the brass to its previous shine before he'd returned it to her. Her grateful tears had almost undone him, because he hadn't wanted her gratitude. If he'd done his job better, he would have prevented the fire in the first place.

The interior of the store had a scent all its own: a combination of new lumber, fresh spices, and wax. Dust didn't have a chance against Lucy and her assistant. Every surface in the place gleamed with the loving care of its owner. Come to think about it, Mitch wondered where Lucy was. It wasn't like her to leave a customer waiting for more than a few seconds.

A movement at the door of the back storeroom caught his eye. Josie Turner backed through the doorway dragging a crate that had to weigh half as much as she did. Mitch fought down the urge to rush behind the counter to help her. If it had been Lucy, he wouldn't have hesitated, especially now that he knew she was expecting. But from past experience, he was well aware that Josie— make that Mrs. Turner—didn't appreciate any man coming too close.

Not that he blamed her. By all reports, her late father hadn't been any more of a prize than her husband Oliver. The thought of Josie breaking her back to earn the few dollars that Lucy could afford to pay while her worthless husband drank himself stupid was enough to make Mitch see red.

He stood by helplessly while Josie tugged and pulled the overloaded crate through the storeroom door. When she finally had it where she wanted it, she stood up straight and dusted her hands on her apron. That was when she noticed she was no longer alone. She took a step backward before she caught herself. Bracing her shoulders, Josie took a position at the counter.

"Can I help you, Sheriff?" Her smile was shy but genuine.

"Yeah, I need a few things," he answered more gruffly than he meant to as he pulled Ben's list from his shirt pocket. He tried to return her smile by way of an apology but wasn't sure how successful he was.

When he held the list out to Josie, she seemed reluctant to take it from his hand. Finally, he tossed it down on the counter and stepped back. He hated the relief that flashed through her eyes. Didn't she know he'd never do a damn thing to hurt her?

Honesty forced him to admit that she had no reason to think so. She probably never saw the man behind the badge pinned to his shirt. Considering how much time her menfolk had spent behind bars, she had no cause to think kindly of lawmen at all—although he had to think that the nights Oliver didn't make it home would come as a relief to her.

As she gathered the few items on his list, her eyes kept flickering in his direction. Realizing that his staring was making her nervous, he walked over to the shelf where Lucy kept a stack of books for people to borrow. Although intended primarily for the women of the Luminary Society, no one seemed to mind much if he occasionally took one to read. In turn, he made a habit of buying a new book now and then to add to the collection.

He did his damnedest to keep his wayward eyes focused on the open book in his hands, but they kept wandering back in the direction of Josie Turner. It went against everything he ever believed in to look at another man's wife, but he didn't seem able to help himself. That he'd never acted on his interest in her was cold comfort.

Mostly, he told himself that it was those brown eyes of hers, huge and anxious, that brought out all the protective instincts he possessed. He'd taken on the job of sheriff because of his need to keep the innocents of the world safe. If no one took up their cause, they suffered and died just like when . . .

The sound of the bell jerked him back from the painful memories of the past. He looked over his shoulder to see who had come in. One glance had him shoving the book back up on the shelf and checking his weapon. Evidently, Jake had released Oliver Turner.

"Josie, let's go," the man snarled.

"It's not time, Oliver. I promised Lucy I would stay until two."

"I don't give a damn what you told her. I'm telling you to come now."

To Mitch's surprise, Josie did her best to stand up to her husband. "No, I won't. I made a promise, and I plan to keep it." She wisely kept the counter between them while she spoke.

It didn't help. In a move surprisingly agile for a man suffering from the effects of too much drink, Oliver's hand snaked out and grabbed Josie by the arm. He dragged her to his side.

Mitch's temper flared at Oliver's rough treatment of

his wife. He edged closer to the counter, making sure that Turner was aware of his presence.

Oliver turned bloodshot eyes in his direction. "This ain't your concern, lawman."

"Sounds like your wife isn't ready to go home, Turner. Why don't you go along peaceful-like and let her follow along when she's done here?"

"And why don't you go straight to hell, Sheriff?" He dragged Josie a few steps closer to the door. "I want my wife at home where she belongs. Turners don't hire out to do menial labor."

Mitch bit back the urge to point out that Oliver didn't work at all. As far as anyone knew, the man subsisted on what little money he won at poker. His father might be wealthy, but the man didn't share much of his money with his son or his daughter-in-law.

"She wants to stay, Turner." Mitch's hand strayed to his gun.

"That's too damn bad. I have need of her at home." He leered at his wife, causing her to go pale.

Damn, Mitch wanted to kill the son of a bitch. The only thing that stopped him was the fact that Oliver Turner was doing nothing illegal. He was acting within his rights as Josie's husband. Most folks would agree that a wife's place was in the home, caring for her man. Despite the best efforts of the Luminary Society to change that attitude, no one would thank Mitch for interfering in the marriage problems of the Turners.

But if Josie wanted his help, he'd give it.

"Mrs. Turner, what do you want to do?"

When she tried to pull free, Oliver only tightened his grasp as he continued toward the door. Mitch started forward, ready to do battle.

"Don't, Sheriff!" Her eyes pleaded for his understanding. "Please."

Josie's plea brought him up short. It took all he had to back down, but the look in her eyes told him that it would only go worse for her if he did interfere. If not now, then later.

Oliver smirked over Josie's head as he yanked open the door. Mitch could only watch as the two of them disappeared down the street, Josie struggling to keep up with her bastard of a husband.

"It's hard to watch, isn't it?"

Lucy Mulroney had joined him at the window. She reached out to lay a comforting hand on his arm, but he didn't want comfort. He wanted to punch something.

"He doesn't deserve her." The words slipped out before he could stop them.

"That's true enough, but there isn't much we can do about it." Lucy somehow managed to lead him from the window and back to the counter. "Now, let's see how far she got with filling your order."

Mitch's gut churned with frustration, but he had to be grateful that Lucy hadn't felt the need to remark on his inappropriate comment. The fact that he hadn't meant to say the words didn't make them any less true.

It didn't take Lucy long to finish collecting the rest of Ben's supplies. When she totaled the charges, Mitch tossed a few bills on the counter, still not trusting himself to talk.

Serenely Lucy handed him his change with a smile as he gathered up his packages. As he walked away, Lucy came around the counter to see him to the door. He braced himself for whatever she felt the need to say.

"Mitch, I don't know how to put this." She frowned as she considered her words. "Josie needs all the friends she can get. I know you mean well, but we have to tread carefully. If Oliver thinks we're ganging up on him, it could go badly for her."

She was right, and he knew it. But that didn't mean he was happy about the situation. He stalked out without saying a word.

Josie closed her eyes and concentrated on keeping her spine ramrod straight and her knees locked. Pride was about all she had left; she wouldn't give it up easily. The door slammed shut, rattling the last unbroken window. She counted off the seconds, waiting for the familiar squeak of the corral gate. When it came, she allowed herself the luxury of leaning against the wall for support.

The shakes started at the sound of hoofbeats passing by the front porch and then fading into the distance.

Alone at last, Josie let a moan escape as she sank to the floor. Grabbing a handful of her skirt, she wiped a small trickle of blood off her face and prayed that Oliver had enough money on him to drink himself into a stupor. With luck, he'd land himself back in Sheriff Hughes's jail cell for a day or two.

She allowed herself the luxury of sitting where she was until the pain faded to a dull throb. Her refusal to beg had almost cost her another split lip, but pride was about all she had left to call her own since Oliver had taken most of their money and their only horse.

That same pride had her using a nearby chair to pull herself back up to her feet. If Oliver came riding back, she didn't want to be caught cowering on the floor. Leaning on the table, she shook her head to clear the last vestiges of dizziness. When she was convinced she could walk without stumbling, she made her way to the pitcher of water by the bed.

Using both hands, she picked it up and poured some into the chipped basin, managing to keep most of it in the bowl. Splashing water over her face and neck, she let the cool liquid soothe both her wounded mouth and her wounded soul. As she reached for the nearby scrap of toweling, the small tintype on the wall caught her eye.

"Pa, you surely didn't do me any favors marrying me off to a rich man's son." She drew a ragged breath. "I know you meant well, but Oliver was not the great prize you thought he was." She let a few tears slide down her face, knowing full well she wouldn't have gotten any sympathy from her father, even if he'd been alive to hear her.

Besides, it wasn't anything she hadn't said to herself on too many occasions to count. It never changed the way her life was going.

She wiped her face clean of blood and tears before preparing for bed. With Oliver gone for the time being, she needed to sleep. She was scheduled to work at the store in town in the morning. Maybe with a restful night the evidence of her latest run-in with her husband wouldn't be so obvious to Lucy Mulroney's all too knowing eyes.

It wasn't as if everyone in town didn't know all about Oliver, his drinking, and the effect it had on his temper. But as long as he only took his bad moods out on his wife, few would lift a finger to do anything about it. The sheriff had been ready to step between them, but Josie hadn't wanted him to do so. He was no doubt acting out of a sense of duty, but Josie didn't want anyone's pity.

She considered Lucy her best friend. But when Lucy and her husband had offered to take her in if she wanted to leave Oliver, that same stubborn pride had forced Josie to turn them down. She would accept help in the form of a job or book learning, but not out-and-out charity.

If a few more tears squeezed out of her closed eyes, she ignored them as she waited for sleep to come. Tomorrow would be a sight better, because she'd spend it in the company of the few women who had gone out of their way to befriend her. And if that weren't enough, the next meeting of the Luminary Society was less than a week away. Clinging to those happy thoughts, Josie drifted into dreamless slumber.

Mitch had split enough wood to last his irascible employee a week or more. Ben grumbled constantly about his rheumatism no matter what the weather, but he still insisted on putting in a full day's work around the farm. This time of year, with its spells of bitter cold, kept the old man in constant pain. Mitch tried to get out to the farm often enough to do some of the heavier work himself.

Besides, splitting wood and pretending it was Oliver Turner fit his mood just fine. He picked up another round and set it on end. He let the weight of the ax do most of the work, but the feel of the sharp blade biting into the firewood gave him a satisfying feel of accomplishment.

"You going to chop down every tree in sight?" Ben came out of the barn leading his favorite mules.

"Not all of them. I want to keep one just in case I need to hang somebody." He gave his employee a dark look before swinging the ax again.

Ben's laugh sounded rusty as he set about harnessing the mules. The tack he used included a heavy chain. "That dead oak finally went down in that wind the other night. Thought I'd drag it in closer for you. No use in cutting it up there and then having to tote it all this distance. Maggie and Bess here won't mind helping out."

The old man patted the nearer mule on the neck. Mitch knew for a fact that Ben preferred the company of most animals over that of his own kind. More than once he'd told Mitch that mules might be stubborn, but he'd never known one yet that robbed or murdered anyone. Considering some of the ugliness Mitch had been witness to over the years, he couldn't argue with that logic.

The sun had finally come out from behind the clouds, but it didn't bring much in the way of warmth with it. Mitch stopped for a minute to look at the surrounding hills. Signs of winter were everywhere, which wasn't much of a surprise, considering Christmas was only a few weeks away. Earlier that morning, there'd been a skin of ice over the water in the trough. The trees had been glorious only a few weeks before, all decked out in oranges, yellows, and fiery reds. Now most of the leaves were on the ground, except for those on the oaks, which would cling to their dying foliage until spring.

Autumn in the Ozarks was about his favorite time of the year, when life seemed to slow down a bit, as if getting ready for the long rest of winter. As sheriff, he had mixed feelings about the approach of cold weather. Men with time on their hands were likely to spend some of it in The River Lady saloon. Although most handled themselves well, the few who didn't made trouble for everyone.

Which brought him back to Oliver Turner.

He swung the ax only hard enough to embed its blade in the stump that he used for splitting wood. Maybe he'd do better helping Ben chain up that downed tree. He picked up his jacket and hiked out to where Ben was maneuvering his beloved mules backward, positioning them near the log.

If he was surprised to see Mitch approach, he gave no sign of it. The two men worked side by side until they had the tree trussed up good and proper.

That done, Ben took hold of the reins and snapped

them sharply over the backs of the two mules. The well-trained pair leaned forward in their traces and moved out in unison. A couple of steps took the remaining slack out of the chain.

"Ho, Bess; ho, Maggie," Ben coaxed as Mitch stood back out of the way. "That's my girls. Pull, damn you, pull." The last few words, shouted as he cracked the reins again, had the two mules straining against their harness. Finally, the tree broke free of the mud and slid forward.

Ben stumbled a bit with the sudden movement, but he righted himself and followed alongside the mules as they dragged the log back toward the house. Mitch secretly enjoyed watching the old man and his animals working together as a team. He'd never admit as much to Ben, knowing full well the man wouldn't appreciate the sentiment.

Back at the house, Mitch helped unharness the mules. He brushed Maggie while Ben saw to Bess. Once the mules were back in their stalls munching contentedly on oats and fresh hay, the two men headed into the house for their own dinner.

It was a contest which of the two was the worse cook, but at least Mitch could brag that he'd never made the two of them sick. That was more than Ben could claim, although he still denied being responsible for the night Mitch had spent doubled up with stomach cramps.

Figuring the old man was immune to his own cooking, whenever Mitch spent time at the farm, he insisted on fixing dinner for both of them. After a few such meals, he was always glad to return to town and the excellent food that Belle served at the hotel.

"What's got you all riled up, anyway?" Ben asked as he held a match to his pipe. "You've been like a bear with a sore paw ever since you got in."

Mitch ignored the question just as he ignored the reason behind his own foul mood. He shoved another spoonful of stew into his mouth and washed it down with some of the tar that Ben called coffee.

"I'll be leaving for town at first light."

"Well, don't wake me up to wave good-bye. I need my rest." Ben guffawed as if he'd cracked a joke.

Mitch sometimes wondered about the wisdom of letting Ben stay on when he'd bought the farm, but he hadn't had the heart to throw the old man out. Far as he knew, Ben had no family left and nowhere else to go. Besides, despite his crotchety nature and reluctance to bathe regularly, having the old coot around beat coming home to an empty house.

"I probably won't be back out here for a few days." Mitch pushed his plate away, figuring he'd eaten enough to hold him until he could tuck into a stack of Belle's flapjacks in town. "Is there anything you want me to bring back with me?"

"A pretty woman would be nice. I'd like something to look at besides your ugly face and those mules out there."

Mitch flinched. He tried to disguise it by stretching his arms up over his head, but he doubted he fooled either of them. Ben was still fussing with his pipe, so maybe he hadn't noticed.

"You'll have to settle for a new pouch of tobacco."

Ben turned his bright, beady eyes squarely on Mitch. "Listen here, boy. You're of an age to be settling down. A man needs a reason to come home at night."

"What would you know about that?"

The old man leaned back in his chair and sent smoke rings floating toward the ceiling. "I had me a woman once. Pretty she was." His eyes seemed to focus on a picture only he could see. "Hair the color of ripe corn, and a smile that lit up a room."

"What happened to her?"

The faint smile around Ben's mouth faded. "Cholera" was all he said. But after a few more rings disappeared above their heads, he added, "We didn't have long together, but at least I have the memories. That's more than you have."

That wasn't exactly true, but Mitch wasn't about to correct him. There'd been a woman in his past, too, but what he had left were more like nightmares. He pushed back from the table and reached for his rifle. "I need some fresh air. Leave the dishes."

He walked out without a backward glance.

Two

Jed Turner glared across his desk at a picture of his son. The sight made him sick. How in the hell had he spawned such a worthless piece of humanity? The thought left such a bad taste in his mouth, he poured himself another shot of whiskey. He had already made sure that he only had one glass in the room. Oliver made a habit of drinking himself stupid on the rotgut they served at The River Lady; Jed wasn't about to waste any of his good sipping whiskey on him.

On occasion he did admit to a certain amount of grudging respect for his son's ability to grovel. The boy had perfected a certain tenacity when it came to begging for money. Although Jed had already decided to give him enough to live on for another month, Oliver would have to earn it by swallowing what little self-respect he still had.

Jed's eyes strayed to the portrait of his late wife, which hung over the fireplace. The cold bitch had always thought she was better than Jed because she could trace her family back to some bigwig or another, while his family had probably stowed away, escaping to America one step ahead of the law. On the other hand, while she may not have thought much of Jed himself, she sure enough liked his money.

He blamed Loretta, pure and simple, for the way their

son had turned out. If Oliver wasn't the spitting image of Jed's old man, he might have accused her of trying to pass off someone else's brat as his. She'd made the boy weak by pampering him from the day he was born. Maybe if Oliver had been forced to scramble for enough to keep himself fed, he would have turned out differently, better somehow. Instead, he thought the world owed him everything without his having to lift a finger to earn it.

Feeling restless, Jed crossed to the other side of the room to stare out the window at the empire he'd carved out of the Ozark hillsides with blood, sweat, and sheer stubbornness. He loved every square inch of his land with a passion he'd never felt for anything—or anyone—else.

Which brought him back to the problem of his son. He still couldn't believe that Oliver had allowed the town drunk to force him into wedding his daughter. Even if Oliver had been dallying with the girl, the boy should have had the gumption to tell the old man to go to hell rather than allow himself to be saddled with an illiterate slut for a wife.

To give Josie her due, she seemed determined to better herself. He'd heard that she was involved in the Luminary Society, where she'd learned to read and cipher. Jed might have admired her efforts if she'd kept to her own kind. Instead, she'd dragged his son down to her level.

Well, no matter how much she gussied herself up, she was still hill trash and not worthy of the Turner name. He could only be grateful that Oliver hadn't managed to breed any white trash children out of her. He'd let his whole empire crumble into dust before he'd see control pass to her spawn.

Reaching for his wallet, he pulled out a small wad of

bills. It wasn't much, but if Oliver was careful, it would last him until next month. Jed allowed himself a small smile. The day would never dawn when Oliver was careful with money. No doubt he'd have every last penny spent within two weeks—three, tops.

And Jed knew his son well enough to know that unless Josie managed to pick Oliver's pockets, she wouldn't see more than a glimpse of the money. He'd been hoping all along that she'd give up on her failed attempt to marry into Jed's money and disappear. Unfortunately, she seemed willing enough to put up with Oliver's abuse as long as he kept a roof over her head.

An abrupt knock at the door jarred him out of his reverie. Jed checked the time. Just as he expected, Oliver was late again. His efforts to show his disdain for his father by keeping him waiting would cost him. Peeling several bills off the stack he had planned to give his son, Jed stuck them back in his pocket. Oliver would know he was being shorted, but not why. If he ever managed to figure out the price of his ill-advised little shows of defiance, maybe he'd grow up a little.

Jed doubted it, but two could play at this game. He let another full minute go by before responding.

"Come in." Jed kept his back to the door, fully aware that it would ruin Oliver's big entrance.

"I'm here."

Counting off a few silent seconds, Jed turned to face his son. A fresh shave and a clean shirt did nothing to disguise bloodshot eyes and the slight tremor in his hands.

"I hear you spent another night in jail." Jed strolled back to his desk, putting the expanse of mahogany between them. He set the money on the desk, just far enough from the edge so that Oliver couldn't quite reach it from his side. "You spend more time there than you do in your own bed."

Oliver rose to the bait all too easily. "That son of a bitch sheriff has it in for me."

"Why don't you do something about it?"

Jed made a point of pouring himself another glass of whiskey. He noted with disgust that Oliver actually licked his lips while he watched the amber liquid splash into the crystal glass. It was one thing to enjoy the taste of good whiskey, but quite another to need it in the same way you needed air to breathe or water to drink. *Weakling.*

"Damned if I won't. One of these days, he'll push me too far."

Jed nodded, letting Oliver think that he agreed with him. But while his son might underestimate Mitch Hughes, Jed knew better. He didn't know much about the man's past, but you only had to look him in the eyes once to know the man had been to hell and lived to tell about it. A hothead like Oliver would never get the drop on a man like that. It was just another way in which Oliver fell short in his father's eyes.

It was time to get down to business. "You wanted to see me?"

Oliver slumped down in the chair that faced the desk. "The bank said my account is almost empty."

"Don't take more out than you put in." Jed shrugged his indifference.

Oliver snapped straight up to his feet. "You don't give me enough for a cockroach to live on!"

Jed glared at him for daring to raise his voice. "Don't take that tone with me, boy!" He slid the money back closer to himself.

With considerable effort, Oliver choked back his temper and dropped back down in the chair. "Sorry. I just get damn tired of living on next to nothing."

"Get a job. I hear your wife has."

"I dragged her out of that store just today. I don't need Lucy Mulroney's charity."

No, but you need mine. Jed figured on poking and prodding at Oliver to see how much he was willing to take just to get his hands on some money. Jed kept hoping he'd finally get up the gumption to tell his father to go to hell and walk out. If he ever did, Jed would welcome him back home with open arms.

But as long as Oliver was willing to grovel, he'd get nothing but the bare minimum it took for him to exist in that pitiful excuse for a cabin that he shared with Josie. Talk about irony—she and her father had plotted to marry her off to Oliver to get at his father's money. Instead, she ended up living right where she always had. Let that be a lesson to the greedy little bitch.

Oliver's hands were twitching, and his foot tapped nervously on the floor. The need for drink must be riding him extra hard this morning. That stuff would kill him if he didn't wean himself from the bottle. Jed didn't figure there was much chance of that happening.

"I still have a job opening for you at the mine."

For once, Oliver didn't try to hide his absolute fury at being expected to earn a living. "I'm your son, not a hired hand." He pounded a clenched fist on the arm of the chair.

"You're a leech and a stupid one at that. It takes knowledge to run a business." Jed pushed the money across the desk but kept his hand on it. "Even if I were willing to turn control of everything over to you, which I'm not, how do you expect to run it when all you know is how to drink, gamble, and spend time in jail?"

Oliver jumped to his feet and leaned across the desk to glare down at Jed. "Go straight to hell, Father. One of these days, I'll take what I want whether you're willing to give it to me or not." He walked away without looking back.

Unfortunately, the effect of his great exit was spoiled when he snatched up the money before leaving. Jed counted the seconds until he heard the front door slam. Leaning back in his chair, he considered his options. Despite his hopes to the contrary, it was obvious that Oliver would never be the son and heir he wanted—needed, even—if his empire was to last beyond the next generation.

No, he was left with no choice but to seek out a new wife and start all over again. This time, he'd see to the raising of his son and make sure it was done right.

Oliver rode his horse hard with little regard for its safety or even his own. Pounding through the woods over game trails played hell with the pain in his head, but his fury demanded action, no matter how useless. He lost all sense of time and direction as they wove their way in and around the hills. Just as they reached the crest of a steep slope, his horse stumbled and almost went down.

Realizing the roan was about played out, he allowed it to slow gradually to a walk. Damning the spavined animal for being worthless, he dismounted, dropping the reins. The horse stood with its head drooping almost to the ground, its sides heaving. He felt a moment's regret, but only because if he had to shoot the animal, he'd have a long walk home.

Grudgingly he urged the horse into a stumbling walk, letting it cool down until it was safe to lead it down to a small creek for a drink.

While he waited for his horse to recover enough to make the long trip back to town, he pondered how much he hated his father. The man tried to act all superior to him, but Oliver knew for a fact that Jed Turner had started out life scrambling in the dirt for enough money just to survive. He had little or no education to speak of and had learned table manners from his wife.

Oliver was grateful that his mother had made sure that he knew the truth about his origins. Her family was something he could be proud of, she'd told him often enough, but the Turners had been little better than beggars. Oliver had always listened to her rantings, but the truth was that he had even less respect for her than he did for Jed.

Jed might have started off with nothing, but he'd ended up a wealthy man. Loretta's family, on the other hand, had started off with the best of everything and lost it all. To recoup their losses, they'd married their one daughter off to the highest bidder and then turned their back on her as soon as Jed paid off their debts. They hadn't even come to his mother's funeral.

Oliver knew his mother would have hated knowing that she was buried in Lee's Mill instead of in her family plot in St. Louis. It served the bitch right for marrying below her station in life. No doubt her relatives had thought she was tainted by her association with Jed Turner.

All of which meant that he belonged nowhere. His mother's family didn't think he was good enough to be one of them, and his father looked down on him for not wanting to start at the bottom of the heap like Jed had. Of course, now Jed owned the heap, but that was no excuse for wanting Oliver to struggle as he had.

He reached for his flask in the saddlebag and took a healthy swig. The whiskey burned clean and hot down his throat. He followed it with another and yet another, despite the objections of his stomach. Ignoring the slight queasiness, he leaned against a convenient tree and waited until he could feel the effects of the alcohol. In only a few minutes, the first hum of the whiskey shimmered along his nerves, sending a pleasant warmth along his limbs and then spreading to his mind.

He should have used the whiskey to calm himself before confronting his father, but he hadn't wanted to confront the old bastard with whiskey on his breath. On the whole, however, he thought he'd played the entire meeting well. Jed no doubt was sitting his office, clucking his tongue over his disappointment in his son. Either that or he was busy counting all the money he was holding back from Oliver.

He could just picture the old man sitting on a pile of gold, happily doling out a few coins at a time to Oliver and thinking he should be grateful for what little he got. Well, that was going to change and damn soon. Just last week, Oliver had met up with a group of men who would be only too glad to help him get what was due him. The very idea had him reaching for the flask again, a private celebration of better times to come.

She must have been tired to not have noticed Oliver coming home and crawling into bed next to her. Moving slowly, she managed to slip out of bed without disturbing him. After hurrying through her morning routine, she skipped breakfast rather than risk his waking up and ordering her to stay home.

The morning was biting cold, the kind of day when breathing hurt. White, lacy frost decorated the dying grass and the few leaves that still clung to the trees. She shivered and hurried away from the cabin, cutting through the woods to where the road swung closest to her house.

Clomping along in Oliver's old coat and boots on the dusty road to town might not be dignified, but her only pair of shoes was worn near through on the soles. It wouldn't take much hard wear for them to fall apart completely. Rather than risk it, she'd reverted back to her childhood days when hand-me-downs had been a necessity, not a choice.

Once she could see the smoke rising through the trees from the chimneys in town, she sat down on a handy rock to pull on her stockings and shoes. She stuffed the oversized boots into a sack she'd brought along for that purpose. Then, after brushing the dust off her feet, she slipped on her stockings and secured them with the garters she had in her pocket. She eyed the stockings with some misgivings. She'd already darned them more than was sensible. Although she was trying hard to save every penny that Lucy paid her, some things were beyond her control.

The price of new shoes and stockings would be a set-back to be sure, but she couldn't work in the mercantile looking like something the cat dragged in. At least Lucy allowed her to buy whatever she had need of at cost, which gave her some comfort. Resigning herself to the expense, she decided to order a new pair of sturdy shoes before winter set in for good.

Figuring she was as presentable as she could be under the circumstances, she set off at a brisk pace along the side of the road, which followed the sweeping curves of the nearby river. The signs of civilization were more frequent now: cabins were scattered in among the trees, and the scent of wood smoke hung heavily in the air.

She hurried around the last turn before the town came into sight. Pausing to catch her breath, she enjoyed the view. She'd never been farther than the neighboring town of White's Ferry, but she thought

Lee's Mill was a right pretty place to live. Most of the damage done during the war had been repaired, giving much of the town a prosperous new look.

She started forward, wanting to make sure she was on time for work. Not that Lucy Mulroney would ever complain about Josie's showing up late, knowing that she had to walk some distance just to get there. She would worry, though, and Josie didn't want that, especially now that Lucy was expecting. It was supposed to be a secret, but Josie had overheard Lucy and Cade talking a few days ago when they didn't think anyone was around.

Their secret was safe with her. She owed them far too much to betray them by spreading gossip, even if it was good news.

It was too early for much to be going on at Joe Tanner's saloon, but Josie hurried her steps anyway. Her husband spent a fair amount of time in the two saloons in town and probably owed both places more money than he could afford. Pride would make her hand over what little money she had if the owner ever demanded it of her. So far, that hadn't happened, but she wasn't going to tempt fate by taking a leisurely stroll past the place.

A familiar voice called out to her as she neared the church on the corner. "Good morning, Mrs. Turner!"

Josie immediately crossed the street to greet the Reverend Hayes. Although he'd only been pastor of the small church for about a year, he'd already managed to establish quite a following. She would have liked him just for himself, but he'd recently married Melinda Smythe, another of the women that Josie counted as close friends.

"Good morning yourself, Pastor Hayes! How is Melinda?"

He fell into step beside her. "She's busier than ever

with school, but she never complains about the work. She loves what she does."

Josie felt a stab of jealousy. She wondered what it would feel like to have both a satisfying job and a man who loved her as much as Daniel Hayes obviously loved his wife. Not that Josie minded working at the store—no, not one bit. Just over a year ago she'd been an illiterate hill girl, so she'd come a considerable way. Never in her wildest dreams had she ever thought to have a job where she was trusted to handle money and serve customers.

"If you're on your way to the store, I'll walk with you. I need to buy more paper and ink before I write next Sunday's sermon."

His twinkling eyes and friendly smile encouraged Josie to feel daring. "Maybe we should do everyone a favor by limiting how much paper and ink you can buy."

To her relief, her companion took her remark as the friendly gibe that it was. He laughed out loud, drawing the attention of several others out on early morning business. Josie felt pleased with her success. It had taken her a long time to realize that not all men were like her father or her husband. She still found it amazing that Lucy and Melinda didn't live in fear of their husbands' tempers. Cade Mulroney, especially, was a force to be reckoned with when his temper was aroused, but his petite wife was his equal when it came to sheer stubbornness.

"By the way, Henrietta Dawson tells me that you've been quite a help with all the sewing for the Christmas gifts. I appreciate all that you've taken on, and I know that she does."

Josie flushed with pleasure. She had about worn her fingers to the bone stitching the candy bags. Henrietta was keeping her well-supplied with work to do. "I have enjoyed helping."

"Well, wait until you see how excited the children are

when they get their bags full of candy." He smiled. "I just hope that you've made a few extras. The children aren't the only ones with a sweet tooth."

"I think that can be arranged."

A familiar figure caught her eye as the two of them stepped up onto the porch of the mercantile. Her heart fluttered as Sheriff Mitch Hughes rode by on his way to the jail down the street. She quickly averted her eyes, not wanting to be caught staring when he dismounted and tied his horse to the hitching post.

Most of the men who didn't frighten her were the husbands of her friends. Although she knew instinctively that the sheriff was trustworthy, he made her uncomfortable for other reasons. There was something about the way he looked at her that made her aware of herself as a woman, not that he was ever anything but painfully polite whenever he came into the store.

The other day was the only time she'd ever seen his temper slip, but his anger had been directed toward Oliver, not her. There was no doubt in her mind that he would have prevented her husband from dragging her out of the store if she had asked him to. Despite her refusal to accept his help, she cherished the memory of someone being willing to protect her.

That hadn't happened often in her life.

She risked one more glance toward the jail before allowing the Reverend Hayes to usher her into the store. Although the door was unlocked, there was no sign of Lucy in the immediate vicinity.

"Give me a minute, Reverend, and I'll get that paper and ink for you."

"Take your time, Mrs. Turner. I'm in no hurry."

Josie stripped off Oliver's coat and the scarf she'd worn wound around her head and tossed them into a corner of the storeroom. Grabbing an apron off the hook, she tied it on over her faded brown dress. After patting her hair to make sure it was still neatly coiled at the back of her head, she hurried out into the store, ready to serve her first customer of the day.

The Reverend Hayes stood near where she'd left him reading a copy of the *Clarion,* the town's only newspaper. She knew what kind of writing paper he preferred, so she let him continue reading while she collected it and the ink and recorded the items in Lucy's ledger.

"Do you want to pay for these now, Reverend, or should I put them on your account?"

Evidently, he'd been more lost in Cade's editorial than she thought, because she had to repeat herself before he realized she'd been trying get his attention. He looked up from the paper he'd spread out on the counter.

"Sorry, I was . . ." His voice trailed off as he got his first good look at her without the scarf around her face. "Mrs. Turner . . . Josie . . ." His distress left him fumbling for what to say.

Shame and embarrassment had her backing away, trying to put some distance between herself and the pity she saw reflected in Daniel's eyes. How could she have forgotten the bruise on her cheek? It had faded somewhat, but obviously not enough.

"Are you all right?" he finally managed to get out.

"I'm fine." Sensing his doubt, she gave him the best smile she could muster. "Really. Now, did you want to pay for the paper and ink now or put it on your account?"

"My what?"

She held the bottle of ink up for his inspection and waited as patiently as she could, especially considering how badly she wanted to slink back to the storeroom and out of sight.

Perhaps realizing that he was making her uncomfortable, Daniel Hayes shook his head slightly as if to clear his mind. "I'll pay for my items now, Mrs. Turner." He put a couple of bills on the counter and waited silently while Josie counted out his change.

"Thank you."

He picked up his purchases and started to walk away. She held her breath, hoping that the whole incident was over, but no such luck. The young minister started toward the door, but then turned back to face her once again.

"I do give thanks for all that you're doing for the children of Lee's Mill, Josie. And know this: my door is always open if you have need of me."

She blinked back the sting of tears. Not trusting herself to speak, she nodded and then turned away, trying her best to look busy. After a second or two she heard the bell over the door chime as the minister left. She gave herself a moment or two to gather herself before going upstairs in search of her employer. Although Lucy frequently left Josie alone in the store for short periods, it wasn't like her not to make an appearance at all.

"Lucy?" Josie didn't want to barge in on Lucy and her family, but she'd never forgive herself if something was wrong and she failed to act. Although it had been months since the attack on Lucy and the store, and the man responsible was in the state penitentiary, it was hard not to worry. Since Lucy now lived in her new husband's house, the upstairs of the rebuilt store now consisted of a small office and the meeting room for the Luminary Society.

Josie went up several more steps and then called Lucy's name again. This time she thought she heard a response, even though it sounded more like a moan rather than words. It was enough to send her flying up the rest of the staircase.

"Lucy, it's me—Josie. Is everything all right?"

She found her employer sitting at her desk with her head down. A rancid smell hung in the air, making Josie want to gag. She hurried across the narrow room to open the windows, preferring the chill of the morning air to the nauseating smell.

"Are you sick?" What a stupid question. Of course she was. She tried again. "Lucy, do you need me to get Cade or Doc?"

Lucy groaned again as she tried to push herself upright. Her attempt at a smile was pathetic. "There's nothing wrong that another month or so won't cure." She drew a shuddering breath. "It's nothing more than morning sickness. It'll pass."

Josie didn't know much about the whole business of pregnancy, but she was willing to do what she could for her friend. "I'll make you some weak tea and get some soda crackers. I've heard that's good for people who are, uh, you know . . ."

Lucy settled her head back down on her arms. "I'd appreciate it."

Josie picked up the basin that Lucy had used and carried it out of the room, hoping the fresh air would help settle Lucy's miseries. She quickly took care of the basin and put water on to boil. Once she had everything set out for the tea, she hurried back upstairs with a pitcher of cool water and a couple of rags.

Lucy was right where she'd left her. She didn't protest when Josie dipped the cloth in the water and then washed Lucy's face. After she rinsed it out, she folded the cloth and laid it across Lucy's forehead.

"That feels like heaven."

"I'll be right back with the tea and crackers."

Josie could only be grateful that it was a slow morning for the store as she made another trip or two to take care of Lucy. Her friend managed to choke down a couple of crackers, washing them down with the weak tea. At last, she had some color back in her face.

"Thank you, Josie. I had no idea I would feel this bad every morning."

"Every morning? What does Mr. Mulroney think about this? I'm surprised he doesn't make you stay home."

Judging by the wicked smile she gave Josie, Lucy was definitely feeling better. "He would if he knew. Luckily, he has to leave for work before I get up in order to take Mary to school. By the time he sees me, most of this has passed." She set her teacup back down and slowly rose to her feet. "I would appreciate you not telling him. He would only worry."

That was when Lucy got her first close look at Josie. Her eyes widened when she saw the fading bruise on Josie's cheek. Her dark eyes sparkled with anger. "What was it this time?"

Josie didn't try to deny anything. Lucy's first marriage had not been a happy one. She knew firsthand what Josie had to live with.

"I won't quit my job." She meant it, too. It was a more a matter of survival than pride.

"Of course you won't. I need you too much." Lucy put her hand on her still-flat stomach. "Now more than ever."

Then she rounded the desk and put her arm around Josie and gave her a quick squeeze. It was a show of support that meant more to Josie than words. No one had ever needed her before. Perhaps Lucy had hired her out of pity, but as Josie had gained experience and confidence, Lucy claimed that she didn't know how she'd ever managed without her.

"I'd better get back downstairs in case someone comes in." She never doubted Lucy's sincerity, but the whole concept of friendship was still new. The emotional bonds were not yet a comfortable fit.

Downstairs she set about doing the daily routine of chores. She dusted all the shelves she could reach easily. The others could wait until she had the floors swept and the stock straightened and counted. She made note of the fact that they were low on sugar and coffee, so Lucy would know to order more.

Finally, she slipped on her coat. The front porch needed sweeping. The wind had come up since she'd walked to town, so she stepped out into the street to get a better look at the sky. Just as she'd feared, it had taken on an ominous look. Dark clouds were moving in from the southwest, bringing with them the threat of a storm. This time of year it could be a cold rain or the first snow of the season.

Or worse yet, it could be freezing rain coming their way. More dangerous than snow, it could cripple the area, making travel all but impossible for days. The weight of the ice would snap tree limbs like matchsticks, sending branches crashing through roofs with no warning.

Common sense told her that she should start for home before the weather changed, but she wasn't about to leave Lucy alone. If she couldn't make it home, surely someone would offer her shelter for the night. As a breeze caught at her skirt and sent a chill through her, she had a guilty thought that it would be a relief not to have to spend the night with Oliver at the cabin.

He wouldn't like it if he was trapped there with no booze and none of his friends for company. Knowing her husband's unpredictable temper, he'd find some way to blame her for the weather. He'd also be mad if she wasn't there to cook his dinner, but at least she'd be out of his reach for a few hours. Her hand crept up to touch her sore cheek. She didn't need another demonstration of his superior strength anytime soon.

If only there were a way out of the mess her life had become. She'd even consider the scandal of a divorce, but that took money she didn't yet have, although she was putting some away whenever she could. Oliver would probably be glad to be shed of her—she knew his father would be glad to see her gone, but Oliver didn't have any more money than she did. And Jed Turner, Oliver's father, doled out money to his son only sparingly.

Footsteps warned her she was no longer alone. She stopped sweeping and turned around. Somehow, she wasn't surprised to find Mitch Hughes standing only a few feet away from her. Her heart tripped over itself when her eyes met his.

"Morning, Mrs. Turner."

"Sheriff." She immediately looked away, not knowing how to react to the strong feelings that washed over her. He stood there, silent and grim, making her feel edgy all over. It wasn't fear—she knew that feeling all too well. No, it was something else entirely.

"Looks like a storm is rolling in."

Looking up at the clouds gave her a safe target for her attention. "Yes, it sure looks that way. The only surprise is what it will bring with it."

"I'm betting on rain and maybe some hail to make things interesting." He stepped closer but still kept a safe distance between them.

"Well, you could be right, because it's warmed up some. An hour ago I would have bet on snow."

The two of them stood staring up at the sky for what seemed like an eternity, neither of them saying a word. Finally, Mitch spoke again.

"Are you doing all right out there at your cabin?"

She didn't know what to say. The cabin was fine? When

Oliver was gone, she was happy enough? Or that he hadn't hit her hard enough to do any real damage?

She settled for a half-truth. "I'm fine, Sheriff."

After a bit, he changed the subject. "I have to pick up a few things for Ben. Can you get them for me, or do I need to see Mrs. Mulroney?"

"No need to bother her. I'll get what you need. I can finish up out here later." Before she had gone two steps toward the door, he stopped her.

"Go ahead and finish. I'm in no hurry."

Feeling self-conscious, she gave the rest of the porch a few halfhearted swipes while trying to keep the bruised side of her face away from the sheriff's observant eyes. He was as likely to react with anger as with pity. She didn't need either, from him or anyone else.

When she figured she'd given a fair imitation of cleaning the rough boards of the porch, she picked up the broom and started for the door. Mitch was there ahead of her, opening for her and then standing back to allow her to enter ahead of him. No doubt, his mama had taught him his manners, but Josie wasn't used to being treated like a lady. She would have handled it better if he'd shoved past her to get in out of the cold.

Once again she headed straight for the storeroom to rid herself of her coat. She didn't give her appearance more than a second's thought, knowing the sooner she waited on Mitch Hughes, the sooner he'd be gone. Maybe then the butterflies trapped in her stomach would settle down.

He'd already set a few items on the counter. "I'll need coffee and some sugar."

It was the third time in two weeks that he'd ordered coffee. "Ben must drink a powerful lot of coffee to need it this often."

To her surprise, Mitch flushed and looked a bit guilty.

"Well, I ended up leaving the coffee I bought last week at the jail for Jake. This time I'm taking it out to the farm."

"How is old Ben doing?" She was still managing to keep her face averted as she put the beans in the grinder and began to turn the handle.

Mitch moved closer to watch her. "About the same—mad at life in general and me in particular."

Josie laughed as she dumped the coffee grounds into a sack and tied it shut. "Sounds like Ben."

"I didn't know you knew him so well."

She shrugged. "He and my father were friends of a sort. I can't say that I know him all that well, but he's been around my whole life. Tell him I said hello."

"I'll do that." Mitch took the coffee from her hand and added it to the small pile of things on the counter. "Can you put all this on my account?"

"Sure thing."

"Tell Lucy I'll settle up with her when I get back to town."

That was when Josie made the mistake of looking at him straight on. As soon as she did, he dropped the few things he'd already picked up, and reached out to cup her chin with the palm of his hand. With more gentleness than she'd known was possible he tilted her face up and to the side.

"Oliver do this to you?"

Once again she was relieved that the hard-edged anger in his voice wasn't directed at her. There was no use in lying about what happened. "Yes."

Mitch's hand dropped away. No doubt he was as disgusted with her as she was for letting herself be treated this way. She shoved her shoulders back and forced herself to meet Mitch's angry gaze head on. "I'll handle my own problems, Sheriff."

Three

Mitch jerked his hand back, fully aware that he'd handled the situation badly. He didn't need to ask who had hit Josie. Everyone in the whole damn town knew about Oliver Turner. There was no call to embarrass her by making her spell it out. He should apologize for intruding and walk away.

But it wasn't in him to do nothing. If she wouldn't take his help directly, then he'd do what he could on his own . . . like arrest her husband on every possible excuse. Oliver might decide he was being harassed, but that was too damn bad. If he tried anything, Mitch would be only too glad to give him back some of his own medicine. Let him see how he liked being hit by someone who was both bigger and stronger.

Jake or Cade would probably be glad to hold Oliver so Mitch could do a better job of it. For now, though, he needed to get away from Josie Turner for a while.

"I'm sorry, Mrs. Turner." Let her think he was apologizing for stepping out of bounds, but that wasn't it at all. He was sorry that a nice lady like her had to put up with an idiot like Oliver.

She was back to acting the helpful clerk. "Well, Sheriff, if that's all you need, I must get back to my duties."

He managed to growl out a halfhearted thank-you as he awkwardly gathered up his purchases and left. His

stop at the store had been a spur-of-the-moment decision, so he didn't have his saddlebags with him to hold
the half-dozen items he'd bought. He'd been in the middle of his morning rounds when he'd spied Josie
working outside. Now he'd have to backtrack to the stable long enough to stow away the coffee and other
things until he left for the farm later in the afternoon.

Ben had already accused him of turning into a squir-
rel for the way he was stockpiling supplies for the winter.
The old man didn't speak much except to complain, but
he wasn't stupid. If he ever ventured off the farm to
spend any time in town, he'd figure out why Mitch
brought home the supplies in dribbles. He was making
a damn fool of himself even though no one knew it, at
least not for sure. More than once Cade had given him
a considering look when the topic of Josie Turner came
up in conversation, and Lucy didn't miss much, either.

Vowing that he'd made his last spur-of-the-moment
trip to the store, he slipped in and out of the stable without having to speak to anyone. When he stepped back
outside, he turned his collar up against the wind, which
had picked up again. There was a sharp edge to the cold,
cutting through his coat and shirt like butter. It didn't
bode well for their chances of a mild winter if it was this
cold so soon after Thanksgiving.

His eyes flickered from one side of the street to the
other as he made note of who had come into town for
the day. The owners of several nearby farms were huddled together on the corner, no doubt talking stock
prices and what to plant come spring. He made note to
check with Ben to see if he would need to make any
major purchases before it was time to plant the spring
crops.

He glanced through the front window of the bank. It looked busy inside, but nothing out of the ordinary. He recognized most of the faces, but there were one or two who were strangers to him. It wouldn't hurt to walk through, just to let his presence be felt.

He needed to check in with Cletus Bradford, anyway. The man served Lee's Mill in the dual capacities of mayor and bank president, so the threat of a new gang moving into the area would be of particular interest to him. Once inside the bank, Mitch caught Cletus's attention, and Cletus motioned him toward his office in the back.

"Morning, Mitch. Have a seat."

"No thanks, Cletus, I won't be here that long. I just wanted to let you know that I have Cade keeping an eye on news from around the state. So far, there's no sign that gang has moved this way. Doesn't mean they won't, but there's been no mention of trouble anywhere close."

"I suppose that's good news, but I'd just as soon know where they are."

He selected a cigar before pushing the box across the desk toward Mitch. Knowing the banker's weakness for good smokes, Mitch accepted the offer.

"I'll send another wire to that sheriff up north and see if he's gotten any new information. Not much else we can do." He struck a match to light his cigar. He allowed himself a few seconds to savor it. "Thanks for this," he said, gesturing with the cigar. "I'd better be on my way."

"Thanks for stopping by, Mitch. I appreciate it."

The line in the small lobby of the bank hadn't gotten any shorter. Everyone must have decided to take care of business before the storm hit. Once again, Mitch looked for strange faces among the crowd. Most folks looked familiar, even if he couldn't put a name to every face.

There was one man at the end of the line, though,

who caught his attention. Mitch was sure he would have
remembered if he'd seen him before, not that the man
was doing anything to draw unwanted attention to himself. But something about his eyes bothered Mitch. They
were never still, instead flickering from one point to another, drinking in every detail in the small room. Then
there was the way his guns rode low on his hips, looking
far too well used.

Rather than confront the man in such a public place,
Mitch strolled on out the door and turned uptown toward the jail. He stopped a few doors down and leaned
against a handy wall to wait. And watch. About ten minutes later, his quarry came out of the bank. If he was
aware of Mitch's scrutiny, he gave no sign of it. He
mounted his horse, a big rangy bay, and rode toward the
far end of town. Judging by his pace, he wasn't in a particular hurry to get anywhere.

There was no crime in being a stranger. But over the
years Mitch had learned to trust his gut instincts, and
they were busy screaming for him to trail that particular
stranger to his destination. There wasn't time. By the
time he could get his horse saddled up and ready to ride,
the man would be too far gone, and the road was too
well traveled to make tracking possible.

But at least he'd gotten a good look at the man. Once
he was back at the jail, he'd compare what he remembered against the stack of wanted posters he had in the
file.

He resumed his prowling, feeling restless and unsettled.
He kept to his usual slow pace as he walked the streets of
Lee's Mill. When he passed by the *Clarion* office, he
glanced in the front window and waved at Cade. There
was no way to avoid passing by the store next door. He deliberately kept his eyes averted to avoid seeing Josie again,
but his anger over the bruising on her face hadn't faded.

As her image formed in his mind, the heavens above opened up, sending a cascade of icy rain pouring down on the earth below. People up and down the way scattered in to whatever shelter they could find. He wouldn't give into the weakness to run. Turning his collar up against the wind, he methodically finished his self-assigned duties.

Finally, he stopped by the jail to make sure that Jake had shown up to take over the care of the town. He mentioned the stranger and asked Jake to keep an eye out for him. Afterward, Mitch resigned himself to a long, cold ride out to the farm, more because the weather fit his mood than because Ben would be glad to see him. Besides, he had all those unneeded supplies to deliver.

At least the old man would be some company. If Mitch stayed in town, he'd either have to hole up in the hotel for the night or else settle for one of the rock-hard cots in a cell. He'd always found it funny that as the sheriff, he spent more time sleeping in jail that most criminals did.

But tonight he wanted his own bed, even if it meant sleeping there alone.

"I saw your sheriff today."

Oliver looked up from his drink and shrugged. "He's nothing to worry about. Hell, our last mayor tried to burn the town down and Sheriff Hughes was one of the last to figure it out."

The outlaw's eyes narrowed slightly, but he kept his thoughts to himself. "He was smart enough to pick me out of the crowd."

That brought Oliver up short. "He recognized you?"

"Not by name. By type, though. One glance at me and he knew I could be trouble." The fool sounded almost proud of the fact.

"Did he follow you out here?"

"How the hell should I know? Do you think the man is stupid enough to try to follow my tracks in the pouring rain?"

Oliver tossed back the last of his drink before getting up to look around outside. His foot caught on Josie's sewing basket, causing him to stumble slightly. After kicking the offending box into a corner with a curse, he managed to make it to the door without further mishap. He needed the man behind him to respect him as an equal, not a simple thing considering the outlaw's growing reputation. Falling flat on his face wouldn't make it any easier.

Outside, he drew a breath of fresh air as he stared out into the gathering gloom of the late evening. The rain that had started earlier was finally slacking off, but he doubted that it would stop completely. It had the feel of a storm that had spent its fury but still had plenty of misery left to spread around.

It dawned on him that Josie should have been home hours ago. Lucky for her that there had been enough of last night's dinner left to offer his guest. She wasn't a bad cook, but that was all that she was good for, the stupid bitch. The only time she'd ever tried to do anything smart was to get herself married up with him.

Lot of good that had done either of them, he laughed bitterly as he lit another cigarette off the last one. His father had been on his case to settle down and get married, but he hadn't approved of Oliver's choice in wives. Not that he'd had much to say about the choosing. Her father's shotgun had been pointed right at Oliver's midsection while the old pastor said a few words over them. That night was such a blur in his memory that he still had no idea why that hellfire-breathing minister had agreed to the ceremony.

Probably thought Oliver had done more than kiss Josie. Well, that joke was on all of them, and especially him, because she'd been a virgin on their wedding night. He'd had a lot to drink before dragging her to his bed, but he couldn't have been mistaken about that. She hadn't enjoyed the experience, and she sure as hell didn't like him much better now.

That pleased him. The door opened behind him.

"You going to stay out here all night? The boys are getting up a poker game and want to know if you're in or out."

"I'm in." He tossed the cigarette out into the rain where it sizzled and died. As he went inside, it occurred to him to wonder who was sharing a bed with Josie for the night. He wished the poor bastard luck, because he was in for a long, cold night if he was expecting Josie to warm his sheets.

For now, he and the men waiting inside had plans to make. And no sheriff, fool or not, was going to interfere.

"You're sure you don't mind?" Josie clutched Cora's extra nightgown in her hands. "I had money for the hotel." Barely, but enough.

"Don't be silly." Cora glanced over her shoulder to make sure her elderly aunt was safely tucked away in her bedroom. "It was nice to have someone for company who stays up past eight o'clock and doesn't snore."

Josie felt guilty for giggling, but she couldn't help herself. "Cora, that wasn't very nice."

"No, but then neither is Aunt Henrietta." Cora fluffed the pillows on the beds and then looked around to see if there was anything else Josie might need.

"I do appreciate her letting me stay over. She doesn't exactly approve of me, you know."

Cora drew in a sharp breath. "She hasn't been rude to you, has she? If so, just tell me and I'll have something to say to her in the morning."

Josie hastened to reassure her friend. "No, nothing directly. I can just tell that she'd rather deal with Lucy when she comes into the store than with me."

"She treats everyone that way, the old biddy." Cora gave Josie a rather forced smile. "Only a few more months to go."

Josie reached out and patted Cora on the shoulder, offering her unspoken support. Once Cora reached the age of twenty-one, she would come into enough money to set herself up in her own house. All the members of the Luminary Society did their best to make her life bearable until that day.

"Well, I'd better go so you can get some sleep. Are you working tomorrow?"

Josie wished she were, but it was Lucy's day in the store. "No, I need to get back home if the weather has broken. Oliver will be worried."

Cora gave her a look on her way out the door that told Josie that her lie hadn't worked. If everyone in the Society knew about Cora's problems, the whole town knew about Josie's. She'd lived with the shame for so long that it didn't hurt anymore—not much, anyway.

"Good night, Cora, and thank you again."

Once she was alone, Josie looked around the room. It might be the smallest room in Henrietta's house, but it was still nicer than any place Josie had ever slept in her life. The bed alone would probably spoil her for sleeping on the straw ticking back home.

She brushed the back of her dress before sitting on the edge of the bed to remove her stockings and shoes. After she unbuttoned her dress, she slipped it off and gave it a good shaking. There was no way that it would look freshly laundered after working in it all day, but she laid it out neatly on the floor anyway.

The gown Cora had left for her was soft and so pretty, edged as it was with small embroidered flowers and lace. It felt good against her skin, even if it did puddle around her feet because her friend was a good four inches taller.

After brushing her hair, she quickly plaited it into a loose braid before crawling into the big bed. The covers were thick and warm, enough to keep her cozy for the night. The storm may have slowed down some, but the temperature was continuing to fall. None of that mattered, because thanks to her friend, she was inside, safe and sound.

And for one night, she didn't fall asleep dreading the sound of Oliver's footsteps.

Despite the weather of the previous day, Mitch stepped out of the house to bright sunshine. He shook his head at the unpredictability of Missouri weather. For the moment, it didn't feel like just a few days after Thanksgiving.

"Don't count on it to stay this way." Ben, always the pessimist, followed him out onto the porch. "It could turn off cold again any minute."

Mitch wasn't going to let the old grouch spoil his mood. "Anything you need next time I come out?"

"No. You'll have to think up your own excuse for visiting that pretty little gal in the store."

Mitch's temper flashed hot as he turned on his hired hand. "What the hell are you talking about?"

Ben evidently realized he'd said the wrong thing, because he backed up several steps before answering. "Nothing, nothing at all."

"Explain yourself." He'd brook no arguments. If folks were gossiping about his frequent stops at the store, he needed to know about it.

"It don't take a genius to figure out that there's someone at the store you like to look at, or else you'd buy everything at once like you used to."

It took some effort to sound calm and rational. "I'm still keeping an eye on Lucy Mulroney and the Society. We don't know for sure that the mayor was acting alone when he set fire to the place. He's just the one we caught."

"I guess that makes sense."

Ben avoided looking Mitch in the eye, but there wasn't much he could do about that. At least the old coot went to town so rarely, he was unlikely to find out about Josie's working at the store. The last thing Mitch needed was someone linking his name to a married woman. From now on, he'd send Jake over to make his purchases for him.

Mitch started for the barn to get his horse. Ben tagged along beside him.

"What do you want me to cook for Christmas this year?"

Now that was an appalling thought. It was bad enough the man couldn't cook eggs without making them taste like dirt. Mitch hated to think what would happen if he tried to fix anything fancy.

"Belle is putting on a big feed at the hotel. Thought I'd eat there." The small look of disappointment that flashed across Ben's face had him adding, "I'll tell her that you'll be with me."

"Well, I don't want to be a burden." The old man puffed up with wounded pride.

"You're already that," Mitch assured him. "However, I don't know how I'd keep this place going without your help." That much was true. The demands of his job kept him from spending as much time as he'd like on the farm.

"All right, then. I'll come into town for dinner." Ben wandered away, trailing a cloud of pipe smoke behind him.

Mitch mounted up and rode toward town without looking back. He felt the same every time he left the farm: a mixture of relief and disappointment. Although he didn't exactly regret buying the place, he still hadn't figured out exactly why he had. It wasn't as if he had time to do anything more than help Ben occasionally.

Maybe he'd been hoping that the farm would come to feel like home to him, a place where he belonged and could set down roots. Looking back, he couldn't remember the last time he felt like he was doing more than just passing through. Even though he'd taken on the job of sheriff in Lee's Mill, he had already stayed longer than he'd expected to. The war had left him feeling restless and hurting.

Once he reached the main road, he urged his horse into a faster pace. He had enough time alone with his thoughts. Back in town, there would be more to do than feel sorry for himself. It wasn't as if he were the only one with problems. There wasn't a person in a hundred miles who hadn't been damaged in some way by the war, no matter which side they'd been on.

For a moment, his memories dragged him back to the smoke and the screaming and the death, the moment more real than the Ozark woods that surrounded him. In his mind's eye, he was back in the middle of it all, fighting to get back to the small house that was the center of his whole world and that held the one person who meant anything to him.

His horse had stumbled, nearly falling. Mitch had been relieved when it found its feet and galloped on.

He'd already had two shot out from underneath him as he dodged the Union patrols. If he lost this mount, he'd run, walk, or crawl if he had to in order to get back home. In the way of dreams and nightmares, time sped forward to when he reached the last rise that overlooked the small valley that had been home to Rebecca's family for two generations.

Nothing in the hell of the battlefield had prepared him for the horror that lay below. . . .

"Sheriff Hughes, are you all right?"

Mitch blinked twice before he realized that the voice was real, in the present, not part of his past. He looked around to see Josie Turner staring up at him with worry clouding her dark eyes.

"I'm sorry, did you say something?"

"Several somethings." She smiled a little as she stepped closer and patted his horse on the neck. "I asked if you're all right. You've been stopped there in the middle of the road for the past few minutes as if you'd turned into a statue or something."

Damn, he'd thought he put these episodes behind him. It had been months since the last one. "Sorry, Mrs. Turner. I was thinking."

"Must have been something pretty serious from the way you were frowning."

"No, nothing that matters." *At least not anymore,* he added silently to himself. "Where are you headed this early in the morning?"

The smile left her face, leaving her looking resigned and tired. "Home. I spent the night at Cora Lawford's because of the weather."

He hated to see her trudging along in the mud, but he couldn't very well offer to let her ride double with him. That wouldn't do at all.

"Do you want me to follow along to make sure you get

home safely?" He started to swing down out of the saddle, prepared to do exactly that.

Josie surprised him by laughing. "Sheriff Hughes, I've been walking this road alone since I was little. I know these woods as well as anybody. If I hear someone coming, I can disappear right quickly."

"Be careful." He knew he sounded gruff, but there was no help for it.

"I will." She patted the horse one more time and then started off down the narrow road.

Mitch watched as long as he dared. When she looked back at him a second time, he knew it was time to be moving along. Jake would be counting the minutes until he arrived. Mitch also needed to collect his mail to see if those promised wanted posters had come in from the sheriff up north. There wasn't a damn thing he could do to improve Josie Turner's lot in life, so he spurred his horse forward toward town. At least as sheriff, he knew what he was supposed to do.

From behind a handy sycamore, Josie watched Sheriff Hughes until he was out of sight. She wondered what he'd been thinking about so hard. She was willing to bet that it hadn't been anything pleasant. His face, always set in serious lines, had looked unusually grim, even for him. And his eyes had looked full of pain. It wasn't her place to worry about the man, but she hoped the rest of his day went better.

She was dragging her own feet, delaying for as long as possible the inevitable fight when she returned home. Not once since they'd married had she stayed gone all night. Oliver made a regular habit of it, but she was supposed to be at the cabin waiting for him. She dreaded confronting him, knowing she'd face his fists again rather than grovel at his feet.

All too soon she reached the narrow cutoff that led to the cabin. She drew a steadying breath, threw back her shoulders, and marched the last distance as if she had not a care in the world. At the last turn, relief washed over her. There was no smoke coming from the chimney, and the corral was empty. She was alone.

Perhaps Oliver hadn't even realized that she was gone if he'd been caught somewhere in the same storm. For the moment, however, she was safe from his temper and accusations. With renewed energy, she hurried across the porch and stepped inside.

One look warned her that he'd been home, all right, and judging by the mess, he hadn't been alone. Her first instinct was to start in on cleaning up after him, but she changed her mind. She'd made do with washing her face at Cora's and dragging a brush through her hair. Now, while Oliver was gone, she could heat water for a real bath. While she waited, she'd see to the chickens and make a start on the other chores that awaited her.

After dragging the washtub into the center of the kitchen, she fetched enough water to fill a couple of large kettles on the stove. Then she brought in some more to fill the tub. By adding boiling water to the cold, she'd end up with at least a warm bath.

By the time the chickens were fed and the bed made, the water was hot. She took a careful look outside the cabin to make sure that Oliver and his friends were not in sight. Alone as she would ever be, she stripped off and sank down into the hot water. It felt like heaven.

Lucy had given her a small bar of rose-scented soap as a present. Here in early December, it brought back memories of summer flowers and warm days. She used it sparingly on her body and hair, hoping to make the

soap last through the winter. Someday, if she could afford it, she promised herself that she'd have flowery
soap for every bath she took. It was the kind of dream
that might just come true.

Lounging in the bath all day wasn't a particularly good
idea, no matter how good the still-warm water felt. There
was no telling how long Oliver would stay gone or if he'd
bring his unknown friends home with him again. Either
way, she didn't want to face any or all of them wearing
nothing more that the scent of roses.

Deciding that she'd dallied long enough, she quickly
rinsed her hair one last time before reaching for the
threadbare towels she'd left within reach of the tub. She
wrung as much water as possible from her hair before
wrapping one towel around her head and using the
other to dry her skin. A new sense of urgency sent her
scurrying into the bedroom to put on a clean dress.

As soon as she was decently covered, she began the te-
dious task of draining the water from the tub. The
ground outside was muddy enough without pouring out
several more gallons of water near the house. She
slipped on the same old pair of boots and filled a pair of
buckets and carried them out to the edge of the woods.
She was returning from her third trip when she heard
the sound of a solitary horse coming toward the cabin.

A quick burst of speed got her to the porch and the
questionable safety of the cabin, leaving her breathless
and shaky. No sooner had she slammed the door closed
and reached the window to peek out, then Oliver rode
into the yard. From her vantage point it was hard to
gauge his mood as he headed for the small lean-to next
to the corral to tend to his horse.

That would give her a few more minutes to finish
cleaning up the kitchen and get her hair combed out.
When Oliver finally stepped through the door, she was

sitting near the fire and pulling a brush through her hair with long strokes.

He seemed surprised to see her. "I thought maybe you'd finally run off."

The teasing tone in his voice confused her, leaving her unsure how to respond. She kept her remarks very matter-of-fact. "I spent the night at Cora Lawford's house because of the storm. I hope I didn't worry you."

He pulled out one of the chairs and turned it around backward to sit on. "You showed good sense staying in town. The weather was a killer last night. A big tree went down just east of here blocking the road in both directions. It could have flattened you."

She wondered if that would have upset him at all. Probably, but only because he would have had to start tending to his own needs.

"Sorry about the mess I left you," he said, gesturing toward the stack of dishes she'd already washed. "I had company last night."

"Anyone I know?"

His laughter wasn't particularly nice. "Not yet. Hell, I just met them myself, but we're thinking about working together."

Now, that did shock her. Oliver's usual way of getting money was either by playing poker or begging his father for some if the cards were running against him.

"What kind of work?" The brush was sliding through her hair easily now. She kept at it, though, not wanting to do anything to spoil the moment. It was only rarely that Oliver let her see this side of him when he was both sober and feeling good. Her question, no matter how innocent the intent, was enough to put him on his guard. His eyes narrowed in suspicion.

"Why?" he demanded. "What have you heard?"

By now she should be accustomed to his sudden

swings in mood, but this one caught her by surprise. "Nothing . . . nothing at all, Oliver. I was just making conversation."

"Well, never you mind." He stood up just as suddenly as he'd sat down. "I didn't get much sleep last night, so I'm going to lay down for a while."

He disappeared into the small alcove that served as their bedroom. She would have to be careful not to disturb him if she wanted to pass a quiet day. There was nothing to be done outside, so that left practicing her lessons or sewing. Since Oliver seemed to resent her efforts to learn, she usually tried to avoid working on her schooling when he was around.

She could, however, do some mending until she was sure he was fast asleep. Surely she'd hear him stirring in time to put her book and slate away before he caught her. Deciding it was worth the risk regardless, she looked around for her sewing basket. She found it wedged between the stove and the wall, the side of the box cracked wide open and the contents spilled and tangled.

No doubt, the innocent basket had gotten in Oliver's way and paid the price. Later, after he was gone, she'd try to repair it. For now, she'd fix the loose button on his favorite shirt and darn a few socks.

Three hours later she reluctantly put away her few school supplies. Now that Melinda Hayes had taught her how to read, she could hardly stand to let a day go by without reading. It was like a hunger that was never satisfied, no matter how many books her friends slipped her to read. But Oliver was bound to wake up soon, and she didn't want to test his temper.

Perhaps they could get through one day without fighting.

Almost without her noticing, her hand crept up to rub the bruise on her cheek. When she realized what she was doing, she jerked it back down and picked up her sewing again to finish the bag she'd started. A few minutes later, she cut the last thread and set her basket aside.

Deciding she needed some fresh air, she slipped on her coat to take a walk outside. When she reached the edge of the woods, the scent of the pine trees brought Christmas to mind. Would Oliver object if she cut some boughs and brought them inside? They'd never really celebrated Christmas, but she would like to this time because so much had happened in her life over the past year that she was truly grateful for. She'd wait to gauge Oliver's mood when he woke up, before asking if he'd mind.

After another turn around the house, she went back inside to do a few more rows on her embroidery project. She'd never had a mother to teach her such fancy things, but several of the women in the Luminary Society had offered to teach anyone who wanted to learn. Josie had mastered the skill well enough that Lucy offered to sell some of her handiwork in the store. So far, she'd sold three pairs of pillowcases and some tea towels. The proceeds had gone right into the small box of money she kept hidden in the back room of the store.

The bank would have been safer, but not if Oliver found out she'd opened an account. He'd either have the money in his pocket or spent within hours of the bank's opening.

A sound in the back of the cabin warned her that Oliver was awake and stirring. She hurried to stoke up the fire in the stove, to start cooking. Even if he was leaving for the rest of the day, he'd want a meal first. His drinking money lasted longer if he didn't have to waste it on food.

She cut off a few thick slices of smoked pork and

dropped them in the skillet. While it sizzled, she sliced some potatoes and snapped the last of the beans from the garden into the hot grease. It wasn't much of a meal, but hopefully it would satisfy Oliver.

He came into the room, carrying his guns in one hand and his boots in the other. She cringed when he came close to setting them down on top of her sewing.

She used the excuse of setting him a place to eat so she could gather her precious linens and move them to safety. He paid little or no atter ion to her handwork, which pleased her just fine. If he took too much of an interest, he might think to ask what happened to the pieces she'd finished. They sure weren't decorating their cabin.

After pouring him a cup of coffee, she served him a heaping plate of food. He grunted his appreciation as he dug into his meal. She fixed herself a smaller portion and sat down across from him. As usual, they passed the entire time without speaking.

Finally, he shoved the plate away and reached for his boots. After slipping them on, he strapped on his guns with such grim determination that she shivered. She wondered where he was going but knew better than to ask. She learned early on that Oliver would tell her what he wanted her to know and nothing more. Asking questions only tested his patience.

"I'm going to see my father before heading into town." He took his coat off the peg by the door and walked out the door without looking back.

She sat frozen in her chair for what seemed an eternity. His trip to town didn't have her worried, but his visit with Jed Turner did. If just the mention of Jed's name was enough to spoil Oliver's day, actually meeting with his father was certain to. She hoped Oliver had enough money to keep himself in drinks after leaving his father's house—a lot of them.

She thought about Mitch Hughes. Maybe he and her husband would cross paths tonight. If so, she might be spared the necessity of facing Oliver before morning. She wondered if it was a sin to pray for her husband to spend the night in jail. Maybe someday she'd ask the Reverend Hayes that question.

As she cleaned up after their meal, it occurred to her to wonder what kind of business Oliver and his new friends were involved in. Maybe he was going to see if Jed wanted to invest. Despite the way Oliver ranted about his father's tightfisted ways with money, he did respect Jed's business sense. Could he be seeking his advice instead of money?

Jed might never accept Josie as Oliver's wife. She suspected that her background reminded him too much of his own. He had every right to be proud of how far he'd come, but he didn't want to give her the same chance. Perhaps he saw his son's marriage to her as a step backward. Despite it all, she always had secret hopes that somehow the three of them could be a family. After all, none of them had anyone else.

For now, though, she had the rest of the day stretching out before her with nothing she had to be doing. With not a little bit of excitement, she reached for the latest book that Melinda had given her. Tomorrow would be soon enough to worry about Oliver and everything else. For now, she could read.

Four

Oliver stopped just out of sight of his father's house and watched for several minutes. Although his father's men were busy green-breaking some horses in the near pasture, there was no sign of Jed himself. Oliver faded back into the trees a little farther to make sure no one saw him. It wasn't as if he was on good terms with anyone who depended on his father for their living.

Each of Jed's employees was handpicked for his loyalty. Jed paid top wages to anyone who'd back his play against all comers, even his own son. Shoving the bitterness back down where he could control it, Oliver studied the house, looking for some sign that his father was home.

It was Jed's regular day to go into town to meet with the banker and take care of other business. If he followed his usual pattern, Jed would stop for dinner at the hotel before returning shortly before bedtime. That gave Oliver plenty of time to carry out his plan.

Earlier in the afternoon, he'd already paid one visit to Jed. They'd had their usual fight over money, but this time his father's refusal to share his wealth didn't particularly upset Oliver. No, indeed, it had only served to seal Jed's fate. Especially when the old bastard casually mentioned that he was going to make a trip to St. Louis soon. Something about looking for a new wife—preferably a young one who could provide him with children. Another son or two. Oliver figured it for a bluff, but it didn't matter.

What Jed wouldn't give, Oliver would take.

If his first attempt wasn't successful, then he'd get help. He'd been currying favor with just the right group of men. He didn't fool himself about his ability to control Baxter's gang. Only the cold-eyed ex-bushwhacker could do that. But for enough money, they'd help Oliver teach Jed a lesson about hoarding his wealth.

As the minutes slipped by, it became more likely that Jed was not at home. By now, the housekeeper should have been cooking dinner, but there was little smoke coming from the chimney. If Oliver remembered right, Jed usually gave her the night off if he was going to be gone. Better and better.

Knowing that the longer he waited the more he risked being seen, Oliver gave himself two more minutes before making his move. Either he'd slip down to the side door of the house or else he'd mount up and ride away. It was unlikely, though, that he'd get a better opportunity.

He pulled his flask out of his saddlebag, telling himself that he didn't need the drink. No, it was more like a toast to the success of his mission. If all went well, by this time tomorrow Oliver would be long gone with enough money to set himself up for life. He drained the flask and tossed it in the bushes, figuring it was the last day he'd have to drink cheap whiskey. He wiped his mouth with the back of his hand and smiled. Damn, he'd love to be able to see old Jed's face when he came home and found his safe empty.

The fool thought that just because he was the richest son of a bitch in fifty miles, no one would dare come against him. He was about to learn that he wasn't invulnerable, not by a long shot.

His decision made, Oliver slipped down the hillside,

hugging the shadows and keeping low, knowing that timing was everything—and mostly luck. He stopped at the edge of the woods, trying to make sure he made his final run across the yard to the door when his father's men had their attention on the action in the corral.

The sound of laughter told him the horse had won another battle, dumping his rider in the mud. Oliver took off running, taking a straight line right for the house. In one motion, he vaulted up the steps, yanked the door open, and went inside. His heart was banging away in his chest so loudly that he couldn't hear anything else. His one worry had been that Jed had taken to locking the doors when he was gone. But no, it would never occur to him that anyone, especially Oliver, would dare invade his territory.

Oliver tried to still his breathing, but it took an eternity before the silence of the house settled around him. Finally, he took several cautious steps down the short hallway before risking a quick look into the kitchen. Empty, just as he'd figured. Next came the dining room and then the door to his father's office.

The thick oak door muffled any noise that might warn him of anyone's presence. He'd come this far; there was no going back. He slowly turned the handle and eased the door open. Once again, he slipped through undetected. There was no time to celebrate his triumph. Each passing second increased the chance of failure. Even now, before he'd actually done anything worse than coming in without an invitation, he'd be hard put to come up with a plausible explanation for his presence.

He shook his head at his father's utter conceit. Most folks tried to hide their safes, but not Jed Turner. He wanted the whole damn world to know that he had money worth protecting in the big steel monstrosity that sat in a place of honor in his office.

His father would not be at all pleased at how easy it had been for Oliver to find the combination, written on a slip of paper and stuck underneath the bottom drawer of the desk. Considering how often Jed opened the safe to play with his money, he had to know the number by now. Maybe he'd forgotten he'd written it there.

But his mistake would be Oliver's salvation.

Three to the right, twelve to the left, and . . . Oliver's fingers froze, refusing to turn the dial to the last number, as the sound of a rifle being cocked echoed loudly in the otherwise silent room.

"Stand up slowly and turn around."

Facing down the barrel of a rifle, Oliver did exactly as he'd been told. He straightened up, his hand outstretched as if still reaching for the dial on the safe.

"I see you're still trying to get your hands on my money without having to lift a finger to earn a penny of it."

Oliver's face twisted in embarrassed fury. "I shouldn't have to. It's as much mine as it is yours."

Jed snarled as he lunged close enough to backhand his son across the mouth. "Like hell it is, boy. I earned every damn dime with sweat and blood. You, on the other hand," he sneered, "have been a leech since the day you were born."

Oliver moved to retaliate but stopped short when Jed brought up his rifle as a reminder to keep his distance. Shaking with barely controlled fury, he spit blood on the carpet.

"And what about *you*, Father? Money doesn't make you any better than the nothing you started out as. Hell, when Mother met you, she had to teach you how to eat with a fork instead of your fingers." He smirked. "She could barely stand to be in the same room with you, much less share your bed."

"And you've done so much better for yourself?" Jed drew himself up to his full height and met his son's gaze head-on. "At least my wife never had to go begging for a job to keep food on the table. I never thought I'd see the day that I had more respect for that illiterate hill girl you married than for my own son. At least Josie expects to have to earn her way. Maybe I'll do the girl a favor and give her enough money to get the hell away from you."

He motioned toward the door with his rifle. "Now get going."

As a final insult, he turned his back on Oliver and walked over to pour himself a stiff drink. Reminding himself that Baxter and his men stood ready to back him on his next attempt to teach his father a lesson, Oliver obediently started for the door. Having thwarted Oliver's first attempt, Jed would no doubt feel invincible. He'd learn differently soon enough.

"While you're at it, I expect you to clear out and never set foot in my home again. I wash my hands of you, you weak-livered, pathetic excuse for a man. Maybe I'll have better luck with my next family."

Jed's parting shot brought Oliver up short. There was no way he'd let the old bastard get by with breeding himself a new litter of trash to steal what belonged to Oliver. "Like hell you will!"

He made a grab for his gun, but Jed had far more experience when it came to fighting dirty. He kicked Oliver in the side of the knee, then swung the his rifle at Oliver's head like a club. Oliver managed to duck, letting the wall absorb the brunt of the attack. The two men crashed to the floor, fighting for control in the narrow space between the desk and the wall.

Jed's fist connected with Oliver's jaw; he retaliated with a telling blow to Jed's gut, doubling him up in pain. The older man recovered quickly and managed to get both hands around Oliver's throat in a choke hold. He was surprisingly strong for a man his age, no doubt due to all of his years of hard physical work. With his own strength rapidly flagging, Oliver fought to get a hand free long enough to draw his pistol, figuring Jed's rifle was useless in such close quarters.

When he felt it slip free of its holster, he gathered one last burst of energy to throw Jed off to the side, hoping to bring the barrel of the pistol against his father's throat. Only a fool would continue to fight when the squeeze of a trigger could blow the top of his head off. Oliver looked forward to doing exactly that. But when he smiled down into his father's eyes, it was his own death he saw reflected there.

To his horror, his father's work-roughened hand closed over his, slowly bending the gun back toward Oliver. The sudden realization that his father had been right all along—Oliver was weaker than the man who had spawned him—gave Jed all the leverage he needed. In one quick move, he had Oliver pinned beneath him and the gun aimed right at his chest.

In full panic, Oliver gave up fighting for control and fought to get free of his father's grasp. There would be time later for retribution, but Jed wouldn't let him go.

"You murdering whelp!" Jed growled. "Think you can get by with threatening me?" He pulled back the hammer. "I've killed better men than you before breakfast."

He slammed the barrel of the pistol across the side of Oliver's face. An agony of pain washed over Oliver as blood gushed from the open gash. Jed got in another blow before Oliver managed to shove him off his chest. This time, all he wanted was to make it to the door alive.

He'd managed to crawl a few feet when a burning pain exploded in his back. He scrabbled for purchase on the blood-soaked floor, but his legs refused to move. Exhausted, he lay still, hoping the pain would stop.

Lord, please give me the strength to run, he begged silently.

He hardly felt the boot in his ribs as Jed flipped him onto his back. Damn, it had to be hell if the whole world had narrowed down to the hatred in his father's eyes. He shivered. Hell wasn't supposed to be so damned cold.

The metallic taste of his own blood bubbled up in his throat, choking the last of his breath. With a gurgling sigh, he felt himself die.

Josie rubbed her aching eyes and decided that enough was enough. She'd indulged herself by reading for over two hours before reluctantly putting her books away. She thought Melinda would be right pleased with how far she'd gotten in the book. And she was pretty sure she had memorized the arithmetic problems she'd been assigned.

But now she had other chores to see to. As she stood up, her stomach rumbled, reminding her that she hadn't eaten in hours. Before she hauled in more wood, she'd take time to put something together just for herself. There'd been no sign of Oliver all afternoon. She'd enjoyed the time alone, figuring it would end soon enough.

While she waited for her soup to heat, she walked out onto the porch. The temperature was dropping steadily—another sign winter was about to set in for good. The air had a definite bite, but it felt good to breathe deeply of its freshness. She could still see the sun hovering over the hills to the west, but it wasn't making much of an effort to shine. Instead, it was a pale imitation of itself with no warmth or color.

The image made her smile. That Shakespeare fellow's fancy way of saying things was slipping into her way of thinking. She shivered one last time before going back inside. It was time to turn up the lamps and stoke up the fire before the cabin got too chilly.

She was reaching for the bucket to bring in enough water for the night when she heard the sound of a horse riding fast and hard for the cabin. Cocking her head to the side, she listened to hear if the horse and rider went past the house to the corral or stopped outside her door.

Something heavy landed on the front porch, followed by the sound of the unknown rider tearing off back down the trail. Caution won out over curiosity. After waiting for several seconds to pass before opening the door a crack, she peeked outside and stared at the disappearing back of an unfamiliar horse and rider. Puzzled, she stepped outside and almost tripped over someone lying at her feet.

"Oliver?" she whispered as she struggled to catch her balance. "What are you doing down there?"

Figuring him to be dead drunk again, she reached down to shake his shoulder but got no response. Her hand came away wet and sticky. Her mind struggled to understand the horror in front of her.

She nudged him with her foot and then again, harder this time. He rolled over to land facedown the mud. A gaping hole in his back oozed with thickened blood. The sight sent her retching into the bushes at the end of the porch.

Josie knew *dead* when she saw it, no matter how hard her mind tried to deny the truth. What should she do? It was awfully late to go running to town, especially if Oliver's killers were still lurking in the nearby woods.

Was tomorrow soon enough to go for help? No, she decided; she wouldn't wait that long. She knew that Sheriff Hughes would know what to do. The tall lawman needed to know that there'd been a shooting. And no doubt, he'd send someone to notify Jed Turner of Oliver's death.

She hated the thought of leaving Oliver out in the mud all night while she went for help. Bracing herself, she managed to pull him back up on the small porch. She was just going inside to get a blanket when she heard a noise. Cocking her head to the side, she listened hard, trying to pick out the sound that had caught her attention.

Riders—several of them—were coming this way. She looked around for something to protect herself with when she spied Oliver's pistol lying a few feet away. She was just picking it up when her father-in-law's voice rang out over the clearing. Her relief at recognizing her visitors was short-lived.

"Hold it right there, Josie!"

He and a couple of his men pulled up a short distance away, their rifles aimed right at her.

"What the hell have you done?" Jed slid down off his horse and ran to where Oliver lay sprawled half in the mud, half on the porch. He knelt beside him and felt for a pulse. "I know he wasn't much of a husband to you, but did you have to do this?"

At first his meaning didn't sink in. When it did, she immediately tried to explain.

"No, Mr. Turner, it's not what you think." She looked around at the others. "We need to go for help. Someone shot Oliver and dumped his body here for me to find." She held up her bloody hand to show him. "Please, can one of you go for the sheriff?"

No one moved. The circle of men looked decidedly grim. She instinctively backed up a step and then another until she ran into the wall of the cabin. What were they thinking? She got her answer soon enough.

"Murdering bitch!" the one closest to her snarled. "I say we hang her now and save the sheriff the trouble."

She tried to protest. "But I didn't . . . I wouldn't . . .

Please, Mr. Turner, you know me. I've never done a thing to hurt Oliver."

The cold that crept into her now had nothing to do with the temperature of the night air. When one by one the other men started to dismount, she turned and ran. Fear had her legs churning as fast as she could go, but Oliver's old boots weren't made for speed. She clomped through the mud as far as the corral before the first one caught up with her. It was Jed Turner himself.

His hand was like an iron clamp that bit down on her arm, jerking her around. Only the strength of his grasp kept her from being flung to the ground like a rag doll.

"You destroyed my son, you worthless bitch!" He shook her until her teeth rattled. "I should hang you myself."

Then he shoved her toward one of his men. "Five of you take her to the sheriff and tell him what happened. Tell him I'll be along shortly." His voice broke as he added, "After I see to my son."

Mitch dozed quietly in his chair. He'd been fighting the need to turn in for the night for the past half hour, but it was too early. The clock had chimed eight times only a short while ago. Another half hour before he was due to walk the streets again.

Maybe another cup of coffee would help clear the cobwebs from his head. He picked up the pot and debated whether to drink the dregs Jake had left him or to make fresh. Deciding he'd do both, he dumped what was left into his cup and refilled the pot and set it back on the stove. He was about to add more wood when a commotion outside had him reaching for his gun.

Damn fools! He'd already run one bunch out of town for the night. Either they were back or another group had decided to start up. He picked up his rifle and stepped outside. To his surprise, the horsemen were heading straight for the jail. It was too dark to recognize anyone yet, but they seemed determined rather than rowdy.

He stepped out into the street, ready to meet them head-on. Cradling his rifle in his arms, he waited for them to pull up. The lead rider was leading another horse by the reins. He wondered if that meant someone was hurt. Or dead.

"Evening, Sheriff."

He recognized the man as Jed Turner's foreman. He couldn't put a name to him, but that didn't matter right now.

"What's the problem, gentlemen?"

The man gestured over his shoulder with his thumb. "Oliver Turner has been killed. We brought you his murderer."

Well, that certainly caught his interest. He walked past the man to get a clear look at the figure sitting huddled on the second horse. When he realized it was Josie Turner, his surprise turned to shock.

"Mrs. Turner? Are you all right? Who shot Oliver?"

Ugly laughter surrounded him. "She did, Sheriff. Hell, if we'd been five minutes sooner, we'd have seen her pull the trigger. As it was, she was standing over his body with the gun still in her hand."

He wanted to hear her deny the truth of their words, but she didn't act as if she even heard their accusations. It was then he realized that she wasn't wearing a coat and had lost one of her boots somewhere along the way. On a cold, damp night like this one, if she wasn't already in shock, she would be soon.

"Let's get her inside where it's warm."

He reached up his free hand to help her down out of the saddle, so intent on Josie that the sound of several pistols being drawn caught him off guard. He froze and then

turned slowly toward the apparent leader of the group,
making sure his rifle was aimed right at the man's chest.

"Put the guns down."

To the man's credit, he didn't even blink. "We're just
backing your play, Sheriff. She's already killed one man
today. Don't want her to get a chance at you."

"It'll be a cold day in hell before I need help from the
likes of you," Mitch said with all the contempt he could
muster.

"Is there a problem here, Sheriff?" Cade Mulroney
walked out of the shadows with a shotgun in his hands.
He stopped outside the circle of men where he could
pick and choose his target if it became necessary. He
nodded at Mitch.

"Seems it took all these big, tough men to help Mrs.
Turner report that her husband has been shot."

Cade grinned at the insult. "Jake said he'd be along in
a minute."

A couple men stirred restlessly, but Cade's shotgun
convinced them to keep their mouths shut. Mitch
showed just how worried he was by setting his rifle down
on the boardwalk before lifting Josie down off her horse.
Her hands were tied together and looped around the
pommel of the saddle.

He resisted the urge to pick her up and carry her inside. "Can you walk?"

She gave no sign that she understood his question, but
after a bit she shuffled forward. He put his hand on her
elbow to steady her after retrieving his rifle. Once they
reached the door to the jail, he shoved her gently inside
before dealing with her captors.

"Mrs. Turner is in my custody now. You all can run
along home."

From somewhere in the back, a voice muttered loud

enough for them all to hear, "I told Jed we should have hung her ourselves."

That did it. Mitch marched back to the edge of the porch. "Any more talk like that, and you'll be spending time in the cell next to hers. I don't take kindly to talk of lynching." He motioned toward the end of town with his rifle. "I'll give the bunch of you five minutes to ride out. Anyone still in shooting distance after that is fair game. Do I make myself clear?"

He felt someone approaching from his right. A quick glance told him it was Jake. Some of his tension eased, now that the odds were a little more even.

"Mr. Turner said he'd be along shortly." The foreman seemed determined to get in the last word.

"Tell him to save himself a trip. I won't be talking to him or anybody else until morning. Now get the hell out of town."

He didn't want to have to resort to gunplay, but he would if necessary. Finally, the whole bunch of Turner's men slowly moved off. He didn't trust them to stay gone, but for now they were leaving. Once they were out of sight, he let out the breath he'd been holding.

"What the hell was that all about?" Jake asked.

"Let's get inside."

Cade moved up beside him. "Do you want me to go get Lucy?"

Mitch thought about it for all of two seconds. "Yes, and tell her to bring some dry clothes for Mrs. Turner. Those damn fools dragged her all the way in here with no coat or hat. She has to be half frozen."

Before Cade had gone two steps, Mitch called after him. "Make sure you announce yourself when you come back. Lucy will have my hide if I accidentally shoot the wrong man."

Now to deal with the problem waiting inside. He

stepped into the relative warmth of his office to find
Josie standing in the center of the room, looking lost.
Jake was busy adding wood to the stove and checking the
coffeepot.

"She's not talking." He looked apologetic, as if he
should have been able to do more than pour them all a
cup of coffee.

"I know. Cade went to fetch his wife. Maybe she'll be
able to get through to her." While they waited, he pulled
a chair close to the stove and eased Josie down.

"Go get Doc. We may need him."

Jake seemed only too glad to escape the confines of
the small room. When he disappeared out into the
night, Mitch locked the door behind him before kneel-
ing down in front of Josie. He pressed a cup of coffee
into her hands, figuring that even if she didn't drink it,
the warmth might help.

"I know something terrible has happened tonight,
Mrs. Turner. I'm willing to listen to your side of things."
He wanted more than anything for her to look at him
with those big, brown eyes and deny the allegations
against her. If there was even a shred of evidence in her
favor, he'd have Lucy and Cade take her home with
them for the night.

A sharp knock at the door had him moving back away
from Josie. No use in giving anyone ideas that he wasn't
acting as a sheriff should.

"Who is it?"

"It's Jake, and I've got Doc with me."

He threw the bolt and opened the door long enough
for the two men to slip inside. Doc immediately headed
for his patient. Josie could have been a statue for all the
attention she paid to any of them.

"What happened to her?" Doc asked as he performed
a quick check of her eyes and breathing.

"I'm not sure. About fifteen minutes ago, a bunch of Jed Turner's men came riding in with her tied to a horse. They claim she shot her husband."

"NO-O-O-O!" The single word came out as a desperate wail. Josie's eyes stared at a horror only she could see as she rocked and moaned again. "No, no, no . . ."

All three men stood over her, helpless and worried. Mitch hoped that Lucy Mulroney arrived pretty damned soon. Maybe the presence of another woman would make a difference.

His unspoken prayer was quickly rewarded.

"Mitch, open up. Lucy is here."

Cade's wife breezed in with Melinda Hayes right behind her. Cade followed them, his arms laden with clothes and blankets. He dumped them on the desk and left, saying he needed to get back to his daughter.

Lucy immediately put her arms around Josie and gave her a reassuring hug. "Mitch, put on a kettle of hot water and then you men skedaddle on out of here for a few minutes while we get Josie out of those wet clothes. Once we've got her dressed and warmed up, I'm sure we'll be able to make sense of this situation."

Jake blushed, no doubt at the thought of a woman undressing in the jail office. Mitch was only too glad to let Lucy take charge of the situation. After setting a pot on the stove to heat, both men picked up their rifles and escaped to the chilly night outside. Doc followed them outside.

"She'll do better under Lucy's care, but let me know if you need me. Otherwise, I'll stop by and check on her in the morning."

"Thanks, Doc."

Mitch and Jake watched him disappear into the darkness. Neither of them was quite sure what to do next, although one of them should make rounds. But if Turner and his men came charging back into town, it could take both of them to defend their prisoner. Finally, Mitch took one end of the building and Jake the other. They stood in companionable silence until Jake noticed a solitary rider heading their way.

"Sheriff." He pointed down the street.

It was too dark for Mitch to recognize either the horse or the rider, but he was willing to bet that Jed Turner had ignored his orders to wait until morning to come by. He was tempted to send the man packing, but he had just lost his only son. Although rumor was that there was no love lost between the two, that didn't mean the man would ignore his son's murder. Or the accused murderer.

Keeping his posture relaxed, Mitch waited to see what Jed had in mind. If he wanted to talk, fine. If he came on strong, blowing smoke and fire, Mitch would send him on his way, at gunpoint if necessary. As if suddenly aware that he was being watched, Turner straightened in the saddle to sit taller.

He stopped a short distance shy of the hitching rail and looked down at Mitch and his deputy. Turner had the bearing of a man who was used to being obeyed at all times. "Sheriff Hughes, I'm here about the murder of my son."

Mitch decided that he needed to set the rules early. "Mr. Turner, I'm sorry for your loss. I will be glad to meet with you in the morning to take your statement."

Turner had been in the process of dismounting. He froze briefly before settling back in his saddle. "I know you'll understand if I want to confront the woman responsible." It was an order, not a request.

"Yes, sir, I understand all right, but that doesn't mean I'm going to invite you in tonight. Mrs. Turner is my prisoner. No one is going to talk to her until I do." Mitch had been leaning against a post, but he pushed away and brought his gun up enough to catch Turner's eye. "Now, you have my sympathy, Mr. Turner, but you need to go on home now. Morning is soon enough."

The two men studied each other, each taking the measure of his opponent. Unfortunately, Lucy Mulroney picked that moment to stick her head out the door. "You can come back in now, Sheriff."

He didn't acknowledge her comment by even so much as a flicker of an eye, knowing that if he did, Turner would be on him in an instant. No one ever accused Lucy of being slow on the uptake. After seeing who was outside, she ducked back inside and closed the door with noticeable force.

"So is it just me who can't see the prisoner, Sheriff?"

The night air seemed balmy compared to the cold in Turner's voice. Mitch had dealt with bullies before. This one didn't impress him much.

"Your men dragged your daughter-in-law all the way here without a coat or even shoes, Mr. Turner." He liked the way the man flinched every time he referred to Josie as a member of his family. "Her clothes were soaked through, and the doctor said she was in shock. I asked a couple of the women in town to bring in some dry clothes for Mrs. Turner and to see to her needs."

"You seem more concerned about a murderer than about the victim."

Because that was true, and it worried him some, Mitch lashed out. "Your son is dead, Mr. Turner, and I'm sorry about that. However, it's my job to make sure the prisoner stays healthy enough to stand trial. Now, move on along before I arrest you for disturbing the peace. It wouldn't be the first time I've had a Turner cooling his heels in my jail."

"You're a real son of a bitch, aren't you, Sheriff? I'll be on my way, but you listen to this: that woman in there killed my son, and she's going to hang for it. The only reason she isn't already swinging from a tree limb is that I'm a law abiding citizen. I figure on letting you take care of that little chore for me."

He yanked on the reins, turning his horse sharply away from the two men on the porch. Mitch was satisfied to see that the bastard left far faster than he arrived. It wasn't hard to guess where Oliver had gotten his temper.

As he watched the older man ride away, he had to wonder at his own response to the situation. Normally, he felt nothing but sympathy for the victim and the family. He even knew that it shouldn't matter what he had thought of the victim when he was still alive. But in this case, all his attention was focused on the accused. Even now he wanted to be inside, offering what comfort he could.

It was a hell of a way for a lawman to react, and damned if he was going to let it show. He'd investigate the case the same as any other. And if all the evidence pointed at Josie Turner, he'd tell that to the judge. She'd have enough witnesses willing to testify to the way Oliver had treated her, so maybe the court would show some mercy. But if not, he'd string the rope to the gallows himself.

Even if it killed him right along with Josie Turner.

Cold. She was cold, inside and out. On some level she was aware of Lucy and Melinda fussing around her, and even more so of Mitch Hughes glaring at her from across the small room. But mostly she was cold.

"Mitch, she needs rest."

He pointed at the cells behind them. "Take your pick."

Melinda and Lucy both gasped in shock. "You can't possibly mean to put her in one of those."

He meant it; he surely did. Didn't they hear the finality in his voice? Josie mustered as much dignity as she could wearing borrowed clothes and someone else's shoes. Slowly she rose to her feet and shuffled toward the back of the room. Determined to show that she wasn't completely beaten, she asked one question before picking her new quarters.

"Which one did Oliver usually stay in?" If her voice quivered, at least her chin did not. It lifted slightly, as she politely waited for the sheriff to answer.

His answer was given only grudgingly. "The one on the right."

She nodded graciously and swept into the left cell. Once inside the small ironclad enclosure, she looked around as if checking out all the amenities of a fancy hotel. In one sweeping glance she made note of the naked cot, a small table that held a pitcher and bowl nicer than the ones she had back at the cabin, and a chamber pot.

Just like home, she thought bitterly.

Then, to save herself the indignity of someone else's doing so, she pulled the cell door closed behind her. It shut with a well-oiled click. Lucy's gasp of outrage helped soothe some of her pain, but only a little. With nowhere to go and nothing else to do, Josie perched on the edge of the bunk to wait for . . . what, she didn't know.

She just knew that if her friends didn't leave soon, she would fall apart again, and this time she wasn't sure she'd be able to pull all the pieces back together again.

Lucy came to the door. "Josie, we'll get you a lawyer."

"I can't afford one."

"Cade and I will—"

Josie forced herself to meet her friend's gaze. "No, you won't. I pay my own way, Lucy." She hadn't meant to be hurtful, but Lucy backed away as if Josie had struck her.

Melinda stepped in between them. "Lucy, we can talk

about that tomorrow. Right now, Josie needs some rest. We all do." She gently tugged Lucy toward the door. "Sheriff, we will be back first thing in the morning."

Alone in her cell, Josie wondered if Mitch Hughes recognized that for the threat that it was. Individually, he might be able to intimidate the women of the town. But since they'd banded together to form the Luminary Society, they'd found strength in numbers. If he didn't watch it, he'd have an office full of women day and night.

With that realization, Josie no longer felt quite so alone.

A few minutes later, she was vaguely aware of the sound of a key turning in the lock of her cell door. Mitch Hughes stepped inside, taking up most of the available space. Slowly she raised her eyes to meet his and waited to see what he wanted.

"Your friends thought you might like these." He thrust a lace-edged pillow and a quilt at her as if they offended him in some way. When she didn't immediately reach to take them, he dropped them beside her on the cot.

She bit back the automatic urge to thank him. Although he'd been the one to send for Lucy and Melinda, she wasn't feeling particularly grateful right now. Frightened, alone, terrified maybe. Gratitude didn't enter into it.

"Is there anything else?"

"No."

"Fine." Mitch stalked out, slamming the door behind him.

Somehow that little fit of temper pleased her. If he wasn't all that happy about having a woman in one of his cells, how did he think she felt? A lot of folks in Lee's Mill had looked down their noses at her for her whole life. Things were likely to be a whole lot worse now. She drew some comfort that Mitch was standing squarely between her and Jed Turner.

But she wasn't going to think about him or her last sight of Oliver, lying in the mud, his eyes open and unseeing. Despite the warmth of the jail, she shivered uncontrollably. Before the tears burning in her eyes broke loose, she grabbed the pillow and laid it at the head of the small cot. Curling up on her side, facing the back wall, she pulled the quilt over her until it covered her head. One by one, the tears fell silently onto Melinda's beautiful embroidery.

Somehow, Josie didn't think she'd mind.

Five

Son of a bitch, she was crying. He knew it as well as he knew his own name. How the hell was he supposed to get anything done with her carrying on like that? Not that she was making a sound. But she was crying all right.

Mitch shuffled through the stack of mail that had come in earlier, none of which was important enough to demand his immediate attention, but he had to do something to keep busy. It wasn't a lawman's job to offer accused murderers comfort, but it was all he could do to keep from doing exactly that. Muttering under his breath, he picked up the next envelope and tore into it. The poster he'd been waiting for had finally come in. He held it up to the lamp for a better look.

Just as he feared, the sketch could belong to damn near anybody. Hell, he knew half a dozen men in Lee's Mill that fit the description: average height, blond hair, blue eyes. A small scar on the man's right jaw was the only real distinguishing mark. According to the note from the sheriff up north, the man used several different names, including Baxter, Barker, and handful of others.

Closing his eyes, Mitch tried to remember every detail he could about the man he'd spotted in the bank. The hair color was right, but the stranger had been sporting a reddish-gold beard. There was a vague resemblance to the poster, but that was all. He wished he'd thought to return to the bank and ask the teller if he'd gotten the man's name. By now, it was unlikely anyone would remember him at all.

Studying the poster again, Mitch doubted the man would answer him honestly if he walked up and asked if, by any chance, he had grown the beard to hide a scar. He could only hope the stranger had just been riding through and he was worried about nothing.

Laying the poster aside, he allowed himself another quick glance toward the cell behind him. Closing his eyes, he listened hard for any sign that Josie was still crying. All he could hear was the slow, regular sound of her breathing. Maybe she'd finally managed to fall asleep. With luck, she'd stay that way until morning.

Leaning back in his chair, he propped his boots up on the desk and closed his eyes. There wasn't a doubt in his mind that tomorrow morning would be busy. Whether he wanted them to be or not, Lucy and Melinda would come pounding on his door at first light or shortly after breakfast, bringing more things to make Josie's stay in jail as comfortable as possible. Although he'd draw the line at lace curtains, most anything else would be all right with him.

And Jed Turner and his men would be right behind them. Jed had enough money to think he could do as he damn well pleased, even if that meant hanging his daughter-in-law. Mitch figured on needing some backup when Jed came calling. To that end, he'd sent Jake on home to get some sleep, saying that he should be back before sunup.

He knew without asking that Cade would be close by. It was more likely that Jed would behave in front of the local newspaper editor. His business interests would suffer if his name was splashed all over the headlines for trying to storm the jail.

Figuring he'd done all the thinking he needed to, Mitch let himself drift off to sleep, hoping he didn't dream about a new widow with big brown eyes.

Jed prowled through the house, restless and angry. Damn, he'd never meant to kill the stupid fool. Oliver was nothing to be proud of, but he was still Jed's son. Maybe he'd have been better off letting Oliver clean out the safe and be gone, but he knew full well the greedy bastard wouldn't have stayed gone.

There'd been enough money in the safe for a reasonable man to set himself up with a solid business somewhere. Jed stared out at the cold, pale moon. The thought of Oliver as a storekeeper or even a saloon owner was laughable. The only thing he'd understood about money was how to waste it on liquor and gambling.

Now, Oliver's wife was a different matter. Jed figured she could have taken the money and made something of herself with it. However, there wasn't a doubt in his mind that Oliver wasn't thinking about his wife and future family when he got caught with his hand in the till. No, he wasn't thinking any further than the next bottle and the next poker game.

Jed headed for his office to finish off the bottle he'd started on earlier. His mind kept coming back to Josie. If she'd been any kind of wife, she would have cured Oliver of his bad habits the first year of their marriage. Hell, his own wife had brought Jed himself up to snuff in less time than that, and he'd been almost as illiterate and ill-bred as Josie was.

No, he'd been right all along. Josie had ruined Oliver's chances for being anything other than a wastrel and drunk the day her papa had dragged the two of them before a minister. That she hadn't actually pulled the trigger that laid Oliver low didn't absolve her of responsibility. She was guilty of Oliver's downfall, pure and simple. And Jed would use every dime at his disposal to see that she swung from a gallows for her part in his son's death.

The whiskey burned down his throat to settle in a pool of fire in his gut. Deciding he'd had enough to help him sleep, he set the half-empty glass down on the edge of his desk. Carefully stepping around the wet spot where he'd cleaned Oliver's blood out of the carpet, he trudged up the stairs to his bedroom. Tomorrow he would check to make sure that no stain still showed. If necessary, he'd rearrange the furniture to make sure no one else saw it—especially that nosy sheriff.

Exhausted by everything that had happened, he was asleep almost before his head hit the pillow.

Josie tried not to move. She had some needs to see to, but she wasn't about to use that chamber pot with Mitch Hughes right out there where he could see every move she made. Waking up in jail was humiliating enough.

"Are you awake back there, Mrs. Turner?"

"Yes, Sheriff."

Her answer was followed by the sound of heavy boots hitting the floor and walking toward her. There wasn't much she could do about her appearance without a mirror and a comb, but she patted her hair to see that it was still neatly braided.

She also rose to her feet, feeling that being behind bars was enough of a disadvantage without cowering in a corner. Mitch stopped to turn up the lamps, casting the room in a circle of yellow light and chasing the shadows back into nooks and corners.

She noticed that Mitch had the keys in his hand, causing her heart to flutter with hope. The grim set to his mouth, however, killed that idea. He avoided meeting her gaze directly when he spoke.

"I'm going to make a trip out back. Though you might need to do the same."

Her relief didn't keep her from blushing with embarrassment. "Thank you, Sheriff. That would be nice."

She cringed at her choice of words. There was nothing "nice" about being escorted to the privy. She supposed it was his job to make sure prisoners didn't escape, but where would she go with no money and a vengeful father-in-law with enough money to track her to the ends of the earth?

Mitch opened the door and then stepped back for her to lead the way. Perhaps he thought it was the gentlemanly thing to do, but she suspected it had more to do with his not trusting her. The whole process took only a few minutes. She supposed she should be grateful that he allowed her the dignity of closing the door, both when she was inside the small wooden building and when he took her place.

Once they were back inside, she let herself back in the cell. For lack of anything better to do, she folded the quilt and straightened the pillow.

"Would you like some coffee?"

It sounded heavenly, even if the offer had been made somewhat grudgingly. "Yes, I would love some."

Mitch poured her a cup and shoved it through the bars to her. It was too hot to drink, but she breathed deeply of the fragrant steam. After a few silent minutes, it was cool enough to sip.

"What do you like for breakfast?"

"Isn't bread and water the usual fare?" she asked tartly, startling Mitch into laughing a bit.

For a few seconds, the deep lines around his mouth

softened. "Well, I figure we could both do with some of Belle's biscuits and gravy this morning."

Her stomach chose that moment to rumble, reminding her that she hadn't had much of anything to eat since the afternoon before. If Mitch heard it, he was kind enough not to say so. "That sounds lovely."

"I'll send Jake down to the hotel when he gets here." Mitch glanced out the front window of the jail. "The sky is getting light up over the hills to the east. He promised to be here before the sun is up."

She wished she could do more than sit and wait, but the cell offered only a limited variety of possible entertainment. She'd already memorized how many bars made up each side of the small room, as well as the number of bricks in each row along the back. Without knowing how long she'd be caged there, she didn't want to spoil all of her fun. She was saving the excitement of counting all the bricks for another day.

Lordy, the tears were starting to flow again. Well, she wasn't going to give in to that particular weakness again. For the moment, she was safe and warm, and a hot meal was only a short time away. It would be a real pleasure to eat someone else's cooking for a change.

And there wasn't anything she wouldn't give to be home, poking at her old stove, coaxing the embers into heating both her coffee and the cabin. She closed her eyes and imagined the scene. She'd have on her nightgown with a coat thrown on over it. The windows would be covered in frost. And Oliver would still be . . .

Dead.

Oh, God, he was dead. He wasn't a good husband, and there were times she almost hated him for the way he treated her. But no one deserved to be shot in the back and left to die in the mud. She clenched her hands into fists to stop from shaking. Who had done such a thing?

A sharp rapping on the front door of the jail startled her.

"Don't worry. It's Jake."

She hadn't said anything, but she must have made some sound, since Mitch felt it necessary to reassure her as he unbolted the front door.

Jake came in bringing a blast of cold air with him. "Damn, Mitch, it's colder than hell out there."

"Yeah, and if you don't watch your mouth, I'll kick you right back out in it to stay." He nodded in Josie's direction. "There's a lady present."

To give Jake credit, he blushed to the roots of his blond hair. "Sorry, ma'am, I didn't mean to offend." Suddenly realizing his manners, he whipped his hat off.

Josie took pity on him. "That's all right, Deputy. I know you're not used to having a woman in your jail."

"Yes, ma'am. Did you pass a pleasant night?"

Mitch stepped between them. "She's an accused murderer, Jake, not a guest."

His words hurt more than they should have, even if they were only the truth. Luckily, he was too busy looking at Jake to notice how she winced.

"Deputy, would you mind keeping an eye on the prisoner while I walk down to the hotel to pick up a couple of Belle's breakfasts?" His tone made it clear that it was an order more than a request.

"Yes, sir, I'll do that." Jake looked more puzzled than offended by Mitch's abrupt manner. "Is there anything else?"

"You might spend some time studying that new stack of 'wanted' posters that came in yesterday, especially the top one. He's the one rumored to be headed in this direction."

Josie watched in stunned silence while Mitch yanked his coat on and slammed out of the door. The room settled back into an uneasy silence as the two of them waited for him to return.

Damn it all, anyway. Now he owed his deputy an apology. Jake was a good man and didn't deserve the raw side of Mitch's temper. And what excuse could he give him for acting like such an ass? For sure, he couldn't tell him the truth—that one look at their "prisoner" made him want to howl with frustration.

Who could blame her for shooting a sniveling son of a bitch who treated her like shit? Hell, if he weren't the sheriff, he would have been tempted to take the bastard down himself just for daring to touch her. How was he supposed to do his job when he felt this way?

The bitter cold did little to calm his temper as he marched down to the hotel. It was too early for the dining room to be open for service, which was just as well. He could place his order and be gone without having to be polite to anyone other than Belle.

He stepped inside the small lobby. Belle's husband was dozing behind the desk. No doubt he'd been up for a couple of hours already, helping her prepare for the early morning rush. Thanks to the quality of her cooking, many of the local citizens regularly ate their meals in Belle's dining room. When the hotel was full, she had to bring in extra help just to keep up.

Mitch quietly slipped past the desk and headed for the door to the kitchen. He knew better than to enter the kitchen without an express invitation from Belle, but she didn't mind if he knocked and waited for her to respond. This time she must have been on her way to the dining room, because the door swung open as soon as he'd finished knocking.

She seemed pleased to see him. "Good morning, Sheriff. You're out awfully early."

"Morning, Belle." He touched the brim of his hat in greeting. "Sorry to bother you before you're really open, but I was wanting to order three breakfasts to take back to the jail with me."

She was obviously curious about his unusual request, but she didn't ask. Instead, she pulled a piece of paper and pencil out of her apron pocket. "What would you like?"

"Some of your biscuits and gravy would be fine. Maybe some eggs, too, if that isn't too much trouble."

"Don't be silly. Why don't you sit down and I'll bring you some coffee to drink while you wait. The biscuits just went into the oven, so it shouldn't take too long."

"Thanks. I appreciate it."

He sat down at his favorite table. Belle was back with his coffee almost before he had time to pull the chair out from the table. Although she wasn't one normally given to gossip, she surprised him by sitting down across the table from him.

"I hear that Oliver Turner finally got what was coming to him."

Mitch knew better than to be surprised at the speed at which gossip traveled. But considering it was fairly late in the evening when Jed Turner's men had brought Josie in, the news must have spread like wildfire.

"I haven't seen the body yet, but that's the story. Someone evidently shot him."

Belle shook her head in pure disgust. "I know we shouldn't speak ill of the dead, but I'm surprised someone hadn't come gunning for him before this. He was a mean drunk and a lousy card player. That's never a good combination."

He couldn't argue with that, but he wasn't going to say

so. Oliver had been a thorn in his side since the day Mitch
had taken on the job of sheriff in Lee's Mill. But if Belle
thought it was one of Oliver's cronies who was responsible, he wasn't going to correct her—at least not yet.

In a pointed effort to change the subject, he asked
about Belle's daughter, who lived up in Columbia. Belle
was only to glad to talk about her grandchildren. After
another minute or two she excused herself and headed
back to her kitchen.

Mitch pondered the dilemma of what to do about his
prisoner. For one thing, come daylight, he'd take a ride
out to Josie's place and then out to Jed Turner's. He
didn't know Jed all that well, but he wasn't going to take
the man's word for what happened without doing some
investigating of his own.

It was common knowledge that Jed and Oliver fought
more often than not. Mitch had to wonder how a man as
wealthy as Jed was reported to be could let his only son
and daughter-in-law live in such poverty while he lived in
one of the fanciest houses within a hundred miles.

No, there was more to the story than Jed was telling.

Before he could follow that train of thought any further, Belle came through the door with a basket full of
food for him. He rushed to take it from her.

"Thanks, Belle. I appreciate you doing this for me."

"No trouble at all, Sheriff. Just send the dishes back
when you've got a chance. No hurry, though."

He took his leave, knowing that Belle was too busy to
stand around chatting. Besides, it would be nice to eat
his meal while it was still hot. He braced himself for the
blast of cold when he stepped back outside. A wind had
come up that bit right through him. He leaned into the
wind and made his way back to the jail.

When he stepped inside, the room was unnaturally
quiet. Josie sat right where he'd left her, her face turned

toward the back wall of her cell. Jake was at the desk, looking decidedly uncomfortable with the whole situation. Mitch decided to mend fences with his deputy first.

He shoved all his paperwork to the far side of the desk and set the basket down. Jake's mood definitely brightened up considerably as Mitch began spreading out the breakfast that Belle had packed for the three of them.

By time he got to the fresh-baked biscuits, Jake was all but drooling.

"I wasn't sure if you'd eaten." Mitch handed him a plate. He dropped his voice to add, "Sorry I about took your head off. I didn't get much sleep last night."

One of the things he most appreciated about his deputy was his basic good nature. If both of them were as moody as Mitch himself could be, their working relationship would be pretty damn explosive. Instead, on the rare occasion when Mitch lost his temper, a brief apology was all it took to get things back to normal.

And some of Belle's baked goods never hurt.

Once Jake had his plate loaded up, Mitch fixed one for himself and one for their prisoner. He was having an easier time of it if he thought of Josie in those terms. After grabbing the keys off their hook, he carried her breakfast over to her cell.

She kept her eyes averted, not acknowledging his approach in the slightest. Fine. Both of them could play at this game. He opened the cell door, stepped in far enough to set the plate down beside her on the cot, and then walked out, shutting the cell door behind him.

Jake was frowning when Mitch pulled a chair up to the side of the desk and started to eat his own breakfast. Despite Belle's best efforts, the food might have tasted like the bottoms of his boots for all the pleasure he took from it. His deputy had no such problems.

"What's the plan for today?" Jake asked as he leaned back in the chair and pulled a toothpick out of his pocket.

Mitch mulled it over. "I think we both need to be here when Jed Turner comes calling. Last night he sent a few of his men to bring Mrs. Turner in and then showed up later by himself. I'm betting he'll have a suitably impressive number of men behind him when he arrives this morning."

Mitch wasn't particularly worried about facing a crowd. He'd dealt with far worse threats during the war and even since. Jed Turner was sadly mistaken if he thought he was going to come riding into Lee's Mill and throw his weight around.

A knock at the door had both men reaching for their guns. Mitch drew his revolver and then edged slowly over to the door. He risked a glance out the window and then immediately reached to open the door. With a blast of cold air, Cade Mulroney slipped inside with Pastor Hayes right behind him.

Upon seeing the gun in Mitch's hand, Cade raised one eyebrow. "Not exactly your usual greeting, Mitch. Hope that wasn't meant for one of us. Who else are you expecting at this hour?"

Mitch shut the door behind the two men and threw the lock again. "Jed Turner never said what time he planned on coming back. I figure to be damn careful who is at the door before I unlock it, especially considering the mood he was in last night."

The pastor didn't join in the conversation. Instead, he walked straight back to the cell door and started talking in a low voice to Josie. Mitch strained to hear what was being said but couldn't make out more than the occasional word.

With his eyes still on the pastor, he offered advice that he figured would likely be ignored. "Tell Lucy to be careful coming around here. I don't want her to get caught in the middle of anything."

Cade shook his head. "You can tell her yourself. I figure she's about five minutes behind me at the most. Melinda dragged poor Daniel over to our house at a ridiculously early hour this morning to start their plan to organize Josie's defense."

Mitch rolled his eyes. He hadn't even had a chance to see the body yet, and already things were spinning out of his control. Hellfire and damnation, he wished everyone would stand back and let him do his job.

"Look, once I know what Jed Turner has in mind for today, I plan to ride out to the Turner place and have a look around. I need to leave Jake here at the jail. Do you want to come with me? I could use another set of eyes."

"Sure thing." Cade helped himself to a cup of coffee.

"Mr. Mulroney? Can I have some of that?" Josie was standing by her cell door holding out her empty cup.

Mitch watched in frustrated silence. If she'd wanted something, why hadn't she asked him?

When Cade had poured her cup, she gave him a tentative smile. "I heard what you said about Lucy. She shouldn't worry about me, especially not now."

"Mrs. Turner, if you know my wife at all, you know she'll do as she sees fit. Nothing and no one will keep her from helping you if she can." He nodded toward Pastor Hayes. "I'm sure the reverend here will tell you the same thing about his wife. You're just going to have put up with the pair of them poking their noses in your business. They won't abandon a friend just because of a little trouble."

If being accused of murdering her husband was a little trouble, Mitch didn't want to know what Lucy and Melinda considered a big problem. Even so, he appreciated the fact that Josie was not going to be abandoned by the women in the Society. No matter how things turned out, she was going to need all the support she could get.

He caught the sound of someone approaching the door. This time, however, he didn't hesitate to open it. No matter how distracted he was by all the commotion, he couldn't mistake the brisk footsteps of Lucy Mulroney and Melinda Hayes for anyone else's.

"Good morning, ladies," he said as he stood back and let them inside. "I do apologize for the condition of the place. Had I known to expect so much company, I would have baked something."

The sarcasm was ignored by both women, as was Mitch himself. They didn't pay much more attention to their husbands as they made a beeline for their friend's cell.

When Lucy stuck her arms through the bars, Josie immediately accepted the awkward embrace. She felt like she'd been holding herself together with baling wire and nerves. The cold metal that held them apart served as a reminder that once again she was on the wrong side of society.

Lucy looked her over from top to bottom. "Are you all right, Josie?"

"I'm fine, Lucy, really," she lied, hoping her friend would realize that.

It was Melinda who threw the truth back in her face. "You're not fine, Josie Turner, and don't go trying to fool yourself or us into thinking you are." She yanked a handkerchief out of a pocket and shoved it through the bars.

"If it isn't bad enough that you've lost your husband, you've had to spend the night in a place like this." She waved her hand around, including the men behind them in the gesture. "Has the sheriff said why he doesn't believe your side of the story?"

Josie didn't know whether to laugh or cry. It hadn't even occurred to her that anyone would accept her version of the facts as the truth. Before she could put together any kind of coherent response, Lucy turned on Mitch. Melinda was right beside her.

"Sheriff Hughes, you have taken down Josie's statement, haven't you?"

Mitch drew himself up to his full height, an obvious attempt to intimidate the two women. Josie could have warned him that it wouldn't work.

"No, I haven't."

"Why not?" Lucy stepped forward. "Surely you aren't foolish enough to think that Josie was capable of killing her husband?"

"It doesn't matter what I think. Facts are what the judge will want to hear. Not my opinion."

"And what would your opinion be?"

Mitch looked past Lucy to meet Josie's gaze head-on. "I think that under the right circumstances, people are capable of terrible things."

Josie knew then that she could talk, she could plead, and she could cry, but it would all fall on deaf ears. If Mitch Hughes believed her capable of shooting Oliver in the back, then she was doomed. Her friends knew it, too, if the horror on their faces was any indication.

She felt a sudden need to be alone.

"Josie, he didn't mean—"

She shook her head. "Yes, he did. If you don't believe me, ask your husbands. They know him better than most."

Silence hung so heavily over the room that it weighed her down. She dropped down on her cot, no longer sure that her legs would support her.

"You all had better be going." She started counting

the bricks again, trying to hold back the tears until her friends were gone.

"But . . ." Lucy protested.

Cade wrapped his arm around his wife's shoulders and gently pulled her toward the door. "You can come back later, Lucy, but it looks like Mrs. Turner needs to rest."

She tried to dig in her heels. "Josie, are you sure?"

Josie managed to muster up a small smile. "I'll be fine, Lucy. Go on home and tend to Mary. You, too, Melinda. I appreciate you coming to check on me."

Then she deliberately turned away from them, willing them all to disappear before she broke down completely. Finally, when there was no one left in the room besides her and Jake, she stretched out on the cot and let the tears drip down her face.

Outside, Mitch was fit to be tied. Where the hell was Jed Turner, anyway? He wasn't going to go riding off, leaving Jake to face Jed and his men alone. On the other hand, the longer he delayed examining the cabin Josie had shared with Oliver, the more likely that any evidence was going to be washed away.

Damn, he wished Lucy Mulroney hadn't put him on the spot like that. He'd said no less than the truth. Life had a way of cornering some people like a treed cougar. Push and prod them hard enough, and they'd come boiling out of their corner, doing their damnedest to fight their way clear.

It didn't come as a surprise to anyone that Oliver Turner had a habit of taking his temper out on Josie, despite the fact she was half his size. The fading bruises on Josie's face spoke volumes about the hell Oliver had put her through. Was it possible that she'd finally had as much as she could take?

Yes. In fact, hell, yes.

Did he think, down in his gut where it mattered, that she'd done it?

He wished he knew.

When the door of the jail slammed open, he held his position and did his best to ignore the venomous looks the two women gave him. Cade murmured something about being ready to ride whenever Mitch needed him. Pastor Hayes patted him on the shoulder as he passed by, offering what comfort he could.

Lucy was right. By now Mitch should have sat down with Josie Turner and asked her about what had happened. It was his job, one he prided himself on doing well. Steeling himself to face those pain-filled eyes of her, he turned to go back inside when he happened to glance up the street.

Jed Turner and what looked like every damn man on his payroll were riding through the middle of Lee's Mill in a military-like formation. He had to marvel at the sheer gall of the man. Most of the time he took his business to one of the bigger towns, making it clear that a small place like Lee's Mill was beneath his dignity.

But now he was riding through town as if he owned the place. Well, he was in for a shock if he thought that Mitch was going to jump to do his bidding. Slowly, so that Jed wouldn't think he'd sent the sheriff into a panic, he opened the door to let Jake know that company was coming.

"Jake, you might want to get out an extra box of ammunition. I don't plan on letting any trouble start, but it may not be up to me."

His deputy, despite his youth, knew how to handle a gun better than most. More than one man had failed to look past Jake's open, trusting face to the competent lawman inside. Most of them were serving time or else weren't going to be trouble to anyone ever again.

Having forewarned his backup, Mitch walked to the edge of the porch and waited for Jed Turner's little parade to reach his end of town. It was still early enough in the day that most folks weren't stirring around yet. The few that were showed good sense by disappearing back inside. Even if they hadn't heard about Oliver Turner's murder yet, the war had taught them all how to recognize trouble when it rode through town.

It didn't take long to ride the length of Lee's Mill, even at a walk. Mitch took the opportunity to study his opponent. The man rode straight for Mitch, looking neither to the left nor the right. If he noticed any of the townspeople staring at him, he gave no indication of it. A line had been drawn last night between the two of them. Enemies both after the same thing: justice for the dead.

"Sheriff."

Jed sat upon the big, rawboned stallion like a king on his throne.

Mitch wasn't impressed, at least not by the man. He wondered what Turner would think about coming out a poor second to the animal beneath him. For some reason, that idea pleased Mitch.

"Mr. Turner."

"I'm here to find out when the trial will be." His eyes flickered past Mitch to the front door of the jail.

Mitch wondered if Josie could feel that hatred right through the brick walls and metal bars. "I'll make sure Cade posts the details in the *Clarion*. You can read about it like everybody else in town."

"When is the judge arriving?"

"He hasn't said."

Turner's infamous temper was starting to show. "I

would have thought that he'd make the case a priority when he heard whose son had been murdered."

There was no use in telling the man that Mitch had yet to send for the judge. He wouldn't, either, until he had a better handle on what had happened out at the cabin. "You've got a pretty high opinion of your importance, don't you, Mr. Turner?"

Jed's eyes narrowed as he leaned forward to better stare down at Mitch. "Don't underestimate me, Sheriff. Other men have made that mistake and paid for it."

"Like your son?"

His barb hit its mark. Jed jerked back as if Mitch had hit him. His lip curled back in a snarl as his hand strayed to his gun. "I should have hanged the murdering bitch last night and saved myself the trouble of dealing with you."

"And if you had, I would have hunted you down for the murder of Mrs. Turner." Mitch's hand found the grip of his pistol and eased it loose from its holster. If he had need of it, he wanted to make sure it came up smooth and easy.

The men behind Turner fanned out on either side of him, their faces set in grim lines. There was no doubt at all that they would do whatever Turner asked of them, including storming the jail and dealing out a little Missouri justice of their own. Mitch would take down as many of them as he could before they got him, but enough would survive to get past him.

He could only hope that Jake had put the bar across the door. The lock was a strong one, but it wouldn't be enough. Resisting the urge to take a step back, he braced himself for the attack that was sure to come.

In the drawn-out silence, Mitch felt another presence. Someone was coming up beside him. He risked a quick glance to the side. He wouldn't have been surprised to

see Cade Mulroney coming to take his side, but instead
it was Pastor Hayes with hellfire in his eyes.

"Mr. Turner! What could you be thinking?" He
stepped directly between Mitch and Jed Turner.

Mitch wanted to throttle him but was afraid if he made
any kind of move at all, Turner's men would have the excuse they were looking for. Meanwhile, Mitch caught
sight of Cade working his way around the back of the riders. He positioned himself to be able to shoot without
worrying about hitting his two friends on the porch.

"You have suffered a terrible loss, Mr. Turner. No one
is questioning that, but this is not the way to handle the
situation. Sheriff Hughes needs time to do his job. If it
were you sitting in that cell, you'd want to know that justice was going to be carried out."

To Mitch's surprise, some of the fury faded from
Turner's face as he stared down at the young pastor. The
crisis had passed, at least for the moment.

"Sheriff, this isn't over, not by a long shot. I'll be
watching and I'll be waiting for you to do your job. But
listen closely: you do your duty soon, or by God, I'll do it
for you."

Once again, he brutally turned his horse away from
the jail. Mitch was surprised the big sorrel didn't dump
him on his ass in the road. Instead, Jed led his men back
down the street and out of town. Mitch didn't make a
move until the last one disappeared around the corner
onto the river road.

Content that they were safe for the moment, he took
some of his foul mood out on his would-be rescuer.

"Damn it, Reverend, don't ever do something that
fool stupid again!"

To his amazement, Daniel didn't back down in the least.
"Don't go telling me how to do my job, Sheriff, any more
than you'd put up with me telling you how to do yours."

Cade stepped up on the porch. "Both of you shut up. You're not mad at each other so much as you were set to do battle and don't have anybody left to fight."

For a moment the three men stood glaring at each other. Something about it made Mitch's lips twitch, as if they were demanding to smile. Finally, a laugh rumbled up from his chest and cleared the air. The other two joined in.

Deciding they'd spent enough time out in the cold, Mitch pounded on the door and waited for Jake to let them inside. He was pleased to see that Jake hadn't wasted any time in preparing for an assault. Three rifles were laid out neatly on the desk, along with enough ammunition to fight off half the Union Army.

He had also remembered to bar the back door of the jail. Mitch's next thought was that somehow their prisoner had managed to escape. But then he noticed a slight movement in the quilt that was draped over the cot in the cell.

"Mrs. Turner, you can come out now. Your father-in-law has gone."

First one foot and then the other popped out from underneath the cot, giving Mitch a glimpse of a particularly attractive ankle. He turned away rather than watch Josie wiggle out from under her hiding place.

"Your idea or hers?"

Jake grinned. "Both. I told her to hide, but she came up with the idea of making it look like the cell was empty."

He could tell by the sound of things that Josie had resumed her usual position of sitting on the end of the bed. She didn't look any worse for the wear, considering she was likely to have heard every word her father-in-law had said.

"Cade, can you be ready to ride out in an hour?"

"Sure thing. I just need to let Lucy know."

"Do you want me to come along, too?"

Mitch eyed the young pastor. "Thanks for the offer, but I'd rather know Jake had someone close by who could go for help if necessary."

Daniel appeared to mull that one over. "All right. I'll stay across the street at the store. I should be able to keep an eye on things from there."

Jake looked like he wanted to protest that he didn't need anyone's help, but Mitch shot him a warning look. He'd explain later, once the pastor was out of hearing. No use hurting the man's feelings.

When Cade and Daniel were gone, he sent Jake out on patrol. Then he dragged his desk chair over closer to Josie's cell and sat down.

"Now, tell me what happened. Don't leave out anything."

Six

The clouds had thickened overhead, but so far the rain had held off. Mitch could only hope that it continued to do so until he and Cade were back in town. The cold was bad enough. Despite his coat and gloves, he was chilled right through to the bone.

He glanced over at Cade, who looked just as miserable as Mitch felt. With one exception: the lucky bastard had someone waiting for him at home who would fuss over him as soon as he walked in the door. The only person who would make coffee for Mitch was Mitch, or at best Jake. Somehow, it just wasn't the same as having a woman there to fuss over a man.

He'd almost had that once, but wars had a way of killing off the innocents and leaving the guilty to thrive. Sometimes he wondered if he'd taken on the job of lawman to pay penance for surviving when so many hadn't. Especially the helpless and the weak.

With considerable effort he jerked his mind back to the present. The trail that led back to the Turner cabin was just ahead. He decided to approach the place on foot rather than add his horse's tracks to the ones already there. Cade dismounted when he saw what Mitch was up to. They both tied their horses to a small sapling near a patch of grass that winter hadn't yet killed off.

"What are we looking for?"

"I don't rightly know. Maybe something that shouldn't be here or doesn't match up with the story we've been told."

"So you don't believe Josie?"

Cade's voice was carefully neutral, but Mitch didn't buy it for a minute. Lucy would never forgive Cade for not siding with her friend, regardless of the facts. Mitch didn't have that luxury.

"I didn't say that. I'm not sure at this point what I believe, but I can't afford to take sides based on anything other than the facts. It's my job." He hoped he didn't sound as defensive as he felt.

"What did she say happened?" The two of them had reached the clearing. In unspoken agreement, they stopped just past the last of the trees.

"According to Mrs. Turner, Oliver left about noon. Seems Josie spent the night before at Cora's because of the weather. While she was gone, Oliver had friends over to play cards and drink."

Mitch walked toward the small, run-down cabin. "She was inside when she heard a horse riding in, running like hell. Seems she usually stays put until she hears if the horse is coming to the door or toward the corral. This time, the horse barely stopped before it took off again. Before it left, though, she heard something heavy hit the ground."

He studied the ground, but there were too many hoof-prints to tell much of anything. "When she peeked out through the door, she saw someone on the ground. At first, she didn't even realize it was Oliver. When she turned him over, she saw blood on his back."

Cade looked up from where he'd squatted down to look at the ground. "His back? She's saying he was shot in the back?"

"Don't really know. Could be that the bullet made a

bigger hole coming out than it did going in. Anyway, she didn't get a good look. By her reckoning, Jed and his men rode in only a couple of minutes after she found Oliver. They had her trussed up and on her way to jail before she could take a deep breath."

There was a dark stain on the porch that caught Mitch's eye. It could be blood, but even it if was, who knew how long it had been there? Still, it did fit with what Josie had said.

Of course, it also fit Jed's explanation of the events. According to him, he and his men had come by to see Oliver when they found Josie standing over her husband with a pistol in her hand. Jed's word against Josie's.

He knew which one he wanted to believe, but he couldn't—wouldn't—let a pair of brown eyes blind him to his duty. All he could do was gather the facts and let the judge do the rest. But by God, he wasn't going to let Jed Turner dictate what the facts were.

More out of curiosity than anything, he opened the door to the cabin and stepped inside. The kitchen smelled vaguely of food left sitting too long—unpleasant but not unbearable. In the dimly lit interior of the cabin, he wandered around, peeking in corners and drawers.

He found a cracked box and lifted the lid. Josie's sewing basket. Maybe he'd take it back to the jail with him. She might appreciate having something to do to keep her hands and mind busy. He set it by the door. Then he found her stash of books and a child's slate. At first he was surprised that she kept the precious items hidden away, until he remembered that Oliver hadn't approved of her efforts to educate herself.

He set the books by the sewing basket. He'd been known to buy a newspaper for his prisoners to read. No one could say he was playing favorites by bringing a few things to Josie. On the other hand, she might not appreciate his efforts, since it meant that he'd been prying into her personal belongings, meager as they were. Although the cabin was clean and tidy, there was pitifully little in it.

And what there was, was old and worn, probably culled from someone else's throwaways. Damn Jed Turner to hell and back. No matter what he thought of his son and daughter-in-law, the man should have pride enough to want to take care of his own.

Cade stuck his head in the door. "Find anything?"

Mitch shook his head. "I wish I had asked Mrs. Turner if there was anything she wanted from here. I thought maybe her books and the sewing basket."

If Cade thought it was odd that Mitch was concerned about what an accused murderer wanted, he gave no indication. "I wouldn't know what to bring. I'd let Lucy take her anything she needs. It's been bothering both Lucy and Melinda for some time how little Josie has. This will give them the excuse to help her out."

It pleased Mitch on some level that Josie had such supportive friends. Considering the fix she was in, their friendship could make all the difference. All he could do for her was try to clear her name. He looked around the cabin one more time, wishing there were more there to be seen. But the log walls were silent.

He picked up the basket and handed the books to Cade. Silently they trudged back through the half-frozen mud to where their patient horses waited.

Cade was limping slightly by the time they were mounted up. The two of them rode most of the way toward town in silence. Once they reached the stable in town, Mitch made short work of unsaddling his horse. He picked up the sewing box and handed it to Cade.

"Can you drop this by the jail and tell Jake I'll be along shortly? I want to stop by the undertaker to see if Jed brought Oliver in for burial. If so, I want to have Doc examine the body to see what he can tell me."

Cade gave him an odd look. "I'd have thought you'd seen enough dead bodies yourself. What can Doc do?"

"I don't know. Maybe nothing." He stopped, trying to choose his words. "Something about this whole mess stinks."

"For instance?" Cade prompted.

"Are you asking as the newspaper editor?"

"Not unless you want me to be."

"No—not yet, anyway." Maybe laying it all in front of Cade would help him make sense of things. "First, let me say that I think anybody is capable of murder if pushed hard enough."

"But . . ."

"Josie's description makes it sound like Oliver was shot in the back. If she shot him because he was hitting her again, why would she wait until he was walking away?"

"Maybe that's the first chance she had to get a gun."

"That occurred to me, but I don't know. It doesn't ring true somehow."

"And maybe you just want her to be innocent."

His voice held a note of sympathy that Mitch tried to ignore. Deciding that there wasn't anything more to be said, he led the way out of the stable. The wind whipped around the corner of the building, almost ripping Mitch's hat off his head.

"Damn, it's cold."

Cade looked up at the sky and frowned. "I wouldn't be surprised if we didn't get our first snow early this year."

Mitch hated the stuff. "Hell, it's not much past Thanksgiving."

Cade turned his collar up. "Speaking of holidays, would you like to have Christmas dinner with us? Mary would be thrilled to have you join us."

Mitch noticed that he hadn't said that Lucy would be happy. "Thanks for the offer, but I already have plans." Some plans—dinner at a hotel with a crotchety old man and a room full of other people who had nowhere else to go. It had been years since he'd done much celebrating at Christmas. If anyone would understand why, it would be Cade, but Mitch wasn't in the mood to discuss his past.

"Let me know if you change your mind."

Mitch nodded and turned off at the next corner to cut through to the undertaker's, the perfect place to suit his mood.

"I can't and I won't." Josie clenched her fists at her side. "I know you all mean well, but I don't want your money." She looked past Lucy to where Cora stood. "And you, young lady, have no business visiting me in jail. Your aunt will have a fit if she finds out."

Cora's face was set in its most stubborn expression. There was no doubt among those who knew her well that she was prepared to dig in her heels if any of them tried to run her off. She managed to sound angry and proud at the same time. "I'm your friend, Josie. That's reason enough for me to be here. If Aunt Henrietta doesn't understand or approve, well, that's just too bad."

Then her lip quivered as she rushed forward to thrust her arms through the bars. Whether she was trying to comfort Josie or seeking some for herself wasn't clear. All Josie knew was that if it weren't for the support of her friends, she would have lost hope.

Cora finally stepped back. "Now, about the money. I've already spoken to Mr. Bradford at the bank. He won't advance me any of my trust fund, but he might consider a short-term loan if my aunt will agree." She stomped her foot in frustration. "I will talk to her tonight. She has to agree. After all, the money will be mine to do with as I see fit in only a few months.

Josie shook her head. "Cora, I don't want to cause you any trouble with your aunt. You know she won't approve, and I don't blame her. Unless someone finds some pretty convincing evidence, you'd be throwing good money away on some fancy lawyer for me."

The door to the jail opened. All four women turned to face the newcomer. Jed Turner strolled in as if he owned the place. He probably thought he did.

"What the hell is this? A meeting of that damned women's group?" He looked around the jail. "Where's the sheriff or his deputy?"

Josie's stomach clenched in fear. Her friends standing shoulder to shoulder between her and Jed helped some, but not much.

Melinda spoke up. "The deputy stepped out back for a minute. He should be right back."

"The damn fool left *her,*" he sneered over their heads toward Josie, "with you to watch her? That's like leaving the fox to guard a henhouse." He casually drew his gun. "Ladies, if you'll step aside, I'll—"

"You'll what?" A voice, deadly and cold, interrupted.

Mitch Hughes filled the doorway, his gun already drawn and ready. He was the same cold-eyed killer she'd seen the day he'd confronted Oliver in the store. He stepped inside, his eyes never leaving her father-in-law for an instant.

"I asked you a question, Turner. I expect an answer."

Moving slowly, as if he knew that one wrong move might end badly for him, Jed turned to face the sheriff. All four women stood rock-still, waiting to see how it all played out.

"I was going to offer to stand guard. Seems your deputy skipped out on you."

"Like hell. I sent him on down to get some dinner." Mitch motioned toward the door. "I suggest you get the hell out of my jail and don't come back unless I invite you." Then he offered up a smile that had nothing to do with being friendly. "Unless you want to take up residence in that other cell, which would be fine with me. Especially if you don't holster that gun pretty damn quick."

For a minute Josie feared that Jed's fearsome temper would get the best of him. His face turned red and then almost purple as he fought to keep control of himself. Perhaps if the other women hadn't been there, he might have tried something. As it was, Mitch was already starting for him when he finally put his gun away.

"I came to ask some questions."

Mitch kept his own gun drawn. "Go ahead. I won't promise to answer."

"Why haven't you sent for the judge?"

"I haven't finished my investigation. I'll send the telegram when I do."

"That's what I thought," Jed sneered. "Well, I've saved you the trouble, Sheriff. Judge McKay is an acquaintance of mine. When I notified him of the details about the brutal murder of my son, he seemed surprised you hadn't contacted him. He should be here by the end of the next week."

"You son of a . . ." Mitch bit off the curse when he remembered there were ladies present. "If I catch you interfering with my investigation again, Turner, I'll throw you in that cell until you rot."

"Those threats had better stop, Sheriff, or that will be something else I bring up with Judge McKay. He'll be damn interested in a lawman who is more concerned with the comfort of killer than he is with justice."

Trying to look self-righteous but not quite pulling it

off, Turner marched toward the door. Mitch stood his ground, forcing the smaller man to walk around him. Turner wasn't content to leave quietly.

He glared across the room at Josie. "We should have hanged you right there by that flea-ridden cabin and then burned the whole damned mess to the ground. Make no mistake, slut. If the sheriff doesn't see that justice is done, I will."

His parting shot sent a new surge of fear through Josie. Judging by their expressions, her friends had a similar reaction. She sought out Mitch, trying to draw some comfort from his strong presence, but he wasn't looking at her. Instead he waited until her father-in-law rode out and then stomped outside, slamming the door behind him.

Lucy and Melinda exchanged glances and nodded. Josie wondered what unspoken message had just passed between the two, but neither of them felt the need to explain. Instead, they pulled three chairs up close to her cell. Cora picked up the stack of books they'd brought with them and passed them out.

Then, as she opened her copy of *Macbeth*, she looked at Josie with great sympathy in her eyes. "That man is odious."

At that moment Josie wasn't sure if her friend was talking about Jed or Mitch, but she wouldn't have argued the point either way. She was more concerned with what Lucy and Melinda were up to. Their calm reaction to her father-in-law's outburst seemed out of character, especially for Lucy and Cora. Melinda, while not quite as outspoken as the other two, should have at least offered Josie some words of comfort.

Instead, Lucy calmly began the reading, just as if she spent every evening keeping a friend company at the local jail. She was definitely up to something. Josie couldn't wait to see what, as long as it didn't land her friends in as much trouble with the sheriff as Josie already was.

Mitch had spent most of the evening trying to walk off his temper. He'd come within a hairsbreath of shooting that son of a bitch Turner right where he stood. He didn't give a damn if the man wanted to throw his weight around, taking advantage of his friendship with the judge.

Having dealt with Judge McKay on several occasions, Mitch knew him for a fair man who would examine all the evidence before rendering his judgement. No, he wasn't worried about him. It was the other threat he'd made—the one about dealing out justice himself—that had Mitch's blood boiling. It wouldn't be enough to convince the judge that Josie was innocent, not if she was to be safe from Jed and his men.

Unless Mitch was able to find the real killer, she would be under constant threat from Oliver's vengeful father. That was another part of the puzzle that had him confused. If Turner and his son had been close, he could understand the man's determination to see Oliver's killer swing. But they hadn't been. In fact, from what Mitch had been able to gather, the two were barely on speaking terms.

In his experience, a man who acted like Jed, did so out of guilt. But guilt over what? Did he regret his treatment of his son? That he'd waited too long to try to mend the rift between them? Or was it something else?

He wished the hell he knew. For now, he'd spent enough time out in the cold. He'd lost all feeling in his toes an hour ago. If he didn't get inside near the stove soon, he'd take all night just thawing out. After a quick stop in the hotel to pick up a couple of dinners, he'd head on back to the office.

* * *

Just as he stepped out of the hotel with a basket filled with Belle's stew and fresh bread, he saw Josie's friends leaving the jail. Relieved he wouldn't have to face them again, he hurried his steps. He was breaking enough rules allowing them time alone with the prisoner. His long legs ate up the distance to the jail.

It felt good to step into the warmth of his office. Josie looked up from the needlework in her lap briefly, but she didn't speak. He set his burden down on the desk to strip off his coat and hat. While he did so, he used the opportunity to study his prisoner. She sat with her head bowed, her delicate features frowning in concentration over the fine stitches in whatever piece of folderol she was sewing.

The iron bars that separated them jarred; they were so out of place with the picture that she made. He'd had enough trouble staying away from her when she was a married woman who came to town occasionally. Being shut up in the same room with her was making him feel things that a sheriff had no business feeling about a prisoner, even a beautiful one.

"Dinner's here."

"Ouch!"

His abrupt words had startled Josie into pricking her finger with her needle. She gave him a reproachful look as she sucked on her fingertip. The image that brought to mind did little to improve his mood.

"Sorry if I caused you to hurt yourself." He began to unload the basket. "We should eat while it's hot."

He dished up a bowl of stew and hacked off a piece of bread to go with it. Josie stood at the door of her cell, waiting for him to shove the food through the space between the bars. On a whim, he reached for the keys instead.

"You can eat at the desk if you promise to behave your-self."

"I promise."

When the door swung open, she seemed reluctant to step out. He wondered what she was thinking behind those huge, dark eyes of hers. Finally, she slipped through the opening and hurried across the room to sit down in front of the desk.

The silence hung heavily in the air. He tried to think of something to say, finally settling on complimenting Belle's cooking. "I eat most of my meals at the hotel. Belle always serves good food."

"I had heard that."

Mitch had been about to take a bite, but her comment brought him up short. "Haven't you ever eaten there?"

She shook her head as she swallowed. "No, sir. Pa never held with paying others to cook for us. Oliver felt the same way."

That was a damn lie. Her husband had been a fre-quent visitor to Belle's dining room. No doubt the bastard had been too cheap to bring his wife with him.

"Well, I'm sure they both liked your cooking too much to want to go elsewhere." He had no way of knowing if she could put together a decent meal, but the compli-ment seemed to please her.

After that, they ate in companionable silence. Once they'd finished off most of the stew, he brought out the pie that Belle had slipped into the basket. Josie insisted that he eat his and half of hers, saying it was more than she could handle. Since he was particularly fond of pie of any kind, he didn't argue long.

When both of them were finished, he stacked the dishes back in the basket, to be returned to Belle on his last rounds. Josie stood up, evidently figuring on re-turning to her cell.

"Do you play cards?"

"A little." Something in her expression warned him that she might not be telling the complete truth on that score.

He pulled out a drawer and tossed her a deck of cards. She shuffled and dealt a hand of poker with all the skill of a professional dealer. When each of them had five cards, she set the deck down and fanned her cards out.

"How many?"

He glanced at his hand. "Two."

She sent that many sliding across the scarred desktop. "Dealer takes three."

When they laid their cards down, she had him beaten with a pair of jacks. He threw his down with good humor. "What shall we play for?"

"You mean gamble?" The shock in her eyes was real. "I don't have any money with me."

He hid his surprise at that remark. As far as he'd been able to find out, she had no money at all. "I was thinking along the lines of buttons or bullets or . . ."

"Let me get my sewing box."

When she returned, she pulled out a small sack and dumped its contents on the desk. She quickly divided the assortment of buttons into equal piles and pushed one toward Mitch. He reached out for it without thinking. When his hand touched hers, a jolt of awareness shot up his arm. His body's reaction to the brief contact was painful in its intensity. The only saving grace was that Josie seemed blissfully unaware of her effect on him.

She was already shuffling and dealing again. He tried to concentrate on the cards; it wasn't easy with her sitting so close by. But no matter how uncomfortable it made him, it was worth it if it took her mind off her troubles for a while.

She played with single-minded determination, winning

her fair share of the pile. After an hour, the buttons were still pretty evenly divided between the two of them. When she yawned for the second time in rapid succession, he knew it was time to call it quits for the night.

He pushed his buttons across the table to her. "It's time I made my final rounds for the night, and you need some sleep."

She put her buttons away and closed up her sewing box. "Thank you for playing cards with me, Sheriff." She glanced past him to where her cell waited. "And for letting me out for a bit. I appreciate it."

Then, without a backward glance, she walked back to her cell and pulled the door shut behind her. A new wave of anger at the men in her life washed over him. If Oliver and her pa weren't already dead, he'd be sorely tempted to take care of that little chore himself.

Then there was Jed Turner. A gentle soul like Josie had no business being locked up like an animal. If it weren't for Jed's threats, he would have been tempted to release her to Cade's custody until the investigation was complete and the trial was due to start.

But she wouldn't be safe outside the jail, not with Jed and his men likely to turn up at any time. He wished he could tell her what he was thinking, but it wouldn't do any good. Reminding her that Jed's hatred was the real reason she was behind bars seemed pointless.

He grabbed his coat and hat and braced himself to step out into the bitter cold. "I'll be back in half an hour or so."

"I'll be here."

He wasn't sure if that was meant as a joke or not, but he didn't wait around to figure it out.

* * *

"Are you sure?"

Lucy shushed her friend with a glance. "We've discussed this to death. She's not safe even in jail, and we all know she's innocent. If we don't get her out of there, it's only a matter of time before something happens to her." She shuddered, remembering the hatred that had glittered in Jed Turner's eyes the other day.

Melinda drew a deep breath and nodded, as Cora slipped up beside them on the porch. "I have the money. Are you sure you don't want me to come along?"

Lucy bit back her first response, settling instead for one that would placate the younger woman. "Sheriff Hughes isn't expecting a crowd this morning. He won't think much about two of us coming this early with breakfast, but he might get suspicious if too many of us show up unexpectedly."

Cora reluctantly slipped back down the alley between the store and the newspaper office.

Melinda clearly had something she was having trouble asking. Lucy finally asked her, "What is it?"

Grimacing, Melinda whispered, "Are you sure we won't hurt him?"

If Melinda couldn't handle the truth, Lucy needed to know before it was too late. "We have to knock him out, Melinda. Of course it's going to hurt."

"That's what I thought." But instead of retreating, Melinda hefted the heavy basket at her feet and girded herself for battle.

The two of them stepped off the porch and tried to act casual as they approached the jail, as if it were a perfectly normal thing for the two of them to be doing before the sun was up.

Lucy rapped smartly on the front door of the jail. When there was no response after a few seconds, she tried again. This time she was rewarded with the sound of a man grumbling as he shuffled toward the door. The two of them stood back and waited for Sheriff Hughes to open the door.

He cracked the door only far enough to see who it was, the barrel of his pistol the only part of him that showed. "What the hell?"

Lucy pasted on a bright smile when he swung the door open wide. "Morning, Sheriff. Mrs. Hayes and I were up early doing some baking and thought we'd bring some over to you and Mrs. Turner while it was still hot."

Mitch looked bleary-eyed, as if he hadn't slept well. "What time is it?"

"Six-thirty."

He shook his head, "Come in, I guess."

Bracing herself for what was to come, Lucy walked into the jail, knowing full well that the action she was about to take might just land her in the cell next to Josie's. She was glad to see that her friend was already awake, although she had to be wondering what Lucy and Melinda were up to. They hadn't told her of their plans, figuring she would refuse to let them get involved in her problems.

"Lucy? Melinda?" Josie looked as puzzled as the sheriff.

"Good morning, Josie. Hope you're feeling well." Lucy knew she was acting too cheery, but neither Mitch nor Josie seemed to notice. No doubt they'd still been asleep when she'd pounded on the door. Perhaps that wasn't a bad thing.

"I'm fine," Josie said, trying to smother a huge yawn. "Why are you here so early?"

Melinda started to give Mitch a guilty look, but Lucy deliberately bumped into her to distract her. "Sorry, Melinda. My delicate condition has left me feeling a little clumsy."

"You should see what we have in this basket for you two."

Lucy prodded Melinda into approaching the cell and pulling back the linen napkin that covered the contents. When Josie peered into the basket, her eyes went round and horrified.

"But why . . . ?"

"Because we worry that you're not eating right," Lucy covered smoothly. "We brought the johnnycake in my best cast-iron skillet, so it's still warm." She looked around. "Let's spread everything out on the desk. If that's all right with you, Sheriff?"

Mitch still looked half asleep. "Sure, go ahead." He shoved some papers to the side. "I'll be back in a minute." He disappeared out the back door of the jail.

Josie waited until the door slammed before demanding to know what they were up to. "Lucy Mulroney, tell me that you're not planning on doing something stupid."

"Now, Josie . . ."

"Don't try lying to me, either of you." She turned her glare on Melinda, too. "Explain yourselves before Mitch comes back."

Melinda took a step backward. "You tell her, Lucy. It was your idea."

"Thanks so much for your support," she said wryly. But as Josie had said, their time was limited.

"We don't think you're safe, even in the jail. Jed Turner and his men have taken to hanging around in the saloons, trying to stir up feelings against you."

She paused for breath. "Cade says Mitch trusts this judge who is coming, but Jed brags that the judge will see to it that justice is done. We don't think he means a fair trial."

She watched as the import of her news sank in. Slowly Josie began to shake her head from side to side, denying the truth of Lucy's words.

Melinda took over. "We need to get you out of here. Away from here, as far as you can go."

"No, that will just make it look as if I'm guilty. I'm not—I'm innocent." Her eyes pleaded with them to believe her.

"We know that," Lucy assured her. "But what we believe doesn't matter. You've got to get out of here."

"But how . . . ?"

The door of the jail opened, causing all three women to jump back guiltily. Luckily, Mitch didn't seem to notice. He was more interested in investigating the basket they'd brought.

"Smells great. How about I make a pot of fresh coffee?"

"You do that while we lay out the food."

Mitch picked up a handful of kindling to stoke up the stove. When he bent down to pick up a small log, Lucy quietly reached for the skillet full of cornbread. Raising it high up in the air, she brought it down sharply on the back of Mitch's head.

With a sharp cry, he fell face forward onto the floor and didn't move.

Seven

"Lucy! Melinda! What are you two doing?" Josie clenched the bars of her cell with both hands as she stared at her friends with utter disbelief.

They were too busy dragging Mitch Hughes's unconscious body into the other cell to answer. Josie watched in stunned shock as Lucy calmly rolled Mitch onto his back and began rifling through his pockets. With a cry of triumph, she pulled out a key. Leaving him where he lay, Lucy immediately shut his cell door before using the key to let Josie out. Then she left the key within Mitch's reach on the floor outside his cell.

"Come on, Josie, there's no time to dawdle." Melinda shoved a bundle of clothes at her. "Put these on."

"But . . ."

"Now, Josie, before he wakes up. I don't want to hit him again."

That was enough to spur Josie into action. With fumbling fingers she managed to unfasten the front of her dress. She let it slip to the floor and stepped out of it. Melinda had a replacement all ready to slip over Josie's head. As she buttoned it up, she realized it matched the dress that Melinda wore. More questions than she could find words for spun through her mind.

Lucy was looking out the front window of the jail. "They're still there."

"Who is there?"

"Jed Turner's men. The past few days, there's been at least one of them watching the jail all the time. We don't like some of the rumors we've been hearing." She looked at Josie with a worried look.

Bracing for the worst, Josie asked the obvious question. "What rumors, Lucy?"

"Your father-in-law doesn't think Mitch will ever force you to stand trial for the murder of Oliver Turner. We think he's planning on taking matters into his own hands."

What had she ever done to the man to make him hate her so? "But I didn't kill Oliver. Why doesn't anyone believe me?"

Her friends immediately ran to her side. "We do, Josie. Never doubt that. So do Cora and Cade and Daniel." Melinda paused to look down at the man at their feet. "We even think Mitch knows you didn't kill Oliver. He's been prowling around and asking a lot of questions, but my guess is that he hasn't been able to find out anything to help your case. That's why you have to leave Lee's Mill."

Lucy nodded emphatically. "Now, before Mitch wakes up and before many more folks start stirring outside."

"But if I run, everyone will think I'm guilty."

"We know it will look bad, but we don't think you're safe here, not even in jail. If Jed Turner manages to stir up folks, there's no telling what will happen. Mitch is a good sheriff, but he's only one man. He can't stand against Turner's men if they come at him all at once."

"But where would I go? And how? I can't just walk out of here, especially if Mr. Turner has people watching the jail."

Melinda pointed at their matching dresses. "I'm going to leave by the back door while you walk out front with Lucy. Those men saw two women come in, and they'll see two go out. They probably didn't pay much attention to what we were wearing, but if they did, they'll see exactly what they expect to. I had a scarf on, so they won't notice that our hair color is different, especially from where they're standing."

"But once I'm out of here . . ."

Lucy shook her head. "There's no time. I'll explain the rest of the plan when we get you to Cora's house."

Josie wanted to refuse, but fear was driving her now. If things had gotten so bad that her friends were willing to jeopardize their good names to save her, then who was she to argue? She accepted Melinda's wrap and the scarf. Lucy tugged her toward the door.

Josie looked down at Mitch with regret. What would he think of all this? Would he give up on finding the real killer to track her down? He was so still that she worried that Lucy had hit him too hard.

"Will he be all right?" she whispered.

As if he'd heard her, Mitch groaned and stirred slightly. Instantly, Melinda disappeared out the back door while Lucy and Josie slipped out the front, carrying the basket containing Lucy's best skillet. The two men who stood leaning against the railing outside The River Lady glanced in their direction but then went back to rolling their cigarettes. So far, Lucy's plan was working.

Moving quickly, but not so fast as to create suspicion, the two of them walked down the boardwalk a short distance before turning off Front Street onto the narrow street that led toward Cora's house. It was hard not to keep looking back to see if they were being watched, but Josie knew that would only draw unnecessary attention to themselves.

Strange as it seemed, she felt exposed and vulnerable without the solid bars of Mitch Hughes's jail cell to protect her. The sooner she got inside, and therefore out of sight, the better she would feel. The house Cora shared with her Aunt Henrietta was just ahead.

Josie stopped midstep. "Lucy, what about Henrietta?"

Lucy responded by looping her arm through Josie's to keep her moving. "Amazingly enough, she's part of the plan."

"What?" Now she'd heard everything.

"Henrietta has her faults, but she has a very strong sense of what is right and proper. She has been absolutely appalled at the idea of our town holding a lady in jail."

Cora's aunt considered her, Josie Turner, a lady? "She actually said that?"

"Several times." From the look on Lucy's face, she was just as amazed by that particular turn of events as Josie was. "In fact, she marched into the bank to corner Mayor Bradford on that very subject. Cade happened to walk in right after she left. He said poor Cletus almost dove under his desk for fear that Henrietta had decided she wasn't finished with him."

The image of the dignified Mayor Bradford huddling on the floor like a small child afraid of thunder struck Josie as funny. She tried to hold back, but a chuckle escaped. And then another. Finally, both women were giggling helplessly only a short distance from sanctuary. Luckily, Cora had been watching for them.

"Will you two hurry?"

The worry in her voice sobered them quickly. They practically ran across the yard and into the house. Cora closed the door and locked it.

"Aunt Henrietta is in the kitchen. She has breakfast about ready. I'll take your things."

Josie followed her friends into the kitchen at the back of the house. Cora's aunt was just pulling a pan of biscuits out of the oven. She set them down on top of the stove.

Straightening up, she turned to greet her guests. "Lucy Mulroney, you have no business skulking around town at this hour in your condition. Sit down now."

"Yes, ma'am." Lucy sank down without a protest onto the closest chair.

Henrietta turned her eagle-sharp eyes on Josie, making her want to shrink into the nearest corner. "And you, young lady—have those odious men been taking proper care of you?"

The unexpected sympathy in her voice was almost Josie's undoing. "I'm . . . I'm fine, Miss Dawson."

"No you're not," the older woman contradicted her, "but you've got gumption enough to stand up to whatever comes your way. Sit and eat. I didn't get up at this ridiculous hour to cook you a hot meal for *my* benefit."

Josie looked to Cora for guidance, but her friend was too busy staring at her aunt as if the older woman had suddenly sprouted a second head. Lucy leaned over and tugged on Cora's sleeve, finally jarring her out of her stunned silence.

Cora blinked her eyes several times and then shook her head. They all knew from her constant complaints that Cora considered her aunt to be so rigidly proper that it was doubtful that the saints would have been up to Henrietta's standards. Now, out of the blue, the woman was supporting the Luminary Society's illegal efforts to help one of their members escape from jail. No wonder Cora seemed stunned.

Finally, though, she took a seat at the table and motioned to Josie to do the same. Once Henrietta had the food arranged on the table to her satisfaction, she took her position at the head of the table.

"I will say grace," she announced.

Dutifully, the three younger women bowed their heads in respect. Josie hadn't grown up going to church, but she'd started attending whenever Oliver hadn't objected to her going. She loved the stories that Pastor Hayes told as he preached love of fellow man and peace on earth. She especially enjoyed the Christmas story. The image of Mary with her son in the manger made her heart swell.

"We thank thee for this meal, Lord. And we ask that you show the men of Lee's Mill, most especially that odious Jed Turner, the error of their ways. Forgive us for taking matters into our own hands, but you know how wrongheaded men can be when they get their hearts set on making fools of themselves. Amen."

Having had her say on the matter, Henrietta served herself some eggs and then passed them on to Lucy. "Help yourselves, ladies. We don't have all morning."

Josie wanted more than anything to ask what was going to happen next, but this was the first hot meal she'd had. To give the sheriff and his deputy credit, they'd been buying her meals from Belle at the hotel, but the food was usually cold by time they carried it all the way down to the jail. Once the weather had turned off cold and wintry, it had stayed that way.

"Miss Dawson, these biscuits are the best I ever ate." Josie meant it.

"You shouldn't exaggerate, Josie Turner," Henrietta sniffed. "However, I do pride myself on my baking." Her piercing blue eyes looked at each woman in turn. "I assume our plans are unchanged."

Cora nodded her head. "Unless something unexpected happens between now and when the stage leaves. Even if Sheriff Hughes remembers what happened, he'd never expect you to be involved."

No one would, Josie thought to herself, but she wasn't complaining. Whatever her friends had planned, she knew they stood a better chance of succeeding with the most self-righteous person in town supporting them. Never in a hundred years would anyone suspect Henrietta Dawson of wrongdoing.

Suddenly, Josie couldn't eat another bite. For a few blessed minutes, she'd been able to relax and enjoy the simple pleasure of sharing a meal with friends. But now she needed to know what was going to happen next. She'd felt so out of control of her own life since the moment she'd found Oliver dead on the porch. She wasn't sure she could live with the constant chaos much longer.

"What is our plan?"

Lucy swallowed her last bite and set down her fork. After dabbing her mouth with a napkin, she pursed her lips as if trying to collect her thoughts.

"You know how Miss Dawson goes up to Columbia the first of every month to see her specialist." She looked at Henrietta for confirmation. "Well, I regret to say that she's taken a turn for the worse."

At first Josie thought Lucy was merely reciting the facts, but then she caught the twinkle in her friend's eye. Miss Dawson's own expression looked awfully cheerful for someone whose health was impaired.

Cora picked up the story. "Yesterday, Aunt Henrietta dragged me up to the stage station to purchase a pair of tickets for this morning's coach. I definitely did not want to buy a ticket. Unfortunately, we caused a bit of a scene at the ticket window."

She didn't sound in the least bit remorseful. "Aunt Henrietta made a point of threatening my allowance if I refused to accompany her to the doctor in her hour of need."

Josie couldn't believe her eyes when Henrietta placed the back of her hand on her forehead and sighed dramatically. "I haven't put on such a fine performance since I left the Riverside Academy for Young Ladies. I do believe the stationmaster was thoroughly taken in."

"Well, I can tell you that Cade heard about the whole incident less than an hour after it happened, Miss Dawson. I only wish I had been there to see it." Lucy allowed herself a small laugh before getting serious again. She checked the time.

"What all this means, Josie, is that in less than an hour Miss Dawson and her niece will board the stage for Columbia."

"But the niece will be me?" Josie appreciated their efforts, but that seemed like a pretty flimsy disguise. All Mitch would have to do is wire ahead to the sheriff in Columbia, and the law would be waiting for her. She told them what she was thinking.

"That's exactly what we want to happen. While he's looking for you on the stage, you'll be right here. No one would suspect that you'd still be in town. Once some of the furor dies down, you can slip away into the woods. As well as you know these hills, no one will be able to find you."

"We have money and food and clothing all put together for you to take."

Tears stung Josie's eyes. The plan was shaky at best, but it would give her a better chance than sitting in jail waiting for the hangman. And they were right. She'd been playing and hunting in the woods that surrounded Lee's Mill since she'd been old enough to walk. It would take a better tracker than any of the men she knew to follow her trail.

"I worry that you have all put yourselves in jeopardy on my behalf, but I do appreciate what you're doing." She tried to look confident in her ability to do her part, but she wasn't sure how successful she'd been.

"What do you think will happen if I run? Do you think

Mitch Hughes will stop looking for the real killer? I mean, won't I look more guilty if I try to escape?" It wasn't the first time she'd asked that question.

"Maybe, Josie. But we figure that isn't as important as keeping you alive."

The sympathy in Lucy's eyes and voice didn't do much to make Josie feel better. She appreciated their good intentions, but Lee's Mill was the only home she'd known. If she ran, she'd never be able to come back or even settle down anywhere else. Not with a man like Jed Turner looking for her.

"I don't want to go." She dared them to argue.

Henrietta took up the standard. "Well, my dear, you can't stay here." She gestured around the room. "I don't mean my home. No matter what happens, you will be welcome here. But the fact of the matter is that unless you want to march back into that jail and face Sheriff Hughes right now, I'd suggest you start thinking about which way you'll leave when the sun goes down."

For a short time they all sat in silence. Finally, Lucy stood up.

"Josie, Melinda and I will weather this little storm in fine shape. Don't worry about us." She leaned down to give Josie a hard hug. "We will make sure the search for the real culprit continues. Remember, you have everyone in the Society on your side. We are a force to be reckoned with."

Cora saw Lucy out, and then she and her aunt began their own preparations, leaving Josie sitting alone at the table.

The walls of the kitchen began closing in on Josie. She had left one cell just to accept another one. Even if she made it to the hills outside town, she wouldn't be free, not by a long shot. Closing her eyes, she tried to imagine what her life would be like, always on the run, always looking back over her shoulder.

But for now, her choices were limited to which direction her flight from justice would take her. She couldn't go toward her own cabin. That would be the first place they would look after they checked out the stagecoach. Downriver might work.

Too many choices and none of them good. Even if she had friends that lived some distance from the town, she wouldn't risk involving them in her troubles. It was bad enough that these fine ladies had taken such chances with their reputations.

What if Sheriff Hughes rounded them all up and threw them into the cell she had just vacated? That particular image made her smile.

"What do you find amusing, young lady?" Henrietta had come back into the room. She had changed into a dress more suitable for traveling.

"Sorry, Miss Dawson, I know nothing about all of this that is funny."

"But . . ." Henrietta prompted.

Josie figured she had little to lose. "If we aren't careful, the next meeting of the Luminary Society will have to be held at the jail because that's where most of the members will be."

Once again Henrietta surprised her. She actually laughed. "Do you think Sheriff Hughes will serve the cookies or pour the tea?"

"He seems to have quite a sweet tooth. I suspect he'd want to be close to the cookies." It felt good to laugh a bit, even if it didn't really change anything.

Henrietta began clearing the table. Josie immediately reached for her own dishes. "Let me do it, Miss Dawson. I'd feel better helping out."

"All right. Make sure you let the fire in the stove die

down, though. Someone might notice if there is smoke coming out of the chimney long after we're gone."

"I hadn't thought about that." Josie poured hot water into the sink and added soap.

"Pastor Hayes says he is expecting even more children at the Christmas celebration. Perhaps you would like to spend the day sewing more of the candy bags. You will find everything you need by my chair in the parlor. By the way, my circle at church is very grateful for all the hard work you've put in already."

Two compliments in one day from such an unexpected source! "I would love to do that." The realization that she was going to miss out on her first real Christmas almost started the tears flowing. One or two escaped before she was able to regain control.

"We must have faith, Josie Turner. Without it, there is nothing."

A few minutes later, Cora came into the room.

"I will get my things, and then we should be going." Henrietta gave Josie another stern look. "You have a good head on your shoulders. Don't panic. Think things through and make the best choice you can. I'm convinced that somehow things will come out all right in the end. Now, I'll leave you two to say your good-byes." She fixed Cora with a stare. "Don't dawdle."

When she was gone, Cora stood there looking totally perplexed. "I have lived with that woman for years. I would never have expected her to do something like this."

"We've always said she wasn't as bad as you thought," Josie reminded her.

"But she's doing this for you, Josie, not me."

"Cora!" Henrietta's voice carried from the front door. "Now, please."

"Now, that's the aunt I know," Cora whispered. She

gave Josie a quick kiss on the cheek. "Be careful, Josie. We'll do all we can to draw them off."

"You've already done more than you should have, especially for me."

Cora's temper flashed in her eyes. She put her hands on her hips. "Why do you say that? Wouldn't you do the same for me? Or Lucy? Or Melinda?"

"Yes . . . but . . ."

"But what? You're our friend, Josie Turner. People stand by their friends. Now, no more apologizing. Who knows? Maybe one of these days, I'll need you to save me." She lowered a small veil from the front of her hat, no doubt part of her disguise.

Josie didn't risk following Cora to the door. So far, they'd been lucky, but if someone happened to be walking by and saw her, their efforts would have been for nothing.

Alone at last, she quickly finished washing the breakfast dishes and then went in search of the needlework. Since the light was best at the table, she settled in at the kitchen table and began sewing.

And while she worked, she considered her options. It occurred to her that there was one person who lived outside town who might take her in. In her mind, she came at the idea from all directions, poking and prodding it until she came to the decision that it was the only sensible choice she had.

She hoped the faith that Henrietta had mentioned would be enough to carry her through.

Why the hell was he sleeping on the floor? Mitch stirred restlessly, trying to find a more comfortable position. Damn, it was cold. If he didn't get the fire stoked up, he and Josie would likely catch their death of cold.

Josie!

He made the mistake of moving too quickly. His senses spun and dipped as a sharp pain cut through his head. He wouldn't make that mistake again.

This time he marshaled his defenses slowly, gathering his strength to push himself up to a sitting position. With his eyes firmly shut, he waited for the room to quit spinning while he tried to remember how he came to be lying unconscious on the floor.

His last clear memory was leaning back in his desk chair with his feet propped up. It wasn't the most comfortable position in which to sleep; in fact, he usually slept on the cot in an empty cell if he had one. But the thought of spending the night with Josie, with only a few bars to separate them, was more temptation that he was willing to risk.

But someone else had been there. . . . A knock at the door had rousted him out of a sound sleep. He'd drawn his gun and peeked outside. Who?

Lucy Mulroney and Melinda Hayes had been standing there, bribing their way past his guard with baked goods. Damn those two for playing on a man's weakness.

He knew even before he opened his eyes that Josie Turner was long gone. He couldn't quite blame her for taking off, not with her father-in-law's promise to take justice into his own hands if his handpicked judge didn't hand down the verdict he wanted.

But now, rather than hunting for Oliver's killer, Mitch was going to have to spend his time tracking down his escaped prisoner. He grunted in pain as he climbed to his feet. How the hell was he going to explain this? He hoped like hell that it was Jake or even Cade who found him locked in his own jail. They'd give him a hard time, but they'd keep it to themselves. Then he spied the key lying on the floor. A few more grunts of pain and a generous helping of cussing, and he managed to reach the key and unlock the door. His head was swimming, but he reached his desk chair without doing himself any further damage. Rather than sit down, he used the rolling chair as a support as he dipped a towel in a pitcher of water.

The chilly water felt like heaven on the back of his head. What had Lucy hit him with? Another vague memory surfaced. Something to do with a skillet. Hell, no wonder his skull felt as if someone had cracked it like an egg. He would have words with that woman, as well as with her accomplice. Who would have thought a pastor's wife would participate in a jailbreak?

If the situation hadn't been so damn serious, Mitch would have found the whole thing funny. Imagine him, always so careful, being taken in by a pair of women swinging a cast-iron skillet. Next time he had a desperado in custody, he'd set the two of them guarding him.

He spied the coffeepot lying on the floor. It had probably got in the way of Lucy's attack. Bending over to pick it up took some fancy footwork on his part, but finally he managed to fill it with water and set it on the stove. Of course, the fire had all but gone out. He'd been stoking it up when Lucy hit him. At least he could take care of that little chore sitting down.

Once the kindling caught, he added a couple of good-sized logs and sat back to wait for both the water and the room to heat up. Then he considered his next move. Despite their actions, he wasn't about to haul two more women in to take up residence in his jail. He had no intention of becoming famous for arresting a record number of women, no matter how much they deserved it.

The clock tolled the hour, giving him some warning that Jake was due to arrive any minute. He'd better come up with a good story and damn quick. His deputy wasn't stupid. If anyone had seen Lucy and Melinda enter the jail, it wouldn't take a genius to figure out what had happened.

Finally, he decided that sticking to the truth as far as he could was his best bet. A few minutes later, when the door to the jail swung open, Mitch had his fingers crossed and his lies ready.

Eight

Mitch turned back toward town, knowing he and his horse had gone as far as they could for the day. Still no sign of his prisoner after almost a week of searching through some of the worst weather Missouri had seen in years. He was beginning to think he'd never have feeling left in his hands and feet.

Not for the first time, he cursed the women of Lee's Mill. Lucy Mulroney and Melinda Hayes were in serious trouble with him, not to mention the law if word ever got out what they'd done. Although he understood their motives—hell, he even agreed with them—they should have trusted him to do right by Josie Turner. They hadn't even bothered to ask him what he thought of the case before banging him over the head with a damn skillet.

He'd had a headache for three days afterward, although he hadn't let it keep him from riding out each day looking for some sign of his escaped prisoner. He hoped like hell Josie was all right, because he was going to throttle her when he found her.

Did she think he wouldn't have protected her from Jed Turner and his men?

Or had she fooled him into thinking she might just be innocent? Rather than torment himself with that thought, he closed his eyes and let the rhythm of his horse's slow walk lull him into dozing. If the poor beast was anywhere as tired as he was, it would be a miracle if they made it back to the stable. Maybe the thought of hay and a warm stall was enough to keep it going.

He, on the other hand, had nothing to look forward to. The jail seemed unnaturally empty without Josie sitting in the corner, quietly sewing or reading. Poor Jake was having to pull extra duty to cover while Mitch was out riding through the hills trying to recover their prisoner.

By now, there wasn't a person within thirty miles who hadn't heard about the big escape. Folks either thought it was the funniest story they'd heard in years or, if they were friends of Jed Turner, they were calling for Mitch to turn in his badge.

So far, he'd ignored both groups.

He doubted even his staunchest supporters would be happy to know that he'd yet to send out any wires asking other lawmen to keep an eye out for Josie. She was in enough trouble without bringing more down on her.

None of the stagecoach drivers had seen her. Cora Lawford had seemed a bit disappointed that her ploy hadn't worked, although he'd been surprised that her witch of an aunt had evidently been in on the whole affair. He'd checked the closest train stations with no luck. So either Josie was on foot or horseback or she'd gone to ground. But where?

His horse jerked its head up to smell the wind. Immediately, it picked up the pace, telling him even without opening his eyes that they were getting close to town.

He dreaded riding through town. If he weren't so damned tired, he'd consider waiting until after dark when he'd stand a better chance of slipping in without having to deal with anyone. Bracing himself for the worst when he reached the last turn, he made the effort to sit up straighter in the saddle, trying to look as if this case weren't beating him down. It felt good to ride into the stable, finally getting some relief from the cold and the wind.

A familiar figure was waiting near the stall the stable owner reserved for Mitch's use.

"Thought you might show up about now."

Cade was one of the few people Mitch could bear talking to. "What brings you out on a night like this?"

He swung down out of the saddle. Both men chuckled when Mitch's horse groaned and shivered, as if relieved to be rid of its burden.

"I've got a proposition for you."

"Can it wait? I'm not sure I could give you a straight answer if you asked me my name." He picked up his tack and stowed it across the stable.

Cade tagged along behind him, carrying Mitch's saddlebags. "That's what I wanted to talk to you about."

Mitch leaned against a nearby railing. "Spit it out, Cade. What's on your mind?"

His friend looked decidedly uncomfortable, as if chewing on something particularly foul. "I feel sort of responsible because you're in this fix."

"Why? Did you kill Oliver Turner?"

Cade didn't dignify that remark with a response. He went on as if Mitch hadn't spoken. "Since my wife is the one that walloped you upside the head, I feel like we owe you, especially when you haven't told anyone what happened."

Of its own accord, his hand reached up to rub the spot that was still sore. The injury to his dignity hurt more. "Go on."

"I figured if I was deputized, temporarily at least, I could take a few shifts at the jail to let you and Jake get some rest. Both of you are so tired now that you're a danger to yourselves, not to mention the town, especially if there was some real trouble to deal with."

"The mayor would have to agree to swear you in."

"He already did." Cade pulled his coat open. A shiny star was pinned to his shirt. "As of right now, I'm on duty until Jake comes in tomorrow morning. He and I will trade off for the next three days. You can go on over to the hotel and get some sleep. When you feel up to it, Ben sent word that he wants you to stop by the farm. He didn't say why."

Maybe it was sign of how tired he was that he felt nothing but relief. Maybe tomorrow he'd be ready to resume his duties, but for now he couldn't see further than a hot meal and a warm bed. "I'll take you up on that offer."

The two men walked back out into the cold. Despite the weather, Mitch felt a new surge of energy.

"I appreciate this, Cade."

"Well, if it weren't for Lucy's interfering . . ." His voice trailed off.

Mitch clapped him on the shoulder. "Look, it's not entirely your fault. I was treating Mrs. Turner more like a guest than a prisoner. If I'd been thinking straight, I would have realized that they were up to something."

Cade gave him a sideways glance. "I take it you haven't had any luck finding Josie's trail."

"Damned if I can figure it out. Near as I can figure, she sprouted wings and flew out of town. No one has seen her since the day she left Lucy and Melinda."

"Well, I think you've done all you can to find her."

"Tell that to Jed Turner."

"I'd rather not. At least since she's escaped, his men haven't been hanging around in town as much."

Mitch frowned. "I'm not sure that's such good news. We could keep an eye on them here. Who knows what they're up to now? What if Jed has them still combing the countryside looking for Josie? For the first few days, they were breathing down my neck everywhere I went. It could go real bad for her if he finds her first."

That thought had him wishing he had the strength to be out on the trail again. But Cade was right—unless he got some rest soon, he'd be no good for anybody.

"Listen. I need to eat something and then get some sleep. Tomorrow I'll need to start looking for her again. If you hear from Ben again, tell him that when I get a chance I'll ride out and check on the farm." He glanced up at the sky. "As long as this break in the weather holds, I need to keep searching. Once it snows again, who knows how long it will be before I can get out?" Or if Josie will live through it.

They'd reached the hotel. "I'll tell Jake what you're planning on doing. If he's got any questions, he can catch up with you before you head out tomorrow."

"Fine." Mitch took his bags from Cade. "And thanks for everything."

Cade grinned. "Least I can do, considering."

"Tell that daughter of yours that I haven't forgotten that game of chess I promised her. And you might let Lucy know that one of her pies would go a long way toward putting her back in my good graces."

"I'll do that, but if I were you, I'd hold out for at least two pies."

Mitch headed straight for the hotel dining room, hoping he could stay awake long enough to eat. Lucky for him, Belle knew a desperate man when she saw one. She was at his table ready to take his order before he had much of a chance to even sit down.

"What can I get you, Sheriff?"

"Something hot and fast."

"As long as you're not picky, I can throw something together in a couple of minutes."

"Perfect."

"Do you want some coffee?"

"No, just food."

She tilted her head to the side. "I'll tell you what. You go on upstairs. I'll bring your dinner up in a few minutes."

"Bless you, woman. Will you marry me?" It was an old joke between them.

"Not this week. My husband might object."

Mitch managed to stand up without help. Considering how tired he was, that in itself was a miracle. "Let me know when you change your mind."

Belle laughed, just as she always did. "Go on with you. I'll be right up."

"I'll be waiting."

"You'll probably be asleep, but don't worry. I don't like to see my cooking go to waste. I'll wake you up if necessary." She made a shooing motion with her apron. "Get moving before you fall down."

He managed to smile before heading for the front desk to pick up his key. People like Belle and her husband were among the biggest reasons he planned on staying in Lee's Mill. That is, if he still had a job after this mess about Josie Turner ended.

He felt guilty leaving Cade and Jake to take care of the town, but the pressing need to find Josie Turner before her father-in-law and his men did was driving him hard. Hell, he even felt bad about taking time out of his search to check on old Ben. He eased his conscience by telling himself that no one would begrudge him a good night's sleep in his own bed. Come dawn he'd be back out riding the trails, crisscrossing the hills in search of Josie.

He ignored the ever-growing fear that it would be her body that he found. Even reminding himself that she'd grown up in those same hills, hunting for small game to keep her and her worthless father fed, wasn't working anymore. Even the most experienced hunters would have a hard time keeping warm and dry with the weather they'd been having: cold rain, sleet, and flurries of snow. Maybe she'd found a cave to hole up in, but she hadn't taken enough with her to survive long outdoors.

Damn Lucy and Melinda for setting her free to die by inches in the brutal Ozark winter. He'd finally cornered the two of them long enough to find out just what they'd scraped together for Josie to take with her. He shuddered at their idea of adequate supplies.

The first few snowflakes of the day danced in front of his horse's nose. Mitch glanced up at the sky, trying to gauge the seriousness of the shift in the weather.

It didn't look good. As much for his horse's sake as his own, he urged the animal into a slow lope. With luck, they'd reach the farm and the safety of the barn before the ground was covered. The sometimes stubborn mare didn't hesitate, convincing Mitch that a wise man would be indoors before the storm hit in earnest.

They almost made it. He figured they were about five miles out when the wind shifted, bringing with it a curtain of white that obscured the trail ahead. He hunkered down in the saddle, trying to make himself as small a target for the icy pellets as possible. Leaning down over his horse's neck, he murmured encouraging words, promising the poor beast that Ben would fix it a warm stall and a hot mash as soon as they reached the farm.

If they'd been on the main road, he would have risked a faster pace, but they'd been following a game trail that led up and over some fairly steep hills behind his home. They made steady progress zigzagging up a slope. But just past the sharp crest, the horse lost its footing on a shelf of limestone, and they both nearly went tumbling down the hillside. At the rate the snow was falling, it would have been the spring thaw before anyone found them.

The close call left him shaken and his horse limping. The footing ahead wasn't likely to improve any. Resigning himself to a long, cold walk, Mitch dismounted and trudged off down the trail, leading his reluctant horse by the reins. If the rocks gave way again, it was unlikely that either of them would survive, what with the horse already injured.

Mitch tried to keep to the trees, figuring the snow would be slower to accumulate under them. The brushy undergrowth didn't make for easy going, though. Finally, he cut across country, heading directly for the farm, figuring the shortest route was the best at this point.

Time passed in an endless blur of stumbling and damn near dragging the horse along behind him. He was almost praying for the cold to numb the pain in his shoulders from yanking and pulling on the reins to keep his horse from giving up. What little luck he had ran out when his boot heel caught on a jagged rock, sending him slip-sliding down a slope of loose rock to land in a heap at the bottom. He would have been all right except for the boulder that broke his fall and damn near broke his head. He sat still for several minutes as he waited for the world to quit spinning around him.

Taking stock of his injuries, he decided none of them would be fatal, provided he got the hell out of the gully and home before he froze to death. After a couple of tries that left him gasping in pain, he struggled to his feet and began the treacherous climb back up to where his horse waited.

Ignoring the traces of blood he left on the branches he used for support, he worked his way up the rock-strewn hillside. Once he reached the top, he grabbed hold of the near stirrup and urged the horse forward.

"Come on, girl, keep going. It will all be over soon." He wasn't lying. If they didn't reach shelter soon, the combination of cold and snow would finish them both off.

After an eternity of stumbling and cursing the horse into taking another step and then another, the outline of a building loomed up in front of him. Convinced that his imagination was playing tricks on him, Mitch blinked several times and swiped at his eyes with the back of his hand, trying to wipe away enough frost to see clearly.

The barn didn't disappear.

This time, the horse needed no urging. It damn near knocked Mitch down in its hurry to reach the sanctuary that lay ahead. Mitch figured he'd done his part to get them both home, so he let go of the reins and let the horse find its own way. Ben would be only too glad to see to the horse once Mitch told him it was hurt and half frozen. No doubt the old man would leave Mitch to take care of himself.

That was fine with Mitch. Right then, he'd settle for a fire in the stove and hot coffee to drink. With his last burst of energy, he made it as far as the porch. Crawling more than walking, he dragged himself across to the door and hit it with his fist. With luck, Ben would be close enough to hear it. If not, come morning he might fall over Mitch's dead body when he went out to feed the animals.

The edges of his mind blurred as he waited and prayed for the door to open. He tried to raise his fist one more time but couldn't quite make his hand obey. Just as he felt himself starting to slip down under the icy darkness in his mind, the door swung open.

Too late. He hadn't made it in time, because it wasn't an ugly old man who reached out from the golden light inside the door, but an angel. As he gave himself over to oblivion, he decided he was glad that God gave angels big, brown eyes.

"How long will he be out?"

Mitch was curious about that himself. He was beginning to think that if he tried hard enough, he might just be able to open his eyes wide enough to get his first glimpse of heaven. He had to admit to being a bit surprised to have ended up there instead of hell, but the gentle voice he'd been dimly aware of for the past little while couldn't possibly come from anywhere else.

"I don't know, missy. It's hard to know about anybody stupid enough to get caught out in this storm."

Now, that voice sounded more like what he expected the devil himself to sound like—rough and cantankerous.

"You know he was looking for me." The sweet voice was colored with worry and maybe guilt.

He didn't want an angel feeling bad about him. He struggled to tell her so. What came out of his mouth sounded like gibberish to him, but evidently it pleased the two who hovered over him.

"See there, Josie, I told you he was too stubborn to die."

"Yes, you did, even though you fussed over Mitch's horse more than you did him."

That comment had Mitch's eyes fighting to open. Maybe this wasn't heaven after all. The only voice he knew that sounded that crotchety belonged to Ben. And it would be just like him to leave Mitch lying frozen on the porch while his horse got a warm place to sleep and something hot to eat.

Sure enough, Ben's ugly old face swam into focus only

inches from Mitch's eyes. It was enough to send him diving back into blissful darkness again. But before that could happen, Ben moved back out of sight, and another familiar face took his place.

"Josie?"

A gentle hand rested briefly on his brow; the sweetness of the touch had him groaning in pleasure.

Ben's callused hand slid under Mitch's head, making him wince in pain. The old man muttered something that sounded like an apology, but he continued in his efforts to prop Mitch up.

A soft, gentle voice coaxed him into cooperating. "I know it's hard, Sheriff, but you need to drink something."

He might have told Ben to go to hell, but he found himself struggling to do anything that would please Josie. Dutifully he opened his mouth and sipped at the cup she held to his lips. The rich flavor of chicken broth eased the dryness in his throat. He paused to savor the taste and then whispered, "More."

"Slow down a bit," Josie chided. "We need to see how much you can handle."

After another few spoonfuls, Ben lowered Mitch back down. Even that small movement had his head swimming.

"Horse?"

"She'll be fine come morning. Nothing wrong with her that a night's rest and some good feed won't cure."

"Limp." He hated talking in single words, but he couldn't seem to string more than that together.

"I saw that, but it doesn't appear to be anything serious. A little swelling, but she wasn't having any trouble standing on it. I figure she'll be ready to ride out long before you are." Ben looked out the window across the room. "If this snow keeps up, nobody's going anywhere soon. I had to tie a rope from here to the barn to make sure I found my way back."

If Mitch wasn't mistaken, the gruff concern he heard in Ben's voice was equally divided between him and the horse. The old man would hate knowing he was that transparent.

There were a hundred other questions he wanted to ask. First and foremost, why was Josie here? And where the hell had she been for the past two weeks?

For now, he'd have to be satisfied knowing he hadn't killed himself or his horse. The rest would have to wait until the pounding in his head eased up. His eyes slipped shut of their own accord as he drifted back down into the darkness.

He was going to wake up any minute, Josie decided as she stood over her patient, watching him toss and turn. And if she was any judge of Mitch's temper, he was going to be madder than . . . Well, he had some cause to be, so she couldn't fault him.

He'd been roaming the hills around Lee's Mill in the rain and the snow while she'd been tucked up warm and safe in his farmhouse. The fact that she'd been waiting for him probably wouldn't make him any happier about the situation. Her patient stirred again, his bare leg kicking itself free of the blankets. He'd already shoved his covers down to his waist, leaving far too much of Mitch Hughes available for her eyes to feast on. She felt her face flush at the sight, but she was too honest with herself to claim it was only embarrassment that had her cheeks turning pink. Determined not to get caught staring, she slipped back out of his room.

Ben was just coming in from the barn. "I see he's still lying abed while honest folks are up working." He hung his coat and hat on pegs by the door and then clomped across the room in his heavy work boots.

Josie knew she should chide him for making so much noise. But in his own way, Ben had been plenty worried about his boss, both before and after Mitch had all but crawled home.

"I'd guess he should sleep . . ."

"Until some old coot comes in making enough noise to raise the dead."

Josie looked over Ben's head to where Mitch stood, propping himself up against the door frame. He had wrapped the sheet around his waist. With some effort she managed to keep her eyes focused firmly on his face.

What looked like a two-day growth of beard did much to hide the bruising along his jawline, but there were several large purple patches down his shoulder and arm, along with some minor scrapes. On the whole, she figured they were more painful than dangerous.

The lump on his head was the one that had her worried. A blow like that could addle anybody's thinking. She shuddered with the knowledge of how close they'd come to losing him. Suddenly, she realized that she'd been staring. All concern about that went out the window when his gaze locked on to hers.

Instinctively she backed up a step, only to find herself cornered against the heat of the stove. "Uh, good morning, Sheriff."

Ben twisted around in his chair to get a better look at his employer. "Hellfire, man, what are you thinking? You can't parade around damn near naked in front of a lady!" He lurched to his feet. "Get back in your room until you get some pants on!"

Josie quickly stifled the urge to laugh at the image the two men made as they grumbled and fussed at each other. Figuring both of them would be ready for breakfast in only a short while, she reached for the skillet. As she sliced off enough bacon for the three of them, she allowed herself a small smile.

She found it flattering for someone to rush to protect her as if she were a real lady instead of a hill girl. For all his bluster, Ben had been nothing but kind to her since she'd appeared unannounced and unwanted on his doorstep. He'd offered her shelter and his own gruff kindness. He'd even argued against sending word to the sheriff that he was needed at home.

And now he was railing at his boss for daring to walk into his own kitchen. Ben knew full well that she'd already seen quite a bit of Mitch Hughes the night before, when they'd struggled to remove his wet clothing and treat his injuries. Maybe Ben figured there was a difference between tending to someone who was unconscious and looking at a man who could look right back.

She glanced back toward the door to Mitch's room and listened. Judging by the muffled noise, Ben was doing his clumsy best to help Mitch make himself decent. She turned the bacon one last time and then broke eggs into a bowl. After a second's hesitation, she added a couple more. She was well acquainted with Ben's healthy appetite and judging from Mitch's size, he'd probably match the older man bite for bite and then some.

Besides, if she kept him busy eating, he couldn't unleash his temper. Maybe it was too much to hope that a hot meal would dim his memories of the past couple of weeks spent out in the wet and cold, but it couldn't hurt.

She closed her eyes and reminded herself once again that Mitch Hughes was not Oliver Turner. Her husband had been handsome and even charming, but underneath the surface he was both selfish and a bully. Before Oliver's death, Mitch Hughes had never been anything but polite and kind to her. In fact, the two times she had seen his temper slip, his anger had been directed at Oliver and Jed Turner, not at her.

In Lee's Mill he had a reputation for treating people fairly. But did that extend to a woman who'd broken out of his jail after being accused of murdering her husband? She hoped so.

The sound of the door opening warned her that she was about to find out. She began spooning the eggs into a bowl.

"Damn it, Ben, I can do it!"

"Fine, I'll watch."

And laugh, if Mitch was any judge of his friend's expression. Well, he'd just show the old bastard who was in charge around here.

Bending slowly, Mitch sank back down on the edge of the bed and tried to work his foot into the leg of his pants. Every joint in his body protested, but he vowed to get dressed all on his own—even if it killed him.

Despite the chill in the room, his face was dripping sweat with the effort it took to get the second foot guided into the pant leg. Feeling rather proud of himself, he started to stand, in order to pull the pants up the rest of the way. A wave of dizziness had him reeling forward.

Ben immediately reached out to catch him, but pride had Mitch waving him back. "I said I would do it."

His shoulder screamed in pain as he tugged his pants up the final distance and buttoned them.

Then he reached for his shirt. If he didn't hurry, he'd use up what little strength he had left and have to crawl back into bed without eating. He sniffed the air. Whatever Josie was fixing out there in the kitchen smelled like heaven. The very thought of eating a hot meal cooked by anyone other than Ben or himself had him struggling to get his shirt on before the food got cold.

About the time he worked the last button through its hole, Ben held out a pair of socks with a particularly smug look on his face. Before he could tell the old man what to do with them, Ben shook his head.

"Pride's going to get you nothing but more pain and cold food."

Figuring he'd proven his manhood with the shirt and pants, Mitch gingerly sat down and allowed Ben to help him with the socks.

"Thanks."

"Didn't do it for you. I figure that little lady out there won't feed me until you're ready. I don't like my bacon and eggs cold."

Mitch accepted Ben's statement for what it was—a way of salvaging Mitch's pride and getting a hot meal for his troubles. Slowly Mitch stood up, using the bed for support. Still unsure how steady his legs would be, he worked his way across the room by holding on to various pieces of furniture. Once he reached the door, he decided that he could make it as far as the table on his own.

Ben hovered just out of reach just in case, although he disguised his efforts by messing with his pipe.

Finally, when Mitch was seated, Ben set the pipe down and took his place at the table. So far, Mitch hadn't acknowledged Josie's presence, not even when she set down a plate heaped with eggs, bacon, fried potatoes, and biscuits that looked light enough to float.

"Miss Josie, you sure have a knack for cooking."

"Thank you, Ben."

Mitch concentrated on lifting his fork to his mouth without dropping it. It didn't take long to know that Ben was right.

"Thank you for cooking for us, Mrs. Turner."

He forced himself to look across the table when he spoke. Josie's face appeared flushed and not a little worried. No doubt she was more concerned about how much trouble she was in than about what he thought of her cooking.

He could have told her. A lot. More trouble than she could imagine. And not only with the law. Sure, she was wanted for murder. Yes, she had broken out of jail with the help of her well-meaning friends. But, damn it, she had left him dangling, worried and scared for her for the past two weeks. She could have sent word that she was safe.

Some of what he was thinking must have been reflected in his expression, because Josie turned pale and dropped her fork. Even that made him mad.

"Go ahead and eat. I promise not to holler at you until after breakfast." He softened his remark with a half smile, knowing the first sign of real temper on his part would fill those eyes of hers with real fear.

He might be mad at her, but only because he'd been so damned worried. Figuring he couldn't very well tell her that, he picked up his own fork and started eating.

Ben, usually totally insensitive to the moods and needs of others, took it upon himself to start a conversation. "I checked your horse this morning."

After waiting several seconds for him to continue, Mitch gave up and prodded the old man. "And?"

"And both you and her are damn lucky to be alive. She's still limping a bit, but nothing another day or two of rest won't cure." Ben gestured toward Mitch's almost empty plate. "Her appetite is about like yours."

"Thanks for seeing to her, Ben. I appreciate it."

Ben struck a match and started puffing his pipe. "Weren't nothing. Besides, that horse is nicer to me than you are."

The sound of Josie's laughter had both men staring

across the table at her. She immediately stopped and covered her mouth. Her gaze dropped to the table and stayed there as the sparkle died.

Feeling like he'd let something beautiful slip away, Mitch tried to apologize. "We didn't mean to stare, Mrs. Turner. A couple of old bachelors like old Ben here and me just aren't used to having a . . ." He choked back the words he'd been about to say. Referring to Josie as a beautiful woman wasn't what a sheriff should say to his prisoner. He managed to finish up with "a guest at our table."

She mumbled something that sounded like "That's all right." The she was on her feet and clearing the table, keeping her hands busy and her mouth shut.

She wasn't the only one who wasn't happy with him. Ben shook his head, purely disgusted with Mitch. "Thanks again for breakfast, Miss Josie. If you don't need me, I'll be out in the barn with the rest of the mules."

At least she didn't laugh, Mitch thought disgustedly. Of course, she did turn away rather abruptly, but if Ben's insult brought back some of the life in her eyes, Mitch wouldn't complain.

Not more than Ben expected, anyway. "Have fun with all your friends."

Ben responded by slamming the door on the way out, rattling the windows and sending a blast of cold air through the room. Mitch shivered, knowing how easily he could have breathed his last out in those freezing temperatures.

"More coffee, Sheriff Hughes?"

"That seems a tad formal, considering you've been living in my house and you just cooked me breakfast. Call me by my given name."

She tried it out slowly, as if the word were a difficult one for her tongue to get around. "Mitch."

She offered him a shy smile. "I'd rather you called me Josie, too. I never got quite used to being 'Mrs. Turner.' That name always belonged to Oliver's mother."

Considering how Oliver and his family had treated Josie, Mitch could understand the logic of that. "Well, Josie it is, then. Would you mind if I lay back down for a while? I'm still a might tired."

She immediately hurried around to his side of the table. "Do you need any help getting back to bed?"

As tempting as the idea of leaning on her fragile shoulders was, he shook his head. He had no business touching her, especially with the memory of her gentle hands touching his face so fresh in his mind.

"No, I can make it." He used the table to push himself up to his feet. Hating the weakness he felt, he walked into his room and shut the door, without looking back once. It may have been the hardest thing he'd done in years.

Nine

Mitch wished like hell he could fall asleep. Instead he was almost painfully aware of the quiet whispers of noise seeping through the thin walls. He'd already tossed and turned for the better part of an hour, listening to the soft scrape of a chair, a muttered complaint when something hit the floor, a tuneless hum.

It seemed strange to think of a woman being in his house. He wondered what Josie thought of the place, and what she had found to do. The farmer who'd sold him the farm had spent most of his time trying to clear the land. There'd been little time and less interest in the little touches that made a house seem warm and welcoming.

The nature of Mitch's job kept him from spending as much time around the farm as he'd like. Besides, with only Ben for company, the evenings seemed to drag on forever.

Finally, he turned his face to the wall, grimacing as his shoulder reminded him to move slowly. He didn't want to know what it would be like to have a woman to share his life with—Josie Turner least of all. Even if she didn't jump like a scared rabbit whenever he looked at her, there was the little matter of the murder charge against her.

He wanted to think she was innocent, but that could simply be because he was thinking with the wrong part of his anatomy. Shifting again, he tried to ease his body's all too familiar response when he spent too much time around her.

It was bad enough when he'd seen her only occasionally, in town or during his frequent trips to the store. He hadn't counted on her invading his home in the same way she invaded his mind. Certainly, he wasn't sure how to deal with any of it, especially with his shoulder aching and his head still pounding. Maybe after he rested, he'd come up with some answers. He wished he could shut out the sounds from the next room as easily as closing his eyes. Doing his best to think of God and country, he drifted off to sleep.

Josie glanced at Mitch's door for about the hundredth time in the past couple of hours. Sooner or later he'd wake up, and then she feared the peace and quiet she'd enjoyed over the past few days would end.

If she were honest with herself, it was a relief to know that the suspense was almost over. Despite her fear of angry men, she was almost looking forward to Mitch yelling and screaming and cursing her for the trouble she'd caused him, both before her escape and since.

Her hands felt restless. She looked around the large kitchen for something to do. Judging from what she saw, it had been some time since anyone had given the room a good scrubbing. Would Mitch mind if she took on the job?

Short of waking him up to ask, there wasn't much she could do but sit and wait. Or throw caution out the dingy window and start in. Figuring he couldn't get much angrier with her than he already was, she fixed up a bowl of soapy water to wash down the shelves. Standing on a chair, she began clearing off the clutter of canned goods and other food supplies.

It occurred to her that Mitch—she savored the right to use his first name as if they were really friends or something—might not appreciate her messing with his things. On the other hand, from the way supplies were scattered all over the kitchen, it was unlikely that he even knew what-all he had. So far, she'd found four different sacks of coffee beans and several pouches of Ben's tobacco. If they had kept the items in some sort of order, they wouldn't have bought duplicates of so many things.

She wrung out her rag and wiped down the first two shelves. Rather than put everything back right away, she decided to leave it all on the table so she could organize the various items before putting them back.

It didn't take long to finish wiping down the shelves. She wished she had some pretty paper to line them with, the kind Henrietta used, but she would have to settle for clean, figuring that alone was quite an improvement.

Whistling under her breath, she began sorting things and arranging them where she decided they logically belonged. Knowing Ben, he'd complain loud and long that he couldn't find anything, but she could handle him. Mitch was a different matter.

Surely he'd see what an improvement she had made once it was all finished.

To that end, she lifted her skirts and climbed back up on the chair to push some empty jars to the far end of the top shelf, knowing they wouldn't be needed until next summer. Unfortunately, she leaned out farther than she should have, causing the chair to tip. Just as she started to tumble, Mitch walked out of his bedroom door. Instinctively she grabbed for him on her way down, sending both of them stumbling backward. His arms clamped around her, pulling her up tight against his chest as he struggled to keep both of them from crashing to the floor.

He lost the battle. In a flurry of flailing arms, the two of them hit the wooden floor with a thud and not a few curse words. Gentleman that he was, Mitch twisted at the last moment to absorb the brunt of the impact, leaving Josie sprawled atop his chest and legs.

The impact knocked all the air out of her lungs. As she tried to catch her breath, she stared down into Mitch's silver-gray eyes. Either her heart stopped or else time did as she became aware of the hard strength of the man stretched out below her. The warmth of his body seeped through the thin cotton of her dress, making her all too aware of her unwilling host.

The expression on his face was impossible to decipher until the side of his mouth quirked up in a half smile.

"Do you often wrestle men to the ground?"

She surprised herself by daring to tease him back. "Only when I'm sure I'll win."

She felt his laugh rumble along the length of her body, making her realize that she was still lying on top of him, her body fitting all too well to the masculine contours of his. Trouble was, she wasn't sure how to go about getting up with any sort of dignity at all.

Mitch solved the problem for them both. He still had one arm wrapped around her. Slipping both hands down to her waist, he lifted her up and to the side. She knew the effort cost him, but he refused her help in getting back up off the floor. When he was standing, he leaned back against the wall, his breath sounding a bit ragged.

His eyes swept the mess she'd made of the kitchen, his focus narrowing in on the clutter of sacks and cans on the table.

"What the hell?" There was no humor in the way he glared at her.

Josie tried to swallow around the lump in her throat before speaking. "I, uh, needed something to do."

"So you decided to destroy my kitchen?"

She tried to see the room through his eyes. He was right. It did look as if she'd been doing her best to wreck the entire room. How could she explain that if he'd slept even another half hour, he would have walked out into a room that gleamed?

"I thought I could earn my keep by doing some cleaning."

He frowned even more. "Who the hell asked you to earn your keep? I sure don't remember saying anything like that. Then, of course, I never invited you here in the first place."

His bitter words pained her. She braced herself to withstand the full power of his fury. Without meaning to, she retreated across the room, trying to put the table between her and Mitch's temper.

"Stop backing away from me," he snapped. "I don't want to have to yell to be heard. My ribs hurt."

She froze, not sure what to do next. Her pulse pounded in her ears, as if she'd been running flat out for a mile or more. When Mitch raised his hand, years of experience had her cowering in the corner with her arm in front of her face to ward off any blows. Her stomach churned with fear as she waited for the pain to begin.

Mitch dropped his hand back down to his side. He'd been going to run his fingers through his hair out of frustration, but he hadn't realized what effect the simple motion would have on Josie.

He was mad, but he was more embarrassed than anything. She was right. The kitchen did need a thorough cleaning, and if it gave her a sense of purpose, fine. He just hadn't expected to see the evidence of his fixation on her lined up in neat little rows: sacks of coffee, more tobacco than Ben would use in six months, enough beans to feed the army for a week. What was he supposed to say if she asked him why he'd bought all that stuff?

For now, he owed her an apology for scaring her. Just the sight of her, frozen in fear, was enough to make him sick. And mad enough to wish Oliver were standing in front of him so he could beat the bastard to his knees. He needed to approach Josie—always a dangerous thing when it came to frightened creatures. If cornered, they sometimes struck out and drew blood.

He hesitated long enough to take a calming breath and then slowly inched forward, not wanting to startle her into running.

Dangling his hands loosely at his side, Mitch cautiously approached the table and then worked his way around the end. He waited to see if Josie would bolt around the other end, but she seemed unable to do more than stand and wait for whatever fate would befall her.

When he was no more than an arm's reach away from her, he slowly raised his hand, careful to keep his fingers spread open and palm up. When he touched her arm, she flinched and made a sound more like a wild animal in pain than the strong woman he'd come to know.

Rather than retreat, he gave up all attempt at caution and gathered Josie's slight form into his arms, cradling her against his chest. It felt as if he were holding a board, stiff and unyielding.

Desperate to break through her shell of fear, he risked a soft caress up and down the length of Josie's back— once, twice, three times, before he was rewarded with a slight softening in her stance. Not one to question success, he continued the rhythm, up and down, up and down, his fingers learning the sweet flow of her back as it narrowed at her waist and then flared out again to hint at the curves below.

Finally, she drew a shuddering breath and then slipped her arms around Mitch's waist and held on for dear life. Her shoulders shook as the tears broke free, soaking through his shirt to burn like acid on his skin. He hated it when a woman cried, not that he saw it as a sign of weakness. But, as with most men, tears scared him worse than facing down an armed drunk.

"That's it, honey, let it out. Let it all out," he mumbled, still stroking her as if she were a frightened kitten he was trying to tame. "I wouldn't hurt you, Josie." *Unless you have to hang her,* a nasty little voice whispered in his mind. He ignored it. "I know you haven't had much reason to trust men, but I swear to God I'd never raise a hand to a woman or a child."

She mumbled something that sounded like "I know" against his chest. Then she straightened up, pulling her head back far enough to look up at him. "I do know. I didn't mean to act like a fool."

She hadn't acted like a fool, but more like a dog that's been kicked so often it doesn't remember anything else. He couldn't very well tell her that, so he settled for tucking her head back against his shoulder.

She accepted his comfort for only a short time before once again struggling to look up at him. "I know you want to yell at me. I promise not to run scared again."

She would if she had any idea what he really wanted to do to her. Now that the crisis had passed, he was becoming aware of her on a whole other level, one that had all his blood rushing to pool up considerably south of his brain. It didn't help that the delicate scent of her hair and skin clouded his senses, making coherent thought all but impossible.

Damn, if he had a lick of sense, he'd shove her backward until he could no longer feel her warmth. He feared that would require more strength than he could muster.

And when she looked up at him with those trusting eyes . . . but now those eyes were drifting down to focus on his mouth. If he didn't know better, he'd think he wasn't the only one affected by the closeness of their embrace. When her lips parted with a quiet sigh, he knew he was lost. Maybe they both were.

Slowly, not wanting to spook her again, he lowered his mouth to Josie's. He brushed his lips gently across hers, fighting for enough control to go slowly. Josie surprised him when she reached out with her hands to hold his head still while she rose up on her toes to close the final gap between them. For one brief second in time, his entire world narrowed down to the sweetness of Josie Turner's kiss.

An eternity ticked by until, somewhere in the back of his mind, he heard the sound of boots stomping across the porch, penetrating the silence that surrounded them. Already the doorknob was turning—too late for them to avoid being caught.

Ben stepped through the doorway, as usual complaining about the weather or the animals or some damn thing. His tirade came to an abrupt stop when he realized what was unfolding right in front of his eyes.

"What the hell?" he demanded as he skidded to a halt a short distance from where they stood. "Damn it, Mitch Hughes, what's gotten into you?"

Evidently, Josie didn't fear Ben's temper like she did Mitch's, a fact Mitch didn't much appreciate. He drew some comfort from the fact that she didn't immediately withdraw from his embrace.

"Ben, try knocking next time."

Josie's comment had his employee sputtering with indignation. "Damned if I will. Until Mitch tells me differently, I live in this house." He glared at the two of them. "Well, do you want me to knock or do you want me to bed down with the mules?" He puffed up in full temper as he waited for Mitch to call his bluff.

Feeling frustrated for reasons that definitely weren't Ben's fault, Mitch was tempted to see if the old man would really go. He knew better than to try it, or he'd spend the rest of the day groveling and apologizing.

Josie settled the matter for both of them. "Ben, don't be silly. Now, both of you get out of the kitchen so I can finish what I was doing."

She practically shooed them both out of the room, leaving them no place to go except their separate bedrooms. Mitch let her have her way, but not completely.

"When you're done, we need to talk." Having said that, he closed his door and sat down on the bed to wait.

"Melinda, we need to talk." Lucy Mulroney shook the snow off her coat as she swept past her friend into the parlor at the rectory. "Is Daniel home?"

"No, he's over at the church." Melinda followed behind Lucy. "You must be freezing. Would you like a cup of coffee or tea?"

"Tea sounds wonderful. The baby seems to object to coffee."

While her friend disappeared into the kitchen to make the tea, Lucy couldn't resist the urge to look down at her waist. Although no one else could see any changes yet, she knew from the way her dresses fit that her waist was expanding. She couldn't wait to meet the little stranger who would join their family in only a few months. Mentally, she counted off the months. In less than two weeks Christmas would mark the end of her third month. Come Easter, she'd be two-thirds through her pregnancy. She closed her eyes and tried to imagine how she'd feel by June when the baby was due.

Cade was so excited, as was his young daughter Mary—now Lucy's daughter as well. The three of them had really become a family. The new addition would just make their lives that much richer.

But today she wasn't here to talk about her pregnancy. No, she was here to get Melinda's help in furthering their investigation into the death of Oliver Turner. So far, the only fact they'd uncovered was that Josie Turner was innocent of the crime. Unfortunately, neither her opinion nor Melinda's would carry much weight when the case came to trial.

She closed her eyes and whispered a small prayer of thanks that Mitch Hughes hadn't seen fit to charge the two of them for the crime of breaking Josie out of jail. She knew that at the very least, they were guilty of assault. Even now she could still remember the sickening thud her best skillet had made when she'd brought it down on the back of his head.

It would really be too bad if her baby ended up being born in the town jail. Before she could depress herself any further, Melinda returned with a tray laden with tea and a plateful of cookies. The next several minutes were taken up with the business of pouring tea and nibbling on Melinda's best sugar cookies.

Finally, Melinda set her cup down and folded her hands in her lap. "All right, Lucy, what's so important that you've closed the store in the middle of a Monday morning?"

"I didn't close the store. Cora is covering for me while Cade is in White's Ferry for the day."

"And you picked today so he won't know what you're up to."

Lucy wasn't at all surprised that Melinda had guessed exactly what Lucy had been thinking. She didn't bother denying any of it.

"Well, I think it's a shame that no one has paid a condolence call on Jed Turner. Don't you think someone should?"

Melinda's response consisted of an arched eyebrow and a wagging finger. "Lucy Mulroney, you have no business whatsoever in going out to the Turner place. If anyone should go, it should be Daniel. He's the pastor, after all."

Lucy gave the matter some thought. "I believe you're right. While he's talking to Jed, we can watch to see if he's lying."

"Daniel won't take us out there." Melinda sounded a little too sure of herself for Lucy's comfort.

"He might, if we're bringing food to the bereaved family."

"Jed's not a 'family,' Lucy. He's a single person, complete with a housekeeper to do all his cooking." Melinda played her trump card. "Besides, Daniel already tried to pay a call on Jed Turner. That awful man didn't even let Daniel in the door."

Melinda sounded outraged on behalf of her husband. Lucy wondered if she could use that anger to her advantage.

"That sounds like something Jed Turner would do. One minute the man is acting as if he owns the town, and the next he doesn't show even ordinary good manners." She did her best to look morally superior. It didn't fool Melinda one bit.

"Lucy, what are you up to?"

"Well, Mitch is busy hunting for Josie, which means he can't be investigating the murder. I don't regret for one minute getting Josie out of that awful place, but I feel we owe the sheriff something for the trouble we've caused him."

"What can we do?"

"I think we should do some investigating on our own."

"Lucy!" Melinda put her teacup down so quickly it rattled in its saucer. "You must be kidding. What would we know about investigating a murder?"

Lucy had been expecting that question and had her answer ready. "The members of the Luminary Society all know how to discuss a topic. And what is discussion but asking questions and listening to someone's response? Based on the information you collect, you develop your own opinion."

"And what would we do with this information we collect?"

She'd known all along that Melinda's own curiosity would be her downfall. Trying to look concerned rather than triumphant, she chewed her lower lip and gave the matter some thought. "We can't tell Cade. He wouldn't approve of us getting involved more than we already are."

"And neither would Daniel."

"That leaves Sheriff Hughes. If we find anything he can use to help Josie, we'll take it straight to him."

Melinda picked up her tea again. After taking a sip, she gave Lucy a worried look. "And if we find something that makes things look worse for Josie? That could happen, Lucy."

The same thing had crossed her mind. There was no easy answer to that particular dilemma, and she said so. "I cling to the belief that since Josie is innocent, no real fact can dispute that. Jed Turner can point fingers all he wants; that doesn't make her guilty."

"Who else could have shot Oliver? And why would they dump his body where it would be found by Josie?"

"I'd have to say, to cast blame on her and away from themselves. As to who might have done it, Oliver wasn't particularly well liked by anyone."

Melinda was getting into the spirit of things. "Maybe he owed someone money."

"But killing him won't help pay off the debt."

"No, but it might serve as a lesson to others who might think about running up bills they can't pay."

"How would we find that out?" Melinda had her limits. "I will not go back in that saloon with you again," she declared, referring to the time the two of them had attended a city council meeting, which were always held in The River Lady Saloon.

"I wouldn't ask you to. No, we'll have to leave that to the men, I think." She pretended to think hard and long. "You know, I still think our best course of action would be to pay a condolence call on Jed Turner as soon as the weather allows. I realize that he and his son weren't all that close, but he may know more than he's let on."

Melinda shivered despite the heat of the room. "That man frightens me. He seems so angry. Too angry somehow. Perhaps approaching him about Oliver isn't such a good idea."

To avoid responding, Lucy busied herself refilling her cup with tea and allowing herself one more cookie. Her gaze wandered around the small room. She noticed the attractive arrangement of greens and holly that Melinda had placed on the mantel. Nodding in the direction of the artful display, she started to compliment her friend when an idea began to form in her mind.

"Melinda, what if we don't approach him about his son, at least not directly?" She paused to think things through. "Christmas is almost upon us. It would be only natural to ask the wealthiest man in the area for a donation to help make Christmas special for all the children."

"We're already giving each of them a bag of candy," Melinda reminded her. She, too, reached for the teapot.

"I know that, but he doesn't. Besides, that's all that some of the children will get. It would be nice to add a few things under the tree. You know, some toys and warm clothes."

"I bet Daniel would know who needs extra help right now."

The excitement in Melinda's voice made it clear that she'd gotten past her reservations about talking to Jed Turner. Having accomplished her purpose, Lucy set her cup down. Cora was perfectly capable of managing the store for a short period of time, but Lucy didn't want to impose on her longer than absolutely necessary. With her usual assistant wanted for murder, she might need Cora's help again.

"Well, I had better return to the store. Cora mentioned something about Henrietta wanting her home soon." She put on her coat and gloves as she spoke.

Melinda followed her to the door. "You take it easy out there. It's slippery in spots. It wouldn't do for you to fall."

Once again, Lucy's hand went to her waist in a protective gesture. "I'll be careful. Thank you for the tea and cookies."

"You're welcome. I'll speak to Daniel about Mr. Turner. Would you like me to see if he'd like to go with us?" Melinda sounded hopeful.

"I'm not sure that's a good idea. After all, Mr. Turner has already turned him away once."

"What makes you think he'll talk to us, then?"

"I don't know if he will. I just know, for Josie's sake, I have to try." She gave her friend a quick hug and then stepped out into the cold. Once outside, she looked up at the sky. Without a doubt, more snow was coming, probably by early evening at the latest. Taking careful steps, she turned down the street that would take her back to the store and safety.

She could only pray that Josie had found some place warm and dry to wait out the storm.

* * *

He didn't know where the bitch was, but he hoped like hell that Josie was buried in a snowbank, as dead and cold as Oliver was. Jed looked out toward the small cemetery on the hill above the barn. Snow had blanketed the area, leaving only the tops of the headstones showing. The burial ceremony had been blessedly brief. He hadn't trusted the undertaker from Lee's Mill to handle the necessary details for him, not with that damn sheriff sniffing around looking for who knows what.

With the winter freeze settling in to stay, he'd had a perfect excuse to hurry the process along. No one would question his rush to get the boy in the ground. And considering the strained relationship he'd had with his son, Jed was somewhat surprised by how much it hurt, knowing that his firstborn was lying in a grave next to his late wife.

The fact that he was the one who'd put him there was beside the point. No matter how badly the boy had turned out, he was still Jed's son. He no longer questioned why he felt Josie was to blame for Oliver's death. If she had been of the caliber of woman that Loretta had been, she would have straightened Oliver out in a matter of months after their marriage began.

And if Mitch Hughes didn't find her soon, Jed would hire the best men he could find to track her down. Once she stood trial and was found guilty, he could stop worrying that somehow that damn sheriff would manage to track Oliver's killer right back to Jed's door.

Maybe if he offered a reward for the capture of his daughter-in-law it would spur folks into finding her for him. How would that look? And how much was enough to be interesting but not raise suspicions? People understood a father's grief, but everyone also knew that he and Oliver didn't get along. If he pushed too hard, it could backlash.

No, he'd give the sheriff another week or so to find Josie, preferably dead.

A soft knock at the door interrupted his train of thought. He sat down at his desk and picked up a pen before he answered the summons. "Come in."

When his foreman stuck his head through the door, Jed pretended to be studying a column of figures. He counted to ten in his head before looking up.

"It's all right, Paddy. Come all the way in."

Looking decidedly uncomfortable, the cowboy slipped into the room. He whipped his hat off, revealing his balding head. "Sorry to disturb you, Mr. Turner, but I thought you'd want to know that the rest of the men made it back."

"And?" He already knew the news wasn't good or else Paddy wouldn't be twisting his favorite hat into knots. His ramrod ran a tight operation, keeping all the men in line. Despite the authority he wielded in the bunkhouse, he had the good sense to be a little afraid of Jed.

"Just like the others, sir. No sign of the woman anywhere. And the sheriff hasn't come back to town for a few days. That Mulroney fellow has been strutting up and down through town sporting a deputy badge. Makes me think the sheriff don't plan on coming in anytime soon."

Jed knew when to reward an employee for his hard work even when the results weren't exactly what he'd hoped for. "Pull up a chair, Paddy, and help yourself." He pushed his cigar box across the desk. "I appreciate all the extra hours you and the men have put in lately."

Now that he knew Jed wasn't going to rip a strip off his hide for not finding Josie Turner, Paddy seemed only too glad to get off his feet for a bit. He reached for a cigar, bit off the tip, and struck a match. After several puffs, he settled back in the chair, content to enjoy a good smoke. For a few minutes the two men sat in companionable silence.

Jed decided it wouldn't hurt to spread the reward around a little bit. He'd always found that he got the best results from his employees by using a careful mixture of fear and generosity. Loyalty was something he depended on. "Would you like a shot before going back out in the cold?"

Paddy was only too happy to accept. "Yes, sir. Some of the good stuff would sure enough hit the spot about now."

In one of his grand gestures, Jed got up and served them both, another ploy he'd found invaluable over the years. No doubt Paddy would spend the evening bragging to the others how the boss man himself had waited on *him*. To add to Paddy's credibility, Jed set the bottle on Paddy's side of the desk after pouring each of them a generous portion.

"When you've finished that," he gestured toward Paddy's glass with his own, "take the rest of bottle out the bunkhouse for everyone to share. Tell them I appreciate their support in these trying times."

Paddy nodded somberly. "I'll do that, sir. If it's all right with you, we'll have a drink in memory of young Mr. Turner."

Considering Oliver's love of whiskey, it seemed a fitting tribute. The damn stuff would have killed the fool sooner or later if Jed hadn't already taken care of that little chore himself. "Thanks, Paddy. That means a lot."

Other than Jed himself, Paddy was the only one who knew the truth of Oliver's death. He'd ridden cross-country, carrying the boy's body back to the cabin and leaving it for Josie to find. Jed had given him a few minutes' lead time before following behind him with the rest of the men. As far as they knew, Jed had been paying a social call on his son and daughter-in-law on the way into town for the evening. He'd even made a point of telling them all that he wanted to make sure Oliver and Josie knew they would be expected for Christmas dinner.

If any of them thought it was mighty convenient that they'd happened by only minutes after Josie had supposedly killed her husband, they had the good sense to keep their mouths shut. High-paying jobs were hard to come by, and they knew it.

Now, if they could only find Josie. He'd already decided that he didn't trust Mitch Hughes to see to it that she got what was coming to her. If necessary, he and his men would take care of that little chore themselves. Let everyone in town think she'd escaped and made her way clear. No one need know that her final resting place would be an unmarked grave somewhere in the backwoods.

She came into the world with nothing. He'd see to it she went out the same way, without even a gravestone to mark her passing. On that thought, he finished the last of his whiskey and said good night to his ramrod.

Once he was alone, he studied the calendar. He'd wait until spring to start the search for a new wife. With luck, he'd be married by summer. He closed his eyes and imagined the perfect wife. She needed to be genteel without being rich. He had no intention of saddling himself with another woman who looked down her nose at him.

Although he didn't require great beauty, she needed to be attractive, with generous feminine curves. He planned to spend a great deal of time and effort to get her with child as quickly as possible. Plump breasts and a nicely rounded backside gave a man something to hold on to when he was planting his seed.

Hell, by this time next year, he could be well on his way to being a father again, and Oliver would be only a dim memory. With that cheery thought, he headed upstairs to his bed to dream of good times to come.

Ten

Josie arranged Mitch's mismatched collection of dishes on the table. Dinner was almost ready. Wiping her hands on the towel she had tucked in her waistband as a makeshift apron, she surveyed the kitchen one last time. To her eyes, she'd made a marked improvement in the room.

Everything was neatly arranged and orderly. The inside of the windows gleamed after she'd scrubbed years of accumulated smoke and grease off, using vinegar and water. If the snow hadn't been piling up steadily all day, she would have done the outside, too.

In her mind's eye, she could see the room come summer. Naked and frozen now, the big sycamore just outside the window would shade the whole house in the warmest weather. If it were her kitchen, the first thing she'd do was sew curtains—something bright and cheery. Perhaps she'd hook a pair of braided rugs for the floor: one under the table and chairs, and another, smaller one by the door.

This time of year called for some fresh greens arranged on the mantle—pine and cedar boughs that would give the whole house a fresh scent. She could just imagine the look on Ben's face if she were to hang stockings for the two men. What would Mitch hope to find tucked into his stocking come Christmas morning?

But who knew where she'd be come Christmas? Most likely back in Lee's Mill, watching out her cell window as other people found their way to the church for the big celebration. She drew some comfort from knowing that she had contributed to making the event special for the children in town.

A door opening down the hall brought her abruptly back to the present. She smiled. She'd been wondering how long the two men who actually lived here would stay banished from the kitchen. No doubt, the smell of chicken and dumplings had something to do with Ben's venturing out again. He'd grumble and complain, but that would end as soon as she dished up supper.

The creak of floorboards in the next room wiped the smile right off her face. Mitch was stirring. She turned back to the stove. Nothing needed tending, but she didn't want to be caught staring at his bedroom door.

Her friends would be shocked if they suspected the secret feelings she had for the man on the other side of that door. They all knew how skittish she was around men of all kinds, but especially men as big and strong as Mitch Hughes. She'd learned early on how a man could use his strength and his temper against women.

Mitch frightened her in ways she didn't understand. Despite her panic earlier, she knew he'd never raise a hand to hurt her. But unless a miracle happened, she would have to stand trial for Oliver's death. If she was convicted, Mitch would hang her because it was his duty to do so. Even after he'd kissed her, he would march her up the steps of the gallows and put the rope around her neck, and the town would watch as she dangled and danced her way to death.

A shiver of breath-stealing cold washed over her that had nothing to do with the winter weather raging outside. Bracing herself for the worst, she listened as Mitch opened his door and stepped into the kitchen.

Damn, he hated the way Josie flinched every time he came near. So far, that was the only sign she'd given that she was aware of his presence. He'd hoped that he'd given her enough time to recover from their earlier encounter. Not that it helped him a bit. He'd dozed off and on, but he'd spent most of the time reliving the brief moment when Josie had surrendered herself to his kiss.

That single moment would likely haunt his nights for years to come, no matter how this mess turned out. He'd always suspected that she would fit perfectly in a man's arms—his arms in particular. But nothing had prepared him for the exquisite sweetness of Josie's kiss. For a woman who'd been married, there was a surprising innocence about the way her lips had shyly met his.

Considering what a brute Oliver had been, it wouldn't have been unexpected for Josie to have turned away from men all together. Hell, with everything she'd gone through, she should have slapped him senseless for daring to touch her.

Her continued silence was making him mad. Reining in his temper, he tried for a neutral subject. "Dinner smells wonderful."

"Thank you."

"Can I do anything to help?"

"No."

She wasn't helping the situation. He tried again. "Where's Ben?"

Without looking in his direction, she gestured toward the door. "He said he wanted to check on the animals one last time."

Casting about for something else to say, he realized

that she'd done a nice job on the kitchen. He hadn't re-alized how much clutter and dirt had built up over the months. The room even smelled cleaner.

"You shouldn't have worked so hard this afternoon."

She rounded on him, fire in her eyes. "I earn my keep, Sheriff Hughes. I'll have you know that . . ."

He held up his hand to stop her tirade. "Let me finish."

She crossed her arms over her chest and waited im-patiently for him to continue. Her eyes were shooting sparks, clearly daring him to criticize one single thing she'd done.

"What I was going to say, Josie, was that you shouldn't have had to work so hard, but I appreciate all that you did. This place probably hasn't looked this good since it was built. Thank you."

"Well, then," she muttered, the steam gone out of her temper. "You are welcome. I find it hard to sit still with nothing to do." She turned back to the stove and lifted the lid on the kettle. "You might give Ben a holler. These dumplings are just about done."

"How about we eat first and then call Ben in if there's anything left for him? I can't remember the last time I had chicken and dumplings."

She gave him a quick glance to make sure he was only kidding before she smiled. "I made twice my usual recipe. That should be enough for both of you to have plenty."

"How about you? Around here, the cook should al-ways get served first."

She cocked her head to the side. She suspected he was teasing, but she wasn't sure what he meant. "And why is that?"

"Because Ben damn near killed me once with his cooking. Now I wait to see if he survives before I risk my own life." He placed his hand over his heart. "That's the God's own truth."

"Well, I've been tasting the broth for the past hour. So far, I feel just fine." She spoiled her solemn speech with a fit of the giggles.

He liked seeing her this way. For the moment, she'd managed to forget her problems. Time had a way of distancing people from their pain. He could tell her all about that, and even warn her how it would be coming crashing back down on her again when she least expected it. He knew because he'd had plenty of experience fighting off grief and pain.

Like now. It had been years since he'd had the pleasure of spending time in a kitchen watching a woman fuss with the last-minute details of a meal. The memories poured into his mind. He shut his eyes, trying his damnedest to make them go away.

Her name had been Rebecca. Willow thin and graceful, with hair like spun gold, her smile could light up the room. The passion that they'd shared had put the sun to shame with its brightness.

She'd loved him despite everything that life had thrown in their way. Her only brother had fought and died for the Union. Somehow, her parents had blamed the loss of their heir on Mitch, but Becky hadn't let their grief and hatred change how she felt. When her parents forbade her to see Mitch, she found ways to evade their watchful eyes.

The time Mitch had spent with Rebecca in his arms had been the happiest in his life. She'd begged him to run off with her, but he'd refused, sure that she would come to regret cutting herself off from her family that way. Once the war was over, surely her parents would forgive and forget. Fool that he was, Mitch had been so sure the future held nothing but good things for them as long as they remained true to their love. But the war changed all that.

Here in Missouri, the battle lines had changed almost daily. He'd done his best to make sure that she and her family were safe from attack, but one man could only do so much. The lines shifted north again, this time right at Christmas, leaving her father's farm behind Confederate lines. Mitch had risked everything to warn her parents that they were in danger of being overrun by the fighting. Instead of listening, her father had run him off at gunpoint.

The old bastard hadn't even wanted to let Rebecca accept the small Christmas present that Mitch had brought her.

Finally, Mitch had left, much to his eternal regret. The next time he'd seen his beloved Rebecca, she'd been sprawled on the front porch where she'd died, her clothes ripped and torn, and her precious blood splattered everywhere. Her parents hadn't fared any better, except that they'd died faster.

He hadn't celebrated Christmas since.

How many nights had he lain awake wishing he'd made it back to the farm in time to save Rebecca? Or, failing that, to have died alongside her? All the regrets didn't change a damn thing.

"You're awfully far away right now, considering you're still sitting at the table, Sheriff."

For the space of a heartbeat, he thought it was Rebecca talking, teasing him with that way she had when she thought he was getting too serious. He blinked several times before he could see Josie clearly.

"Sorry, my mind tends to wander at times."

Rather than ask the questions that hovered in her expression, Josie reminded him again to call Ben in from the barn.

"Tell him to hurry if he wants to eat while it's hot."

Grateful for the distraction, Mitch reached for his coat

and stepped out onto the porch. The cold air cut like a knife. By the looks of things, the snow was already ass-deep and with more still drifting down from the sky. For the moment, the wind had died down some. If it picked up again, the drifts would reach as high as the windows on the house.

"Ben, you old buzzard, get your worthless hide in here now!"

Mitch paused to listen for a response. He called again. "Damn it, Ben, if my dinner gets cold, I will send you back out to sleep with the mules."

The door of the barn slid open enough to allow Ben to slip through. He came trudging across the yard, having to plow his way through the snow. Mitch considered going out to meet him, but Ben wouldn't appreciate the gesture. The old cuss had enough pride for two men. No one would have a moment's peace if Mitch managed to offend him.

When he was sure Ben was going to make it on his own, Mitch stomped the snow off his own boots before going back inside.

"He's coming."

Josie began setting food on the table while Mitch washed his hands. Ben came in. He hung his coat over the back of a spare chair and pulled it close to the stove to dry.

"Everything all right out there?"

"Yep. Your horse's leg seems to be fine now."

"Thanks for taking care of her for me."

"Yeah, well, I had to go out there anyway."

Ben took his normal seat at the table. He immediately took notice of the changes Josie had made in the kitchen. "Girl, you just couldn't leave well enough alone. Now how am I supposed to find anything?"

"Ben!" Mitch didn't mind his employee taking his bad

mood out on him, but he wouldn't let him turn it on Josie. "You may be afraid of soap and water, but the rest of us appreciate a little cleanliness."

"It's all right, Sheriff. Ben has been fussing at me as long as I can remember. As contrary as he is, I just assume he means the opposite of everything he says." The gleam in Josie's eyes invited him to share the joke.

Ben glared at the two of them equally before serving up a double serving of the tender chicken and doughy dumplings. He kept his eyes on his plate as he began shoveling the food into his mouth. Mitch motioned to Josie to serve herself before accepting the heavy bowl himself.

One bite and he groaned in pleasure. "This is even better than it smells, and that's saying something."

"Thank you, Sheriff."

"I thought you were going to call me Mitch," he reminded her. Maybe he shouldn't encourage the familiarity under the circumstances, but he liked the sound of his name when she said it.

For the remainder of the meal, the three ate in silence. When the last drop of broth was gone, Ben lit up his pipe. He squinted through the cloud of smoke.

"How's that hard head of yours?"

"Better. Nothing another night's sleep won't cure." Mitch leaned back in his chair and stretched.

A gust of wind shook the windows. Ben took his pipe out of his mouth to fiddle with the tobacco some more. "Looks like we'll be snowed in but good come morning."

"How long do you think this will last?"

Josie probably thought she sounded as if she were just making polite conversation, but there was a thread of tension running through her voice. She knew she was safe as long as the roads and trails were impassable.

"Depends on the temperature. You never know around here. Could be a week or more before we see any melt-off. Just as likely to be gone in a couple of days." Ben struck another match. "I'd figure on staying put for several more days." He glanced at Mitch. "Both of you."

"I'm not in any hurry to be anywhere." Mitch pushed away from the table and started picking up the dishes. When Josie jumped up to help, he gently pushed her back into her chair. "You cooked. Ben and I will clean up."

"But a woman's supposed to . . ." Josie protested.

"Honey, if Ben and I waited for a woman to clean up after us, we'd be hip-deep in dirty dishes and dirty clothes. We've been looking after ourselves for a long time now."

With Ben's reluctant help, Mitch had the last dish dried and put away in short order. He'd been all too conscious of Josie's eyes following his every movement. He wondered what she was thinking about. How it had felt to be in his arms? Or how soon he'd drag her back to Lee's Mill to stand trial?

Probably a little of both.

Ben tossed his towel down on the side of the sink. "I've done enough for one day. I'm going to bed."

Mitch and Josie sat in silence as Ben shuffled down the short hallway to his bedroom. When the door slammed closed, Mitch chuckled and smiled.

"If that man worked any harder at being grumpy, he wouldn't have time to do anything else."

Josie nodded in agreement. "He's been that way as long as I've known him. On the other hand, he didn't hesitate to take me in. Somewhere inside that crusty outside beats a kind heart."

"I wouldn't say that to his face. He'd be insulted to think he grumbles and complains all the time for nothing."

Mitch looked around for something to occupy his hands, if not his mind. Finally, he had to ask, "Did you happen to come across a deck of cards when you were cleaning?"

"A couple of them."

She looked up and down the length of the shelves a couple of times. Finally, she gave him a triumphant look as she stood on her tiptoes, trying to reach the top shelf. Mitch walked up behind her and reached over her head and picked up the well-worn deck of cards.

He knew he should back away immediately, but the need to be close to Josie was riding him hard. She slowly turned to face him, leaving only inches between them. He could have sworn that he could feel her heart beat in time to his. Damn, he knew better, but if she kept looking up at him with questions in her eyes, he'd have to do his best to answer them.

As much as it pained him, he stepped back and then put the width of the table between them. He pushed the extra deck over to her side of the table and then began shuffling his cards. Feeling only marginally safer from temptation, he dealt himself a hand of solitaire. He tried to concentrate on his next play, but he was almost painfully aware of each move Josie made.

For several minutes she wandered around the room, straightening this, adjusting that. She hadn't been kidding about her need to keep busy. Finally, he gathered up his cards and dealt out two hands.

"Do you know how to play gin rummy?"

She was staring out at the snow and didn't appear to hear him. He repeated the question. This time she answered him.

"I can play most card games. My pa taught me."

"Then pick up your hand."

"You don't mind?"

"If I did, I wouldn't ask. Now, play." He sounded more gruff than he meant to, but she didn't seem to notice. Considering her background, she probably thought all men acted that way all the time.

Once again, he'd made a mistake. He'd thought playing cards would keep his mind focused on something other than Josie. Instead, he found himself watching her slender fingers fan out her cards. He'd never realized that the way a woman bit her lower lip when she concentrated was sexy as hell.

And the way her tongue darted out to lick her lips whenever she made a big play about did him in. All he could hope was that she didn't take notice of his fixation.

"Mitch, can I ask you a question?"

Anything to distract him. "Sure."

"What are you going to do about my friends?" She looked up from her cards, her eyes wide with worry.

He knew what she was asking, but he wasn't going to make it easy for her. "What about them?"

"You know, the way they helped me."

She drew another card from the pile and tossed an ace on the discard pile. He snapped up that card and picked one of his to get rid of. He needed a seven to win.

"I thought that's what friends were for. What would you have me do?"

"Mitch Hughes, you know what I mean. They broke me out of jail."

She was so intent on pulling an answer out of him that she got careless with her cards. He'd already picked up one seven. She threw another one down. With a triumphant smile, he pounced on it.

"Gin," he crowed, spreading his cards out on the table for her to see. She didn't seem to care. "What's the matter?"

"You're avoiding my question. Why?"

He gave in. "No one knows who broke you out of jail. Not for certain. Of course, some folks have their own theory."

"*You* know."

"Sorry, but my memory is addled. Probably something to do with being bashed over the head with Lucy's good skillet. Now, that is a mystery." He shook his head sorrowfully. "How do you think some stranger managed to steal her skillet, knock me over the head with it, and then return it to her house?"

He dared her to contradict him. "You might be a trifle more in trouble with the judge for hightailing it out of there. But the way I see it, it shouldn't come as a surprise to anyone when a prisoner seizes an opportunity to escape. Lucky for you that some stranger was trying to steal something from the jail."

She stared at him as if he'd lost all good sense. Hell, maybe he had, but he wasn't about to put a pregnant woman and a pastor's wife behind bars. And the thought of locking up Henrietta Dawson where she could rail at him day in and day out was enough to drive a sober man to drink.

He studied Josie's face while she studied her cards. Something was still bothering her, and knowing her, she wasn't going to let up until she had all the answers.

"Spit it out, Josie."

"What?" She probably didn't realize how easy it was to read her thoughts from her expression.

"Whatever you're chewing on." He pointed at the discard pile. "You've thrown down three eights in a row. If your mind isn't on your cards, it's on something else. You might as well tell me."

"It's nothing." She looked up from her cards. "Really."

He didn't believe her, but there wasn't much he could do to force the issue. Sooner or later she'd get around to it. He drew a card and almost threw it away before he realized it was the one he'd been hoping for.

"Gin."

He laid the cards down in a neat pile. When he

reached out to scoop up the others to shuffle, Josie
shook her head.

"If it's all right with you, I'd like to go to bed now."

"Go ahead." He dealt a hand of solitaire.

"You can play the red three."

Mitch picked it up and put it where it belonged. "I
thought you were going to bed."

"I just realized that I don't have anywhere to sleep."

Of course she didn't. The house only had two bedrooms: Ben's and his. Had she been sleeping in his bed?
Lord, he didn't need that image to plague his thoughts.
Her honey brown hair spread out on his pillow. The
scent of her skin clinging to his sheets. How could he
not have noticed?

"You've been using my room." It wasn't a question.

"Ben insisted. But I didn't feel right sleeping in your
bed . . ."

He noticed that she stumbled on that last part. Maybe
he wasn't the only one who had problems with that idea.

"So I've been sleeping on the floor. I hope you don't
mind."

"Mind what? That you slept on a cold floor instead of
using a perfectly good bed?" He wasn't sure why that
made him so mad, but it did. He shoved the cards into a
pile.

When he glared across the table at her, she flinched
again. "Damn it, Josie, quit doing that."

"Wh-what?"

"Jumping like a scared rabbit every time I get a little
aggravated."

"I'm sorry."

Her eyes flickered to the side, as if she were trying to
find the safest escape if he chose to make a grab for her.
That did it. He lashed out with words but managed to
keep his hands still.

"Listen and get this through your head." He waited until she forced her eyes up to meet his. He leaned across the table, his hands splayed out in front of him. "I will not hit you. And when I do put my hands on you, it will be because you want me to." He let his own gaze linger on her face and then wander on down to study her womanly curves. "I assure you, it won't have anything to do with anger."

He let the words hang there in the air between them and waited to see how she would react. The tension in her face changed as the meaning of his words sank in. Slowly she nodded. He wondered if it was because she understood that he wouldn't hit her, or because she knew that some time he had every intention of doing a whole lot more than touch her.

Satisfied that he'd gotten his message across, Mitch leaned back again. "Now, about sleeping arrangements: you can have the bedroom; I'll sleep out here."

"But . . ." Josie started to protest, but one look at his expression and she stopped. "I'll make up a pallet for you."

Since her chin had taken on a stubborn tilt, Mitch let her win that particular skirmish. "Fine. Let me know if you need any help."

He picked up his cards and started shuffling again. Once again he closed his eyes and enjoyed the sound of a woman fussing around the house. Like always, he wondered what his life would have been like if Rebecca hadn't died. Would they have still been happy? He'd like to think so. Her death had left a festering wound somewhere inside him—one that had yet to heal completely.

Josie had disappeared into his room and closed the door. Perhaps he was making a mistake by treating her as a guest rather than a prisoner. No matter how good his intentions were, he couldn't let himself forget who and what he was. He'd sworn to stand up for the law. There was nothing in that oath that would let him off the hook just because he felt something for the accused—not and still live with himself.

He glanced behind him. The soft glow of the lamp still peeked out from under the door, telling him that Josie was still awake. Knowing her, she was probably reading one of the books that he always had lying on the shelf above his bed. He wished he'd thought to pick one out for himself before she'd gone to bed.

For a brief instant he thought about knocking on the door to see if he could come in. He squashed that idea immediately. It was one thing to imagine Josie in his bed and quite another actually to see her there. It would take a far stronger man than he was to resist the temptation of climbing under the covers with her.

A worn-out deck of cards was damn poor company. But the only women he was going to spend time with tonight were made out of paper.

Eleven

Lucy paced back and forth across the front of her store, never retreating more than a few feet from the front window. Where was Cora? It shouldn't take this long for her to get to Melinda's house and back. She'd counted on Melinda's being home, since it was Saturday and there was no school. If the two of them didn't hurry, they'd miss the opportunity they'd been waiting for.

She pulled the curtain to the side and peeked out the window again. He was still there, looking as though he owned the place. Probably thought he did. She knew it was wrong to hate—Pastor Daniel had preached on that very subject only a couple of weeks ago. But in Jed Turner's case, she was willing to make an exception.

No matter which way she looked at it, something about the way he was acting the grieving father did not ring true. The most generous interpretation of his behavior, considering the poor relationship he'd had with Oliver, was that he was motivated by guilt. After all, everyone in town knew that Jed had treated his son, and therefore Josie, like poor relations. Now that it was too late to mend fences, Jed was playing the devastated father with a little too much enthusiasm.

Right now, Jed was standing outside The River Lady with several of his men. As cold as it was, she couldn't imagine him staying there much longer. Any minute he was going to head for her store. She knew he was coming, because earlier he'd sent one of his men in to place an order. He'd included a message that he would be stopping by to settle his account and pick up the supplies. It was the first time in years that he'd purchased much of anything in her store. She had to wonder why. Was he after more than beans and flour? Perhaps he needed a public stage on which to practice his performance.

Whatever the reason, his timing couldn't have been better, since she and Melinda had planned to pay a call on him as soon as the roads were passable again. Instead, he'd saved them the trip by coming into town—something he'd almost never done before Oliver's death.

For a brief second, she was tempted to run next door to see if Cade was available. He'd understand that she was nervous about facing Oliver's father, since she was directly responsible for Josie's escape from jail. But even if Jed suspected as much, he couldn't prove a thing. For some inexplicable reason, Mitch Hughes had chosen to keep that little bit of information to himself.

But as comforting as it would be to have Cade close by, she rejected the idea. He already thought the Luminary Society had taken too active a role in Josie's defense. He'd object loud and long if he thought she was going to confront Jed Turner directly. Once again, she hoped her friends would hurry; otherwise, she would have to deal with him on her own.

She forced herself to go back to stocking the shelves. If Jed did come in before her friends arrived, she didn't want to get caught watching him. No, it would definitely look less suspicious if she kept herself busy. After dusting an already immaculate shelf, she went into the storeroom in back for another half-dozen boxes of nails.

She was just putting the last box in place on the bottom shelf when the bell over her front door chimed. She straightened up and turned slowly to greet her customer.

"Mr. Turner."

His eyes raked her over from the top down. She did her best to hide a shiver of distaste. Although she'd only seen him up close once or twice before, she could see a strong resemblance to his late son. But where the effects of liquor had taken their toll on Oliver's looks, Jed showed no such weakness in his appearance. A nasty intelligence seemed to glitter in his eyes, and his mouth quirked up in a sardonic smile.

"Mrs. Mulroney."

He edged closer. She moved a step backward before she caught herself. This was a man who would walk all over anyone who displayed the slightest hint of weakness.

"I'd like to say how sorry I was to hear about your son."

Jed was busy pulling off his gloves. He paused and shook his head. "Why, Mrs. Mulroney, I wouldn't think the wife of a newspaperman would stoop to lying."

"Excuse me?" She couldn't believe her ears. She'd never expected so direct an attack from him. Perhaps she should have sent for Cade.

"I knew my son very well, and I knew what he was capable of. He was a brute when he was drunk, which was most of the time. I imagine his wife gave your little society an earful about how he treated her." He finished removing his gloves and stuck them in his pocket. "Not that she didn't deserve whatever she got."

Lucy knew full well he was trying to goad her into saying something she shouldn't. Well, two could play at that game. "Josie was a good wife to Oliver, even if he didn't deserve her."

His nostrils flared as his mouth flattened into a straight line. Her remark must have hit a nerve.

His voice, however, was coldly calm. "The truth is that

she was born a nobody, Mrs. Mulroney, and that's how she'll die. The minute her father forced my son to marry her, his life was ruined. For that alone, she'll pay."

Lucy gasped, but before she could respond, the door of the store opened. Melinda and Cora walked in together.

Jed ignored them as he flashed Lucy a smile that made her skin crawl. "Now, Mrs. Mulroney, if I can have my supplies, please."

Enough was enough. She drew herself up to her full height. It was no match for his, but she still managed to give the appearance of looking down at him. "No, sir, you may not. I would appreciate it if you took your business elsewhere."

"You don't want to make an enemy of me, Mrs. Mulroney." He glanced at the counter where she'd set the sacks that contained his order. "Those look like they're for me. I'll just be taking them now. How much do I owe you?" He pulled out his wallet and drew out several bills.

"Take the supplies if you need them so badly, Mr. Turner." Knowing she was prodding a rattlesnake, she added, "However, keep your money. I know how important it is to you. Good day."

With that, Lucy swept past him to join her friends. Together the three of them presented a united front of feminine outrage. Jed was right. He wasn't a man to trifle with, but Lucy didn't care.

Turner tossed the bills on the floor and picked up his packages. Ordinarily, Lucy would have at least opened the door for a customer, but Jed was on his own. When he was about to leave, she picked up the money he'd left behind. In a voice loud enough to make sure he could hear her, she announced, "Look, Melinda, Mr. Turner has made a sizable donation to the Luminary Society. Imagine how many books we can buy."

The slamming of the door was his only response. As

soon as she knew for certain that he was gone, Lucy found herself needing to sit down before she fell down. Melinda sent Cora for a glass of water and a cool rag.

"What happened, Lucy? What did he say that has you so upset?"

Lucy closed her eyes and waited for the room to quit spinning. Finally, she managed to pull herself together. "He's going to kill Josie, no matter what."

"He said that?"

"Not in those words, but he might as well have." She tried to recall exactly what he'd said. "He said that Oliver's life was ruined when he married her. And for that alone she would pay."

While Melinda was obviously dismayed, Cora looked more thoughtful. "Why do you suppose he said it that way? I mean, you'd think he'd want her punished for killing Oliver."

"That's right, but he didn't say that. What do you think that means?" Her momentary dizziness gone, Lucy stood up. "I'm going to go talk to Cade. Maybe he'll have some idea."

"Do you want us to go with you?"

"No, I'll be fine. I'd feel better, though, if both of you kept an eye on the store for me—unless you'd rather I closed up for a few minutes."

Cora, always the brave one, immediately shook her head. "We can't let him have the satisfaction." She marched over to the counter and stood behind it. "Take as long as you need. I'll be fine." Her bravado was belied by the way she clenched the ledger tightly enough to turn her knuckles white.

"I won't be gone long."

She took her wrap off the peg on the wall and hurried outside. Before leaving the relative safety of the store, she looked up and down the street to make sure that Jed was well and truly gone. Although she recognized one of his men standing by the saloon, Jed himself was nowhere in sight.

Lifting her skirts slightly, she headed for the newspaper office next door. At this time of day, Cade should be about finished putting the *Clarion* to bed for the day. When she stepped into the front office of the paper, her senses were assaulted with the familiar smells of ink and newsprint. Will, Cade's assistant, looked up from a copy of the paper, probably checking it for accuracy before running the rest of the print run.

"Howdy, Mrs. Mulroney," he said, nodding in her direction. He wasn't much for talking, probably because the sooner he finished printing the paper, the sooner he could join his friends across the street at the saloon.

"Hello, Will. Is Cade in his office?"

"Yes, ma'am."

She maintained her calm facade until she saw her husband. When she stepped through his door, Cade looked up from the article he was proofing. One glance at her face, and he was on his feet and around the desk. He didn't ask any questions until she was safely wrapped in his arms.

"What's wrong?"

She snuggled against the powerful comfort of his embrace. "Jed Turner came into the store."

Cade waited for her to go on. She did her best to gather her thoughts before speaking again. "I thought it was strange that he'd place an order for supplies from me. I mean, he's always gone elsewhere for what he needed."

"Did he threaten you?" Ice wasn't as cold as the anger in his voice.

"Not me, not exactly. He warned me that he wasn't a man to be trifled with." She shivered. "But he did threaten Josie."

Cade's hold on her relaxed only slightly. "Can't blame him for that. He believes she killed his son."

Lucy put a little distance between them so she could look her husband in the eye. "But that isn't why. He said she ruined Oliver's life when she married him. He said she'd pay for that alone."

Cade frowned. "Are you sure that's what he said?"

She nodded. "Almost exactly. What do you think it means?"

"I'm not sure, but Mitch will want to hear about this. If he's not back by tomorrow afternoon, I'll take a ride out to his place and see if he's been there."

Satisfied that she'd done all she could to help Josie for the moment, Lucy smiled up at her husband's beloved face. "Cora invited Mary to spend the night with her tonight. I said that was fine with us."

Never let it be said that her husband was slow-witted. "I take it you have plans for us tonight." It wasn't a question.

"What do you think?" She traced the contours of his chest with her hands and then let one drift downward until Cade caught it in his iron grip.

"Hold that thought, darling," he whispered as he drew her up close for a bone-melting kiss. "I'll make a point of finishing up early. I wouldn't want to interfere with your plans."

A few minutes later, she left the newspaper office feeling much better about life in general. She'd send Cora and Melinda on home and finish up the few things she still needed to do. After all, the earlier she closed up the store for the day, the sooner she could place her plans for the evening in motion.

In the early hours of the morning, Josie lay awake listening to the soft rasp of the snow blowing against the house. If it weren't so cold, she'd be tempted to look outside. But even the beauty of a snow-covered landscape wasn't worth leaving the warmth of Mitch's bed.

It was a real bed, too. The wood wasn't as fancy as the furniture at Henrietta Dawson's house, but it was sure a whole lot nicer than any other bed she'd ever slept in. She'd have to ask if he'd bought it or if it had come down through his family. The quilts showed someone's fine hand with a needle. Brushing her hand across the soft fabrics, she wondered if the bits and pieces of cloth held any memories for Mitch.

Had his mother pieced it from clothing too worn out for anything else? Or was it made by some other woman from his past? Somehow, that idea seemed to ring true to her, although she had no reason for thinking so. Maybe it was because she couldn't imagine that no other woman had ever looked at Mitch Hughes with a powerful want in her heart.

She closed her eyes and tried to imagine what Mitch had looked like at a much younger age. His smile alone would have drawn women like bees to honey. He probably always did have a serious side to him, but she'd seen enough ex-Confederates to know that the war had left its share of shadows in his eyes.

But none of that mattered. Dreams were dreams, no matter how badly she wanted them to be real. And considering that she had no future to speak of, she shouldn't be wasting time on dreams at all.

That idea was enough to have her throwing back the covers and sitting up on the edge of the bed. Mustering her courage, she touched the floor with her bare foot, jerking it back when she found it was cold enough to hurt. She braced herself for the worst and clambered out of the bed to grab her clothes. Shivering from her hair on down, she struggled to pull on her stockings, the petticoat Cora had given her, and the warmest of her three dresses.

The various layers of her clothing did little to blunt the edge of the cold. She made quick work of straightening the bed and then slipped out of the room and into the kitchen. Mitch was stretched out on the floor just inside the other room. If she hadn't been moving slowly, she would have tripped right over him.

She'd already fallen on top of Mitch once. Even now, hours later, her body remembered the feel of Mitch's strength stretched out beneath her. For a heartbeat, just from thinking about it, the heat of embarrassment stained her cheeks. Or maybe the warmth coursing through her had nothing at all to do with the awkwardness of the moment.

Lifting the hem of her skirt, she edged around Mitch's still form. If she was quiet about it, she could start the fire and get some heat going. That way she'd be the only one who had to suffer from the cold.

She picked out some kindling from a crate near the wall and knelt down to arrange it in the stone fireplace. She used another piece to stir the ashes, to expose the last few coals from the night before. After laying a split pine knot directly on the glowing embers, she was satisfied that the fire would catch. Next, she turned her attention to the stove and to making a fresh pot of coffee. In just a few moments, the scent of fresh-brewed coffee filled the air.

"That smells good."

Mitch's sleep-roughened voice startled her. She spun around to see him still stretched out under his covers, his hands locked together supporting his head. His cheeks were shadowed with a day's growth of beard. It gave him a dangerous look that had her heart thumping.

"I didn't mean to wake you," she stammered.

"Don't worry about it. I'm an early riser most of the time. Besides, I'm only too happy to have someone else brave the cold to get the fire started instead of me."

"Seemed like the least I could do, considering you had to give up your bed for me."

"I didn't mind."

He started to sit up, which had Josie spinning away. She didn't need to see his chest—or anything else. It didn't help when he laughed.

"Josie, I appreciate you trying to respect my modesty, but it was too damn cold to sleep without my clothes on."

Josie kept her back turned anyway until he was up and walking around. She risked a peek. He hadn't exaggerated—he was covered from the neck down with at least two layers of everything.

He sat down at the table and pulled on his boots. "I need to check on the animals. While I'm outside, I'll clear a path around back for you."

She'd been wondering how she was going to wade through all that snow to the privy out back. Feeling shy about discussing such a personal situation, she merely nodded and began measuring out flour for biscuits.

Mitch disappeared out the door in a blast of cold air. She shivered, grateful for the heat that was slowly warming the room.

Humming softly to herself, she cut the lard into the flour and baking powder. She added enough milk to make a soft dough and then kneaded it into a smooth ball. In no time, she had a pan full of biscuits ready for the oven.

She counted to make sure she had enough eggs left from the day before for the three of them. Deciding to fry them, she put bacon on to cook. Once it was done, she'd have the grease for the eggs.

The door down the hall opened. Ben came trudging into the kitchen, still fastening the straps to his overalls.

"Where's Mitch?" He scratched his head and glanced around the room, his rheumy eyes blinking and looking bleary.

"He went out to check on the animals. I expect him back any minute."

"Dang fool, he's got no business wading through all that damn snow. Hell, just yesterday he could hardly stand up without help."

Josie recognized the anger for the concern it really was. She moved aside to let Ben look out the window.

"If he's not back in five minutes, I'll have to go dig him out of a drift somewhere." He muttered awhile longer before announcing, "I see him. He's coming from around back."

Josie hurried to pour each man a cup of coffee as soon as she heard Mitch stomping the snow off his boots on the porch.

Moments later, the three of them were sitting around the table finishing off the last of the eggs and biscuits.

"Girl, you're going to spoil us." Ben took another long drink of his coffee. "You'll have to show me how to make those biscuits. Mine always turn out . . ."

"Like rocks," Mitch finished for him. Before Ben could complain, he continued, "Of course, we used mine to build the stone wall out by the corral."

Josie giggled, and even old Ben started to smile before he caught himself.

"He keeps insulting me like that, missy, and he'll find himself working this place by himself."

Josie wasn't about to add to Ben's woes. "I'm sure it's all a matter of handling the dough the right way. A man as strong as you are probably has a hard time kneading the dough gently enough."

"I never thought about it that way. Maybe you're right."

Josie shot Mitch a look that dared him to contradict her.

As soon as they finished eating, Josie slipped on her coat and boots and made a quick trip outside. Even though Mitch had broken the path for her, she still found the going hard. She stumbled back inside the cabin, glad that both the fireplace and stove were working hard. After hanging her coat back on a peg, she rubbed her hands to get them warm before washing the dishes. As cold as her hands were, the hot water from the reservoir would likely scald them.

Mitch came into the kitchen to fill a pitcher with hot water. His braces were dangling down from his waist, and the top few buttons on his shirt were undone. "I'm going into my room and wash up some. Before I do, do you need anything out of there?"

She fought to keep her eyes averted from that tantalizing glimpse of his bare chest. "No, uh, not right now. I was going to do the dishes and then maybe sew for a while. If you have anything that needs mending, set it on the table for me."

Mitch frowned at her. "I've told you before that you don't have to earn your keep around here."

"And I've told you that I need to keep busy."

He glared at her, clearly frustrated when she stood her ground. "Fine, if that's the way you want it."

"It is."

Mitch gave her a look of pure masculine frustration before he disappeared into his room with a bang. To her own surprise, she quietly chuckled at his antics. She must be getting used to the sound of slamming doors. At least they didn't frighten her the way they used to when it was her pa or Oliver doing the slamming. She considered that thought for a moment. How odd to feel like laughing at Mitch's little display of temper.

A small smile tugged at the corner of her mouth as she began scrubbing the skillet clean.

He'd been an ass. Again. Damn, he was getting tired of the way Josie brought out the worst in him. What was so wrong with not wanting her waiting on him and Ben? She wasn't exactly a guest, but neither was she a servant. The worst part was that he could get used to having her around.

And not just underfoot, but under him. He groaned at his body's all too familiar response to that particular idea. It had taken him hours to fall asleep last night, and not because of the cold or even the hard floor. Hell, he'd spent the war years sleeping on every damn rock in the Missouri Ozarks with no problem. No, it was the idea of Josie sleeping such a short distance away in his bed. Alone. Without him.

Son of a bitch, he had no right to be thinking that way. He listed off the reasons. First, she'd lost her husband only a short time ago. She deserved some time to be a widow without someone lusting after her. Second, she may have killed the worthless bastard herself, not that anyone except Jed Turner blamed her for that. Third, she was supposed to be his prisoner. Fourth . . . Hell, it didn't matter what the fourth reason was or wasn't.

He'd never forced his attentions on a woman in his life and wasn't about to start now. He leaned closer to the small mirror on the wall and stared at his image. His reflection frowned back at him. Had his eyes always had those tired-looking lines around them? By calendar years, he wasn't all that old. He'd turned thirty just a few months ago, but right now he felt decades older.

His razor stung as he scraped it down the side of his face. Washing off the wad of soap and whiskers in the basin, he took another stroke down the other side. For the moment he concentrated on getting a clean shave with a minimum amount of bloodshed. Finally, he wiped the last little bits of lather from his skin.

He looked around for something else to do within the confines of his bedroom. There wasn't much choice. He could straighten the bed. He could scrape the frost of the window and stare out at the snow. He could lose his mind.

It was time to have that talk with Josie about how she had come to take up residence in his house. He buttoned up his shirt and checked his appearance as much as he could in the mirror. What a damn fool thing to be doing. He was a lawman, not a beau come a-courting. If he wouldn't have felt foolish for doing so, he would have pinned his badge on, more to remind himself rather than Josie of who and what he was.

At least he had the presence of mind to rein his temper in before confronting her. It was hardly her fault that he couldn't look at her or even think about her without wanting to drag her off to the nearest bed. He counted to three and then quietly let himself out of his room.

It didn't take long to confirm that they were alone. Josie was sitting at the table, weaving a needle in and out of a small piece of fabric with precise, delicate motions. She seemed oblivious to his presence, but then she spoke.

"Ben is out in the barn. He said something about preferring the company out there." She picked up her sewing and bit through the thread. "I put on a fresh pot of coffee. It should be about ready if you'd like some."

Anything to put off their discussion. Mitch poured them each a cup and carried them over to the table. He took the chair across from hers. She was squinting at a needle, trying to slip the thread through the narrow hole. It took several tries, making him wonder if her hands were a little unsteady, and if so, why.

Josie adjusted the length of her thread and then, in a move too quick for him to follow, she knotted the end of it. Before picking up whatever she was stitching, she looked over at him.

"You want to talk." She turned to face him directly.

There were so many questions he could ask, but he started with the one that had him most puzzled. "You got away clean. Why did you come here?"

Nodding as if she'd been expecting that very question, Josie fiddled with her sewing for a few seconds before looking up to meet his gaze. "I had nowhere else to go."

That made no sense. "There's a whole, wide world out there. What do you mean, you had nowhere to go? If you didn't know any place yourself, you could have asked one of your helpful friends. I'm sure they would have had some ideas for you. God knows they have opinions on every other subject."

That brought a smile to her eyes. "Well, they did have some suggestions, but none of them seemed right. For one thing, Jed Turner won't stop until he finds me, and he can afford to pay men to do his looking for him. I doubt I would have made it as far as St. Louis or Kansas City before they caught up with me."

"So you went to ground within spitting distance of where you started." Her choice still made no sense to him. "There has to be a better reason than that."

Josie left the table to stand by the window. She rubbed a clear spot in the frost and stared out into the sun glaring off the snow. "I didn't kill Oliver, no matter what Jed thinks." She looked back at Mitch. "No matter what anybody thinks." Her chin came up, daring him to disagree.

"I'm not your judge, Josie. It's my job to look for facts to present to the court."

"And the fact is, Oliver was a miserable husband, and no one would be surprised if I had decided to end our marriage with a gun." She wrapped her arms around her waist, looking so damned sad. "Then there's the little matter of Jed's men riding up to the cabin to find me standing over Oliver's body and holding a gun. I know it looks bad, real bad, for me."

"So why here? You have to know that I'll have to take you back to jail soon as this all clears out."

"You're the only man I knew I could trust to be fair. I would have never left the jail in the first place if my friends hadn't practically dragged me out of there. You would have kept me safe from Jed and his men."

Her words hit him as hard as Lucy's skillet had. Even knowing he'd do his job, she trusted him? How would she feel when the judge banged his gavel and declared her guilty? Women didn't get hanged often, but it happened. It didn't bear thinking about.

"I've asked you before, Josie, but think about it again. If you didn't kill Oliver, somebody else did. Who could it be?"

She came back to the table and picked up her sewing and then dropped it again. "Oliver bragged about some new friends he'd met up with. He said they were going to do business together, but that's all he told me. I will say he acted as if he wasn't going to have to worry about money anymore."

Mitch thought of the stranger whom he'd seen in the bank a few days back. "Did you ever get a look at any of these friends?"

"No. As far as I know, the only time he had them over to the cabin was the night of the storm when I stayed over at Cora's. They left the place a mess, but they were gone when I got home. You remember—I passed you on the road the next morning."

He did remember. That was the day she'd caught him stopped in the middle of the road, his mind lost someplace in the past. "I don't suppose he said what kind of business it was?"

Once again she shook her head. "No, except I think it had something to do with his father. Maybe Oliver just wanted Jed's advice."

That didn't seem likely, considering what he'd learned so far about Jed and Oliver. The two barely spoke. More than ever, he wanted to track down these so-called new friends of Oliver's. If they were such good friends, why hadn't any of them come to pay their respects? Although Jed had buried his son on his own place, Mitch had ordered Jake to watch the proceedings from a safe distance. From what his deputy had seen, the only people in attendance were Jed and the men who worked for him. Other than the pastor from the next town, no one else had made the trip out to the Turner place for the burial.

Interesting.

"Tell me about your marriage. From the beginning."

Josie's eyes filled with tears. "Why? Everybody in Lee's Mill knows how it was."

"I know what everyone thinks, but none of them really knows. It will help me understand why you married him."

Her fingers clutched one of Ben's shirts in a death grip. "My pa died before you moved to town, but I know you've heard all the old stories. How he was the town drunk, how he forced Oliver to marry me." She looked to him for confirmation, so he nodded.

"Pa used to be a different sort of man, when my ma was alive. But when she died of a fever, he started sinking into the liquor bottle and never came out. I kept hoping he'd find something that made him want to go on."

To Mitch's way of thinking, the fool did have something worth living for—Josie herself. On the other hand, maybe if Mitch hadn't felt responsible for his men in the war, he might have sought solace in whiskey when Rebecca died. He was in no position to judge.

"Anyway, Pa got it into his head that my mother wouldn't have died if he'd had money. He wanted better for me." She frowned at the memory. "He was the one who brought Oliver around to meet me. Truth be told, between drinking and playing cards, the two of them spent more time together than Oliver and I did. Then one night, Pa came home with the old preacher. The two of them accused Oliver of trifling with me."

It was none of Mitch's damned business, but he asked anyway. "Did he?"

"He'd kissed me. Nothing more." Her eyes were huge in her face as she stared back into her memories. "I tried to tell Pa that Oliver hadn't done anything more than steal a few kisses, but he wouldn't listen. He had already convinced the preacher that I'd been wronged. Between the two of them, they had Oliver and me all married up before either one of us knew had happened."

"Is there anything else I should know? Anything at all?"

Josie fiddled with the pile of darning that Ben had given her. From the way she avoided looking at him, something had to be bothering her. He used his best lawman glare and waited. She reached her breaking point.

"I was fixing to leave Oliver. For good."

That had him sitting tall and at attention. "When were you going to do that? And why?"

"Lucy pays me to help her in the store, but she also displayed some of my needlework for folks to buy. No one ever knew about that part except Lucy and me. I kept the extra money in a box in her storeroom."

"I take it you never let on to Oliver that you were making more money than he knew about." Not if she was smart, anyway.

"I know it's wrong for a wife to keep things from her husband. But if he'd known about the money, he would have taken it. Oliver didn't much like me working, but he liked the money I brought home just fine."

There was a touch of bitterness underlying her words, not that Mitch blamed her a bit. Oliver Turner hadn't done a lick of work in his life. Why should she have to turn over every last penny she made, for him to spend it on liquor, cards, and other women? Mitch wondered if Josie had any idea how much time and money Oliver had spent upstairs at The River Lady. He didn't know much about women, but he couldn't imagine Lucy or Melinda or even Belle putting up with such behavior.

Had Josie found out about that? Had that been the final straw in their marriage?

"Why had you decided to finally leave Oliver? Did anyone else know about your plans?"

She considered her answer. "It's no secret that I am— no, I *was*—an uneducated hill girl. My pa's cabin may not be much, but it was mine. If I left that, I had nothing." Suddenly, there was pride in her voice and in the way she held her head high. "But thanks to the ladies of the Luminary Society, I can read and do some arithmetic. I figured out that if I struck out on my own, I could earn my keep."

Damn, but he was proud of her. It would have been easy to take all that life had heaped on her head and sit around feeling sorry for herself. Instead, she had seen her chance and grabbed on with both hands. If Oliver had been too closed-minded to appreciate what a gem he'd found in Josie, the bastard deserved to lose her.

But if she was going to leave him anyway, why would she

have killed him? If she was telling the truth about her hidden cache of money, then Mitch was more convinced than ever that she was innocent.

Which meant that someone else had a strong interest in seeing Josie stand trial and hang for Oliver's death. In fact, whether or not she ever came to trial, as long as everyone was convinced of her guilt, the real culprit would walk away free. Would anyone look any further for Oliver's killer?

No one, except Mitch. He needed to get back to town, and soon. The trail was already cold. He cast around for ideas of what he could do that he hadn't already done.

For one thing, those new friends of Oliver's had to have gone to ground somewhere for the winter. If he could track them down, he could find out more about the business they had with Oliver. Maybe it was nothing, but somehow he didn't think so, especially if it involved Jed Turner. He couldn't quite picture Jed investing in anything Oliver had cooked up.

Second, he wanted to talk to some of Turner's men. He might not get any of them to tell him much, but sometimes he learned as much from what they didn't say. Mitch was convinced that Jed's outrage over Oliver's death was an act, at least in part. Did he know more about his son's death than he was letting on?

Mitch glanced at his prisoner. During his silence, Josie had turned her attention back to her sewing, giving him an opportunity to study her. Now that the last of her bruises had faded away, her skin was flawless if a bit pale. Her dark eyes, framed by equally dark lashes, were warm and lovely. But it was her mouth that drew him.

Perhaps a little too wide for her face, it was as if the sun had come out after a long darkness when she smiled. There was surprising strength in her slight build, and her body molded perfectly to his. As if she felt his gaze, her eyes flickered in his direction and then went back to her sewing. Damn, he needed to do something other than sit there and stare. Maybe Ben needed help in the barn.

"I'm going out to check on Ben. Do you need anything?"

"We could use some fresh eggs, but that's all. I thought I'd put some ham and beans on to simmer for dinner tonight. I think you've got the makings for cornbread to go with it."

"Sounds good. I'll see if I can't scrounge a few eggs for you."

He grabbed his coat and hat and braced himself for the cold. To his surprise, though, the temperature had risen considerably since he'd been outside earlier that morning. He paused to listen. Sure enough, he could hear the steady drip of snow melting off the roof and the trees. If it kept up, he should be able to get back to town by tomorrow afternoon at the latest.

Before he left, he'd have to decide what to do about Josie. Her friends had felt she wasn't safe in the jail, and maybe they were right. If he dragged Josie back there, what would Jed Turner do? Was Lucy Mulroney right in saying that Jed had plans to do Josie harm before she could come to trial?

For now, she was safe since no one knew where she was, other than him and Ben. Ben might be a cantankerous old cuss, but it was obvious he had a soft spot for Josie. He was a fair hand with both a rifle and a shotgun; no one would get past him easily. Mitch only had Josie's word that she had nowhere else to go, but he believed her. For now, he'd go about his business as if he were still hunting for her, so no one would suspect where she was. As long as he knew, the hell with everybody else, especially Jed Turner.

Tomorrow he'd ride back into town. Cade and Jake would probably be damn glad to see him, even if he

returned empty-handed. Once he gave them a day or
so of relief, he'd take back to trailing after Jed's men
to see what they were up to. And it wouldn't hurt to
call on Jed himself. Considering the man's temper, if
Mitch poked and prodded enough, he just might let
something slip.

Feeling more in control than he had in days, Mitch
headed for the barn to explain his plan to Ben.

Twelve

"Sheriff Hughes rode back into town this morning." Melinda sounded breathless. No doubt she'd come running as soon as she'd seen their missing lawman's return.

"Was he alone?" Lucy finished folding a length of fabric that she wanted to set aside for a new dress for her stepdaughter. She put the rest of the bolt back on the table for her customers.

"Yes, he was."

The reassurance that Josie had yet to be caught did little to relieve Lucy's worries. She gave voice to the question they were all asking themselves. "Do you think she's all right? I mean, what with this weather and everything, how far do you think she's gotten?"

Her friend shrugged. "I don't know. After all, as far as we know, she was on foot when the storm hit. Surely she knew to take shelter somewhere."

Lucy looked out at the piles of snow that had yet to melt away. "Cade tells me not to worry, because Josie knows how to take care of herself, but how can I not? We were the ones who sent her out on her own."

Not for the first time, she blinked back tears. Her pregnancy had made her more emotional than usual. But even allowing for that, she was almost sick over the whole mess. Melinda handed her a handkerchief. She dabbed at her eyes and offered up a silent prayer for the welfare of their friend.

"What did Cade say about Jed Turner's behavior when he was in the store?" Melinda asked as she fingered some fabric that caught her eye.

"He agreed that we would no longer welcome Mr. Turner's business, but otherwise there wasn't much he could do about it. He said if the man comes in again, I'm to slip out the back and go right to the newspaper office."

"That sounds like a reasonable plan. I must admit that man scares me." She held the fabric up to the front of her dress. "Would I look good in this shade of green?"

"I think it was made for you, especially the way it brings out the red highlights in your hair. How much do you want?" Lucy unrolled the fabric and reached for her shears.

"Enough for this new pattern I bought last week." She pulled it out of her purse. "I've been looking for just the right fabric for the Christmas service at church."

The two women conferred over the pattern and then measured and cut the necessary amount of fabric. As Lucy folded it and figured the price, Melinda picked out some trim to go with it.

"You know, Josie was really looking forward to the Christmas service this year. Her father never brought her to town for such things, and Oliver never attended church either. My Daniel had made a point of inviting her himself, so she'd know how much we wanted her to be there. This would have been her first time to be part of the celebration."

Lucy marked down Melinda's charges and set the ledger aside. It was hard to concentrate when she was so worried about Josie. "I know. She loved making all those little bags to hold candy for the children. And

Henrietta was pleased with the baby clothes that Josie sewed before she left."

This time it was Melinda who looked ready to cry. "I keep telling myself not to give up hope for her. After all, Christmas is the season of miracles. Maybe there will be one for Josie this year."

"We can only hope so."

The bell over the door chimed, announcing the arrival of another customer. Lucy wiped her eyes again and prepared to offer up a bright smile. It faded immediately when Mitch Hughes stepped up to the counter. He tipped his hat at the two of them, acting as if everything were normal. Sometimes Lucy wished he'd yell at them or something, considering how guilty she felt for how they'd treated him.

"Hello, Sheriff. I heard you were back in town."

"Word travels fast." He glanced in Melinda's direction, showing he knew exactly who had carried the news. "I'll be leaving again tomorrow, but I wanted to talk to the two of you before I go."

"All right. Would you like some coffee or anything first?"

"That sounds good." Without waiting for her to fix it, he pulled a chair close to the stove and sat down.

Knowing how much he liked sweets, Lucy sent Melinda to get a plate of cookies from upstairs and then carried the tray over to where Mitch waited. He'd leaned back in the chair and let his eyes drift almost shut. It wasn't hard to see that he was tired.

He sat up and accepted both the coffee and the cookies. "Thanks." He took a careful sip from his cup and then ate two cookies in quick order. "Now, let's talk. Cade tells me that Jed Turner paid you a visit."

Once again, he was ignoring their part in his current troubles. Well, she wasn't going to bring it up if he didn't. "Yes, he sent one of his men with a list of supplies, saying Jed would pick them up himself."

"I take it that's pretty unusual even though you own the only store in town."

She nodded. "As far as I know, he does most of his buying over in White's Ferry. I guess he never got along with either my father or my first husband. We didn't miss his business, though. He's not an easy man to please."

"Did he order anything that seemed out of the ordinary?"

"No, mostly the same things everyone needs: flour, beans—you know the sort of stuff I mean."

"What did he say that upset you?" Despite his relaxed posture, it was clear from the expression in his eyes that Mitch was listening carefully to what she said.

"He said that Josie ruined Oliver's life." She paused for effect. "Then he said for that alone she would be punished."

"Not for killing him, just for marrying him, huh?" Mitch thought that one over for a minute. "Now, that's interesting."

Without another word, he stood up and walked out. The two women followed him to the door and watched as Mitch hurried down the street toward the stable.

A sudden rise in temperature had melted the snow faster than it could drain away. Almost overnight the roads changed from slippery ice to ankle-deep mud. He didn't want to risk hurting his horse again, but he couldn't afford to wait in town for conditions to improve. For the moment, Josie was safe at his farm.

But just for the moment.

All it would take for everything to go straight to hell was someone stopping by unexpectedly and finding out that he had a unexplained guest. Hell, even Cade would have a hard time understanding why Mitch hadn't dragged Josie back to jail through the snow and ice. And once the weather had broken, Mitch had no excuse at all for leaving her in the questionable custody of old Ben. Hell, he didn't understand it himself.

His horse plodded on, each step more of an effort than it should be for the poor animal. Mitch would get off and lead it along the trail, but that would only slow them both down. Besides, the last time he tried that, he almost killed them both.

He glanced at the sun's position in the sky. It would be well past sundown before he made it back to town, but he'd planned it that way. After some discreet inquiries, he'd managed to find out that Jed Turner made a habit of going into White's Ferry to see to his business concerns and to have dinner with his attorney every week.

Mitch had every intention of having a long talk with Jed in the very near future. But for now he'd content himself with a careful look around Jed's home without the man's knowledge. With the caliber of men that Jed kept on his payroll, it was doubtful that Mitch would actually get near the house. Even so, he thought it was worth a look, figuring he'd learn a lot about the man himself by studying where he lived.

He'd been there before, but always under the watchful eye of Jed himself. This time he wasn't going to ride up to the front door. No, he was approaching from the back, hoping to get close without being seen. If he'd judged things correctly, Jed's house should be visible from the top of the next rise. Any other time of the year, the thick foliage of the surrounding woods would allow Mitch to get fairly close without any danger of being seen.

Now, though, with all but the oaks bare of leaves, any movement would be obvious if anyone happened to be watching. Something told Mitch that Jed probably had guards posted all the time right now, even if that was a new development. When a man had something to hide, he tended to guard his privacy pretty tenaciously. In fact, if Jed had surrounded his home with armed men, that in itself was significant.

He dismounted just short of the ridge. After considering his options, he tied his horse to a handy sapling where it could reach some grass that grew in the protection of an outcropping of limestone. It was mostly brown, but the horse wouldn't care. Although Mitch would remain close to his horse in case he needed to beat a hasty retreat, he figured he stood a better chance of remaining undetected alone.

Slipping from tree trunk to tree trunk, he paused at each new position to study the terrain below. When he reached a thick clump of brush, he knelt down and stared at the scene below. From his current position, he counted two—no, make that three—men with rifles standing watch. Unless he missed his guess, there were at least one or two more on the far side of the house.

Interesting. Damn interesting, in fact. Jed Turner had never been known for his hospitality, but this was taking it to extremes.

Mitch moved farther down the hillside. There wasn't a chance in hell that he'd be able to make it to the house unobserved, but he hadn't really thought he would. It was enough to know that Jed Turner needed hired guns to feel safe.

But why? Mitch would give a year's salary to know the answer to that question.

The sun had dropped low in the sky. If he didn't start back soon, he'd run the risk of riding across country in the dark. With that thought in mind, he waited until the closest guard turned back to walk in the other direction before dropping back into the trees. He was so intent on watching Turner's men that he forgot to watch where he was going. His boot caught on a root, sending him stumbling backward until he grabbed on to a branch to stop his fall.

He froze in the awkward position until he was sure that his clumsiness hadn't drawn unwanted attention. Slowly he straightened up, this time taking more care where he stepped. He'd gone no more than a step or two when the flash of something shiny caught his eye. He backed up a couple of feet to get a better look.

He swayed back and forth slightly, trying to catch the sun at the same angle. On the second pass, he spied it again, under the bottom branches of a scrubby bush. After checking again on the whereabouts of the sentries, he picked up a stick and poked at the object half buried in the leaves and mud. To his surprise, it was a rather expensive-looking flask. After wiping most of the mud off with a handful of wet leaves, he unscrewed the lid and took a whiff.

Cheap whiskey was his best guess. He put the lid back on and studied the outside of the flask. The lack of tarnish led him to assume that it hadn't been lying out in the elements all that long. He hefted it in his hand. Judging by the weight, it had cost someone a fair amount of money. It was hard to imagine that it had come to be resting under that bush by accident. If the owner had tired of it, he could have sold it easily enough.

Maybe money wasn't important to the former owner.

There'd be more time to study the flask in more detail later. For now, he shoved it in his saddlebag and swung up in the saddle. He wanted to get back to town, to relieve Jake for the night. Cade had been great about helping out, but Lucy would appreciate having him home for dinner.

Tomorrow Mitch planned on doing some scouting for
Oliver's friends, and figured on talking Cade into riding
with him. Only a fool would ride into a nest of Oliver's
acquaintances without someone to guard his back.

Despite the mud and the cold, his mood had improved considerably. He didn't know the significance of
the flask, but the first time Mitch felt like he'd taken a
step closer to the truth of how Oliver Turner came to be
dead.

The day dawned bright and sunny—and damned cold.
Mitch pulled on an extra pair of socks and his warmest
gloves. He stepped outside the hotel and looked around.
At least the weather was still keeping most folks at home.
A few brave souls had ventured out, but not many—all
the easier to keep Josie's whereabouts a secret.

He hurried to the stable and a chance to get in out of
the wind for a few minutes longer. Cade hadn't arrived
yet, so Mitch set to work saddling up both of their
horses. He was giving the cinches one last tug when his
friend showed up.

"Damn, I swear if it got any colder out there, my blood
would freeze up solid." Cade's words came out in puffs
of steamy breath.

"It's not much warmer in here." Mitch tossed Cade
the reins to his horse. "Hopefully we won't have to be
out long." He'd already explained to Cade what he
hoped to accomplish. If Cade wondered why Mitch was
looking for Oliver's friends instead of his missing wife,
he didn't ask.

"Where we headed?" Cade led his horse out of the
stable before mounting up.

"First to Mrs. Turner's cabin." It felt strange to call
Josie by her more formal name, but Mitch hoped that it

sounded more professional. "Folks have reported seeing fresh tracks leading off in that direction and smoke coming from the chimney. I figure someone has helped himself to a warm place to hole up for a while. With luck, it's the men we're looking for."

"Still figure them to be that bunch the sheriff up north warned you about?"

"Could be, but so far they've behaved themselves around here."

Mitch turned his collar up against the wind and took the lead. Cade rode up even with him after a bit. "If we don't find them at the Turner place, do you have any idea where to look next?"

Mitch had been thinking about that very thing. "You know where the river bends back up to the north and then snakes around a couple of small islands?"

Cade nodded. "Yeah, about a mile and half up past White's Ferry."

"Well, there are some caves up along the bluff that are big enough to live in."

"Damned cold way to live." Cade gave him a puzzled look. "Besides, how do you know about the caves?"

"I'd guess the same way these men would have found out, if that's where they are. Back during the war we kept supplies hidden in them. If things got tough, we crawled inside ourselves until the bluebellies moved back north."

Cade shuddered. "Even in the winter?"

"Especially in the winter. A dry cave beats tents all to hell." Memories flashed by, trying to suck him back in time again. With considerable effort Mitch closed his eyes and shoved the whispers from his past back where they belonged. When they were silenced, he urged his mount into a quicker pace, trying to put some distance between himself and the shadows that had trailed him since the war.

His companion understood enough not to ask any more questions. Mitch knew that Cade had spent a good deal of the war in a prisoner-of-war camp. He'd been captured after being shot in the leg during a skirmish near Columbia, leaving him with a slight limp as a reminder of the whole experience.

Considering everything, both of them had been damn lucky.

Mitch slowed down when they reached the cutoff toward Josie's cabin, debating the best way to make their approach. Trouble was, until he knew who he was facing and how many, it was impossible to gauge what sort of welcome he'd get. Rather than risk both of them, he motioned for Cade to take off through the trees to his left.

Once he had disappeared into the woods, Mitch started forward again. Before going any distance, he checked the slide of his pistol in its holster. If any shooting started, he wanted to know he could defend himself with no mishaps. Listening for any indication that he was no longer alone, he kept his eyes trained on the clearing up ahead.

He knew before he left the trees that the cabin was deserted. Cade joined him.

"Think they've been here?"

Mitch threw his leg over the saddle and slid down to the ground. "I'll take a look around inside. I know Josie hasn't been back since she was arrested. If anything has changed since we were here, that should tell us something."

It didn't take long to know that somebody had been there. There hadn't been much worth having in Josie's small home before, but now what was left was little better than kindling. Son of a bitch! He wanted to punch something. Hadn't she lost enough without having someone destroy the little part of the world that she called home? He settled for kicking a broken chair, sending it rattling across the room. He stomped back outside, his mood worsening by the minute.

Cade had dismounted and was studying some tracks. He pointed in the direction of the river. "Whoever was here went that way. Looks like you might be right about those caves."

"Let's go take a look."

Both men mounted up and set off at a fast pace. The only good thing about the mud was that it made it easier to follow the trail. After a bit, Cade cleared his throat and spoke.

"Ah, Mitch, can I ask you something?"

Mitch nodded, although something told him he wasn't going to like the question.

"You sounded pretty sure that Josie hadn't been back to her place since she was arrested. How do you know that, if you haven't seen her since she escaped?"

Damn, he'd hoped Cade hadn't caught that little slip, but he should have known better. A reporter to the bone, Cade would pick up on the slightest scent of a story.

"I didn't see any of her tracks in the mud." It wasn't much of an explanation, but it was the best he could come up with on short notice.

"You've got to do better than that if you're going be a convincing liar, my friend."

"Drop it, Cade."

"Consider it dropped," Cade grinned, "but when this is all over, you can tell me the real story over a bottle of scotch."

"I'll even buy a couple of those fancy cigars you like so much."

"Fair enough." Then, to change the subject Cade reached into his saddlebag and brought out a pair of sandwiches wrapped in paper. He tossed one to Mitch.

"Lucy sends her love. She thinks eating something will help ward off the cold."

Mitch bit into the thick slices of bread and ham. It tasted great and had the added advantage of making it difficult for either of them to talk. They were just finishing up the supply of cookies she'd also included when they caught sight of the river through the trees.

"How do you figure on approaching the caves without getting shot?"

"I'll show you." He rode straight for the edge of the river and stopped on the gravel bar that jutted out into the water. After listening to the silence for several seconds, he whistled two long notes and followed with a trio of short ones. When he didn't get the response he wanted, he tried again, this time varying the pattern a bit.

Cade hung back, watching upstream for any sign of activity, his rifle in hand. "See anything?" he whispered.

Mitch pitched his voice to carry no farther than where Cade had stopped. "We won't, unless they want us to. That's how we . . . they survived the war—by being damn near invisible most of the time." He hadn't seen any sign they were being watched, but he'd bet his last dollar that someone had his rifle aimed right at the middle of his back.

For several more minutes there was no sound except the rippling water and the occasional bird call. He wished to hell someone would make up his damn mind. Feeling more like a target than a sheriff at the moment, he decided to press the issue. Drawing his rifle, he fired off a couple of shots, figuring that should catch someone's attention.

It didn't take long. One minute the woods behind them were empty, and the next, a handful of men rode out from the trees, rifles drawn and their expressions grim.

Mitch guided his horse alongside Cade's and waited.

Most of the newcomers pulled up just as they cleared the woods. One rider approached Mitch and Cade, looking pretty damn unfriendly. "Where did you learn to whistle like that?"

"Same place you did. In fact, I spent a fair amount of time in some of the caves along this river a few years ago." He didn't have to specify that it was during the war or that he'd worn a butternut-and-gray uniform at the time.

"I take it you wanted something?"

Mitch did a silent head count and then doubled it. If there were four men in front of them, there were probably close to that number coming up behind them. Standard tactics from the war. He knew without looking that they'd be wearing bits and pieces of their old uniforms.

"I want to talk to the man in charge." He kept his stance relaxed, realizing that fear or belligerence would just increase the chances of him and Cade getting shot— or worse.

"So talk."

Mitch smiled and shook his head. "Unless I'm mistaken, you're not him. Leastwise, you're not the one who was scouting out the bank in Lee's Mill."

That caused a stir among them. And just as he expected, he heard voices whispering from across the river behind them. Finally, a man afoot strolled up from around the bend in the river. He had his rifle in hand, but it was resting pointed backward on his shoulder. Of course, it was easy to be cocky with an armed band of men ready to back his play.

"Well, Sheriff, I was wondering when we'd meet up again." He tipped his hat in salute. "And Mr. Mulroney, we haven't met before, but my compliments. My men and I think you print a fine newspaper."

"Thanks." If Cade was surprised that they recognized him, he gave no sign of it.

Mitch took note of the fact the man said *when* they'd meet again, not *if*. He decided to dismount and approach the as yet unnamed leader. It was easier to gauge a man's reactions when looking him in the eye. Cade followed suit. The man motioned for one of the others to take care of their horses.

"It's cold. Let's go have some coffee."

Nothing more was said until he'd led them back around the bend in the river to a campfire tucked up near the bluff. There was a pot of coffee on the fire, but nothing else that suggested this was their actual camp. The three of them sat down on a convenient driftwood log.

Cade spoke first. "You seem to have us at a disadvantage, sir, since you know our names, yet we don't know yours."

"Mr. Jones will do for our purposes, Mr. Mulroney." The twinkle in his eye invited them to play along with his obvious lie. "Now, why don't you tell me what brought you out here to see me."

"Oliver Turner."

He raised his eyebrows in mock innocence. "I believe I read in the *Clarion* that someone by that name was murdered recently. You don't think I had anything to do with that, do you?" Some of the friendliness was gone from his smile.

Mitch shook his head. "No, as a matter of fact I don't. However, I heard rumors that you and your men had some business with him. I was curious what kind of business that might be."

"Why?"

"Curiosity mainly. Oliver never had two dimes to rub together. I was wondering what kind of business investment he might be involved in." Mitch accepted the cup of coffee and cradled it in his hands. "I'm still trying to find a motive for his murder."

Mr. Jones looked honestly puzzled. "I thought his wife was the one who pulled the trigger." He sipped his own coffee. "A couple of his father's men got into a poker game with two of my, ah, associates. They said old Jed was offering top dollar to who ever dragged her back for hanging."

Son of a bitch—he hadn't heard about the reward. What could he say to that? Luckily, Cade was better with words.

"Despite what Oliver's father has to say on the matter, Josie Turner is well thought of by people in town. It's going to take a lot more than Jed's opinion to convince a judge to hang a woman in these parts."

Mitch would have to thank Cade later. He'd phrased it exactly right by making it look like the townspeople were demanding that Mitch keep searching for facts at the same time he was searching for Josie.

Their host considered what he wanted to say. "I haven't met Jed Turner myself, but I can tell you that Oliver never had anything good to say about him. Seems like the old man was a bit tightfisted with his money."

That was an understatement. "And this business of Oliver's?"

The man shrugged. "It was all talk as far as I can tell. Oliver was sure he'd come up with a scheme to get his father to part with a substantial sum of his money. Oliver was going to approach Jed himself first. If it didn't work out, he thought maybe I could help negotiate the deal."

Mitch could imagine what form that negotiation would have taken. He wondered if Jed had any idea how close he'd come to facing the business end of Mr. Jones's rifle. Maybe he did. That would account for the armed guards surrounding Jed's house.

"Did I tell you anything helpful?"

"Yes, as a matter of fact. There's one more thing." Mitch reached into his coat pocket and pulled out the silver flask he'd found in the woods outside Jed's house. "Have you seen this before?" He tossed it across the fire to Mr. Jones, who caught it easily.

The outlaw leader turned it over to study both sides. Then he unscrewed the lid and took a sniff. His nose wrinkled in distaste. "I'd say it belonged to Oliver Turner. He carried one like it, and it even smells like that cheap whiskey he drank all the time."

It had been an outside shot to see if Oliver's new friend would recognize the flask. "When was the last time you saw that he had the flask with him."

"Does it matter?"

"It could."

"He was drinking out of it the night I stayed over at his cabin. Unless I'm mistaken, that was the day before he died."

Mitch had gotten far more from Mr. Jones than he'd expected to. He owed the man something back, so he pulled a folded piece of paper from his other pocket and passed it over to Mr. Jones. He waited until after the man had a chance to look at it before saying anything.

"Thought you might like to know that a certain sheriff up north was circulating these to all the lawmen in this part of the state. I'd recommend you keep the beard. It hides the scar."

"Why are you warning me?" The man rose slowly to his feet.

"Partly because you told me more than you had to and partly because I lived in caves like these myself." He allowed himself a small smile. "Besides, you've been in my area for a while now and haven't caused me any problems." He tossed the dregs of his coffee into the fire, sending a shower of sparks flying skyward. "I'd like to see things stay that way, if you get my drift."

Mr. Jones stood up. "I'm assuming you'd rather we didn't use this spot as the center of our various, uh, enterprises."

Mitch nodded his agreement. "You'll find I'm easy enough to deal with as long as you stay on my side of the law, Mr. Jones. I would remind you that I found you easily enough this time. Next time I won't whistle to warn you that I'm coming." Then, in a move that surprised him as much as it did Mr. Jones, he held out his hand.

Reluctantly Mr. Jones accepted the offer of a handshake. "I wish you luck in dealing with Jed Turner, Sheriff."

He didn't make any promises about his future plans for himself and his men, but then, Mitch hadn't really expected him to. A certain type of man had survived the war but hadn't been able to give up living on the edge of risk. Against his better instincts, he was inclined to like Mr. Jones or Baxter or whatever name the outlaw was using. He'd hate like hell to have to hunt him down.

It would do no good to tell him so. If the man was going to find a way to leave the war behind, he would have to find his own path. He and Cade had made peace with their past. It wasn't easy, but it could be done.

"We'll be going now."

"My men will have tied your horses up near where you rode in. You shouldn't have any problem finding them."

"Thanks for talking to us."

"You're welcome. Always happy to help the law."

If his laugh was a bit ironic, Mitch didn't say anything. As they walked away, the outlaw leader had one more thing to say.

"And, Sheriff, thanks for this." He held up the wanted

poster. He rubbed his whiskers and grinned. "It's nice to know my beard does more than keep my face warm."

He turned his back on them and disappeared into the tumble of rocks along the river. The lawman in Mitch was tempted to follow him at a distance to see if they were in the caves he knew about or if they'd found some of their own. Hell, the whole Ozark area was riddled with the damn things.

But the voice of caution kept him and Cade moving on along. The man had granted them safe passage, but he hadn't done so without having someone watch to see that Mitch and Cade left as they were supposed to.

When they were out of hearing, Cade murmured, "Do you hate having guns aimed at the middle of your back as much as I do?"

"Damn straight, I do. That's something a cautious man never gets used to."

Their horses were tethered right where they were supposed to be, much to Mitch's relief. The two men mounted up and rode out at a faster clip than they'd ridden in.

Thirteen

Damn, he didn't want to spend the night in town, but Cade would be sure to wonder why Mitch felt the need to ride through the dark and the cold just to spend a few hours at the farm. Logically, he knew it would be better to wait until after he got off duty tomorrow evening, but that didn't mean he had to like it.

But for Josie's sake, he'd wait. He'd already made one slip in front of Cade. Luckily for Mitch, Cade was in no hurry to see his wife's good friend back behind bars. Other folks may not feel quite so generous.

For now, he stared at the flask on his desk. His gut told him that he was right—the flask had belonged Oliver Turner. It had just the sort of flashy style that would have appealed to the man, but what an idiot. Even though he'd had a woman waiting for him at home who was worth more than all the silver flasks in the world, he'd been too stupid to appreciate what he'd had. He chose instead to spend his short life drinking and carousing.

The war had taught most of those who survived it to appreciate the simple things that made life worth living: a good woman, a family, a place to call home. Looking back, he sometimes wondered if Rebecca would have settled for his small farm. Her father had always bragged about how he'd spoiled her, spending large amounts of money to suit her every whim. The man had never really

approved of Mitch, saying he'd never amount to anything.

Would Rebecca have even liked the man Mitch had
become? Considering that Rebecca and her father were
long dead, Mitch felt guilty thinking such traitorous
thoughts. Rebecca had loved him; that was the memory
he should cherish.

He also knew he had no business comparing Rebecca
to Josie Turner. The two women had very little in common
except for the strong feelings that Mitch had for each of
them. The only explanation he could come up with was
that Rebecca had attracted the attention of him as a young
man, full of the kind of dreams that youth cherished.

But he wasn't young anymore—maybe not so old by
the calendar, but war had a way of making a man feel
older than his years. He wanted a woman who could
make a house feel like more than boards and furniture.
Even in the short time that Josie had been under his
roof, she'd made little changes that were impossible to
ignore—more than just the way she cleaned the kitchen
and the darning she'd done. There was just something
damn special about spending the quiet of the evening
with a woman. And possibly the long hours of the night.

Which brought him back to the flask. If he could follow its trail back to the real killer, then with luck he
could clear Josie's name. Once the burden of guilt was
laid at the feet of the real culprit, then she would be free
to . . . free to live her life as she saw fit. One kiss gave him
no claim on her, and considering her experience with
men in general, he wouldn't blame her for wishing that
every man she met would go straight to perdition.

But she had kissed him. The memory of that moment
was never absent from his thoughts for more than a few
minutes at a time. He wanted to kiss her again. And
more, so damn much more.

Feeling too restless to be cooped up in the jail, he decided to make his rounds early. Grabbing his coat and hat, he stepped out into the cold night air.

Josie stared out into the night, too tired to do anything, too restless to sleep. The moon had risen high in the sky, blanketing the countryside with its eerie silver light. Ben had already disappeared into his room for the night, leaving her alone to prowl the confines of Mitch's house.

She missed him.

On one hand that didn't particularly surprise her, but how much she missed him did. Considering she'd spent most of her life alone, with only herself for company, she'd come to depend heavily on Mitch's presence since the day this whole nightmare had begun.

She shuddered.

What was Mitch doing now? Considering how late it was, he was probably dozing in his chair at the jail. Of course, it could be Jake's night to be on duty, but she didn't think so. Didn't want to think so. If Mitch was off, she wanted to think he'd be here at his farm. With her.

She wanted him.

That thought had her shaking her head. She had no business thinking such thoughts. She'd been a widow for such a short time, not to mention that she was in no position to be making any kind of plans for the future. She may not even have one, especially if it was left up to Jed Turner, with his determined men and his unlimited money.

She should go to bed.

But in her current mood she knew sleep wouldn't come. Even though she'd put clean linens on the bed, every night when she lay down, she was uncomfortably aware that it was Mitch's bed—his blankets, his pillows, his scent. It took all the self-control she could muster to keep from burying her face in his pillows to breathe in the clean, masculine scent that was his alone. She had no right to take such liberties. If he hadn't ordered her to continue to use his room in his absence, she would have made up a pallet for herself on the kitchen floor.

She wondered if he remembered their one kiss.

Turning from the window, she looked around for something to keep her hands busy and her thoughts off Mitch Hughes. She spied her sewing, still sitting where she'd left it. Maybe she was fooling herself that all the small bags she'd made for Christmas candy would get used this year. Even if she managed to smuggle them back to Melinda and Lucy, would parents want their children to have a gift made by an accused murderer? The impulse to sew disappeared as quickly as it came.

She turned out the lamp and sent herself to bed. Alone.

It was time to pay another visit to Jed Turner. This time Mitch planned on riding straight up to the house rather than slinking around in the woods. More and more the need to confront the victim's father was riding Mitch hard.

He just wished he knew if he could trust his own judgment. Was he wanting to focus on Jed simply because he didn't like the man? Or because he felt more than he should for Josie? No, by God, he'd been a lawman too long to let his own personal prejudices interfere with the job. From the first night, when Jed's men dragged Josie to the jail, something about the entire episode had bothered him.

And he finally knew what it was. According to everyone he'd talked to, Jed Turner had practically disowned his son for failing to live up to his expectations. Oliver's marriage to Josie had only reinforced Jed's opinion of his son as a failure. Mitch made a mental note of another question to ask Josie.

How often had she been invited to Jed's home for any occasion, let alone a holiday dinner? He was willing to bet that it wasn't very damn often, if at all.

And if he was right about his suspicions, it had been an amazing coincidence that Jed had been overcome with the need to spend time with his estranged son and the daughter-in-law he actively disliked right when Oliver was being murdered. In Mitch's experience, if a man's story didn't ring true, didn't make sense, then chances were that the son of a bitch was lying to save his own skin. The only question was, what was Jed lying about?

As the Turner house came into sight through the trees, Mitch mentally took note of where each hired gun was standing. He studied the two who had first noticed Mitch's approach. There was more tension in their stance, but neither one made any kind of threatening move toward him. Evidently, they recognized him from town.

If he had to guess, neither one of them had ever made their living with just their guns. Most likely they had worked for Jed in some other capacity, but standing guard had been added to their duties. He thought of another question he'd like to ask their boss.

Just who was Jed so afraid of?

Mitch ignored the two guards much as they ignored him. He stopped short of Turner's porch and dismounted. Before his foot touched the ground, he heard footsteps running toward him. Immediately, the memories of another time, another threat, stole the present from him, replacing it with the need to find cover and protect himself from the attack.

Using the last little bit of sanity he could muster, he forced the memories, the scents, the screams back where they belonged. He drew one breath of the winter air, the cool scent of the present, and then turned to see who was approaching him in such a hurry. Despite the remnants of confusion in his head, he placed the man immediately: Jed Turner's ramrod.

The man slid to a halt just about an arm's length away from Mitch. Since he didn't particularly like being crowded by anyone, much less one of Jed's men, Mitch glared and held his ground. Maybe it was petty of him, but he enjoyed the small victory when the smaller man backed up a step and muttered, "Sorry, didn't mean to startle you, Sheriff. I'm Paddy McCain, Mr. Turner's foreman."

"I'm here to see Jed Turner," Mitch announced, looking past McCain toward the house. He may have been stating the obvious, but he wanted to make it clear that dealing with one of Jed's underlings would not suffice.

"He's busy working in his office."

"Tell him I'm here." Mitch planted his feet solidly, another sign that he wasn't going to be put off.

Paddy's eyes flicked toward the house and back, clearly not wanting to interrupt his employer. He licked his lips and shifted his weight from one foot to the other while he considered his options. Mitch didn't give him any.

"Either you can tell him I'm here or I will."

"What is it you want to talk to him about?" Paddy asked, already moving in the direction of the front door.

"Why is that any of your business?" Mitch stood, immovable, waiting for Paddy to do his bidding.

"Wait here." Paddy didn't bother to knock before entering Jed's house, but he was careful to wipe his boots before stepping through the door.

Mitch figured on giving Paddy about two minutes to deliver his message and other five for Jed to keep Mitch waiting before showing his face. It was all a matter of power—who had it and who didn't. Paddy didn't. Jed did. And whether Turner knew or not, Mitch had it in spades.

Mentally he ticked off the seconds. Jed surprised him by arriving thirty seconds before Mitch had expected him.

"What the hell do you want?"

Interesting. A show of temper before he even knew why Mitch was there. What would he do if Mitch did a little more pushing?

"I have some questions for you. I figured you'd rather answer them here instead of in my office in town."

An expression flashed across Jed's face that looked a lot like fear or guilt. It was gone, replaced by his usual glower, before Mitch could decide for sure. Either way, the man was not at all happy to have the law come calling. Interesting. In fact, damn interesting.

"Wouldn't you spend your time better out searching for my son's murderer?"

"Sir," Mitch said with a respect he certainly didn't feel, "I assure you that catching the person responsible for your son's death is extremely important to me."

Jed's eyes narrowed in suspicion. "Then why don't you have his murdering wife back behind bars? I'm tired of paying my own men to do your work for you." He waved a fist in Mitch's direction. "As soon as we find her, I will make sure the judge shows up to see that justice is served."

"I never asked you to do my job, Mr. Turner, and I don't appreciate you trying." He stepped forward, using his height to his advantage. He glared down at the two men. "I'll tell you what, though. Until the town of Lee's Mill says otherwise, I'm the law in these parts. If you do anything—anything at all—to interfere with my job, I'll throw you and as many of your men as necessary behind bars and let you rot there."

He included both men in his glare. "And furthermore, I'll tell you what you *will* do, Turner. You *will* answer my questions. You *will* keep you and your men out of my way. If you're lucky, you will be the first to know when I have enough evidence to convict your son's killer."

By now Turner was sputtering with fury while the hapless Paddy looked around for a way to escape. Mitch had to wonder why Turner wasn't calling for help. Maybe he wanted to know what Mitch was up to more than he wanted to get rid of him.

"Paddy, why don't you go do something useful?" Turner didn't even spare his employee a glance. Jed waited impatiently for Paddy to move out of hearing. "Now, ask your questions."

"Have you seen this before?" Mitch pulled the flask from his pocket, careful to let Turner get a good look without getting his hands on it.

"It looks like the one I gave Oliver for Christmas the year before he let himself get hitched to that hill trash."

Mitch forced himself to relax his hands, fighting the urge to take his building frustration out on the man in front of him. As satisfying as that might be for the moment, it would only cause Mitch more problems in the long run. Especially considering the number of armed men who were being well paid to side with Turner.

"When was the last time you actually saw the flask in Oliver's possession?"

"How the hell am I supposed to remember something like that?" Jed ran his fingers through his hair, clearly having to struggle to control his temper. "My boy had a weakness for liquor, Sheriff, but he knew better than to show it around me. I can't abide weaklings, and I made sure Oliver knew it. When he'd come begging for money, he always made the effort to be sober." Forgetting for the moment who he was talking to, he snorted in disgust. "Fool, only thing more pitiful than a drunk is a lazy drunk."

Then, as if realizing he wasn't exactly sounding like a grieving father, he changed tactics. "I kept hoping that he'd change. You know, it broke my heart to bury him, knowing he'd never have a chance to make something of himself."

In Mitch's opinion, Oliver had already made something of himself—a bad-tempered, brutal drunk. And in his experience, men like that never changed. They used alcohol to bolster their courage until one day they made the mistake of crossing the wrong man. As far as he was concerned, it hadn't come as a surprise that Oliver died with a bullet in his back. The only question had been when.

Jed interrupted his thoughts. "Look, I'm a busy man, Sheriff. Are we done here or do you have other questions?"

"Just one. How often did you have your son and his wife over for a family dinner?" Mitch was willing to bet the answer was next to never, but he waited for Jed to answer.

"Looking back, not nearly enough." This time Jed saw the question for the trap that it was. If it weren't for the chill in his eyes, Jed would have sounded like a father still reeling from the tragic loss of a favored son. He stared off at the surrounding hills. "A man always thinks there will always be more time, but it doesn't always work out that way. I kept thinking if Oliver proved himself worthy, I could hand over the reins to my business and take it easier. Since that plan wasn't working, I wanted to try another way. Maybe if I made him welcome in my home again, he'd step up and meet the challenge."

Jed shook his head and sighed. "Just when I wanted to offer my son . . ." His voice trailed off. "Sheriff, make damn sure you find his killer." Then he walked away, back into his house, and closed the door.

Mitch watched him go, wishing like hell that he knew more about how the man thought, how he worked. It would be so easy to believe Jed Turner's portrayal of a father broken and battered by the loss of his son. But once again, Mitch's gut was telling him a different story. He just wished he knew if he could trust himself to know the truth when it came to Josie Turner.

Josie turned away from the window, disappointment leaving a bitter taste in her mouth. She'd been so sure he would have returned by now. Even Ben had thought so. He'd left for town himself earlier in the afternoon, saying he needed to see Doc about something. He planned to stay over the night and come back some time tomorrow morning.

Ben had refused to tell her exactly why he needed medical care. She'd noticed he'd winced in pain when he sat down on the seat of the buckboard. Maybe it was just his rheumatism acting up. His last words had been to reassure her that Mitch should be back soon.

That was hours ago and here she was, alone and pacing the floor, all because Ben had gotten her hopes up that Mitch would arrive soon. She had managed to concentrate on her sewing for a while after Ben left. There was a tidy stack of candy bags sitting on the table, waiting for someone to make the taffy to go in them. Then the realization that she wouldn't be with the rest of the Society when they got together to fill the bags had hit her hard.

Next, she'd swept out the entire house, not once but twice. If it hadn't been so cold outside, she would have taken to doing the laundry just to keep herself busy. Now there was nothing left to do except . . . She remembered seeing a stack of books on a shelf in Mitch's room. If they weren't too hard, maybe she could read one of them. He wouldn't mind—at least, she didn't think so.

None of the titles she sounded out were familiar to her, so she selected two at random and carried them back into the kitchen where the light was better. She pulled a chair near the window and settled in to enjoy herself. The first book turned out to be a volume of poetry. The thought of their tough sheriff sitting around reading poems brought a smile to her face. She knew he had a fondness for books because he borrowed them from the Society once in a while. But poetry?

His secret was safe with her, but she might have to tease him about it just a little.

A sound outside the window dragged her attention away from the book in her hands. She heard it again—the sound of a horse approaching at a slow pace. It was enough to make her realize that anyone riding up to the house would have a clear view of her through the window. What an idiot! Ben and Mitch had both warned her to make sure she wasn't seen.

Slipping from the chair onto the floor, she crawled across the room to where Ben had left a loaded shotgun for her. Her skirts made the going awkward, but she made it in good time. Now that she was armed, it was time find out who had come calling.

Sliding up to the window, she drew a breath and then peeked outside. Relief swept over her as she recognized Mitch's horse. The man himself had already disappeared into the barn, obviously intent on seeing to his horse's needs before coming inside. But now that he was home, she panicked. Had he come back to tell her that she had to go back to jail?

Had he found out anything new about Oliver's death? Was her hair a mess?

She ran into Mitch's bedroom to look at herself in the mirror. It was a foolish, woman thing to do, but she couldn't face him with her hair stringing down around her face. Helping herself to his brush, she quickly unbraided her hair and ruthlessly dragged the brush through it. Once the tangles were out, she plaited her hair, winding it into a neat coil at the back of her neck.

Back in the kitchen, she cast her eyes around, trying to figure out what she should do with the last few minutes she had before Mitch finished stabling his horse and headed for the house. He'd be hungry, just the way every man she'd ever known had been whenever he walked into the kitchen.

Thank goodness Ben had filled the wood box before he left. She grabbed a handful of kindling and stirred the fire in the cookstove to new life. After setting the stew she'd served for lunch on to reheat, she wrapped a towel around her waist for an apron and began mixing up a batch of corn muffins. Mitch stepped through the door just as she started beating the eggs.

He sniffed the air and smiled wearily. "If that tastes half as good as it smells, I'm a happy man."

The comment pleased her, but she didn't know how to respond. Compliments had been few and far between in her life. She managed to mutter, "It's just stew left over from noon. Ben didn't complain too much, so it must be at least edible. I would have made something fresh, but I didn't know that you'd be here for dinner."

"No way you could have. Besides, my ma always said stew and soup were always better the second time around."

Mitch hung his coat and hat up before taking a seat at the table. The lines around his eyes and mouth looked deeper than usual, as if he'd had a long, hard day. Or several of them.

"Speaking of Ben, where is he? Kind of early for him to have turned in already."

She looked up from the pan she was greasing. "I'm sorry—I should have told you right away that he went to town and won't be back until tomorrow."

Mitch sat up straight and angry. "Why the hell did he do that? The old bastard promised he'd stay here and keep an eye on you!"

Her own temper rose to meet his. "And why should he have to do that? I promised you that I wouldn't go anywhere. Isn't my word good enough for you?" She glared across the table at him, her hands on her hips.

The smile that played at the corner of his mouth didn't help her mood one bit. "I didn't mean that the way it sounded. I knew full well you'd be here, but Ben wasn't supposed to leave you alone. I wanted him around in case someone showed up unexpected-like."

Not ready to be shed of her anger, she studied his face for a minute or two before deciding he was telling the truth. "I don't think he wanted to go, but he needed to see the doctor about something. He wouldn't tell me what."

Mitch frowned, his eyes full of concern. Despite the way the two men snapped and snarled at each other, it was clear that Mitch cared about his hired hand. "Did he seem really sick? Ben never has much use for doctors."

"Not exactly, but he seemed to be in pain when he climbed up on the buckboard. I thought it might be his rheumatism." It occurred to her that if Mitch had been in town, Ben would have stopped in to see him. "Where were you today?"

"I was out paying a call on your father-in-law."

Her stomach clenched in fear. "Is he still sending his men out to look for me?"

"He may have a few out, but I warned him to keep them out of my way. I don't know if he'll listen."

She shoved the muffins in the oven and quickly set the table.

Mitch eyed the single plate she'd placed before him. "Aren't you going to eat?"

"I had something earlier," she lied. Just the thought of Jed Turner had her belly churning something fierce. If she did eat the stew, she wasn't sure if she could keep it down.

"Don't let Jed worry you. I can handle him."

"He hates me."

"Maybe he does, but I don't think he cared much more for Oliver. Which brings me back to why I went out to see him." He leaned back in his chair far enough to reach the pocket of his coat.

"Do you recognize this?" He set a tarnished silver flask down on the table.

"It looks like Oliver's." She picked it up and turned it over in her hands, running her fingertip along the smooth surface. "Even when we didn't have a dime to our names or food on the table, Oliver hung on to that. He was right proud of it." Tears stung her eyes, although she didn't know why. "It was the only thing I ever knew him to take pride in. Maybe because it was fancy or maybe because it was a present from his father. Of course, that was before we were married, back when Jed had no call to hate his only son." The tears started in earnest. Before she knew what was happening, Mitch had rounded the table to enfold her in his arms. He held her close to his heart while the tears continued to fall, as if a dam had broken.

Finally, she decided enough was enough. As much as she enjoyed the protection of Mitch's arms, the problems were hers alone to deal with. She pushed against him to get free. Mitch immediately backed away, giving her the room she needed to regain control of herself.

She swiped at her eyes with the corner of a towel. "I'm sorry. I don't know what brought that on. Let me get your dinner on the table."

A blast of heat bathed her face as she opened the oven door to check the muffins. They'd risen nicely. She gingerly poked the nearest one to see if it was done. The small dent sprung back immediately, so she gathered up a towel to protect her hand when she lifted the pan out of the oven.

After removing the muffins from the pan, she arranged them on a plate to set on the table. She finished by ladling up a bowl of the savory stew and handing it across to where Mitch was seated.

"Are you sure you don't want to join me? I hate to eat alone." Without waiting for her to answer, he snatched up a muffin and immediately slathered on a thick layer of butter. He was already reaching for a second one before she had a chance to sit down.

For the moment, she was content to watch him enjoy the meal she'd prepared. Oliver had never cared much about food one way or the other. As long as it was hot, he'd eat it. Besides, in his mind, it was a woman's duty to have a meal on the table whenever her man was ready to eat. He never felt the need to praise her for doing just what was expected of her.

"Is there enough for seconds?"

She smothered the urge to smile. "There should be plenty."

When she started to rise, Mitch motioned her to stay seated. "I'm not helpless. It's enough that you cooked." He filled his bowl from the kettle and sat back down. The first helping must have taken the edge off his hunger, because he wasn't in such a rush to shovel the food in his mouth.

After he had finished his fourth muffin and second bowl of stew, he pushed back from the table with a satisfied smile. "That hit the spot."

"I'm glad."

She quickly gathered up the dirty dishes and washed them. Once again, Mitch pitched in and helped by drying everything and putting the clean dishes away, whistling an off-key song as he worked. Between the two of them, the kitchen was spotless in a short time. Mitch picked up a deck of cards and started dealing solitaire. When he had the cards arranged to his liking, he glanced over at her.

"Do you want me to finish telling you what I've been doing?"

Her good mood died. "Do I have a choice?"

"I suppose, but since it all affects you, perhaps you should know."

He was right, no matter how much she didn't want to listen. She folded her hands on the table and nodded for him to continue.

"I tracked down those friends of Oliver's that you mentioned. I don't know exactly what kind of business Oliver had in mind, but I know it wasn't legitimate. His friends are wanted in several counties for bank robbery and similar crimes."

She gasped. She knew Oliver didn't have many upstanding citizens for friends, but she'd never expected him to take up with actual criminals.

"But what was Oliver going to talk to his father about? Jed would never get involved with outlaws." She may not like her father-in-law. He had a reputation of driving a hard bargain, but no one had ever accused him of being anything other than basically honest.

"My guess, Oliver was tired of his father doling out his money a little at a time. If Jed didn't willingly hand over a fair amount of cash, I suspect your husband was going to use his new friends to take it from him." Mitch scooped up his cards and dealt again. "Does that fit with what you know?"

"I hate to admit that it sounds like Oliver. He thought Jed's money was just as much his. Every time Oliver had to go ask Jed for more, he came home in a bad mood." Of its own accord, her hand touched her jaw in memory of some of those episodes. When she realized what she was doing, she jerked her hand away from her face, aware that Mitch had taken note of her response.

She kept her eyes on the table, not wanting to see the pity in his eyes. Then, gently, as if well aware that a man's hand coming close to her face might bring back bad memories, Mitch reached across the narrow table to lift her face. She resisted briefly but then gave in. When her eyes met his, her heart fluttered a bit and then almost slowed to a stop.

It wasn't pity she saw reflected there, nor was it ridicule. No, it was something hot and sweet and so very gentle. The warmth of his hand on her skin slipped inside her mind, soothing her fears, tempting her to trust. She was so tired of being alone and being scared. It took almost the last ounce of strength she had to pull back, because she knew in her heart that Mitch could hurt her in ways that Oliver never had.

The difference was simple. Mitch made her care—about him, about her, about what could have been between them under other circumstances. But wishing didn't change anything. He was still the sheriff. She was still his prisoner. And unless they found the real killer, he could very well be her executioner.

Waves of pain started in her chest and rolled through

her. Whimpering with the agony of it, she shoved away from the table and ran for Mitch's room. She quickly closed the door, putting the flimsy barrier between them, hoping it would keep Mitch out long enough for her to gather her scattered thoughts and emotions.

She should have known better. Not that he came barreling in. No, with that wicked gentleness he could show, he turned the doorknob slowly, probably trying to give her a chance to protest. When she didn't say anything, the door opened far enough for him to see in, but still he stayed outside the room.

"What did I do?" Despite his mild tone there was anger in the way he stood there, as unmovable as an Ozark Mountain.

"It's not you."

"If it's not me, why did you run?"

Feeling cornered and not liking it one bit, she turned away. "I didn't run. I walked."

That brought him into the room. His room. His bedroom. She looked for a means of escape and failed to find one.

"Josie, I'm tired of repeating myself, but you don't seem to hear me. I won't hurt you. I'm not Oliver."

All the fight went out of her. He would hurt her, but not in the way he meant. "Sheriff Hughes, believe me, I know that you aren't Oliver. You couldn't be."

"Then why do you back away from me all the time."

He moved closer yet, crowding her with his words and his body. The nearness of his warmth and his strength had her aching to step backward into his arms, but he had to hear what she was thinking.

"I'm still your prisoner."

He hurled a curse toward the ceiling that should have had her blushing. Instead, it felt good to know that he found their circumstances as irritating as she did. He gave up all pretense of keeping his hands to himself. He spun her around so fast that it took her breath away.

"To hell with that. I've spent every day since the day your worthless husband finally ran out of luck trying to find out who killed him. I won't stop until I clear your name. And do you want to know why?"

"Because you're the sheriff, and it's your job."

"Josie Turner, if you believe that's all it is, then you are the dumb hill girl Jed says you are."

Her fragile hold on her emotions shattered. "Don't you dare call me dumb, Mitch Hughes. I've listened to that my whole life, but I don't have to take that from anybody. Not anymore." She fought the urge to pick up the pitcher on the nightstand and heave it right at Mitch's head. "Not even from you."

A slow smile spread over Mitch's face, his eyes smoldering with something bone-melting hot and suggestive. "You're right, Josie Turner. You don't have to take that from me." He crowded her, forcing her to back away until she ran right up against the wall. "But you just might have to take this."

Then his mouth crushed down on hers, cutting off anything she might have to say on the matter.

Fourteen

Mitch just plain couldn't help himself. He'd tried and tried to keep his hands to himself, but damned if he'd waste another minute of his life without kissing Josie Turner again. He'd always been attracted to her, but he found this new, feistier Josie irresistible. Even if he'd startled her with his sudden kiss, she definitely wasn't fighting him off.

No, indeed, she certainly wasn't. Her hands grabbed on to the front of his shirt and held on for dear life as she rose up to meet him halfway. To his pleased surprise, she was the one who insisted on deepening the kiss. Her tongue danced along his lips, tasting and teasing until he met her challenge. She tasted honey-sweet and spicy hot.

Desire for her burned through him to settle in a hot shaft of need, making him want to lift her high against the cabin wall and take her right there. Or on the floor; it didn't matter.

He fought for control, knowing that although Josie had been married, he had no idea what her experience in the marriage bed had been like. Having no wish to add to the collection of bad memories she already had, he reined his hunger and gentled his touch.

She'd have none of that. As soon as he put half an inch of distance between them, she closed it. He tried again, struggling to give voice to all the questions he knew he should be asking. He had to know that she wanted what was about to happen, that she wanted him, not just the comfort that any man's arms could offer.

"Josie?" was all he manage to say.

She was every bit as smart as he knew she was. She not only understood the question, but she answered with a hot, wet kiss of her own.

Her dark eyes, filled with the secrets of a woman's desire, met his as she smiled. "Mitch Hughes, I need you to teach me how good it can be between a man and a woman. Please."

Happier than he could remember being for a long time, he pulled her close. "That would be my pleasure, ma'am." Then he winked at her. "No, make that *our* pleasure."

Sweeping her up in his arms, he startled her into a pleased giggle. Together they tumbled onto the bed, tangling arms and legs and tongues. When he rolled onto his back, he sent her sprawling across his chest. At first she was too startled by the unexpected change in positions to do more than stare down at him, looking puzzled.

"I thought you might like to be the one in control of the situation."

"Me?" she sounded both curious and incredulous.

"Yes, you." He tugged her down for a quick kiss. "I don't want to rush things, so I'm letting you set the pace."

As he spoke, he traced the line of her cheek with his fingers before slipping them around to start tugging the pins out of her hair. After pulling out the last one, he scattered them on the floor before slowly unplaiting her braid. The honey-gold silk of her hair tumbled down her shoulders. He cherished the feel of it against his face.

"You can touch me, too, you know." He kept his tone light and easy, but if she didn't kiss him soon he was afraid he'd lose all claim to sanity.

She tilted her head to one side as if to consider what to do next. He thought he'd die with the feel of her sweet breasts crushed against his chest. When she pushed herself up over him to kiss him, he groaned and clutched a handful of the quilt to keep from ripping off all the clothes that kept his skin from touching hers. And more.

Between kisses, he begged her to tell him what she wanted him to do next. At first, she clearly had no idea what he meant, telling him for certain that Oliver had been the kind of lover who took his own pleasure with no regard for hers. Fortunately, she was a quick learner.

She moved to lie beside him. Blushing furiously, she whispered, "Touch me."

So he did.

Using his fingers and hands, he learned all that he could of the woman in his arms, starting with the delicate shell of her ear, following the flowing curves from her cheekbones down to her shoulders, and finally to the plump softness of her breasts. Her eyes opened wide and then drifted closed as she gave herself over to his tender ministrations.

One by one, he undid each of her buttons to push her dress down off her shoulders. She tugged her arms free from their sleeves and tangled her fingers in his hair as he nibbled kisses across the tops of her breasts.

"Mitch!" she moaned as she arched up off the bed.

He took less time in untying the ribbon at the top of her plain cotton chemise. Before she could protest, he suckled one rosy-tipped breast while kneading the other gently with his palm.

Her hands became frantic as the flames of heat between them continued to intensify. He needed her so badly that his skin hurt. With what little self-control he could muster, Mitch pulled away long enough to strip away the rest of her clothing before starting on his own.

His fingers fumbled with his belt and his buttons and even his boots.

In only seconds that took an eternity to pass, he had them both completely and gloriously skin to skin, heat to heat. But in just that short a time, Josie's need had cooled, no doubt from being naked and therefore self-conscious. She tried to cover herself with the quilt, but he would have none of it.

"Lord of mercy, Josie, I've waited so long to have you with me like this. Do you have any idea how beautiful you are?"

And she was. He wished she could see herself through his eyes. Her skin was the color of cream, a wonderful contrast to the golden brown beauty of her hair and dark eyes. He begged for the privilege of kissing her, which she granted him. Their mouths met, lips to lips, tongue to tongue. Her hands became as daring as his, caressing his chest, his back, and gradually daring to travel lower down his body.

When first she touched him, her hand at first retreated but then ventured back to learn the feel and texture and center of his need. It was difficult to believe that this sort of mutual exploration might be new to her. Finally, he tugged her hand away.

"Did I hurt you?" she whispered, her voice full of concern.

"Not at all, quite the contrary," he reassured her with smile. "It felt *too* good. I want this to last."

He slid his leg over hers, letting her get used to the weight of him pressing her down into the mattress. This time when he kissed her, he rocked against her, letting her feel how much he wanted her. She delighted him by wrapping her arms around his neck and wiggling from side to side to rub her breasts against his chest. They both moaned with the sweetness of it.

"Take me, Mitch," she whispered, her voice sounding husky with desire.

Still concerned that he might frighten her with the power of his need for her, he forced himself to go slowly as he moved up and over her to settle between her legs. The second he pressed against her, she moaned again in obvious invitation to continue showing her new wonders.

He didn't need to be asked twice. In one swift thrust, he took her, claiming her with his body and with his need. He knew he should give her a chance to grow used to the sudden invasion of her body, but she would have none of it. She arched up under him, encouraging him to continue.

Withdrawing partway, he thrust forward again and again because nothing had ever felt so damn good. He whispered encouraging words to her as Josie dug her nails into his back and lifted her legs high around his waist, pushing him that much deeper. All hope for control exploded in the need to ride her hard and fast, plunging repeatedly into her welcoming heat.

Seconds later, in a heated rush, they climaxed in an agony of jubilation.

Her heart and her breath fought to return to normal, but it didn't seem possible for anything to ever be normal again. How on earth did she live all those years as a married woman without once feeling this way? As soon as she silently asked herself the question, she knew the answer.

She had never loved Oliver. Not for one instant. Somehow that seemed unutterably sad—all those years wasted between two people who had no real feelings for each other. Oliver had been no kind of husband to her at all, but she now realized that she hadn't been any more of a wife, except in the most basic ways. She'd cooked his meals, done his laundry, and even shared his bed, but not because she'd loved him or even liked him very much.

Maybe Jed was right—if she'd been a better wife to Oliver, maybe things would have turned out better for both of them.

And now she was being just as unfair to Mitch Hughes, especially because he was the reason that she knew how shallow her ties to Oliver had been. Somewhere between being thrown in jail and ending up in his bed—or maybe even before—she'd fallen in love with Mitch Hughes, completely, totally. But until she found out if she was going to be hanged or proved innocent, she had no business tangling her life up with anyone else's.

"You're being awfully quiet," Mitch murmured as he shifted around, lifting her, to pull the bedding up over them. The soft patchwork quilt was like a cocoon, shutting out the cold and the world.

She knew she shouldn't hide there in the warmth and the darkness, clinging to the shimmering aftermath of making love with Mitch. If she were a woman of honor, she would crawl out of the bed, pick up her scattered clothing, and find her way back to the jail cell where she belonged.

But she wasn't that strong. Not yet. Perhaps by morning she'd find the courage to walk away—or crawl if necessary. She didn't want to hurt Mitch, but far better to hurt him now than later, when he had to put a rope around her neck.

"Josie, honey, are you all right?"

She reached up to caress the side of his face, his beard feeling rough and so very dear against the palm of her hand. The touch led to a kiss; the kiss, to another, until the passion flared between them again. She gave herself over to the sensations of being surrounded and possessed by the man who also held her heart.

First light, she would find the strength to stand alone. But tonight, in the shadows and moonlight, she would make as many memories as her mind and heart would hold.

For the final few seconds when his mind hovered between sleep and consciousness, Mitch was happy. Last night he and Josie had come together more times than he could count, until both of them had been sated and exhausted. Even as he'd tucked her close by his side, too tired to do more than give her one last kiss, he'd been thinking of how much he'd enjoy waking her up when the night hours faded into dawn.

But then reality set in when he realized that he was alone. Not just in the bed. Maybe Josie had slipped outside to use the privy, but he didn't think so. The quiet was too absolute. Anger and worry cleared out the last of the cobwebs in his mind as he threw the covers aside and stood up.

Ignoring the cold and the fact that he was bare-butt naked, he searched his bedroom and then the kitchen, looking to prove his suspicions right. Immediately, he noticed that her clothes were gone. Not just the dress he'd stripped off her last night, but her coat and boots as well. Just in case, he opened the door to look outside.

"Josie!" he hollered. "If you're out there, answer me."

He kept hoping that she'd come running from around back or peek out of the barn to see why he was raising such a ruckus. But he knew better. She'd packed up and moved on.

But where would she go? And why?

Last night had changed everything. At least, he thought

it had. Didn't she realize that he loved her? Granted, he hadn't told her so in words, but he sure as hell had in every other way. Did she think that nights like they had shared came around more than once in a lifetime?

Damn, what had gotten into her?

Besides him, that is. He closed his eyes and tried to remember every detail he could of the past twelve hours. Not once had she acted as if he'd frightened her in any way. In fact, the last two times they'd made love, she had been the one who reached out to him.

What were his options? He immediately rejected all thoughts of just letting her go. With that decision made, he stomped back into his bedroom to gather up his clothes and get dressed. But instead of finding his clothes thrown every which-way, the way he'd left them, they were folded neatly on his bureau.

She'd taken time to straighten up after him even as she was sneaking out of his bed and his home. He had half a mind to paddle her backside for that little trick alone. Except that he wouldn't. More than once he'd promised he'd never raise a hand to her, and he'd hold to that. But by damn, as mad as he was at the moment, he found the idea sorely tempting.

He yanked on a clean shirt and yesterday's pants before returning to the kitchen. Before riding out, he'd have to see to the basic needs of the animals in the barn. Normally, he'd leave the chores to Ben, but he didn't dare until he knew why the old man had sought medical care. There was always the chance that Doc would need to keep Ben close at hand for longer than one day.

He was heading for the door when his stomach rumbled, reminding him how long it had been since dinner the night before, not to mention how much energy he'd burned during the night. Looking around for something quick to eat, his eyes lit on the last of the muffins

Josie had baked for him. He picked up one and shoved the whole thing in his mouth.

Two more went in his coat pocket. Reluctantly he used up a few more minutes scribbling a note to Ben, so at least someone knew where Mitch had gone and why. When that chore was done, he pulled on his boots and headed for the barn. He'd make sure the horses and mules had water and hay, throw some feed to the chickens, and then light out after his wayward woman.

Half an hour later, Mitch led his saddled horse out of the barn. Before mounting up, he crisscrossed the barnyard and then the trail that led away from his place, looking for some sign of Josie's passing. He didn't know if it was better or worse that she hadn't taken one of the horses when she left. Knowing the backwoods as well as she did, she stood a better chance of hiding her trail by walking, but a horse would have carried her farther, faster.

It took him an irritating amount of time to find his first trace of her footsteps. She'd skirted the muddiest parts of the trail, but in a couple of places she'd left a clear heel print. Using his past experience in tracking and sometimes just wild luck, he kept at it until he realized where she was going.

Unless she doubled back somewhere, she was headed straight for Lee's Mill. What was she thinking of—that is, if she was thinking at all?

Had last night addled her brain? No, they'd been good together, but as hot as the sex had been, it hadn't been enough to damage her ability to think straight. Not if she'd managed to get dressed, fold his clothes, and sneak out of the house without disturbing his sleep.

There was no telling how long she'd been gone, but he

figured he stood a good chance of overtaking her if he hurried. With an apology to his horse, he spurred it into a ground-eating gallop, determined to catch up with his woman before she ran into some of Jed Turner's men.

During spring and summer, he would have taken the long way around, following the road. But the winter had stripped most of the trees of their foliage and killed back a good part of the undergrowth. He could knock off a mile, maybe two, by going cross-country.

Low branches whipped across his arms and face, stinging like hell. As much as possible, he leaned out low over his horse's neck. He'd had plenty of practice riding in just that manner during the war. Of course, back then he'd been dodging bullets. Getting slashed with the occasional branch had been no more than a minor inconvenience.

Up ahead he could see that the trees were thinning out, signaling that he had circled back up to the road. He reined his horse back down to a slower pace. A smart man knew that it didn't pay to go rushing into anything—even though he had last night.

But nothing and no one could have stopped his headlong rush to get Josie Turner into his bed. Hell, he knew better than most that the woman was a tangled mess of problems, not the least of which was the chance that he was wrong about her innocence. She wouldn't be the first woman who'd picked up a gun to stop the beatings.

But had he been wrong about her? He would have sworn that she didn't have a dishonest bone in her body, but she had already admitted that she'd been secretly saving money in order to run away from her late, unlamented husband. Maybe Oliver had found out and tried to stop her. If she were capable of running out on her lawful husband, what would hold her to a lover of just one night?

The doubts flashing through his mind hurt as much

as the branches that he kept trying to dodge. For some reason, they only served to strengthen his resolve to find Josie and drag her back to their . . . make that *his* home. It scared him clean through to realize how quickly she had made herself a part of his life.

His horse gathered itself up to jump a downed tree, forcing Mitch to concentrate more on hanging on than worrying about Josie Turner. Once they were safely on the other side, he had to decide which way to go on the road. Without knowing how long Josie had been gone, he could only guess how far she might have gone.

He turned in the direction of town rather than back toward the farm. If she had gotten past this point, it wouldn't be long before she ran into someone. At best it would be someone who didn't know her, but that wasn't likely. She'd gained a certain notoriety for being the first woman to be locked up in the Lee's Mill jail.

Mitch figured there was little chance Jed Turner had taken him seriously about calling off his men. If Josie ran into any of them, she could be dead before Mitch found her. Stupid woman, what was she thinking of? Even if it was Cade or Jake who found her, she'd end up back in her same cell. This time Jed would have the judge there before Mitch could prevent it.

Once again, he urged his horse to pick up the pace. He had to find her before anyone else saw her.

Every so often he stopped long enough to lean down and study the ground. So far, he hadn't seen anything that showed, one way or the other, if Josie had come this way or this far. The road was too well traveled, despite how bad the weather had been, for him to pick out any one set of tracks. His jaws ached from the growing tension.

How could he have slept through her leaving? He'd been a light sleeper his whole life, but the war had ruined him for anything more than that. When the lives of his men depended on his quick reactions, he'd learned to make do with only a minimum amount of sleep. Too many years of living that way had taken their toll on his ability to sleep soundly, yet Josie had managed to slip past his guard.

He stopped again, figuring he was no more than a mile and a half from town. Fear for Josie's well-being was threatening to send him into an all-out panic when a familiar figure came around the bend just ahead, driving a wagon.

He forced himself to remain outwardly calm while he waited for Ben to reach him.

Ben glared at his employer. "Mitch, what are you doing out here instead of back at the farm? I thought you were against leaving the little gal alone."

"Keep your damn voice down. Besides, I didn't leave her—she left me." He got more disgusted every time he thought about it. "I take it you didn't see her on your way out of town."

Ben whipped his head back around to look back in the direction he'd come from. "Should I have?"

Mitch wasn't sure if he should be relieved or not. Maybe she hadn't gotten this far after all. "I don't know. She snuck out some time early this morning. Heaven knows what kind of fool notion she got in her head."

"How did you miss her stepping right over you?" Ben's eyes narrowed in suspicion. "Unless of course you weren't sleeping across the doorway."

Mitch amazed himself by blushing to the roots of his hair. He could only hope that Ben's eyesight wasn't sharp enough to notice. He wasn't that lucky. The older man let loose with a string of cusswords that would have shocked most folks.

"I knew I couldn't trust you to keep your hands off of her. You've been mooning after that girl for months."

Aw, hell, how had Ben figured that out?

"It's not what you think," he started to protest, but Ben would have none of it.

"Don't lie to me or to yourself," he ordered, giving Mitch a look of pure disgust. "Even a blind man could see how you look at Josie with a powerful hunger. And then there's the fact that she's been looking back. It don't come as a surprise to this old man that the two of you found some pleasure together."

Clearly agitated, he pulled his pipe out of his pocket and started messing with it, leaving Mitch to stew for several minutes while he got it lit and burning to his satisfaction. Squinting up at Mitch through the smoke, he asked, "Assuming you didn't do anything to scare the girl, why would she take off on you? You didn't do something stupid like threaten to haul her back to jail?"

"Hell, no. I thought she was happy living at the farm. At the very least, she felt safe there." Mitch yanked his hat off his head and dusted it against his leg. The sudden motion startled his horse into dancing sideways. "I managed to follow her tracks through the woods until I knew she'd headed this way. I'm worried she's run into Turner or his men."

Ben sat up straight in his seat. He winced in pain but took a firm hold on the reins. "I'll go on up the road toward the farm. Why don't you wait a few minutes and then follow along inside the trees? If I know Josie, she'll work hard at not being seen."

Although the need to find Josie quickly was topmost in his mind, Mitch hadn't missed the flash of pain on Ben's face. If the old man was sickly, he needed to know. "Josie said you went into town to see Doc. Are you all right?"

"That girl talks too much," Ben grumbled. "I had me a boil lanced, if it's any of your damn business. Now go after your woman." He slapped the reins, setting his mules off at a smart pace. "If we don't find her on this sweep, we'll turn around and try it again."

Mitch couldn't come up with a better plan, so he waited until Ben was out of sight and then took to the woods. He hadn't spent much time in church since Rebecca died, but he risked a small prayer that Josie was safe and would stay that way.

Josie sat down on a convenient rock and hiked up her skirt to check her knee. She'd been watching the road ahead more than where she was walking. From out of nowhere a root had jumped up and sent her tumbling forward onto her hands and knees.

She wiped her hands clean on the hem of her skirt. A trickle of blood ran down her leg, staining her stockings and the bottom edge of her only petticoat. The cut was shallow but bloody. Figuring she had no choice, she tore a strip off the bottom of her petticoat for a bandage. She wrapped it around her leg twice before tying it off.

Rather gingerly she stood up. Her knee felt sound, even if it hurt something fierce. Figuring it would only stiffen up if she didn't get moving, she started off back down the road. She'd gone only a few yards when she heard a wagon heading her way. In the wink of an eye, she skedaddled into the trees, putting a good thirty feet of thick woods between herself and the road.

She ducked behind the broadest tree she could find and waited for the wagon to pass. When it was dead even with her, she risked a quick look to see who was driving. Unless she was mistaken, it was Ben on his way back to Mitch's farm. She edged forward, trying to get a clear view of him. He was calmly smoking his pipe, apparently enjoying a leisurely trip home. Evidently, whatever he'd needed to see the doctor about hadn't been too serious.

And since he hadn't seen Mitch, he hadn't heard about her most recent escape. Between the sheriff and her father-in-law, she already had two angry men searching for her. She didn't need to add someone else to their ranks. Another minute went by before Ben was out of sight and out of hearing. Time was pressing on her. The sun was gaining height in the sky, so she figured Mitch had discovered her absence by now.

Torn between the safety of the woods and the speed of the road, she chose the latter in order to make the best time. Her hope was to reach town before Mitch did, so that she could turn herself in to the deputy. With luck, she'd be back behind bars before Mitch caught up with her, because she knew without doubt that he would come after her.

The only question was, would he be riding as the sheriff of Lee's Mill looking for his missing prisoner or as her lover? She pulled her coat closer around her, wishing as hard as she'd ever wished for anything that she could have stayed tucked in that fancy bed next to Mitch. She let her mind drift back to the sweetness of lying next to his lean body, his strength a comfort rather than a threat. No matter what happened, she'd always cherish the memories they'd made during the night.

But until her life was hers to live as she saw fit . . .

A rider came plunging out of the woods heading right for her. She froze, knowing that it would do her no good to run. Her ability to disappear into the woods wouldn't work against a man on horseback who was already almost on top of her.

Just as he'd been a good part of the night before.

His horse skidded to a halt just inches from where she stood. Silently Mitch held out his hand, offering her a boost up in front of him. She immediately shoved her hands in her coat pockets, just as wordlessly refusing his command. His eyes, so warm last night, were icy cold as they stared down at her.

"Josie, this is not the place to be stubborn. Any second now, someone could come riding down this road and see us. You've obviously decided you no longer want to stay at my farm. Fine. But I'm afraid I can't let you go waltzing back into Lee's Mill right now."

She hated being ordered around by a man, even this one. "And why not? I want to turn myself in to the law there."

"I'm the law there, and I said I won't let you do that."

Didn't he realize that she couldn't let him jeopardize his career for her sake?

"You don't have the right to make my decisions for me, Sheriff Hughes. Now, get out my way and let me do what I have to do." She tried to walk around him, but he managed to keep his horse firmly planted between her and the road.

"Why do you have to turn yourself in now, Josie? Is it because of last night?"

It was, but not in the way he meant. She closed her eyes against the sting of tears. If she cried, she'd never convince Mitch that she wanted no more to do with him. Digging her fingernails into the palms of her hands until the pain overrode her need to cry, she looked him dead in the eye and lied. "I wanted to make sure that last night couldn't happen again."

He jerked back as if her fist, rather than her words, had battered him. At first she thought he was going to call her bluff, but he didn't. Instead, he absorbed the pain with a shuddering breath before again holding his hand out to her. Just that quickly, his face was a mask she couldn't read.

"You're not safe in the jail. I'll take you back to the farm before I ride back to town. Stay with Ben until I get this mess straightened out. Once we know for certain who killed Oliver, you'll be free to do what you want."

He kicked his foot free of the stirrup as she took his hand. She put her foot in the stirrup and let him yank her up in front of him in the saddle. She tried her best to sit upright without touching him, but it was impossible with his arms surrounding her. Finally, she settled against his chest, figuring the easier she made it for them to ride double, the quicker he'd get her back to the farm.

The trip took an eternity. She'd never known that silence could be so painful, leaving little doubt that she'd accomplished her goal—Mitch wanted no more to do with her. Once they reached the front of his house, he more or less dropped her to the ground and left her to fend for herself. He wheeled his horse around and rode out without a single glance back in her direction. She knew that for a fact, because she stared after him long after the trees hid him from sight.

The door opened behind her. "You're not going to stand there mooning after Mitch all morning, are you? There's chores to be done."

"I'm not mooning after him."

"The hell you say. He might think you took off because you were purely disgusted by what went on here last night, but I figure he's dead wrong." He pushed past her on his way to the barn.

The meaning of his words hit her about two seconds later. "Ben, what did you mean by that?"

He either didn't hear her or else he'd decided to ignore her. She caught up with him at the barn door. "I asked you a question. Now, answer me. What did you mean back there?"

His old eyes seemed to see straight through to her soul. "He was right about you running scared, missy, but he got the reason all wrong. You didn't take off because you hated him touching you. You liked it too much and that terrified you."

"Listen here, Ben, you don't know everything about Mitch or me. He's a good man, and he deserves better than a hill girl like me. The last thing he needs is to be tangled up with a woman he might just have to hang." This time there was no holding back the tears.

Ben muttered under his breath, but that didn't keep him from wrapping his big old arms around her and patting her awkwardly on the back. He'd probably leave bruises, but she appreciated his rough comfort.

When the tears slowed to a trickle, she squirmed herself free. "I'd better see to the chickens."

Ben stopped her. "I don't claim to know how all of this is going to end, but Mitch won't leave a single Missouri rock unturned until he gets at the truth. He won't let anything happen to you until he does."

She didn't point out that Mitch had already done a powerful amount of searching and was no closer to the truth now than he had been the night Oliver was murdered. Feeling older and more alone than ever, she followed Ben into the barn.

Fifteen

"Thank you for keeping me up to date, Paddy. I appreciate it." Jed was lying and they both knew it.

"I'm sorry, sir, but I'll send the men back out in the morning."

Paddy backed out of the room, evidently a little hesitant about turning his back to Jed. Of course, he was the only one who knew for a fact that Jed had shot Oliver in this very room. In the back, too, come to think of it.

Jed managed to wait until he heard the outside door close before he reached for the nearest book on the shelf and heaved it at the wall across the room. It helped some but not nearly enough to burn out the anger that had settled in his gut. He sent another one flying through the air, and then another and another.

Finally, he sank down in his favorite chair and sulked. There was no other word for it. How in the hell had Josie managed to elude capture this long? There was always the possibility that she'd died in that big snowstorm, but he didn't think so. She was too savvy for that.

And she had friends, damn each and every one of them.

One would think that he would be the one to get sympathy from those fools who lived in Lee's Mill. After all, he'd lost his only son. But no, everyone in town treated him like a leper, whispering behind his back how concerned they were about Josie. Where was the justice in that?

He laced his fingers together in his lap while he thought long and hard about what to do next. Nothing had worked so far—not money, not threats, not a damned thing had produced any results at all. What else could he do?

It didn't help that the sheriff remained unconvinced of Josie's guilt. Of course, he wasn't probably thinking with his brain. Jed snickered before he remembered how mad he was. The poor son of a bitch probably thought that piece of hill trash was worth bedding.

Jed toyed briefly with the idea of selling her off to a brothel but immediately discarded it as being too impractical. It would be too risky to haul her to St. Louis or even Kansas City. Besides, he had enough problems with the townspeople now. If word ever leaked out that he'd done something like that, they'd have him strung up.

Of course, unless they found Josie, he couldn't do much of anything with her. Or about her, for that matter.

A soft knock at the door interrupted his brooding. He toyed with ignoring the summons, but he wasn't accomplishing anything sitting there staring at the wall.

"Yes, what is it?"

The door opened a crack, just enough to reveal a portion of his housekeeper's homely face. "Mr. Turner, your dinner is about ready." Just as quickly she pulled the door shut and disappeared.

He sniffed the air. Unless he was mistaken, that was fried chicken he smelled, one of his favorite meals. For the moment, he would put his problems out of his mind. No use in spoiling an excellent meal over a worthless nobody like Josie.

He was about to head for the dining room when it occurred to him to wonder why the sheriff had wasted valuable time making a trip out here a few days ago. After all, his main focus should be tracking down an escaped prisoner. Unless, of course, he already knew where she was.

Now, that idea was worth thinking about. In fact, he'd dedicate the rest of the evening to doing just that as soon as dinner was over. Feeling better than he had for days, he followed the scent of fried chicken and all the trimmings straight to the table.

By the time the sun rose, Jed had been in the saddle for over an hour. Not knowing where he'd find the sheriff, he'd made sure to get an early start. Last night he'd made the decision to leave his men behind at the ranch. To make sure they'd stay there, he had strolled out to the bunkhouse after dinner with half a dozen bottles of whiskey, to find Paddy.

He'd told his foreman to give the men the next day off except for the basic chores that had to be done. After thanking them for putting in so many long hours in the saddle ever since Oliver's death, he returned to the house knowing they'd been far more interested in good liquor than they were in his motives. He doubted a single man would awaken for hours after he'd ridden out in search of the sheriff.

But that left him wondering where to start looking for Mitch Hughes. He couldn't very well walk up to the jail and ask for him without arousing suspicion. Of course, there was always the chance that Hughes was at the jail in the first place.

Finally, he decided to start by having breakfast at the hotel. That Belle woman and her husband always seemed to know what was going on. If Jed asked them the right questions, he might get the answers he needed. The only

problem was that if he aroused their suspicions, Hughes
would hear about his interest in his business.

He'd have to be damn careful.

By the time he'd reached town, he was no closer to
having a plan. That in itself worried him. He'd been
many things in his life but never indecisive. It was one
more indication that he needed to get this whole matter
resolved and behind him. As soon as Josie Turner was arrested and hanged, he could get on with his life. But
before that could happen, he had to find her.

Despite the early hour, there were several horses tied
outside the hotel. He wished he'd paid more attention to
the sheriff's horse when he'd been at the ranch. If he were
able to recognize the animal, he'd already know if Mitch
Hughes was one of those having breakfast at the hotel.

After tying his own horse at the end the rail, he
stopped long enough to glance up and down the street
before walking inside. Just the fact that he was there
would draw some attention, although he frequently ate
at the hotel when he was in town. But as far as he could
remember, he'd never been there for breakfast. Damn,
he wished he had thought of that before now.

What excuse could he give for being in town at this
hour? The bank wouldn't open for hours and neither
would the store. Not that Lucy Mulroney would welcome
his business, the uppity witch. If she didn't have that
cold-eyed husband of hers to back her up, he would
make a point of making her life miserable. She and that
damned society of hers were directly responsible for his
current problems.

But stewing over a bunch of biddies wasn't going to
help him now. He studied the various businesses on the
far end of town, rejecting them one by one until he got
to the telegraph office. That was it. He could claim to be
expecting a telegraph from one of his business associates

from back east. No one would know one way or the other if he was lying. Hell, he could even make a trip down to check on the telegram after he ate. How sad that he'd come all this way for nothing.

Just that quickly, his mood improved. What could be better? Belle's good cooking and a plan guaranteed to work. He walked through the hotel lobby and straight into the dining room. The place was busy, but he was able to find an empty table in a front corner right by a window. He'd be surprised if anyone dared sit down with him without an invitation, which meant he'd be free to watch who came in. The window offered only a limited view of the street, but he'd be able to see anyone who was headed out of town.

"Mr. Turner, have you had time to decide what you'd like?" Belle held a small tablet in her hand, ready to take his order.

He studied the chalkboard by the entryway listing his options. "I'll have two eggs, bacon, and a side order of flapjacks."

"I'll be right back with your coffee."

Jed stared after Belle, trying to decide if her smile had seemed a bit forced. She stopped to take two more orders before disappearing into the kitchen. She didn't linger to talk to them either, so maybe she was feeling a bit rushed. After all, every table in the room was occupied. There was no reason to think that she'd singled him out.

As usual, there was a stack of yesterday's newspapers sitting on a table across the room. Normally, he'd ask Belle to fetch him one, but he didn't want to wait that long. He made his way through the crowded room to pick one up. Before he got back to his table, someone else had taken his seat.

If it were anyone else, Jed would have sent the squatter packing. However, he'd have a hard time dislodging

Cade Mulroney if he was determined to stay. There was the little matter that he'd never seen the newspaperman when he wasn't wearing a gun. From the easy way it rode on his hip, it was safe to assume that he knew how to use it.

"Sorry if I took your seat, Mr. Turner." Mulroney's apology definitely lacked something in sincerity. The bastard was positively smirking.

"That's fine. Belle seems to have her hands full this morning." Jed pulled out the opposite chair and sat down.

"Nice to see you reading my paper." Again, his words had an edge to them.

"Something to pass the time." But instead of reading the paper, he left it folded on the side of the table. "I would have thought that lovely new wife of yours would have fixed your breakfast."

Cade's eyes turned a shade colder. "The town provides my meals."

"Pretty generous of them to feed the editor of the paper. Is that so you'll go easy on the mayor and the town council?"

"You misunderstand, Mr. Turner. They provide meals for the sheriff and his deputies." Cade pulled his jacket to the side to reveal a badge pinned to his shirt underneath. "I'm just going on duty."

Damn, that probably meant that Hughes was not in town. Dare he risk asking Mulroney? He decided to use a more roundabout inquiry.

"How long do you think you'll remain on as a deputy?"

Cade shrugged slightly. "As long as it takes."

Belle approached their table with a pot of coffee. Neither of them felt inclined to say more until she was safely out of hearing. Jed picked up right where they'd left off.

"As long as what takes, Mr. Mulroney?"

"Why, I would have thought you'd know that, Mr.

Turner. None of us will rest comfortably in our beds until your son's murderer is behind bars."

Now, that was good news. "I must say that I'm surprised that my daughter-in-law has managed to elude capture for so long."

Cade's eyes narrowed. "Well, from what I've seen of her, Josie is a quick learner. I wonder if you haven't underestimated her." Then he gulped down the last of his coffee and stood up as if to leave.

Jed wasn't finished quizzing him. "I thought you came in for some breakfast."

"Seems I've lost my appetite."

Then Cade walked away, leaving Jed to eat alone and wonder how close the sheriff was getting to finding Oliver's killer. The idea that Mitch Hughes wasn't looking for Josie but for Jed himself sent a chill right up his spine. He thought back to when Oliver had made light of the sheriff's intelligence. At the time Jed had considered his son a fool for underestimating the man.

Maybe he should have paid more attention to his own advice.

He wished that he could walk out of the hotel, but enough people had taken note of Mulroney's abrupt departure. If Jed followed hard on his heels, folks would be whispering about it all day long. Rather than stir up more trouble for himself, he picked up the newspaper and pretended to read until Belle brought his breakfast.

Thirty minutes later Jed sopped up the last of his eggs with a piece of bread. Despite his foul mood, he had given Belle's excellent meal his undivided attention, figuring he'd have time later to plan his next move. He left some money on the table and headed back out into the cold.

Once again he paused long enough to look around the town. He spied the pastor hurrying down the street, probably heading back to the church. Cade Mulroney was just coming out of his wife's store. If he noticed Jed watching him, he gave no sign of it as he crossed the street toward the jail.

Deciding there was nothing more to be learned in Lee's Mill, Jed mounted up to ride out. But where? He still wanted to find out what Hughes had been up to since he last saw him. If the man wasn't hanging around town, where else would he be? Was he trailing Josie, or did he already know where she was?

And if so, where would he stash her that he would consider safe? Obviously, it wasn't the jail. That was Jed's fault. If he hadn't told his men to hover around town to keep an eye on things for him, Josie's friends wouldn't have decided that she wasn't safe there.

He let his horse pick its own way along River Road. Not having a destination in mind meant Jed was in no hurry to get anywhere while he considered various possibilities.

If she'd been incarcerated in a jail in one of the neighboring towns, he would have heard about it by now. Josie had friends in town, more than he'd imagined, but they wouldn't dare harbor a fugitive for this long. No, she wasn't in Lee's Mill or White's Ferry. So that left the countryside.

Who did she know that lived outside town? He knew for a fact that she'd never been more than a few miles from that hovel she'd called home. It had to be someone with ties to the town, someone she'd met through that blasted society or through that job she'd taken at the store. That didn't leave many possibilities, especially since it had to be someone the sheriff also trusted.

The sheriff.

Jed yanked back on the reins. He needed to think this

through. Josie had known the sheriff before Oliver was killed. Mitch Hughes had been acting pretty damned protective of her from the minute he'd taken her into custody, to the point of sending for her friends to tend to her needs. Had Josie taken up with Hughes even before Oliver died? Not that he gave a damn, but if she had, it only increased the likelihood that it was the sheriff who had offered Josie a safe haven.

Especially since the man owned a farm tucked up in the hills, not five miles from town.

Should he round up his men before paying Mitch Hughes an unannounced visit or scout the situation out by himself first? He rejected the idea of riding in with a posse of armed men behind him until he knew for certain whether he was right. If he was mistaken, he could slink back into the woods unnoticed.

But his gut reaction told him that finally he was on the right trail. He savored the idea that he was about to find his long-lost daughter-in-law. If she was alone, perhaps a single shot would solve all of his problems for him. The sheriff wouldn't be able to do much about it, considering he was breaking the law by offering her the sanctuary of his home.

Feeling decidedly better about the situation, Jed urged his horse into a jaunty trot. Despite the overcast sky, the day seemed definitely brighter as he set off to find his elusive daughter-in-law.

The day had been a long one already, and it wasn't even noon. Earlier Ben had already accused her of trying to wear a path across the kitchen floor. Of course, unlike her, he was free to come and go as he pleased. Normally, she could while away the hours, content to sew or read. But not this time.

Josie was restless and frustrated and desperately afraid
she'd made a serious mistake. Actually, she was sure
she'd made a mistake—the only problem was that she
had no idea what it was. She honestly believed that she'd
done the right thing by trying to leave. But instead of
helping Mitch, somehow she'd succeeded only in hurting him. The chill of the winter wind had nothing on the
cold way he'd treated her when he'd fetched her back to
the farm. No amount of explaining was going to smooth
that over. She couldn't very well smile nicely as she explained that she'd only been thinking of his future.

She wondered if Ben would change his mind about
letting her help in the barn. Earlier he had shooed her
back to the house after she'd fed the chickens and collected the eggs. She knew better than to think he
considered mucking out stalls to be men's work, so in his
own gruff way, he was being protective of her. Mitch had
said she was safer in the house, and Ben would back his
decision on the matter.

She sidled up to the window, trying to see outside
without being seen herself. Staying clear of the windows
was another of Mitch's rules, even though in all the time
she'd been at the farm not a single person had stopped
by. Neither man was in the habit of encouraging friends
to come calling.

Ben had to be wanting his midday meal soon. If she
put together a quick lunch for the two of them, she
would have an excuse to leave the house long enough to
call him in from the barn. Granted, it was a poor excuse,
but if she didn't breathe some outside air soon, she was
going to lose her mind.

Feeling slightly cheerier than she had been a few minutes ago, she stoked up the fire in the stove and started
peeling potatoes. As the smell of ham started filling the
kitchen, Josie found herself humming a song her

mother used to sing. She couldn't remember the words, but the melody made her think back to when her mother was alive and her father was sober.

Sometimes it was easy to forget that her father had ever been anything other than a bitter drunk. But if she tried hard enough, she could pull images out of the back of her mind that spoke of happier times. Maybe Ben could help her remember more of that period of her life.

The door behind her opened. She stirred the potatoes one last time before picking up the skillet to put it on the table. As she set it down, she looked up, intending to compliment Ben on his timely appearance. Instead, she found herself staring down the barrel of a rifle.

"Well, daughter-in-law, I'll bet you're not exactly thrilled to see me."

Jed Turner's smile scared her straight through. It was the same one Oliver used to have on his face right before he was going to hurt her, either with his fists or in his bed. If she made a grab for a carving knife . . .

Jed correctly guessed her intentions. He lunged forward, his rifle only inches from her head. "Don't try it, bitch. I knocked that old man in the barn out cold. But if you try anything, I'll go back and finish the job." He motioned toward the door with the rifle. "Now, let's get going."

If she did as he said, she knew she was as good as dead. If she didn't, she was still dead, but so was Ben. It wasn't much of a choice. Fear had her rooted to the spot. With a great deal of effort, she forced her feet to move one step at a time toward the door. Jed kept enough distance between them to keep her from trying to attack him but remained close enough to kill her pretty damn quick.

He didn't offer to let her get her coat, no doubt figuring she was going to be cold permanently in short order. Her one hope was that Ben stayed unconscious long enough for them to get away. She couldn't bear the thought of the old man dying because of her. Jed shoved her from behind, sending her tumbling down the steps into the dirt.

He grabbed her by the hair to jerk her back up onto her feet before reaching for the rope on his saddle.

"Hold your hands out." When she complied, he quickly wrapped her wrists with the heavy rope and knotted it. He yanked on the rope to make sure that she couldn't slip her hands free.

"Now we're going to go find us a nice quiet place in the hills. There's some unfinished business between us."

He swung up in the saddle and ruthlessly kicked his horse in the ribs. The startled animal lunged forward, pulling Josie stumbling along behind. She struggled to keep up, knowing Jed would drag her, if necessary, to get where they were going.

For a short time he followed the road, but then he cut off through the woods. That slowed their pace down slightly, but the footing was worse. Her lungs burned with the effort it took her to keep up with her captor, giving her little energy left over for worrying about what was to come.

Her only comfort was that Mitch would never let Jed get away with killing her over the death of his son. Jed might have his revenge, but he would pay for his vengeance with his life. His money wouldn't buy off the one witness—Ben. That is, if he hadn't been lying about Ben only being unconscious. A lump of fear settled in her chest, making it even harder to breathe.

Jed stopped for a minute or two to look around. Josie sank to her knees, gasping for breath and trying to ignore the pain in her wrists and arms. At least she was leaving a trail that Mitch should have no trouble following. There wasn't much chance of his getting there in time to save her, but at least she wouldn't end up buried in an unmarked grave somewhere.

"Get on your feet."

She didn't bother to argue. Using the tension in the rope to pull herself up, she regained her feet just as Jed's horse started forward. They continued for maybe another mile before Jed stopped again. This time she resolved not to go another foot, no matter what he did. Cooperating with the man wouldn't change a thing. She might as well show him what she was made of.

When he dismounted, he untied the rope from the pommel of his saddle and started toward her. As much as she wanted to collapse in fear and exhaustion, she braced herself and met his hate-filled gaze head-on.

"I didn't kill your son, Mr. Turner." Whether he believed her didn't really matter; she'd live or die with the truth between them. "Someone else did."

Jed backhanded her across the face, knocking her to the ground. "You may not have pulled the trigger, but you're the reason he's dead."

She struggled back to her feet, the bitter taste of blood in her mouth. She wiped her mouth on her sleeve, leaving a trail of blood on her arm. "But if you know I didn't kill him, why are you blaming me?"

"Because if you and your father hadn't schemed to get my money, Oliver would have married a woman worthy of the Turner name—someone who would have made something of him." He spit on the ground at her feet. "Instead he ended up shackled to the likes of you. Hell, no wonder he drank! The embarrassment alone would be enough to drive a man to the bottle."

Small flecks of spittle appeared at the corners of Jed's mouth as he ranted on. He cursed her father, her, and even Mitch Hughes for delaying her well-deserved hanging. The whole time, he kept watching back the way they'd come, as if he were expecting someone to join them.

She tried to get through to him one more time. "Think what you will, Mr. Turner, but I did my best by Oliver. I know you don't believe me, but I did not shoot your son."

He whirled around to knock her backward again. "Hell, I know that—I shot him myself. The poor dumb fool thought he'd get away with robbing me."

This time she stayed down as she stared up at insanity. "But . . . why. . . ? He was your son."

Jed chose not to answer. Instead, he dragged her over to a nearby tree and threw the end of the rope over a thick branch. He began hauling on the rope, slowly pulling her up until her toes barely reached the ground. Pain shot through her shoulders as he wrenched her up even further. Then he tied the rope around the tree, leaving her to dangle there, spinning slowly around.

After testing the rope to make sure it would hold, he slapped her again. "Now I'm going to go wait for your sheriff friend to come riding after you. Once he's dead, I don't suppose anyone else will bother looking for you." Then he swung up in the saddle and disappeared back into the woods.

Josie managed to hold back her tears until he disappeared. Fear and dread settled in her chest, making it difficult to breathe. Even in her nightmares, dying at the end of a rope had at least been fast. Instead, Jed had taken her worst fears and made them ten times worse.

Refusing to give Jed the satisfaction of her praying for her own death, Josie tried desperately to muster up some kind of hope. She started by listing the people who had befriended her—the women of the Society and even their husbands. Next she savored the memories of being included in the plans for the Christmas celebration for the first time in her life, and how it had felt to be a part of something so wonderful.

And then there was Mitch, an honorable man who had taught her the sweetness of a man's touch. She closed her eyes as she recalled every detail of the night she'd spent in his arms. Maybe someday he'd forget how much she'd hurt him and realize she'd done so out of love. Then, finally, she remembered Mitch's promise to keep her safe. He'd take it really hard about letting Jed get his hands on her, because he had the kind of honor that Jed and Oliver never had and never understood.

If he wasn't already searching for her and Jed, he would be soon. And because she loved him, she prayed that he'd find Jed Turner before Jed found him.

Mitch rode hard from the minute he'd left Cade until he reached the trail to the farm. Only years of hard-earned experience kept him from charging the last distance at a breakneck pace. If Jed Turner had figured out where Josie was, he could very well have laid a trap for Mitch as well. And if Mitch got injured or even killed, he'd be of little use to Josie or old Ben.

He made his approach slowly, gun drawn and ready. The bad feeling that had been haunting him all day had just gotten a whole lot worse. When he'd made another trip out to the Turner place, Paddy had reluctantly informed him that Jed had evidently ridden out at first light and hadn't returned. A little more prodding on Mitch's part had Paddy confessing that Jed was alone because all of the men had slept late.

If the rest of them looked as bad as Paddy had, they probably felt damn near dead. All because Jed had plied them with his best whiskey. When a man who always had

several armed men at his side suddenly changed his
ways, it had to mean something bad.

Mitch had lit out for town to see if Jed was there, but
no such luck. Cade had seen him at breakfast, but no
one had seen him since. And though Mitch might have
no use for Jed, he didn't make the mistake of underestimating the man. It was a miracle that he and his men
hadn't stumbled onto Josie's whereabouts before this.

And now Mitch was staring at his own house, his stomach roiling with a cold dread. The front door was
standing wide open, and there was no smoke coming
from the chimney. Slowly he urged his horse forward
until he reached the porch and dismounted, at each step
wondering if Jed had him in his sights. Fearing what
he'd find, he forced himself to walk into the kitchen.

A skillet of cooked potatoes sat on the table. He stuck
his finger in the white globs of grease. Stone cold.
Damn. Next he checked the bedrooms, breathing a sigh
of relief when he didn't stumble over Josie's body or
Ben's. But where were they?

There was no sign of a struggle, only the abandoned
food and open door giving evidence that Josie had left
unexpectedly. He set off for the barn at a long-legged
lope. The door was slightly ajar, giving him a clear view
of a pair of legs wearing boots and overalls sticking out
of the farthest stall. The feet were bound together with
rope. Mitch charged in without waiting to see if it was a
trap, desperate to see if his friend was all right or even
alive.

He knelt down by Ben and gently shook his shoulder.
"Ben, Ben, wake up."

The older man stirred and blinked up at Mitch.
"About damn time you got here. Where's Josie? Is she all
right?"

"I don't know. She's not in the house, but her coat is

still hanging on its peg. It looks to me as if she was interrupted in the middle of cooking."

"Then he's got her." Ben rolled over on his stomach. "Cut me loose. We need to go after them."

Mitch didn't have to ask who Ben was talking about. He pulled out his knife and worked the blade between Ben's hands, trying not to cut him. Then he did the same to his feet. Ben pushed himself up into a sitting position, wincing in pain. "How long have they been gone?"

"I'd guess since about midday. I was just fixing to go in and eat something."

Mitch pulled out his watch to check the time. They'd been gone at least one, maybe two hours. Damnation, there was no telling how far they'd gone or in what direction. Ben was still talking.

"The bastard got the drop on me. I thought it was Josie sneaking back out of the house." It wasn't hard to see the guilt he felt. "He's going to kill her, Mitch. We've got to hurry."

Mitch didn't want to hurt his friend's feelings by refusing his help, but it was clear that Ben was in no shape to ride long or hard. Before he told him so, though, he helped him up off the ground. Feeling the strength of Ben's grip, Mitch had an idea. Maybe he could last as far as town to get help.

"I'm going to need Cade and Jake. Think you could get them rounded up for me?"

Ben was rubbing his arms, probably trying to restore the circulation in them. He stopped to frown at Mitch. "I know I'm not as young as I used to be, Mitch, but I can still ride when I have to. And you're going to need all the guns you can find." There was hurt pride and anger in his words.

"Damn it, Ben, I know that. But I need their help, too. Jed appears to be doing this alone, but he's had plenty of time to round up his men. I need to get right on his trail. But if it's a trap, Josie's going to need more than just me and you coming after her."

"If you're sure . . ."

"You come back with them. I'll do my best to leave an easy trail for you to follow."

Ben picked up his tack and saddled his horse. He handed the reins over to Mitch. "You take her. She's fresh. Your horse will last long enough to get me to town, and I can pick up a fresh mount at the stable."

"That blow on the head didn't slow down your thinking, Ben," Mitch said, meaning it. "Make sure you pick up extra ammunition at the jail while you're there."

The two men left the gloom of the barn together. After a quick trip into the house for food and his extra guns, it was time to set out after Josie and her captor.

Sixteen

Ben had been gone about fifteen minutes before Mitch hit on the first clear indication of Jed's trail, destroying any hope that Turner was simply taking Josie back to Lee's Mill to stand trial. They were headed in the opposite direction. As Mitch squatted down to study the tracks, a cold fury washed through him. He had expected Jed and Josie to be riding double, which would slow their pace down considerably and cause Jed's horse to tire before long. Jed was riding, all right, but he was dragging Josie along behind him on foot. From her tracks, she was definitely struggling to keep up with her captor.

Jed would pay extra for that.

But the time for anger and retribution would come later. For now, Mitch needed to keep his wits about him as he tracked a kidnapper and his captive. If he thought too much about it being Josie, he might make a mistake that might cost her—and him—dearly. He kept his eyes focused on the ground, trying to read Jed's intentions from the trail he left. Some broken branches caught Mitch's attention about half a mile farther down the road.

He dismounted to get a closer look. Someone had definitely left the road there, but it was impossible to tell how recently. Rather than assume that it was Jed, Mitch continued up the road for a short distance. When he found no further signs of Josie's footsteps, he was convinced that their trail had veered off into the woods. He pulled off his bandanna and tied it to a tree to mark his path for Cade and company. Then he led his horse off the road, staying afoot for the first fifty feet or so, until he had a general idea of which way Jed was headed.

Finally, he mounted up and risked a faster pace, stopping every so often to check for tracks. At one point, it looked as if Jed had stopped for a while, probably to see if they were being followed. When they'd moved on, he had changed directions slightly, making no effort to hide their trail. Which meant that he expected—even wanted—Mitch to be coming after them.

Mitch slowed to a stop and studied the surrounding woods. A trap waited ahead. He could almost smell it.

It was time to make some of plans of his own. If he wasn't careful, he might just stumble into whatever surprise Jed had waiting for him. For Josie's sake, he couldn't risk being captured or killed.

Finally, he decided to leave his horse behind and circle off to the right. The ridge dropped off too steeply for a rider to traverse safely, but a man on foot could easily cross. If he kept to the low side of the ridge, Jed would have a hard time spotting his approach, especially if he were watching for a man on horseback. Mitch picked up his rifle and set off down the hillside.

The woods were almost unnaturally quiet, even allowing for a large proportion of the animals being in the middle of their winter naps. At the very least, a few birds should be fussing around in the trees above. But something or someone had scared them all off. Mitch stopped to listen, wishing like hell that he knew what Jed was up to. His gut feeling said Josie was up ahead somewhere, serving as bait in the trap Jed had laid for Mitch.

He wouldn't let himself think that she might be already dead. He kept telling himself that Jed knew a corpse wouldn't entice Mitch to come rushing to the rescue. No, she was alive but under Jed's control. And once Mitch had her tucked away safe, he was going after Jed with everything he had. It would likely cost him his badge, but he planned on making damn sure that Jed never bothered Josie again. The thought brought him rough comfort, no matter how today's events played out.

The narrow ridge was turning back up toward the top of the hill. He paused to catch his breath and check his watch while he was still far enough down to avoid being seen. More than enough time had passed for Ben to reach town and be on his way back with help. But no matter how fast they rode, it might be too late.

Jed wouldn't wait forever. Any minute now he could change his mind and decide to end it all. Mitch picked up his rifle and started forward as fast as he dared. When he reached the top of the hillside, he listened for any clue that someone was around.

The continuing silence was too much like the lull before battle for Mitch's comfort. During the war, he'd hated the waiting the most, especially knowing that the enemy was close by, ready to attack. Once the shooting started, he could distance himself from the fear and react with a cold clarity. The only comfort was that Jed was obviously alone, since Mitch hadn't come across any tracks other than his and Josie's. Mitch figured he and his opponent were evenly matched.

He braced himself for battle and eased up over the top of the ridge. Staying crouched low, he ran forward from tree to boulder to tree until he ran across Josie's tracks again. He shadowed her trail for a bit before dropping back to where the trees were thicker. Despite the cold, he worked up a sweat as he walked, ran, and damn near crawled over the rough Ozark hills.

Finally, he spied a clearing a short distance ahead.
Josie's tracks headed straight for it. He stopped to consider his next move. If she was there, Jed would be
nearby as well, no doubt ready to shoot the first person
who cleared the trees.

Mitch decided to detour around the clearing and approach it from the rear. With luck, he'd spot Jed without
giving himself away. Once the shooting started, though,
he'd have no choice but to go charging in and hope that
he could free Josie.

The passage of time pressed hard on him, driving him
onward as he wound through the undergrowth. About
halfway around the clearing, he edged close enough to
see that Josie was indeed there. She was, but that bastard
Turner had left her hanging from a tree, just like a
hunter did with his game. With no coat, she had to be almost frozen, but her eyes were open and alert. Mitch
wished like hell that he could let her know that she was
no longer alone, but he couldn't risk it. The best he
could do was position himself for the best attack.

He'd almost reached his goal when a twig snapped
under his foot. He crouched low to the ground and
started running as a shot rang out. Bark exploded from
the tree right over where he'd been standing. Son of a
bitch!

"Mitch! He's waiting for you!" Josie screamed out a
warning.

Jed retaliated by shooting into the dirt at her feet. The
message was clear—she would live only as long as he allowed it. Mitch needed to find the crazed fool before he
got careless with his shots. Maybe if Mitch threw something into the woods, he could flush Jed out. Thanks to
the rocky Missouri soil, he didn't have to look far for a
rock of the right size. He drew back his arm and heaved
it as far as he could.

Jed fired off three shots in as many seconds. He was shooting from behind a cluster of boulders and trees on the opposite side of the clearing, leaving Josie directly in the line of fire. Mitch kept circling, going as fast as he dared.

"Sheriff Hughes!" Jed called out. "I know you're out there!" He sent another volley of shots dancing across the dirt in the clearing, stopping only inches from Josie. She whimpered as she tried to swing clear.

Mitch kept quiet. Taunting Jed would only make him madder, as well as letting him know right where Mitch was.

"Don't be coy, Sheriff," Jed called. "I'm going to kill her anyway. It's up to you if she dies fast and easy or slow and painful. If you'd done your job, she'd already be dead and buried, and we wouldn't be here now."

There wasn't a doubt in Mitch's mind that Jed meant every word. But maybe if he kept Jed talking, he could gain enough time for Cade and the others to arrive.

"My job is to find Oliver's killer." Mitch moved off to the left as he spoke, trying to confuse Jed.

"She's the one who ruined him."

"But she didn't pull the trigger." This time Mitch moved closer to the clearing as he moved back to the right.

"Who gives a damn if she did or not? I want her dead just like my son, so I can start over." He paused, then added, "This time, I'll make sure my son grows up strong like me."

What the hell was he talking about? What did he mean about starting over? The worst part was that Jed sounded so calm and reasonable.

A bird whistled directly behind Mitch. At least it sounded like a bird. He searched the woods, waiting for it to sound again. This time when he heard it, he saw a movement back down the hillside some distance away. He watched closely until he picked out the unmistakable sight of two men heading right for him. If they'd been Jed's men, they wouldn't have warned him that they were coming.

It had to be Cade and Jake. He backed down the slope until they caught up with him. He didn't have to tell them to keep their voices down.

"Jed Turner has Josie strung up to a tree in a clearing up ahead. Near as I can tell, he's in a cluster of boulders up above her on other the side, daring me to try to cut her free." His hand shook more than he liked when he pointed toward where Josie was. "Think you two can circle around and come against him from both sides? When you're in position to get a clear shot at him, whistle again. Maybe you can distract Jed while I cut Josie free."

Grimly both men nodded. "What are you going to do until then?" Cade asked as he checked his weapons.

"Keep him talking until you have time to get in position."

Jake asked the one question Mitch had no answer for. "And if he gets tired of talking?"

"Pray it doesn't come to that."

He started back toward the clearing, hoping that Jed was feeling chatty.

Josie's arms screamed in pain, but that was the least of her worries. Right now she was far more concerned about her father-in-law and what he might do next. Lord of mercy, she didn't want to die, and more than that, she prayed that Mitch didn't die trying to save her. She closed her eyes, ignoring the tears she couldn't stop, and wished she'd told Mitch how much she loved him.

"Jed!" It was Mitch calling out. He sounded closer than

he had last time. "Let's talk about this. It's not too late for me to haul Mrs. Turner back to stand trial. With your influence, I'm sure the judge would be here damn quick."

She braced herself for another round of shots aimed in her direction, but the woods were quiet. What was Jed doing now?

"Jed, I'm willing to hear what you have to say. Why don't we sit down together?" Mitch was still moving, probably trying to keep Jed from knowing exactly where he was.

"I'll tell you what. I'll throw down my guns and walk out into the clearing. You come out and we'll parley."

"You must think I'm plumb stupid, lawman. You can parley all you want, but it won't change a damned thing."

Josie about jumped out of her skin as Jed's voice echoed through the trees. Maybe she could help keep him talking.

"Mr. Turner, you make it sound like you've got big plans. We won't stand in the way of them." Her throat was dry, making her sound hoarse. "I know the sheriff will agree."

"And how do you know that, bitch? How long after my son's death did you go crawling into the sheriff's bed?" He sent off another round of shots, throwing up dirt and rocks. "Nothing would surprise me. You were a slut long before Oliver met you."

Josie whimpered in fear, wishing she could disappear into the mud at her feet.

"Good girl. Keep him talking."

Mitch's whispered encouragement came from right behind her.

"Mitch, you need to get away. He'll kill us both before he's through." She resisted the urge to twist around in his direction. "He killed Oliver himself, but he's convinced himself that it was my doing."

"Hold on for a little longer, Josie. Help is coming."

A whistle echoed through the woods, followed by a series of shots ringing out over the clearing. She screamed, thinking that Jed had decided it was time for her to die. But then she realized that the gunfire was coming from up behind her where Jed was hiding a short distance away. At the first shot, Mitch charged out of the woods, running straight for her, knife in hand. He slashed at the rope where Jed had tied it to the tree.

Before he had time to cut through it, though, her father-in-law ran into the clearing with his guns drawn, ready to fire. His left sleeve had a jagged tear in it, his hand covered in blood. The second he spotted Mitch cutting the rope, his right hand came up, ready to fire.

"Mitch!" Josie screamed.

Instead of running for cover, Mitch slashed at the rope one last time before throwing himself between Josie and Jed. Josie picked up her feet, dropping her full weight against the remaining strength of the rope. After a brief hesitation, it snapped in half, sending her and Mitch tumbling to the ground. There was no time to think. As soon as they quit rolling, Mitch all but dragged her into the scant covering of the undergrowth inside the trees.

Jed screamed his outrage at their attempt to thwart his plans, as he peppered the ground and trees around them with bullets before disappearing again. Mitch shoved her face almost into the dirt to keep her out of the line of fire. At the same time, he drew his own gun but didn't make any effort to shoot back. Before she could ask what he was waiting for, he answered her unspoken question.

He leaned in close to her face and whispered, "Cade Mulroney and Jake are out there somewhere. I can't risk shooting until I know where everyone is." He pulled out his knife again. "Hold out your hands."

Somewhat awkwardly she managed to roll to her side and hold up her wrists. The ropes were slick with blood where they'd rubbed her wrists raw. Mitch cursed Jed under his breath as he sawed through the ropes. When her hands were free, he gently turned them over.

"I'm sorry I let him do this to you."

She tugged her arms out of his grasp. "You're not responsible for anything Jed Turner does or doesn't do, Mitch."

Ignoring what she was trying to tell him, he peeled off his coat and drew it over her shoulders. "Put this on and keep down."

She caught him by the shirtfront. "I mean it, Mitch. None of this is your fault."

"I'm the sheriff—it's my job." He kept his gaze over her head as he watched for signs of either Jed Turner or his friends.

She'd been dragged, hanged by her arms, and scared within an inch of her life. She wasn't about to put up with being ignored. "Is that all I am? A part of your job?"

The answer was there in the angry glitter in his eyes. Mitch was fighting some powerful emotions, and not all of them had to do with Jed Turner. She risked a gentle touch to the side of Mitch's face. "I'm sorry." There was so much more she wanted to say, but now was not the time.

"Listen, Josie . . ."

Both of them froze when there was a rustling in the brush off to the right. Ben poked his head up over a rock for a quick look around before ducking back down out of sight. Mitch motioned for Josie to stay still before he started for Ben, half crawling, half running across the forest floor.

"Ben!" he called softly, making sure his friend heard him before he got too close. The two men talked briefly and then Mitch disappeared. A few seconds later Ben settled down onto the ground next to Josie. He handed her a pistol and a box of bullets, keeping his favorite shotgun for himself.

He kept his eyes moving, watching for any sign of movement. "Mitch is going to track down Jake and Cade. Together, the three of them will take care of Turner."

Her father-in-law wouldn't give himself up easily. He had far too much to lose: his reputation, his money, his freedom. And if Mitch could make a convincing case against him, Jed could very well end up dying at the end of a rope instead of Josie.

A long, low whistle carried on the wind, followed by a burst of gunfire. Considering there were only four men out there, they made a powerful racket as they tried to end the standoff. After a few seconds, the woods settled back into silence.

Ben stared off in the direction of the shots. "Sounds like Mitch and the others have cornered Jed."

"He won't surrender. He wants me dead." She had never let herself care too much about how Oliver's father had treated her, but it hurt to find out that he'd really hated her.

Ben gave her a rough pat on the shoulder. "Listen, missy, folks like Jed and his son are born twisted up inside. I can tell you this much, though. I had me a daughter once. If she'd have lived, I would have been right proud if she'd turned out like you."

He tolerated her emotional hug before backing away. "Stay low. No use making a better target of yourself before we're sure Mitch has taken care of Turner."

"It's a shame you won't be around to see that." Jed walked out of the trees behind them, his rifle aimed right at Ben. His eyes flickered in Josie's direction as the two of them quickly stood up.

Before Ben could bring his shotgun up, Jed smiled and squeezed the trigger. Josie screamed and threw herself between the two men, hoping to draw Jed's fire. A sharp pain shot up her arm as the ground came up to meet her. The air exploded in noise and yelling and smoke as Mitch ran into sight, his guns spitting fire and death. Before the dust had settled, a pair of hands appeared from nowhere and lifted her up.

"Damn, she took a bullet meant for me," Ben shouted. "Somebody see how bad it is!"

Jake gently pulled her arm free from Mitch's coat and pronounced it a shallow graze. When he sounded relieved, she wanted to tell him that it still hurt. At first her eyes refused to open, but she didn't need them in order to know it was Ben who cradled her in his lap. Finally, they cooperated enough for her to look up at him with a worried smile.

"Ben? Are you all right?"

"I'm fine, damn it."

Mitch appeared briefly in her line of vision. "What were you thinking of, Josie?"

"Couldn't let him hurt Ben." She was feeling so very tired, but there was one more question. "Jed?"

Ben looked over behind them and pulled her closer to his chest. "Mitch made sure Turner won't be bothering you anymore." There was a definite grim satisfaction in his words.

Jake, or maybe it was Cade Mulroney, moved past them. "I'll go round up the horses."

A bandanna dropped down over Ben's shoulder. "Wrap her arm with this. It might not look bad, but Doc will check it once we get back in town."

The other three men came and went, leaving Josie to rest. She was having difficulty following the sudden burst of activity. It couldn't have been long before Cade rode up leading several horses.

"I'll hand her up to you." Mitch crossed to where Ben still supported Josie. He lifted her up to Cade.

She tried to protest. "I can ride by myself." And if she had to ride double, she wanted to be with Mitch, not Cade.

"Don't argue, Josie." That was Ben. "The man has a job to do."

That hurt. Again, all of this was only because of Mitch's job. She reminded herself to be fair. He was, after all, the sheriff. Even if he'd saved her life, she wasn't feeling particularly grateful. She wanted desperately to be something other than a duty for him. But there was nothing more to be done now except let Cade take her back to Lee's Mill. Her life was no longer in danger, but without Mitch would it be worth living?

The knock at the door wouldn't be ignored. As much as Josie wanted to, no one dared deny Henrietta Dawson, especially in her own home.

"Josie Turner, it is time to quit hiding in there."

A stickler for propriety, Henrietta would never intrude on a guest's privacy by entering a room without permission. She would, however, stand outside the door until she wore Josie down. Giving in was easier than fighting her, so Josie crossed the short distance to the door and opened it.

Henrietta swept in, somehow filling the room with her presence. She clucked her tongue when she saw that her guest was still in her dressing gown. Josie instinctively pulled it close around her, as if Henrietta could see through it to what a tangled up mess she was on the inside.

"I must say, Josie Turner, that I thought you had more gumption than this." She perched on the one chair in the room. "I will admit you have been through more trouble the past few weeks than most folks see in a lifetime. However, you cannot hide in here forever. I won't allow it."

Her words hit Josie hard. She knew that she needed to return home to her cabin; she just hadn't expected it to be this soon.

She drew herself up straight and tall. "I'll leave today. I want to thank you for your kindness."

Henrietta snorted in a very unladylike manner. "'Kind' is not a word people often use to describe me, my dear, but that is not the point. It is time for you to decide what you want to do with your life. No one else can make that decision for you."

As if it were that easy. She'd never been alone before, having gone from being a daughter to a wife. Now there was no one left to make demands on her time or to make decisions for her. She felt as if she were still dangling from that tree, unable to put her feet down solidly on anything.

"I'll be returning to my cabin. Once I've set it to rights, I'll talk to Lucy Mulroney to see if she'll let me come back to work."

Henrietta gave her a nod of approval. "That will do for a start. Mind you, I don't want to think you need to be in a hurry to leave my home. Christmas is only two days away. Wait until then before you go." Having accomplished her goal, Henrietta started for the door. On her way past Josie, she reached out and patted her on the arm. "You've come through all of this stronger than you think. Remember, you have people who care very much about you." Then, as she walked out the door, she turned to add, "And not all of them belong to the Society."

"Thank you again for everything."

Once the door was closed, Josie slumped down onto the bed and considered her options. As tempting as it was to stay under Henrietta's roof a few more days, she wasn't sure she could bear to stay in town for the holiday. She knew her friends in the Society would welcome her. Henrietta had made it clear that she wanted her to stay. Even Cade Mulroney had stopped by to check in on her.

But one specific person hadn't, and that made all the difference.

It was time to go home, even if it meant being alone for Christmas again and for all the days to follow. The cabin might not be much compared to what other folks had, but it was hers. She could cook what she wanted and when she wanted. There was no question about where she could sleep or when she could go outside.

Yes, it was definitely time to gather her meager belongings and walk home.

"She's gone where?!" Mitch jumped to his feet, knocking his desk chair to the floor. "Are you out of your mind?"

Henrietta Dawson looked him up and down, and from the expression on her face, she definitely found him lacking. "Very possibly, Sheriff Hughes, but that is my problem," she told him rather tartly. "However, I want to know what your intentions are regarding Josie Turner."

He wondered what the penalty would be for throwing an interfering old woman in jail. "How is that your business?"

"I've chosen to make it my business, young man. She has no family to speak for her. It is obvious that you've trifled with her emotions. I shall have to speak to Pastor Hayes if you continue in such a manner."

"My intentions are my business—and Josie's."

There, let her make of that what she would. Apparently, it was enough to satisfy her.

"I will trust that you will do right by her, Sheriff Hughes. She deserves that much."

Her stiff skirts rustled across the floor as she walked out, leaving Mitch staring after her, totally at a loss. He wondered what the old woman would do if she found out that he'd trifled with far more than Josie's emotions. Probably have him run out of town on a rail. The interfering old biddy.

He righted his chair and sat back down. Damn, he was tired. It had taken him the better part of two days' hard riding to catch up with the judge in Columbia. Another one before all the paperwork had been settled. After allowing himself only a few hours sleep, he'd ridden far too many hours to return to Lee's Mill. And Josie Turner.

Only to find out that she had left the safe haven of Henrietta Dawson's home to walk back to that damn wreck of a cabin. It occurred to him that he'd never told her that someone else had torn the place apart. She might have a roof over her head but not much else.

Jake was due to return in a few minutes. Mitch had planned on getting a good night's rest before seeking Josie out to discuss her future and, hopefully, their future. But he wouldn't sleep at all, knowing she was huddled on the floor, alone and cold. The only good news was that he'd stopped off at the barbershop for a hot bath and shower as soon as he'd reached town. At least he wouldn't have to face her with five days of whiskers and the stink of the trail still clinging to his clothes.

* * *

A few minutes later Jake walked in to find Mitch pacing the room, his coat on, and counting the minutes until he could set out after his woman.

"I'll be back tomorrow." He pushed by Jake.

"No hurry. I'm staying in town for the Christmas celebration tomorrow night anyway." Jake tried to choke back a grin but failed. "Tell Miss Josie hello for me."

Mitch didn't bother to respond, since he had no way of knowing just how warm his own reception would be. He'd specifically asked Cade to let Josie know why Mitch had lit out right after bringing Jed Turner's body back to town. He'd gone to Columbia to clear her name, after stopping at Turner's place to notify both Paddy and the housekeeper that their boss would not be coming home.

Once he'd explained what had happened, Paddy had rather guiltily confessed that he'd known all along that Jed had killed his own son. After knocking the man to the ground, Mitch had hung around long enough to take Paddy's sworn statement.

Then he'd ridden straight for Jed's friendly judge to get the business of Oliver's death settled once and for all. He wanted there to be no doubt whatsoever that Josie was innocent of all charges. Once he confronted the judge, news of Jed's death traveled fast. Even before Mitch left for Lee's Mill, the less successful members of the Turner clan were digging in, ready to fight long and hard over his money.

Mitch figured all of his good intentions might have been for naught since neither Cade nor Henrietta had seen fit to tell anyone, most especially Josie, where he'd gone. He'd like to think that the one night she'd shared his bed had been enough to convince Josie she meant something special to him. But he feared several days of unexplained silence might well have destroyed their fragile ties to each other.

After making one quick stop to deliver a message, he hired a fresh horse from the stable and set off at a gallop.

Josie eased down carefully onto the makeshift bench she'd pieced together from her broken table and chairs. It wasn't much, but at least she didn't have to sit on the floor. She poked at the fire, sending a shower of sparks up the chimney, and wished she'd had the sense to stay at Henrietta's another few days.

She looked around the shambles of her cabin. Had it always been this small and dingy? In her mind's eye, she compared it to Mitch's snug house, where the wind never found its way through the cracks in the walls and all the smoke went up the chimney. Drawing her thread-bare blanket around her shoulders, she forced herself to think cheerier thoughts.

Lucy had asked her to work more hours until and even after the baby was born. Without Oliver to drink up her cash, she'd have plenty to live on and maybe even put some aside. The small stash of money she'd retrieved from Lucy's storeroom would go a long way toward replacing her broken dishes and furniture.

Her friends in the Society had pressed her to make the trip back to town for the Christmas celebration. But she wasn't sure she could, not if Mitch would be there. Maybe after some time passed, she'd get over the strong feelings she had for the man, but right now they were too new, too raw.

No one seemed to know where he was or when he'd be back. Remembering the nightmares she'd had the past few nights about Jed and his plans to kill them both, she prayed Mitch was safe.

The sound of a horse riding hard for the cabin shattered her thoughts. For a heartbeat she thought it was

Oliver coming home, drunk and mean, before she remembered he was dead. It was a sorrowful thought that
she could only feel relief.

But that didn't explain who was out there or if she was
in danger. After picking up her rifle, she waited by the
door for her uninvited guest to identify himself.

"Josie Turner, I'm coming in."

Her knees went weak as soon as she recognized
Mitch's voice. Her first reaction was relief and joy that he
was all right, but it quickly changed to anger. Where had
he been?

She threw open the door and confronted him. "Do
you always come calling on people, bellowing like that?"

He stood on her porch, glaring down at her. "What do
you mean moving out here all by yourself? Haven't you
got a lick of sense?"

That did it. She'd been pushed around by men her
whole life, but no more. She simply wouldn't stand for
it. "This is my cabin. I own it free and clear. Where else
should I be?"

He yanked his hat off his head and twisted it in his
hands, possibly wishing it were her neck. The idea
pleased her. "You could have stayed with Henrietta until
I got back. Or better yet, out at the farm with Ben." He
stepped closer. "Somewhere you'd be safe until I got
back."

"And how was I supposed to know when that would
be? Besides, you never told me that you wanted me back
at the farm." *Where I desperately want to be,* she added
silently.

"Look, can we discuss this inside? It's getting colder by
the minute, and you don't have a coat on."

She backed away from the doorway, giving him room
to come in. Once inside, he looked around, his mouth
set in a grim line. She tried to see it through his eyes: the

patched-up bench, the cracked dishes, the pallet of blankets on the floor for a bed. Embarrassment and shame left her feeling angry.

"If you have something to say, make it fast. It's getting late, and you have a long ride back to town." She turned to face the fire, not wanting to know if she'd find pity in his eyes.

"First of all, Cade was supposed to tell you where I'd gone. If you're mad at someone because you didn't know why I wasn't around, at least be mad at the right person."

Why would Cade withhold the information? "Maybe he figured it was none of my business."

"How should I know? As I said, ask him." Mitch joined her at the fire, standing far too close for her comfort.

"Secondly, I was in Columbia to get these." He thrust a thick envelope of papers at her. "You can read them later, but that's a signed order from a judge clearing you of all charges."

"He believed you?" She didn't ask if the judge might change his mind if he ever found out that she and Mitch were lovers, even if it had only been for one night.

"He didn't have to. One of Jed's men confessed that he knew all along that Jed had killed Oliver."

She had to know how Mitch really felt. "How long did you really know I was innocent?"

He reached out to run a stray strand of her hair through his fingers. "I think I knew it all along, but I had to have proof if you were ever to be truly free of Jed and his accusations. I knew it for sure when I found the flask. I have a witness who saw Oliver with it right before he was killed. Oliver had to have been at his father's house the day he was killed."

All of her anger drained away, leaving nothing to hold off the strong need she felt for this man. "I'll read through these tomorrow." She moved away to set the papers down in a safe place. "Thank you for bringing these out to me, but they could have waited." With some effort, she managed to look him in the face. "You'd better be going now. It's late and I'm tired."

"I'm not going anywhere without you."

Had she heard him right? "What are you talking about?"

Just that fast, she found herself cornered between him and the closed door. He put one hand on each side of her, effectively pinning her in place. Once again she was reminded just how big and strong he was. Not that he frightened her at all. Instead, she rather relished the safety of being enclosed in his arms.

"I asked you a question, Mitch Hughes."

Very slowly he smiled. "You sound like Henrietta Dawson."

Now, that was definitely an insult. "I do not."

"Yes, you do. Just today she demanded I tell her my intentions regarding you."

"She did, did she?" Her voice cracked. "And what did you tell her?"

He leaned in even closer. "I told her the matter would be settled between you and me."

Could he mean . . . ? She had to know. "What would?" she whispered, her eyes captivated by the sight of his mouth moving ever closer to hers.

"This." Then he was kissing her.

She'd almost convinced herself that she had exaggerated how powerful and sweet it was to kiss him, but she hadn't. No, not at all. If only he'd put his arms around her and carry her over to the blankets on the floor, her world would be perfect. It wouldn't be as comfortable as his bed, but it was the best she could offer him.

He broke off the kiss, sounding as if he'd been running a long, long way. "Josie Turner, I want you so bad I hurt."

She blushed to find herself saying, "My bed's over there."

His smile was back. "We'll get there soon enough, but not before I ask you one more question."

If he didn't kiss her again soon, she'd die. "Go ahead and ask it."

"Would you be happy living with a simple farmer?"

He was talking crazy. "You mean Ben?"

Mitch seemed to find that right funny. "Well, I'm afraid he's part of the deal. If you marry me, that is."

"You aren't making sense. You aren't a farmer. You're the sheriff."

"Not anymore, not if you'll have me. I've had enough of guns and fighting to last a lifetime. All I want now is to settle down with a good woman and maybe raise a passel of kids."

Her heart pounded, and her lungs refused to fill up with air. "You mean me?"

He pretended to look around the room. "Do you see anyone else in here?"

"You're sure?" She wanted to dance around the room and holler.

He picked her up and swung her around the small room, laughing at her surprised shriek. "I'm as sure as I've ever been about anything." He turned serious. "Josie Turner, will you be my wife?"

"I'm pleased to hear your intentions are honorable, Mr. Hughes," she teased, doing her best to sound like Henrietta at her snootiest.

"Is that a yes?" he demanded, already swinging her up in his arms.

"That's definitely a yes," she assured him.

"You'll marry me?" He slowly lowered her to lie down on her mother's best quilt.

"Yes, I'll marry you," she whispered as she pulled him

close for another long kiss. Each touch of his hands felt like heaven.

"Good thing, since I already told Pastor Hayes that we'd be wanting him to say the words over us tomorrow night."

He kept her from protesting, by the simple act of kissing her until she lost all coherent thought.

Epilogue

If anyone objected to the Christmas Eve celebration's being taken over by a sudden wedding, Mitch didn't hear about it. He supposed it was rather high-handed of him to order Pastor Hayes to make room in the service for a marriage ceremony, especially before Mitch had even proposed to Josie. Checking his appearance in the mirror, he decided he didn't care. If Daniel had protested, Mitch would have found some way to change his mind. After all, Mitch had the weight of the Luminary Society on his side. No man in town stood a chance against them.

But he had waited far too long to find a woman like Josie to delay a single minute longer. Besides, they'd already started the honeymoon. If by chance they'd also already started a family—and he'd sure enough worked hard at trying—he wanted everyone to know he'd married her because he'd wanted to, not because he'd had to.

There had been enough gossip about the circumstances surrounding her first marriage. She didn't need to go through that again.

Ben and Cade joined him. Cade was to stand up as Mitch's witness. Ben was giving the bride away.

"Is she here?"

"Not yet, but she'll be here." Cade slapped him on the shoulder. "I warned you against these long engagements trying a man's nerves."

Pastor Hayes joined them. He grinned at Cade. "As if you had any engagement at all. As I recall, Lucy had all of five minutes from the time you asked her to marry you and until you both said 'I do.'"

"Well, no sense dragging things out when you know you've found the right woman." Cade gave the young minister a knowing look. "Seems to me that you and Melinda didn't wait much longer."

A knock at the door interrupted their discussion. Henrietta Dawson was waiting outside. "It's time."

Mitch waited for his friends to file out ahead of him. Daniel solemnly led Mitch and Cade to their positions at the front of the church. When the music started, Mitch looked over the congregation toward the back of the room to where Ben stood with his hair slicked down, looking nervous in his new store-bought suit.

Then she was there, holding Ben's arm and walking down the aisle toward him, right where she belonged.

Josie knew without a doubt that she would have collapsed in a heap if she hadn't been holding on to Ben's strong arm. Step by step, the two of them filed by their friends and neighbors on this most special night of the year. The scent of pine boughs and cinnamon filled the air, while red bows decorated the pews. Candles flickered in the windows and on the huge tree set up in the front corner, filling the room with soft yellow light.

She knew all this loveliness was in honor of Christmas to celebrate the Holy Child's birth. But somehow she didn't think he'd mind sharing a little of it with her and the man who'd made such a difference in her life. Somehow it seemed fitting and proper.

She did her best to smile and nod at the people who had made all this possible. But once she saw Mitch standing in front, looking so tall and handsome, her eyes and heart went straight to him and stayed there. Finally, they reached the end of the aisle that had never before seemed so long.

Ben gave her an awkward kiss on her cheek before handing her off to her future husband. Mitch leaned in close to whisper, "You still sure about this?"

Josie smiled serenely up into his teasing eyes and nodded. "I couldn't have wished for a better Christmas present."

"For both of us."

The final strains of "O Come All Ye faithful" faded away as the two of them held hands and turned to begin their life together.